PRAISE FOR THE NOVELS OF
MAUREEN MCKADE

"A story that will tear at your heart . . . terrific."
—*Rendezvous*

"Watch out when sparks start to fly!" —*Affaire de Coeur*

"A Maureen McKade novel is going to provide plenty of excitement and enjoyment . . . Another triumph."
—*Midwest Book Review*

"Well-done, uplifting, and enjoyable."
—*Rocky Mountain News*

"With a clever story line and sparkling dialogue she's created a town that will live in her readers' minds and keeper shelves forever . . . *Untamed Heart* is one of the must-read romances of the year!" —*The Literary Times*

"One of the most original romances I've read in a long time. I look forward to reading more from this talented author." —*All About Romance*

"Hard to put down . . . A great story." —*The Best Reviews*

A REASON TO LIVE

MAUREEN MCKADE

BERKLEY SENSATION, NEW YORK

THE BERKLEY PUBLISHING GROUP
Published by the Penguin Group
Penguin Group (USA) Inc.
375 Hudson Street, New York, New York 10014, USA
Penguin Group (Canada), 90 Eglinton Avenue East, Suite 700, Toronto, Ontario M4P 2Y3, Canada
(a division of Pearson Penguin Canada Inc.)
Penguin Books Ltd., 80 Strand, London WC2R 0RL, England
Penguin Group Ireland, 25 St. Stephen's Green, Dublin 2, Ireland (a division of Penguin Books Ltd.)
Penguin Group (Australia), 250 Camberwell Road, Camberwell, Victoria 3124, Australia
(a division of Pearson Australia Group Pty. Ltd.)
Penguin Books India Pvt. Ltd., 11 Community Centre, Panchsheel Park, New Delhi—110 017, India
Penguin Group (NZ), Cnr. Airborne and Rosedale Roads, Albany, Auckland 1310, New Zealand
(a division of Pearson New Zealand Ltd.)
Penguin Books (South Africa) (Pty.) Ltd., 24 Sturdee Avenue, Rosebank, Johannesburg 2196,
South Africa

Penguin Books Ltd., Registered Offices: 80 Strand, London WC2R 0RL, England

This is a work of fiction. Names, characters, places, and incidents either are the product of the author's imagination or are used fictitiously, and any resemblance to actual persons, living or dead, business establishments, events, or locales is entirely coincidental. The publisher does not have any control over and does not assume any responsibility for author or third-party websites or their content.

A REASON TO LIVE

A Berkley Sensation Book / published by arrangement with the author

Copyright © 2006 by Maureen Webster.
Cover art by Judy York.
Cover design by George Long.
Interior text design by Kristin del Rosario.

ISBN: 978-0-7394-7225-5

BERKLEY SENSATION®
Berkley Sensation Books are published by The Berkley Publishing Group,
a division of Penguin Group (USA) Inc.,
375 Hudson Street, New York, New York 10014.
BERKLEY SENSATION is a registered trademark of Penguin Group (USA) Inc.
The "B" design is a trademark belonging to Penguin Group (USA) Inc.

PRINTED IN THE UNITED STATES OF AMERICA

For Alan, my very own hero, for serving his country faithfully for twenty-one-plus years. All my love.

$\mathscr{P}$ROLOGUE

Virginia, March 1865

LAUREL Monteille Covey ducked out of the tent and stretched, pressing her palms against her aching lower back. The filthy, worn canvas couldn't mute the low moans and cries from the wounded soldiers in the makeshift hospital but she'd learned to shut them out. She'd had to.

She wiped at her eyes, tearing from kerosene fumes and the stench of gangrene, blood, and unwashed bodies. However, being outside gave her little respite. A half mile away, the battle raged against the Yankees, and black smoke from cannons and rifles blotted the sky and drifted through the camp. The sight had once inspired fear, but now she felt only resignation.

A man's scream from the amputation tent sliced through the groans of misery but Laurel felt . . . nothing.

When was the last time she'd smelled fresh air—air free of death and dying? Or listened to birdsong without human sounds of anguish and pain as accompaniment? Or looked at a field untrammeled by war?

Exhausted in both mind and body, Laurel wanted nothing more than to sleep in her childhood bedroom and dream of dancing horses and rings of posies. But that life was gone forever.

She shook her head, refusing to dwell on the past. There was nothing left back there for her. There was only the present.

An ambulance wagon pulled by two bony mules halted less than ten feet from Laurel. Half a dozen blood-covered soldiers were unloaded from the back by stretcher-bearers and set on the ground around her. Snapped out of her bleak musings by the battle's casualties, she scanned the wounded men with an experienced gaze, noting one young man was already dead.

Determining which soldier was the most seriously injured, Laurel dropped to her knees by his side.

"Grapeshot," one of the stretcher-bearers mumbled as he shook his head and shuffled past her.

Two years ago Laurel would've flinched at the grim announcement and grimmer picture. No blanket covered the young soldier, so the wounds to his belly were obvious. It was also evident he had only minutes left on earth.

Black powder couldn't hide the bone-white pallor of his face. Unspeakable pain and anguish filled his striking blue eyes. His jaw was clenched, as were his fists at his sides. He was no more than sixteen or seventeen, like so many other boys who'd died for the Confederate States of America.

Surprisingly, Laurel fought tears. She thought she'd forgotten how to cry. She swallowed the odd block in her throat and managed a smile. There was nothing she could do but ease the boy's life into death. "You're a brave man," she said, her voice shaky.

"I'm d-dying," the boy said. Blood bubbled across his lips and coated his chin.

Laurel considered lying, telling him that he'd be as good as new in a week or two, but something in the young man's expression stopped her. She stroked his furrowed brow and swept back a hank of greasy hair from his forehead. "Yes, you are," she said gently.

Panicked fear flashed through his dirt and smoke-blackened features, but there was also gratitude for her honesty. "N-never thought . . . it would . . . end l-like this."

Ignoring the gory sight of his gaping belly wound, Laurel clasped one of the boy's hands between hers. Empty words of comfort lodged in her throat.

"M-my pa was right." The boy closed his eyes and his breath rasped loudly.

"About what?"

"Killing . . . the War."

She nodded even though she wasn't certain what he meant.

The young soldier stared at her with eyes far too old for his age. "Tell my p-pa . . . t-tell him that he's the b-bravest man I know."

His expression relaxed and for a moment, Laurel could see the carefree child he'd been. "I will." She leaned closer and whispered, "I promise."

The boy seemed to sigh, then his eyes became unfocused as he stared unseeingly into the desolate sky.

A single tear rolled down Laurel's cheek and dripped onto his lifeless body. She hastily brushed the moisture from the tattered uniform and drew back her shoulders. She didn't have time for sorrow.

She methodically went through his pockets and found his ration card with his name, Lyman Eaton, and where he was from in his jacket, and a pocket watch in his trousers. She'd record his final words in her journal and add his name to the one hundred and thirty-three other soldiers who'd died in her care. She glanced at the other boy who was already dead and found his card, also in his jacket pocket—Austin Forrester, who was from the same town in Texas.

Her gaze moved from the one dead boy to the other and she wondered if they'd been friends—children playing a game of war together, except this time the weapons were real and they'd paid the ultimate price. Together.

Ignoring her soul-deep weariness, Laurel tucked the watch and the two ration cards in her smock pocket. There were wounded boys who needed her assistance.

$\mathcal{O}$NE

Six months later

February 7, 1865. Private Jeremiah Hoskins from Chapel Crest, Tennessee. Wounded at the Battle of Hatcher's Run on February 6. Brown curly hair, hazel eyes, scar on his chin, eighteen years old. Cause of death: minié ball to the upper right chest. "Tell my Jenny I love her and tell Ma and Pa I made them proud."

LAUREL Covey's thin bonnet was little protection against the hot Tennessee sun and she felt the tickling sensation of sweat rolling down her back. She ignored the irritation. It wasn't difficult. She'd had over two years to learn how to overlook annoyances.

The memory of the hospital tent filled with wretched moans invaded her thoughts. Her nose wrinkled at the remembered odors of blood, sweat, urine, and rotting tissue. Laurel held her breath and when she finally gulped in air, there was nothing but the scent of damp soil. With a shaking hand, she wiped the beaded perspiration from her brow. Funny how the stench hadn't bothered her during the

War, but now her stomach roiled simply from the memory.

She shifted her backside on the wagon's unforgiving oak seat, glad for the discomfort to keep her thoughts from straying again. She glanced down at the cloth bag that held her precious journal and the remaining possessions to return to families. Soon, she'd be passing on his final words to his loved ones—to Jenny and to his parents. Instead of merely names scrawled in her book, they would become real people. There would be tears and anger, just as there had been at the last fifteen places where she'd taken messages from dead sons, husbands, or brothers.

For a moment, desolation swept through her, bringing bleak emptiness. Despite the heat of the day, she shivered. She reminded herself that the War was over and had been for four months. There would be no more soldiers dying, and no more words to record and pass on to loved ones. There were only those remaining messages in her journal.

Promises to keep.

The pockmarked road ran through a thick copse of trees, which opened as Laurel rounded a curve. A small shack, made of warped wood, weathered gray by the sun and rain, stood amidst three rooting pigs and a dozen scrawny, scratching chickens. She halted her mule, Dickens, and remained seated in the wagon. Although there was an air of poverty surrounding the home, it didn't look like it had been touched by the ravages of war like so many others.

A lean, stooped man wearing faded overalls and carrying an ancient rifle came out of the house. A stained floppy hat with more than one hole covered his head and shaded his face. The way he held the gun told Laurel he was the distrustful type. Not that she blamed him. It was difficult to tell the difference between friend and foe nowadays.

"Whaddya want?" he called to her in a gruff voice, keeping his weapon aimed in her direction.

"Is this the Hoskins home?"

He spat a stream of brown tobacco juice onto the bare ground. "Who wants to know?"

"My name's Laurel Covey and if you're Mr. Hoskins, I have a message from your son, Jeremiah."

His grip tightened on the rifle as pain flashed through his gaunt face. "My son's dead. Got me a letter that said so."

Laurel glanced down at her gloved hands and blinked away the moisture filming her eyes. Taking a deep breath, she raised her head. "I know and I'm sorry for your loss. I was with him when he died. He asked me to pass on a message."

Hoskins remained as still as a statue and Laurel could feel his measuring gaze. Despite the urge to look away, she kept her own eyes steady. One of the pigs wandered closer to the wagon, and his snuffling snorts distracted her and gave her something on which to focus.

The rifle barrel wavered and finally lowered. "I'm Jeremiah's pa." His voice echoed with weariness. "C'mon in. The missus just put on some coffee."

He turned back toward the house, leaving Laurel to clamber down from the wagon alone. She set the brake and tied the reins, grabbed her journal, and followed Hoskins's hunched figure into the shack.

Laurel stepped across the door's threshold and blinked in the abrupt darkness. Greasy smoke hazed the room, blurring the corners and the simple, hand-hewn furniture that occupied it. A movement caught her attention and she spotted a thin woman moving about the kitchen. Another woman, younger and with a rounded belly, kneaded bread dough.

"Says she got words from Jeremiah," Hoskins announced to the two women.

The younger one ceased punching the dough and stared at Laurel. The older woman, probably Jeremiah's mother, froze for only a moment, then said, "Sit. Would you like some coffee?"

Laurel nodded. "Yes, please." Three small steps carried her to the table and she lowered herself to a rough chair gingerly. She removed her gloves and laid them aside.

Mrs. Hoskins brought two cups of coffee and set one on the table in front of Laurel. The other she gave to her husband, then she stepped back and eyed Laurel.

To allow herself a moment to gather her composure, Laurel sipped the coffee that tasted like hot dishwater. But she couldn't begrudge their hospitality. Food was in short supply and the price reflected its scarcity.

Keeping her expression blank, she laid her hand on the journal that she'd set on the table. "I was a nurse during the War," she began in the suffocating silence. "Jeremiah was wounded during the battle at Hatcher's Run and brought to the tent hospital where I worked."

The young woman, obviously in a family way, wiped her hands on a threadbare towel and joined them. "So you seen him afore—" she glanced away. "Afore he passed?"

Seeing her close up, Laurel was shocked to find the young woman was actually a girl, maybe thirteen or fourteen years old. She stifled her surprise and nodded. "Yes, I did. Are you Jenny?"

"Yes, ma'am." She lifted her dainty chin. "Jeremiah was my husband."

For a moment, Laurel felt much older than her twenty-seven years. She managed a smile. "I didn't know him well, but I could tell he was a good man." *Even if he was only a boy himself.*

Jenny's lower lip trembled and her eyes glittered with tears before she blinked them back. "He died a hero."

Laurel's stomach churned. There was nothing heroic about fighting a losing battle. But she forced herself to nod. "His last words were for you and his parents."

Mrs. Hoskins gasped and moved closer to her husband. "Wh-what did he say?"

Laurel opened the journal to where she'd left a blue ribbon to mark Jeremiah Hoskins's entry. She licked her lips and read his words. "Tell my Jenny I love her, and tell Ma and Pa I made them proud."

Jenny covered her mouth with her hand as her expression paled and two tears trickled down her cheeks. Mrs.

Hoskins tried to stifle a sob but Laurel heard and felt it, like a knife twisting in her heart. Jeremiah's father looked away, his lips curling into a grimace of anguish.

Laurel stared down at the words in her journal but all she could see was a vivid picture of Jeremiah's final moments. The futile desperation and horrible realization that death was close at hand had brought tears to the boy's eyes. He'd sobbed his last words to her and died with panic etched in his face.

Mr. Hoskins cleared his throat, bringing Laurel back to the present. She lifted her head and met his watery gaze.

"He was a good boy," the man said with an emotion-roughened voice.

Although Laurel hadn't known him, she nodded.

"He was so damned scared the war was gonna end afore he could sign up." Hoskins drew a gnarled hand across his eyes. "Didn't wanna be left outta the glory."

Glory. There was no glory in drowning in your own blood.

"Me and him married a week afore he left," Jenny said, a hand curved protectively over her round belly. "Said he'd come back a hero."

Bitterness rose in Laurel's throat but she choked it back. "He died doing what he believed was right," she said.

Mrs. Hoskins threw her arms out and resentment spilled through her voice. "He was a damned fool. I told him he ought to stay home with his wife and not go gallivantin' off to war."

Jenny clasped her mother-in-law's hand. "Don't, Mama Hoskins. He's gone. Ain't nothing going to bring him back. And it don't do no good to be blamin' him."

The older woman snapped her mouth shut and her fury fled, replaced with grief.

Laurel eyed the girl, taken aback by her mature words. She swallowed her own anger and tried to ease some of the sorrow that filled the tiny cabin. "Jenny's right. Jeremiah's last thoughts were of his family, so I know he loved you all very much."

"Did he suffer?" Hoskins suddenly asked, pinning her with a penetrating gaze.

Laurel glanced down and ran her hand over the smooth surface of her journal. "No," she lied.

Hoskins stared at her for a long moment then nodded. He straightened his spine. "Would you like to stay for supper?"

Laurel's belly protested at the thought of food and she shook her head. "No, thank you." She stood. "I should return to town." She faced Mrs. Hoskins, who was being held by her petite daughter-in-law. "I'm very sorry for your loss."

Jenny managed a slight smile. "Thank you, Miz Covey. It comforts me to know my Jeremiah had someone by his side when he died."

He shouldn't have died. The angry words leapt to Laurel's tongue but she pressed her lips together to keep them from springing forth. Instead, she merely nodded.

Hoskins walked her out, his damning silence preying on Laurel's conscience. He awkwardly helped her climb up into the wagon then he shoved his hands into the sides of his overalls. "I 'preciate you lyin' 'bout how my boy died. His ma and wife don't need to know he suffered in the end."

Laurel licked her dry lips, surprised by his astuteness. She looked over his shoulder, to the peaceful setting of green trees and the colorful flicker of flitting birds. It was a scene she'd despaired of ever witnessing again. "If it's any comfort, Jeremiah faced his death like a man."

Hoskins's chest puffed out. "I didn't raise no crybaby. Taught him to be tough, like a man."

Afraid to say anything more, Laurel released the brake and slapped the leather reins across the mule's rump. As she drove away, she wondered if she'd done the right thing. But then, what was another white lie or two if it gave a grieving family some solace? Speaking the truth would only bring more pain. No, she had no reason to taint their memories with the harsh realities of war.

Her thoughts roamed as Dickens plodded along the road

back to town. Sixteen families contacted, with only five more remaining. Not that there were only twenty-one soldiers she'd seen die, but those were the ones who left final words to pass on to their families. Most relatives lived in Virginia where she'd been at the end of the War so it hadn't been difficult to find them. However, those left ranged from Tennessee to Texas.

But what else was left for Laurel besides delivering deathbed messages? Her own parents had disowned her. They'd made it perfectly clear that the Massachusetts Monteilles were not traitors to their country, unlike Virginia-born Richard Covey who'd died at Gettysburg. Laurel had chosen her husband over her family and continued to pay the price for her loyalty.

The sudden cessation of bird trills brought Laurel out of her dark musings. Dickens's large ears pointed upward and he kept swinging his knobby head to the right, toward the heavy woods that lined the road.

Icy tendrils of alarm spread down Laurel's spine, but it was still a shock when two men on horseback abruptly charged out onto the middle of the road in front of Dickens. She instinctively drew back on the reins, halting the skittery mule.

Stiff with tension, she gazed at the men, dressed in familiar ragged gray pants and shirts. They'd obviously been soldiers in the Confederate army but that observation brought no comfort. Desperate times bred desperate men.

"Afternoon, ma'am." The older of the two drawled a polite greeting.

Laurel nodded, her pounding heart lodged in her throat. "Good afternoon."

They continued to stare at her, their hungry gazes resting on her breasts. Dread slithered down her spine. With their horses blocking the road, she didn't have a chance of escape. "Can I help you?" she asked, keeping her voice even.

"Reckon you can," the younger ruffian said. "After you give us your money and fancy jewelry."

His meaning was obvious and Laurel shuddered with revulsion and more than a trace of fear. "Please, don't do this." She hated the pleading in her voice.

As the men shifted to opposite sides and moved toward her, she struck the mule's rumps with the reins. Dickens jumped and brayed, then surged forward. The younger outlaw reached down to grab his traces, halting the animal. Metal jangled and hooves hammered the ground, but there was no getting away from the brigands.

Laurel's heart plummeted.

The older one approached her and leered, revealing brown teeth. "Now that weren't very friendly of you. We ain't even got to know each other yet."

The stench of his unwashed body wafted across her as her breath quickened in terror. Had she survived the conditions of the hospital camps only to be robbed and assaulted by two men she might have nursed during the war? If the situation weren't so dire, she would've laughed at life's irony. Still, maybe it was a fitting recompense for someone who'd lived when so many others had died.

CREEDE Forrester drew back on Red's reins, stopping the chestnut mare. He removed his broad-brimmed hat and dragged his forearm across his sweat-soaked brow. The light breeze ruffled his shaggy hair, cooling his scalp and the back of his neck.

Squinting up at the sun's position, he reckoned it was mid-afternoon sometime in early September although he'd be hard-pressed to come up with the exact day. What did it matter if he didn't know if it was a Tuesday or a Saturday? The last day he had more than a scant recollection of had been the day he received the letter. It had been the eighth of March, and gray clouds holding the elusive promise of rain had scudded across the sky. He could even recall how one of those clouds had been shaped like a smithy's anvil. Funny how he could picture that easier than he could remember his son's face.

He slapped his hat back on his head and urged his mare into motion once more. He idly wondered if he was on a fool's errand, yet what difference did it make if he was? What did he care if his cotton farm languished under the scorching Texas sun? There was no son to leave it to, no wife to give him another child. At thirty-eight years old, Creede was back to where he'd started twenty years ago.

"Leave me alone!"

The woman's cry straightened Creede's spine and, before he made a conscious decision, he dug his heels into Red's sides. Coming around a tree-lined bend, he immediately sighted a mule-drawn wagon flanked by two men. One of them was attempting to drag a woman out of the wagon.

Creede reached back and pulled his rifle out of its casing. Even before his horse stopped, he fired two rounds into the air. For a second, the frozen scene was almost comical with the men's mouths gaping and the woman's eyes wide. Then the man shoved the woman back and she flailed as she fought to keep from tumbling out of the wagon. Regaining her balance, she dropped heavily onto the plank seat.

Before Creede could draw a bead on the outlaws, the scraggly men fled in the opposite direction. He considered chasing after them, but suspected the woman might need some assurance. Kneeing his horse forward, he neared her slowly, careful to keep his arms open and his expression nonthreatening.

The woman regarded him warily as she readjusted her bonnet, tucking long wheat-colored hair beneath it. Even though her face was the color of ripe cotton, her brown eyes were steady and her chin raised.

"Thank you," she said with an amazingly strong voice.

Creede slid his rifle back in its scabbard and inclined his head. "You're welcome. Did they hurt you, ma'am?"

Her gaze darted away but returned to him almost immediately. "No. Your arrival was most timely."

He replayed her words and the cadence of her speech in

his mind, and it struck him that there was an absence of the genteel southern drawl. "You're not from around here."

She appeared, for the first time, uncertain. "That's right."

The way this woman spoke her words brought to mind a long-ago acquaintance named Boston Bill, who'd been as handy with a gun as he was with fancy words. "You from Massachusetts?"

Surprise was followed closely by a skittishness that he'd seen in an orphaned fawn he'd found over ten years ago. His son had persuaded him to bring the young deer back to the house, and they'd bottle-fed the fawn until it just up and left one morning. Austin had been heartbroken. Creede shook aside the bittersweet memory.

"Where I come from is of no concern of yours, Mr.—"

"Forrester, Creede Forrester." He tipped his hat using his thumb and forefinger.

She narrowed her eyes. "If I were a gambling woman, I'd say you were from Texas."

Creede almost smiled. "Yes, ma'am."

"You're a long way from home, Mr. Forrester."

"You and me, both, ma'am."

Her lips tilted upward but her eyes remained somber. "Mrs. Laurel Covey originally from, as you ascertained, Massachusetts."

Lightheadedness assailed Creede as he stared at the woman for whom he'd been searching for over two months. Mrs. Covey was the nurse who'd been working in the hospital tent where his son had died.

"Are you all right, Mr. Forrester?"

He blinked her concerned face into focus and the dizziness receded. Part of him wanted answers to his questions immediately, but another part of him lacked the courage. Clinging to the foolish hope that it was all a mistake and his son was still alive, he chose to hold his questions for the time being. He didn't even attempt a smile to reassure her. "Just a touch of heat. So what brings you to Tennessee, Mrs. Covey?"

She stared over his right shoulder. "Promises, Mr. Forrester."

Her vague reply brought more questions, but Creede suspected those were questions she had no intention of answering. He hoped she'd be more forthcoming when he found the courage to ask about his son. "Where are you headed?"

She smoothed her dress over her lap. "Back to town."

"Is your husband waiting for you?"

Sorrow darkened her features momentarily, then she shook her head. "No."

Was she a war widow? If so, had her husband been in the Confederate Army? That would explain why a woman from Massachusetts had been a nurse for the South. Creede crossed his wrists on the saddle horn, keeping his questions unasked. "If you don't mind, I'll ride along."

She turned to glance in the direction the outlaws had bolted. "Do you think they'll return?"

He shrugged, hiding the flare of protectiveness she engendered. He assured himself it was only because he wanted to keep her safe until he could talk to her about his son. "They skedaddled pretty fast, but it's hard to tell. Besides, I'm going in the same direction as you, so it's not out of my way." He paused, his gaze probing to see past her cool composure. "That is, if you don't mind."

Indecision chased across her flushed features, but when she met his eyes, there was no hint of hesitancy. "Thank you, Mr. Forrester, I accept your offer."

Relief eased the coil in his belly. "Would you like me to handle the mule?"

"I'm fine." She smoothed a gloved palm across a bag sitting on the seat beside her, as if whatever was inside was something precious.

Without another word, Mrs. Covey stirred the mule into motion. Creede rode beside the wagon, close enough to engage the woman in conversation. However, by the set of her jaw, she didn't seem inclined to talk. That suited him fine since he wasn't certain how long he could stall his questions.

Thirty minutes later the settlement, a haphazard collection of sun-faded wooden buildings, came into view. It wasn't much different than a hundred other towns Creede had come through since leaving Texas.

"Where are you staying?" he asked.

"The Brand Hotel. It's the only hotel in town."

He didn't say anything more but merely continued to ride along until she stopped the mule in front of a livery. Creede dismounted and moved to the wagon. Lifting a hand to her, he waited while Mrs. Covey made her decision. Finally, she laid her hand in his hand and he held her slim fingers in his palm, grasping them snugly.

Once down on the ground, she quickly pulled her hand back to her side. Creede didn't blame her for being jumpy. From what he'd gathered, the two outlaws had wanted more than her money.

She reached up to grasp the cloth bag sitting on the seat. "Thank you for your assistance, Mr. Forrester."

"Are you staying in town long?" he asked.

"Not long. Why?" Suspicion colored her tone.

"Would you be interested in having dinner with me?" Creede preferred to speak with her someplace more private than the livery.

Laurel stared at him and opened her mouth as if to decline his invitation. But she seemed to reconsider and smiled slightly. "Thank you, Mr. Forrester. I'd like that."

Although he'd hoped she'd agree, he was surprised by her acceptance. "Does the hotel have a restaurant?"

"Yes. Perhaps we can meet in the lobby at six?"

"That would be fine, Mrs. Covey."

The woman took a step back. "Thank you again, Mr. Forrester. Until six."

Creede watched her walk to the hotel but his dark thoughts didn't allow him to appreciate her womanly shape. In a few hours, he'd get the answers he'd ridden over a thousand miles to acquire.

But would they be the answers he hoped to find?

$\mathscr{T}$WO

AS Laurel crossed the street, she could feel Mr. Forrester's gaze upon her. However, she sensed no hint of malice in his scrutiny and her tense shoulders slumped with fatigue.

She greeted the hotel desk clerk with a nod and climbed the stairs to the second floor. Once inside her room at the end of the hall, she placed her journal on the crude chest of drawers. Keeping her mind blank, she removed her bonnet and gloves and set them beside the book.

The trembling started then, and she lowered herself to the narrow bed. Recognizing the delayed reaction as an aftereffect of the danger she'd faced didn't help her gain control of her body's response any quicker. The only thing she could do—as she'd told countless soldiers during the War—was ride out the tremors.

She lifted her legs onto the bed and curled her knees into her chest. Sweat coated her brow and dampened her palms. She expected her mind to replay her brush with the outlaws, but instead she saw bloodstained wagons filled with wounded soldiers. During the War, it had been a rare day when no ambulance came to the hospital tent. And those days were usually spent nursing the soldiers and cleaning the tents, including the ones where the amputations were done.

Laurel opened her eyes to stop the memories from gaining a firm foothold. She'd already experienced the reality once; she had no wish to relive those days. Thinking about the two ruffians was infinitely safer than letting her mind take flight on its own.

Finally her shakes lessened and she straightened her stiff legs and rolled onto her back to stare at the water-stained ceiling. She took a deep breath to chase away the lingering pictures. She was alive and unharmed, and that should be all that mattered.

Now able to think more clearly, she considered Mr. Creede Forrester. He'd saved her from being robbed and worse, yet she suspected there was more to his well-timed arrival than mere coincidence. Yet if he had his own nefarious reasons for chasing the thieves away, why did he escort her safely into town?

She wiped her perspiration-coated brow. Perhaps she should simply be grateful that Mr. Forrester had crossed her path. She'd almost declined his invitation to dinner, but since she owed him a debt of gratitude she'd gone against her better judgment and agreed to meet him. Besides, it might be nice to eat a meal in the company of another human being. Ever since she'd begun her quest to deliver the soldiers' last messages, she'd spent much of her time alone . . . or in the company of ghosts.

The start of a headache throbbed through her temples. It wasn't unexpected. After relaying a final message to a family, a headache would usually strike. She stood and dampened a cloth with some water from the pitcher, then lay back down and set the cool cloth on her forehead. She hoped the headache would be gone or severely lessened by dinnertime, or she would have to cancel her dinner engagement.

Regretting her acceptance, Laurel hoped that would be the case, but a part of her—the young girl she had been—yearned to spend time with her handsome rescuer.

* * *

CREEDE nervously plucked at the string tie around his collar, not so much worried about how he looked but fearful of the answers only Mrs. Covey could give him. He sat in one of the worn overstuffed chairs in the hotel's lobby. At one time the Brand Hotel probably outshone anything else in the small town, but now its finery was faded and moth-riddled. Its shabbiness was either a result of the War or time, or both.

"Mr. Forrester?"

Creede jumped to his feet, surprised he'd missed Mrs. Covey's approach. "Ma'am."

She'd changed out of her simple skirt and blouse, and now wore a rust-colored dress with tiny green and yellow flowers sprinkled across it. No hat covered her head, and her golden-brown hair was gathered in a loose bun at the nape of her slender neck. Stray ringlets framed her face, softening her plain features.

He offered her his arm and she slid her hand through the crook, allowing him to lead her to the dining area. Less than half the tables were occupied, and Creede escorted Mrs. Covey to one at the back of the room where he could observe the comings and goings of the patrons. It was a habit he thought he'd laid to rest years ago.

After the waitress brought them coffee and took their orders, awkward silence fell between Creede and his dining companion.

"So what brings you to Tennessee?" Mrs. Covey asked, obviously more concerned with breaking the uncomfortable impasse than the answer to her question.

Creede stared down at his hand resting on the table. The time for answers had arrived. He raised his head and met Mrs. Covey's steady gaze. "You."

Her lips formed an O but no words emerged. She closed her mouth and tried again. "Do I know you?"

He shook his head and tried to find some moisture for his sand-dry mouth. "No, but you may have known my son."

Confusion vied with wariness in her expression. "Where did I meet him?"

Creede's gut knotted so tightly he had trouble drawing air into his lungs. "During the War, in your hospital."

Her brow furrowed and Creede could almost see her mind spinning. He knew the moment she recognized the name by the way sympathy replaced her confusion.

"Was your son's name Austin?" she asked softly.

Creede nodded as shivers swept through him. He fought the impulse to run, to hold onto hope for another minute, another hour.

"I'm sorry. He was dead when they brought him in," she said, her eyes filled with compassion.

Denial rose in Creede, black and desperate. "Are you certain it was him?"

"The ration card in his pocket had his name on it." She leaned forward and laid her hand on his fisted one. "There was nothing anybody could've done for him."

Moisture burned in Creede's eyes and the room swam in blurriness. The last fragile thread of hope was cut. Austin was dead. Gone to his mother, who'd been killed ten years ago. Now there was no one left—no wife or son—and the last seventeen years of Creede's life were erased, as if they had never happened. Everything he'd built—a home, a prospering cotton farm, a new life—was for nothing.

"Mr. Forrester, our food is here," Mrs. Covey said.

He blinked and absently watched the waitress set their plates on the table. Although his stomach protested even the smell of food, he forced himself to pick up his fork and put some potatoes in his mouth. They tasted like wood.

"Are you all right?" Mrs. Covey asked, her own meal untouched.

No. Nothing will ever be right again.

"I'm fine," he replied curtly. "You should eat before it gets cold."

She frowned but picked at her food. "Do you have other children?"

"No."

"What about your wife?"

Creede set his fork down and took a drink of coffee to cover the fresh anguish, the knowledge that his family was no more. "She died ten years ago."

"My husband is gone, too, so I know a little of what you're feeling."

Anger slid like red-hot fire through his veins. "Is your only child dead, too?"

Her face blanched but her gaze didn't waver as she shook her head.

"Then don't tell me you know how I'm feeling," he said in a low, raspy voice.

She drew back, as if slapped. "I apologize. You're right. I'll never know what losing a child feels like."

Her words, spoken with stiff civility, dissolved his fury. He rubbed his brow and sighed. "No, I'm sorry, Mrs. Covey. I had no call saying what I did."

"You had every right. Losing a child . . ." She cleared her throat. "I've seen other parents, felt their grief and anger at their loss. I wish I could've saved them—all those sons who died—but I couldn't."

Creede roused himself from his own sorrow to recognize the regret and self-reproach in the former nurse. "I don't know what it must've been like for you, Mrs. Covey, but I have fought battles, and in battles men die." He cleared his throat. "Boys, too. It's not your fault. You didn't pull the trigger."

"No, I didn't, but I also didn't do anything to try to stop the bloodshed. Once the soldiers' wounds were treated and they were able to walk, we sent them out into the carnage again."

Was that what had happened to Austin? The letter Creede received stated that his son had been injured. But by the time Creede arrived in Virginia, the War was over and Austin was dead. Had the doctors declared him fit for duty, then sent him back to the fighting, only to have him mortally wounded the next time?

Mrs. Covey dabbed her lips with a napkin. "Now that

you have the information you sought, Mr. Forrester, I will take my leave."

Creede glanced at her barely touched plate of food. "But you aren't finished eating."

"I've lost my appetite."

"Won't you stay for a few more minutes?"

"Why? It's obvious you wanted more than I could give you regarding your son's demise." A hint of bitterness wove through her tone.

Creede didn't have an answer for her, only a wish not to be alone for a little while longer. "I like having someone to eat with."

She glanced down as pink tinted her cheeks. When she lifted her head, she nodded. "I'll stay and finish my coffee."

Unexplained relief flowed through Creede. Even though Austin had been dead when he arrived at the hospital, Mrs. Covey had been one of the last persons to see him. That reason alone was enough to want to spend more time in the woman's company.

He picked up his fork, but set it down when he realized he, too, was no longer hungry. "How did your husband die?"

Mrs. Covey rested both elbows on the table as she held her coffee cup between her slender hands—hands that had touched his son's lifeless body. Creede forced his gaze back to her face.

"Gettysburg. He was pierced with a saber," she replied.

"I'm sorry."

"It wasn't your fault," she said, throwing his words back at him. Her gaze became unfocused. "He was an officer. It was his decision to fight." She cleared her throat, but her expression remained collected. "And die."

"Nobody chooses to die."

Mrs. Covey's attention returned to him and infinite sadness reflected in her eyes. "You're wrong, Mr. Forrester. I knew men who chose death rather than live without an arm or a leg. They simply gave up and willed themselves to pass."

"It seems to me a man ought not to give up, that he should fight until the end."

"Those are easy words to say when you haven't been in their position, Mr. Forrester."

Creede clenched his jaw, not certain if she was mocking him or merely stating a fact.

"How did you find me?" Mrs. Covey suddenly asked.

He leaned back in his chair, shrugging off his irritation. "I spoke with a doctor you worked with—James Lampley. Dr. Lampley told me you were visiting the families of some of the soldiers. He gave me some of the names of the towns you were traveling to."

"I wanted one person to know." Then she added quietly, "One person who cared."

Mrs. Covey's tone was lacking self-pity, which made Creede all the more sympathetic. He leaned forward. "What of your family? Didn't they try to stop you?"

"I have no family, Mr. Forrester."

She rose and Creede scrambled to his feet.

"Thank you for your timely intervention this afternoon, Mr. Forrester," she said. "I don't want to think about what might have happened if you hadn't arrived when you did." Her voice was as steady as her gaze.

"What about the next time?"

She blinked, losing her composure for a moment. "What do you mean?"

"You're a woman traveling alone. You're inviting trouble."

Anger sparked her eyes. "I'll be prepared next time. Goodnight, Mr. Forrester." She spun around, but paused and said over her shoulder, "Thank you for dinner."

Creede scowled at her retreat. A strange combination of irritation, protectiveness, and admiration wound through him. However, underlying it all was bone-deep grief for his son and a vast emptiness where he could easily lose himself.

Suddenly craving the oblivion only liquor could give

him, he dropped some coins on the table for the meal. As he strode out of the hotel lobby, he ripped off his tie and stuffed it in his pocket. Where he was headed, he wouldn't need it.

LANTERNS swayed in the breeze, casting obscene shadows across the stretchers bearing wounded soldiers. Laurel ignored the battle of dark against light and focused on her gruesome task. She knelt beside the first man and immediately recognized the damage from a saber. His right arm remained connected to the rest of his body by little more than a flap of skin.

She called for someone to carry the wounded soldier to the amputation tent, which was far enough away to keep his screams muted from the rest of the crude hospital.

"No, please don't take my arm." A tear rolled down the man's cheek.

Laurel leaned over him and beneath the blood and dirt, she recognized her husband. She fell back as a scream crawled up her throat . . .

Suddenly Laurel awakened and stared wide-eyed into the darkness. Confusion clouded her mind as she tried to figure out why she wasn't at the field hospital. Her husband . . . No, Robert was dead.

She glanced around. *Why am I standing in the hotel hallway?* Heavy footsteps coming up the stairs roused her out of her bewilderment. She frantically cast her gaze about to find the door to her room, and fled to it as her thin nightgown flapped around her bare legs. Fortunately the door wasn't locked and she scrambled inside, clicking it softly behind her.

Leaning against the door, she panted in the thick, humid air. Sweat rolled down her face and chest, dampening the front of her gown.

She awakened from nightmares often with a scream caught on her lips, but always before she'd been in her bed. Tonight, she had no memory of rising and walking out her door. What if someone had found her sleepwalking in the hall? They would think she was crazy.

Of course, that wasn't far from the truth.

She slid to the floor and wrapped her arms around her drawn-up legs. Why had she dreamed of Robert's death? She hadn't even been at his side when he died. She'd been at the Richmond hospital because Robert hadn't wanted her near the front lines. So while he lay dying, she'd been wearing her spotless, pressed nursing smock, tending men who would end up back in their units to fight—and maybe die—another day.

Laying her cheek on her knees, she lost the strength to fight the memories. The familiar ghosts paraded through her mind. Some were missing an arm or a leg, a few were short two limbs, another's eyes were gone, and still another had half his face burned away. She knew them all. She'd helped save their lives, only to have the gift of life spurned.

Minutes passed until Laurel roused herself. She lifted her head, surprised to see her gown where she'd laid her face was damp with tears. She pushed herself to her feet and splashed some water on her hot face, then crawled back into her rumpled bed. If she were lucky she'd fall back asleep for a few more hours and not dream.

Laurel was never that lucky.

STANDING in the livery's open door, Creede squinted against the low-hanging morning sun and tried to close his ears to the birds' shrill songs. The problem with the morning—besides the fact it came too damned early—was he felt emptier now than he had last night.

His stomach rolled and pitched and he pressed a hand to his belly to stave off another bout of vomiting. He didn't know how there could be anything left in his gut. It was a good thing he'd decided to sleep in the livery instead of getting a room at the hotel—it would've been a waste of money. He couldn't have staggered that far after polishing off the bottle of rotgut last night.

Rubbing a hand over his grizzled cheeks and jaw, he decided to forego a shave. As much as he was shaking he'd probably slit his throat, which wouldn't bother anyone except the livery owner who'd have to clean up the mess.

Fresh grief welled up in him. Although he kept reminding himself that Austin was dead, his heart refused to accept it. He'd accepted his wife's death because he'd seen her shot and held her in his arms while she'd died. But the last time Creede had seen his son was the night before he'd run away to join the Confederate Army. Sixteen-year-old Austin had been alive and whole . . . and intent on doing his share to preserve the South despite his father's objections.

Creede shook his head to clear his mind then wished he hadn't. His head spun and his stomach followed. He managed to stave off the nausea by panting through his mouth.

"Mr. Forrester?"

The feminine voice startled him into opening his eyes. In front of him stood Mrs. Covey, dressed in a brown skirt and loose white blouse. A wide-brimmed hat covered her head and shaded her face, and her slender hands were encased in black gloves.

Creede reached for the brim of his hat and realized he wasn't wearing it. Glancing down at himself, he was relieved to see he was wearing trousers and a shirt. "Mornin', Mrs. Covey. You're up early."

She raised her head to study the slant of the sun. "It's nearly nine o'clock. I would hardly call that early." Bringing her gaze back to him, she frowned. "Are you all right?"

Heat flushed Creede's cheeks. It was one thing to get stinking drunk and nurse a hangover the next morning, but it was another to have someone notice his less-than-respectable condition. "I'm fine." It was then he noticed she was carrying two bags and the same cloth sack she'd had yesterday. "You going somewhere?"

Irritation flickered across her face. "Yes." She brushed past him into the barn, calling, "Mr. Miller."

Creede followed, curiosity getting the better of him.

She stopped in the center of the barn and the livery owner—Miller—joined her.

"I'll be leaving this morning," Mrs. Covey told the big-bellied man wearing a pair of faded overalls.

Miller mopped his round face with a yellowed handkerchief. "I'll get your horse and mule ready, ma'am." He trudged away to carry out his task.

"I thought you had a wagon," Creede said, leaning against a post to keep upright.

"I rented it. I travel by horseback."

For some reason, that made Creede angrier. "For being such a smart woman, you sure don't have any sense when it comes to traveling alone."

Mrs. Covey's eyes flashed with indignation. "And I suppose it was sensible of you to drown yourself in cheap whiskey last night."

Creede's face heated beneath her rebuke, knowing she was right, but damned if he'd admit it. "A woman riding alone is inviting trouble."

"I didn't have any trouble getting from Virginia to Tennessee by myself."

Creede's head pounded from his hangover, increasing his impatience. "You were damned lucky. Do you think those two men planned on only robbing you yesterday?"

Her cheeks flamed but her stubborn chin didn't waver. "No. They also said they were going to have some fun." Her nostrils flared. "Which meant they planned to violate me, too."

Creede's mouth gaped. He hadn't expected such a blunt reply. "You're willing to chance that happening again?"

Shadows flitted in her eyes. "I have no choice."

"Yes, you do. You can go back home."

She straightened her backbone and her icy gaze nearly froze him. "My parents disowned me for marrying a Southerner. My husband's parents despise me because I'm a Northerner. Pray tell, where is my home, Mr. Forrester?"

At the best of times, Creede would've been hard-pressed to give her an answer. Having a hangover gave him no chance at all. "Go back to that doctor friend in Virginia."

"Dr. Lampley has no room for a widow in his home with a wife and four children. Or are you suggesting I insinuate myself as his mistress so he'd give me a place to live?"

Creede flinched at her caustic tone. Damn it, he needed a drink.

Miller, the liveryman, led a dun mare and a bony mule toward them and held the reins while Mrs. Covey strapped her bags to the mule's frame pack. The cloth sack she slipped into one side of her saddlebag.

Mrs. Covey took the horse's reins and the mule's rope from Miller. "Thank you."

"Have a safe trip, ma'am." Miller turned to Creede. "Are you wantin' your horse saddled, too?"

"I can saddle my own damned horse," Creede grumbled.

Miller shrugged and wandered off.

"There's nothing you can do for your son, Mr. Forrester. Go back home to Texas," Mrs. Covey said. Then she turned to mount her horse.

Creede grabbed her arm. She spun around, her nostrils flaring.

"I'm riding with you," he stated.

She jerked her arm out of his grasp. "In your condition, you'd be more of a hindrance than a help."

He couldn't argue that, but the same protective instincts that had tried to safeguard his wife and son now rallied to protect Mrs. Covey. He didn't understand, but he couldn't ignore it either. "Dr. Lampley told me your last stop was somewhere in Texas, so since I'm going there anyway, we'll ride together."

Mrs. Covey pressed her lips together then climbed up onto her horse's saddle before Creede could protest. She adjusted the reins in her right hand and held the mule's rope in the other. "I ride alone, Mr. Forrester. Good-bye."

She heeled her mare's flanks and was out of the livery barn before Creede could stop her. But he'd noticed a flicker of something in her eyes, something that reminded him of that orphaned fawn.

Angry at the memory and even angrier at himself for caring, Creede stomped over to Red's stall and saddled his mare. Whether she wanted his company or not, Mrs. Covey was stuck with him.

$\mathcal{T}$HREE

LAUREL was grateful Dickens didn't balk as they left Chapel Crest—and Creede Forrester—behind.

After six weeks together, Laurel and her two traveling companions had fallen into a familiar routine. Laurel settled into a comfortable slouch in the saddle and slackened the reins, allowing Jeanie, her dun-colored Kentucky Saddler, to travel at her own speed. Dickens plodded along behind, occasionally voicing his displeasure at something or other. The mule could be contrary when he wanted to be, which was more often than not, but he'd behaved like a gentleman this time.

Unlike Mr. Forrester who appeared to have spent the previous night immersed in a bottle of cheap whiskey. It was also obvious he'd been sick this morning as his body tried to rid itself of the poison he'd ingested. Laurel's husband had imbibed on occasion, but she'd never seen him drunk. The closest he'd come was when he'd been promoted to captain and even then he had stayed in control of his faculties. He'd slept in the spare bedroom rather than subject Laurel to his "baser nature."

A humorless smile tugged at Laurel's lips. Oftentimes

she thought it funny that Robert was so concerned about offending her sensibilities. She'd been trained as a nurse and was inured to those same bodily functions of which Robert had been so sensitive.

However, Mr. Forrester appeared to have no compulsion about exposing his "baser nature" to women. Or maybe it was only she he felt no compulsion to treat as a lady. She frowned. Although she held no fondness for him, that assumption bothered her.

Laurel reminded herself it was doubtful she'd see Mr. Forrester again. He'd probably found a pile of straw to sleep off the rest of his drunk.

Disappointment twinged her. For a few moments last evening Laurel had felt like a woman again. The last time she'd dined in a restaurant with a man was when Robert had taken her out to eat for their first anniversary, which had been a month before shots had been fired on Fort Sumter. Mr. Forrester's attention had made her feel young and pretty again. But it had only been wishful thinking. The only reason he'd invited her to dinner was to learn of his son, another casualty of the conflict.

Which was why he'd found comfort in a bottle of whiskey last night.

Shaking aside her melancholy thoughts, Laurel patted the saddlebag that held her precious journal, assuring herself it was still there, then firmly directed her mind to her next destination. The town was situated at the far southwest corner of Tennessee. There Laurel would deliver another message.

Although it was only midmorning, the sun already heralded another hot, sticky day. Now that she was some distance from town, Laurel unbuttoned the top two buttons of her blouse and rolled her long sleeves above her elbows. She debated ridding herself of the gloves but didn't relish gaining a palm full of blisters from the reins and Dickens's lead rope. After glancing around at her deserted surroundings, she defiantly tugged her skirt hems above her knees.

Dickens brayed and Laurel stuck her tongue out at the mule. "If the sight of my legs bothers you, don't look."

Dickens bared his teeth and shook his head.

Laurel didn't bother to retort. Dickens always got in the last word.

In the lulling warmth of the sun Laurel thought back to her innocent years, when death was only a word and war a noble battle of good versus evil. She'd shared secrets with her older sister and spied on her younger brother. Constance had been her matron of honor when Laurel had married Robert. Lester had been attending his second year at Harvard but played hooky to be one of the groomsmen.

Constance had kept in contact with her until the start of the War. With the country split in two, lines of communication between the North and the South were eliminated and few posts made it to their recipients. So even if Constance had sent her a letter, it would have become lost somewhere along the way.

Laurel had considered sending a missive to her sister when the war ended, but so much had changed, including Laurel herself. Besides, their father might get angry with Constance for ignoring his edict. No, it was better to cut the family ties completely than be rebuffed again. The rejection wouldn't hurt any less a second time.

Dickens snorted, which was Laurel's only warning before nearly being dragged out of the saddle by the mule's abrupt stop. Jeanie halted and blew noisily.

Laurel turned in her saddle to scold the mule and her mouth dropped open. Creede Forrester, unshaven and frayed around the edges, sat astride his horse with his hands braced against the saddle horn. For a split second, she didn't recognize him and feared another incident like the one he'd interrupted yesterday.

He dipped his head slightly. "Mrs. Covey."

Laurel snapped her mouth shut and glared at him. "Are you following me?"

He removed his hat and raked a hand through his sweat-flattened dark hair. "My mama taught me to take care of womenfolk."

Anger surged through her. "As I told you already, Mr. Forrester, you don't have to take care of me."

His gaze swept down her, lingering at her neck and legs, then returned to her face. Suddenly realizing her state of undress, Laurel blushed but indignation followed closely on the heels of her embarrassment. She had no intention of being even more miserable in the heat because Mr. Forrester intruded upon her. She'd treat him just as she treated Dickens—if he didn't like what he saw, he needn't look.

He replaced his hat, throwing his grizzled features into shadow. "That may be so, Mrs. Covey, but seeing as how we're both headed in the same direction, it makes sense to travel together."

"I thought you were going back to Texas."

"I am."

"Then your sense of direction leaves something to be desired."

His shoulders lifted in an indolent shrug. "I'll get there sooner or later."

Frustration made Laurel tighten her grip on the reins. "Why do you insist on accompanying me?"

"The hell if I know, ma'am." There was a sardonic tilt to his lips. "Maybe I'm not as bright as I look."

Laurel bit her tongue. At the moment, he didn't appear very bright at all. First drinking himself into a stupor, then following someone who clearly didn't want company pointed to a man of little intelligence. However, the set of his jaw revealed a stubbornness that would do Dickens proud. "Fine. Suit yourself, Mr. Forrester, but don't expect any stimulating conversation."

"That's the last thing I want, Mrs. Covey."

She frowned, wondering if she'd been insulted. However, his wan complexion and bloodshot eyes explained his disinclination to converse. For a moment, she considered chatting only to irritate him, but realized she, too, had no desire to talk. She could only discuss the weather for so long, and anything beyond that was more than she cared to reveal to a virtual stranger. So, she'd say nothing at all, and after a few days, he'd grow bored in her silent company and leave her to travel alone once more.

With her plan set, Laurel gave him a curt nod and turned forward. She tapped her heels to Jeanie's sides and spoke over her shoulder to the mule. "Come on, Dickens."

She heard a rusty chuckle from her unwelcome companion and ignored him. What did she care what Creede Forrester thought of her mule's name?

What did she care about anything Creede Forrester might be thinking?

CREEDE couldn't help thinking he was a damned fool. Following a woman who didn't want his protection, under a blazing sun that made his throbbing head want to explode, wasn't exactly the smartest thing he'd ever done.

Texas was hot, hotter than Tennessee, but the air seemed thicker up here, like he was breathing through heavy fog. His sweat didn't go away, but soaked into his shirt and trousers, making the cloth stick to him like a second clammy skin.

His only consolation was that Mrs. Covey seemed almost as miserable as he was. That was the only explanation he could come up with for her raised skirt hem and unbuttoned blouse. It'd been a long time since he'd seen a lady's calves or the shadowy cleft between her breasts. Not that he thought of Mrs. Covey "that" way. Not with her stiff back and pursed schoolmarm mouth. But there were some things a man just couldn't control—things that a finely curved leg or the pale slope of a breast did to him. Especially a man who'd not been in the company of a woman for too damned long.

The setting sun brought only a small margin of relief

from the heat. Shadows lengthened and birds started their evening chorus.

Mrs. Covey veered her horse off the path and the mule followed without raising a ruckus. Creede stayed behind them, far enough back that the ornery mule couldn't kick him. Dickens had already gotten his hooves too close for comfort more than once during the day. As far as he was concerned, the mule should be called Lucifer instead of being named after some writer.

Minutes later Mrs. Covey stopped and slid out of her saddle. Creede eyed the clearing, impressed by her choice of a campsite. Maybe she acted and sounded like a city woman, but she appeared to have the common sense needed in the wilderness. But then, she'd been a Confederate nurse, too, and he suspected those living conditions had been much worse than out here.

Creede dismounted and turned to the silent woman. "I can take care of your horse and mule, Mrs. Covey." She didn't appear to have heard him and he repeated, "I'll take care of the horses and mule, ma'am."

She leaned close to the mule's twitching ears. "Did you hear an irritating buzz, Dickens?"

Creede listened closely, but couldn't hear any insects, then cursed under his breath. She was obviously referring to him. If his mother had known Mrs. Covey, he doubted she would've been so determined to teach her sons to be protective of a woman. But his mother had, and even if he didn't like Mrs. Covey, he couldn't ignore a lifetime habit.

"Fine," Creede said. "It doesn't change a thing."

He caught a glimpse of her down-turned lips and felt a measure of satisfaction. At least he'd gained a reaction from her.

The evening passed uneventfully in thick silence. Mrs. Covey didn't offer him any of her meal, so Creede ate a dry biscuit and some jerked meat. It was better than nothing, but not by much. After drinking some water from his canteen, Creede laid out his bedroll between the fire and the animals and settled in for the night. He closed his eyes and listened to the quiet rustle of Mrs. Covey's clothing as she, too, retired for the evening. It wasn't long before he heard her steady breathing from the other side of the dwindling campfire.

Creede scowled at the stars. If he had any brains, he'd leave right now. Mrs. Covey obviously didn't want his protection and her silent treatment told him she also didn't want his company.

Then the memory of his wife's lifeless body and his son's laughing face struck him. His gut clenched in anguish and he savagely wiped away the single tear that rolled down the side of his face. He'd killed them as surely as if he'd pulled the trigger himself. Leaving behind his life as a hired gun eighteen years ago hadn't changed a damned thing.

Mrs. Covey shifted restlessly and Creede turned on his side to gaze at her lumpy figure beneath the blanket. She had no one but her horse, her mule, and her damnable pride. If he had the sense God gave a jackass, he'd leave her to them.

Suddenly his blanket was jerked away and he sat up, only to see Dickens toss it aside then grin with his big ugly teeth. Hell, even the mule wanted him to leave.

But the memories of his mother, his wife, and his son demanded that he protect Mrs. Covey better than he'd protected them. And the only way he could do that was to become the man he'd once been.

Swearing under his breath, he stood and retrieved his bedroll. With the blanket in one hand, he stopped in front of the mule. "I'm not leaving." Dickens laid back his ears and Creede glared at him. "I can out-stubborn you so don't even try."

Creede lay back down, feeling a sense of satisfaction.

"Do you feel better now, Mr. Forrester?"

Mrs. Covey's quiet voice startled him and he glanced at her, catching the flash of white teeth in the dim oval of her face.

His face warmed. "I was just telling him how it is."

"Ah, I see." But the humor in her voice said otherwise. With a grumble, Creede rolled over and closed his eyes. One thing was for certain—traveling to Texas with Mrs. Covey would prove he was more mule-headed than even a . . . a damned mule.

LAUREL awakened, feeling more tired than when she'd lain down last night. Her eyes gritty and her muscles stiff, she threw off her single blanket and rose. Pressing her palms to her lower back, she stretched.

She dropped her arms to her sides and gazed at her unwanted traveling companion who continued to slumber. Resentment crested and waned in a matter of seconds. Although he was the reason for her lack of rest, she couldn't blame him for his behavior. Grief made a man do strange things and Mr. Forrester had come face to face with the cold fact that his son was dead. A horrible burden for anyone to bear, especially when he bore it alone. Perhaps acting as her guardian gave him something to cling to, a reason to return to Texas.

However, it didn't make his presence any easier to tolerate. There were things about her she didn't want him—or anyone else—to know. And it was the nights she feared the most. Nightmares were becoming as real as the earth beneath her feet, forcing her to consider that she might be afflicted with the same darkness that stole soldiers' minds and hearts during the War.

Shying away from that thought, she focused on her crude morning toilette then prepared breakfast. As coffee brewed, she checked on Jeanie and Dickens. Recalling how the mule had stolen Mr. Forrester's blanket, she smiled and gave the animal's rough coat an extra pat.

"Were you planning on waking me or just riding out?"

Startled, Laurel turned toward the man. She opened her mouth to reply then closed it, remembering her silent tactic. A tactic she'd forgotten last night, but seeing Mr. Forrester talk to Dickens had been too difficult to resist.

He sighed and scrubbed a hand through his mussed hair. "I figured as much."

Laurel returned to the fire and poured herself a cup of coffee. Manners dictated that she ask Mr. Forrester if he wanted some, but she clamped her lips together. Manners be hanged. She wanted to be rid of him, not encourage him to stay.

Glancing up, she spotted him shaving with a straight edge and using a small rectangular mirror hung crookedly from a tree branch. Four years disappeared and Laurel was once again a new bride to the dashing Robert Covey. Shaving a man in the hospital was simply another duty, but watching Robert shave was an intimacy from which she'd taken guilty pleasure. She'd longed to take the razor from his hand and perform the intimate act herself. The one time she'd suggested it had been her last.

Depressed by the memory, Laurel returned to the present just as Mr. Forrester wiped his face with a rough-looking cloth. She had to admit he appeared almost civilized this morning. He'd even used a comb after sluicing water over his head.

As he put away his shaving items, Laurel set her gaze on the steaming coffee in her hand. She listened to him approach and was surprised when he reached for the pot.

"I'd ask for some, but I suspect you wouldn't answer me so I'll just help myself," he said, pouring coffee into a tin cup.

Laurel scowled at his presumption but didn't offer an argument. She'd have to speak in order to do so.

After she ate a handful of crackers, she readied Jeanie and Dickens. By the time she was prepared to leave, Mr. Forrester was sitting atop his own horse, his wrists crossed on his saddle horn as if he had all the time in the world. He hadn't even offered to help her. Not that she would've taken him up on the offer, but it was the fact that he didn't that galled her.

Don't be foolish, Laurel. You're the one who doesn't want him around.

Angry with herself as much as him, Laurel adjusted her wide-brimmed hat and mounted Jeanie. After taking Dickens's lead rope in hand, she returned to the road to continue her journey, all the while conscious of her so-called protector following in her wake.

Throughout the day Mr. Forrester remained mute. Laurel should have been pleased, but found herself irritated by his continued silence. If he spoke she could ignore him. But as long as he was quiet, she couldn't. However, his presence gave her mind a diversion from the messages she carried in her journal—both journals—and the pictures she carried in her memory. It was the only positive thing that came out of Mr. Forrester's company.

That evening after choosing a campsite, Laurel dug out her journal and the map, which had every destination circled. Those places she'd already left her messages had a black "X" through the circle. Sitting close to the fire for light, she counted each mark on the map. Sixteen circles with X's in them, and five without—only a fourth left. It gave her a disconcerted, unsettled feeling.

"What's the next stop?" Mr. Forrester asked.

"Fordingham," she replied without thinking, then realized she'd acknowledged him. Lifting her head, she glared at him sitting cross-legged across the flickering fire. "Are you happy now?"

A smug grin captured his lips. "Yep."

She shook her head but froze when she noticed the revolver in his hands. "What's that?"

He turned the gleaming weapon over in his hand. "I reckon you know."

"Where did it come from?"

"My saddlebag."

Irritated, she flicked her gaze to his gear, including the rifle propped against a nearby tree. "What of your rifle?"

"It's good for game, but poor for close fighting."

"Surely you don't expect to shoot anyone."

Mr. Forrester continued to wipe the gun with an oiled rag. "I don't expect anything, ma'am. But I do believe in being prepared." He motioned to her journal with his chin. "What's that?"

Laurel pressed her palm to the cover. "Nothing that concerns you."

He shrugged. "Just curious is all."

She suddenly bit her tongue. What in the world was wrong with her? Why was she conversing with him?

As if reading her mind, Mr. Forrester smiled. "I knew you wouldn't be able to keep that mouth of yours shut forever, ma'am. It's just not natural for a woman to be so closemouthed."

Laurel wanted to scream her frustration, but choked it back. "Why do you insist on accompanying me when you're clearly not wanted?"

He sobered and studied her for a long moment. "What kind of man would I be if I *didn't* stay with you?"

Laurel didn't know how to counter his quiet, straightforward reply. She wanted to argue, but there was a simple truth in his words that she couldn't dispute.

Mr. Forrester stood and slid his shiny revolver into a gunbelt he hadn't been wearing when they met. The fire's light gave him an ominous appearance, especially with the low-slung belt around his narrow hips. She shivered. She knew relatively nothing about him, save the fact that he was from Texas and his son Austin had died in the war.

What kind of man would I be if I didn't stay with you?

But then, perhaps that was all she needed to know about him.

A rustle in the brush caught her attention and Mr. Forrester became a blur of motion. Shocked by how quickly he'd drawn his revolver, Laurel didn't know what she should be more afraid of—him or whoever was hiding in the brush.

Four

A pitiful meow broke the tense tableau and Creede released the air in his lungs with a gust. He slid the revolver back into its holster. Eighteen years of disuse had lessened his speed only slightly, and the gun butt still felt natural in his palm, like the return of an old friend. In fact, the gun felt too damned good in his hand.

"Is this what you need your revolver for—to protect yourself from helpless cats?" Mrs. Covey asked, her voice a mixture of teasing and mockery.

Creede swallowed back his embarrassment and kept his mouth shut. His vision adjusted to the dark and he could make out a gray blur with glowing eyes.

"It could be hurt," she said matter-of-factly.

Cats had their place in keeping a home free of mice, but out here they were nothing but another feral animal. Creede placed his hand on his revolver. "I'll put it down."

"Wait."

He frowned. "He'll just as likely claw you as let you near him."

She looked up at him from where she knelt on the ground. "We won't know until we try, will we?"

Even in the evening's dim light, he could see the spark in her eyes. He cursed under his breath, but she ignored him and stretched her hand out to the animal.

"Come here, kitty. It's all right. I won't hurt you."

Creede stifled an impatient sigh. It was Mrs. Covey who should worry about the cat hurting her. However, the woman seemed unafraid, or maybe unaware of the damage a feral cat could exact with its claws.

The cat backed away with a low hiss, but Mrs. Covey kept coaxing it as she eased nearer.

"Be careful. Don't get too close," he warned.

The cat dashed back into the brush and Creede sighed in relief to have the animal gone. He expected Mrs. Covey to move back to the fire, but she remained still and silent.

"Mrs. Covey."

No reaction.

Creede leaned over and touched her shoulder. Mrs. Covey exploded into motion, crabbing backwards, away from him. Her eyes held a wild look, not unlike the cat's.

"Mrs. Covey. Laurel," Creede said, holding up his hands.

She gasped and stiffened, then slumped.

Creede hunkered down beside her. "Are you all right, Laurel?"

She blinked and stared at him a moment as if trying to remember his name. Then the familiar stubbornness crept back into her features. "I'm fine."

Her obvious lie made Creede's own voice curt. "You didn't look fine."

She glared at him and pushed herself to her feet, forcing Creede to stand and retreat. "I'm going to sleep."

His mouth twisted in a scowl, Creede watched her ready her bedroll then lie down without once glancing at him.

What happened? What had caused her to lose her usual control? Had she seen something? If so, why wouldn't she tell him?

He recalled the look in her eyes and a shiver swept through him. For a moment, she wasn't there. It reminded him of the vacant look in a dead person's eyes, something he'd seen more often than he cared to confess.

He glanced at her, knowing she wasn't asleep by the stiff way she lay in her bedroll. He could protect her from outlaws on the trail, but what bothered her now was beyond his control. But then, he hadn't volunteered to be her friend. He had his own problems to contend with and that was more than enough to handle.

Sighing, he slid into his bedroll and turned his back on the woman.

Laurel heard Mr. Forrester retire and relaxed minutely. She closed her eyes and saw the same image that haunted her minutes ago.

"Keep away from me, you damned Yank. You come any closer and I'll slit yore throat!"

Laurel pressed her hands to her ears, but the apparition refused to leave her. She clearly remembered the Confederate soldier, waving a big knife as his insides were spilling from a saber slice across his belly. She'd wanted to help him, but her Northern accent had confused the fevered man. In his delirium he was convinced he was surrounded by Yanks, and had been near death's door by the time anyone could get close to him.

Another failure. Perhaps if she'd kept her mouth shut or allowed someone else to help him, he would have survived.

And then what? He would've healed and been sent back to fight . . . to die another day?

Laurel commanded the ghost to leave and the memory faded away. But she knew he would return to haunt her again, and she hoped the next time she'd be alone.

Her cheeks burned with humiliation. Mr. Forrester had seen her weakness, but at least he didn't see her accompanying shame. Why wasn't she strong enough to fight the ghosts? Why did she keep remembering the past so vividly? She hadn't fought on the bloody battlefields or killed others with her bare hands. She'd only been a nurse.

Laurel's head pounded, but she didn't mind. It meant

she'd sleep little tonight, which would keep the nightmares at bay.

She turned onto her back and pillowed her head on her arms to stare at the night sky. Diverting her thoughts to the stray cat, she couldn't help but wonder where it came from. Was it as wild as Mr. Forrester thought it was? Or was he only using that excuse to employ his revolver?

She shook her head, ashamed of herself for thinking him that kind of man. Despite his own sorrow and grief, he seemed truly concerned for her welfare. If he wasn't a decent man, he would have shown his true colors earlier. Instead, he'd endured her childish pout and kept her safe even though he had nothing to gain. She vowed to behave in a more civilized manner tomorrow.

A plaintive meow sounded from the brush, telling Laurel the cat hadn't gone far. She already had more than enough traveling companions, but it wasn't in her to ignore the animal's plight, either. After glancing at Creede, who appeared to be deep in slumber, she eased up to a sitting position. She quietly dug into her saddlebags and found a piece of dried meat, which she tossed in the direction of the meow.

"Only this one time, cat, then you're on your own," she whispered.

Tomorrow the cat would be gone and no longer her concern. The last thing Laurel wanted was the responsibility of another life, even if it was some stray, bedraggled cat.

THE morning dawned with coral-tinted clouds illuminating the horizon. Flies and mosquitoes swarmed around Creede like honeybees around clover, making it miserable for man, woman, and beasts. Although he didn't like the insects, he was accustomed to them. The way Laurel—Mrs. Covey—ignored them told him she, too, was no stranger to the buzzing pests.

"Coffee, Mr. Forrester?" Mrs. Covey asked.

Wiping his face after shaving, Creede turned around to
see if she was taunting him. Instead, he found her holding
up a cup. He slung the damp cloth around his neck and accepted the peace offering. "Thank you, ma'am."

"Breakfast will be ready shortly. I hope you like bacon
and flapjacks."

Too startled to speak, Creede nodded. He gazed at Mrs.
Covey, noting the red flush in her cheeks and wondered if
it was the fire's heat or something else that caused it.
Grease crackled in the pan, followed by the pleasant tang
of bacon. How had she managed to get the meat? Food-
stuffs were in short supply because of the loss of men
working the fields, which inflated the cost of supplies. Severe taxes were levied against folks whose only crime was
that they'd thrown in with the losing side of a war, making
money needed for overpriced food even scarcer. Maybe
her Massachusetts accent had helped her procure food
from Northern traders.

What did it matter where she got it? The War was over.
At least for sane people. But there were still Confederate
soldiers who refused to acknowledge the loss and formed
guerrilla groups who acted more like outlaw bands. That
was one of the reasons he insisted on riding with her.

"Here you are, Mr. Forrester."

Creede blinked, surprised to see Mrs. Covey holding
out a plate. He accepted it and set down his now-empty
coffee cup. "Thanks."

With a plate of food less than half of what Creede had,
Mrs. Covey settled cross-legged on the ground. It seemed
odd to see this correct woman sitting in such an unladylike
way. Times like this, he could see her working under the
primitive conditions of a field hospital. The straight backbone and ability to make do would've done her well during
the War.

"How did he look?" Creede suddenly asked.

Mrs. Covey froze with a piece of bacon halfway to her
mouth then set the meat back down on her plate. She lifted

her cup to her lips, but he could tell it was more to gain time than actually drink coffee. Surprisingly, she understood his question.

"To be honest, I don't remember much about your son," she replied. "His face was thin, but most were. Toward the end of the War supplies were almost nonexistent, and I'd often see men arguing over a dead rabbit or squirrel." Her cheeks lost their pink flush. "I'm sorry. Your son was one of so many."

For a moment, it looked like she would cry but her chin lifted and she continued eating. Creede finished his breakfast, but the pleasure of the meal had disappeared with Laurel's account.

There was a slight rustle of grass to the side and a scraggly cat peeked out of the long stalks. Although he wasn't certain, Creede figured it was the same one who'd visited last night.

There was nothing pretty or distinguishing about the animal. It was dingy gray, black, and white, and had part of an ear missing, as well as tufts of hair—probably a result of a fight with another cat, or maybe some other wild animal.

Before he could say anything, Laurel approached the creature, crooning in a low voice. Creede didn't waste his breath cautioning her, but made sure his hand was on his revolver.

The cat took a dainty step forward and stretched out his nose to smell Laurel's fingertips. After familiarizing himself with her, the cat pressed his head against Laurel's palm and started purring.

"I'll be damned," Creede muttered.

Laurel curled her fingers around the animal's middle and picked it up to examine it more closely. "No recent wounds, but he's skinny as a rail."

"Just hungry."

She nodded and placed the animal back on the ground. She picked up the pan she'd used to fry the bacon and scraped the drippings onto her plate, then set the dish in front of the cat. The stray didn't waste any time, but immediately lapped at the grease.

"You realize it'll probably follow us now," Creede said.

Laurel jerked her head up, her eyes flashing with something akin to panic, but it disappeared so quickly he couldn't be certain. She shook her head. "It won't be able to keep up with us."

Creede shrugged. "I've seen stranger things."

She merely rolled her eyes. "Really, Mr. Forrester, it might try but it's not foolish enough to continue."

He didn't bother to argue.

"I'll wash the dishes," he volunteered after the cat sat back on its haunches and began to clean its face with a front paw.

She handed him the frying pan along with the other utensils. As he walked away from the camp, he recalled their brief conversation about his son. He paused and said over his shoulder, "I'm sure you did the best you could for Austin and all the others."

She lifted her head, startled, but looked away without a word.

Creede carried out his task and when he returned to the camp, Mrs. Covey had her horse and mule ready to go. Her usual hat covered her head and most of her wheat-colored hair. "Where's the cat?"

"It disappeared." She took the things from Creede's hands and tucked them into her pack. "I told you it wouldn't follow us."

Creede expected a smug expression on her face, but instead a genuine, albeit small, smile tugged at her lips. "That you did, Mrs. Covey."

He readied Red for traveling with quick efficiency and climbed into the saddle. He glanced around the camp, looking for anything they had missed, but spotted nothing.

Laurel sat atop her horse, her relaxed seat telling him how comfortable she was on the dun-colored mare. As they rode side by side, with Dickens behind them, Creede asked, "What kind of horse is that?"

She patted the animal's arched neck with a gloved hand. "A Kentucky Saddler. My husband's family raised them on their Virginia plantation. Jeanie was given to me as a wedding gift."

"Jeanie?"

Her gaze drifted away, as if embarrassed. "I named her after Mr. Foster's song, 'Jeanie with the Light Brown Hair.' It seems silly now, but back then . . ." She shrugged. "I was a young, romantic fool."

Creede cleared his throat. "We all were young romantic fools at one time."

"I find it hard to imagine you as one."

He remembered how he'd promised to give up his gun and stay with Anna forever. Only forever came sooner than he had expected and his revolver was back on his hip. Even hired guns could do foolish things in the name of love. "Appearances can be deceiving, Mrs. Covey."

"You called me Laurel last night."

So she'd heard him. "I'm sorry."

"Don't be. If we're to be traveling together, we don't have to hold to ceremony. Call me Laurel."

"Creede."

Another smile tugged at her lips. "Creede."

Although they didn't speak again, the silence wasn't awkward as in the previous two days. Instead, it was a comfortable quiet that rode with them except for Dickens's outbursts every ten or fifteen minutes. Creede figured it was the mule's contrary nature and tried to ignore the obnoxious braying.

Around midmorning they took a break alongside a small clear stream. While the animals drank, Creede and Laurel filled their canteens a few yards upstream.

"How much farther to this Fordingham?" he asked.

"We should be there this evening."

"So what do you have to do there?"

Laurel dipped a handkerchief in the stream and wrung it out, then wiped the back of her neck. "I have to meet with someone."

"Who?"

"The mother of a young soldier."

Creede flinched and glanced away. "He dead?"

"Yes. His last words were for his mother."

Envy clawed Creede's gut. At least the boy's mother would have something. But Creede had nothing—no son and no last words. His stomach churned and his vision grayed. Anguish cut through him like a dull scythe. Although it wasn't Laurel's fault there'd been no final message from his son, Creede couldn't stop the flood of irrational anger.

"Are you ready?" he asked gruffly.

She glanced at him in puzzlement but only nodded and tied the damp scarf at her throat.

As they straightened, the stray cat trotted out of the grass toward them.

Laurel's eyes widened and Creede might have laughed at her comical expression if his lungs weren't so tight.

"Stop following us," she said to the skinny animal.

The cat merely stared up at her.

Laurel shook her finger. "I mean it. Go back home."

The green eyes remained unblinking.

Laurel stepped over to it, picked it up and tossed it a few feet away, in the direction from which it came. The cat turned around and walked back to her then rubbed against her ankles.

Creede watched the proceedings from atop his horse, his somber mood lightening. "You made a friend, Laurel."

She glared up at him. "I don't want a friend." Her attention turned back to the stray. "I won't carry you, so go back where you came from."

She turned away and climbed into her saddle. Without giving the cat another look, she heeled her horse and the dun mare headed back down the road.

The cat followed.

Puzzled by Laurel's sudden indifference toward the stray creature, Creede urged Red after her. It wasn't long before the cat fell behind and Creede forced himself to ignore the pitiful meows that grew fainter and fainter. Once or twice he thought he caught Laurel sneaking peeks behind them, but figured it had to be his imagination.

When the sun was high in the sky, Creede and Laurel took a break to rest the animals and eat lunch. While they sat on rocks and gnawed on jerky, the two horses and the mule grazed on the lush green grass.

Laurel finished her repast and pulled her legs up onto the rock, wrapping her arms around them. She peered around at the kaleidoscope of different shades of green that surrounded them. "When I look around here, it's hard to believe there was a war."

"Texas is a lot the same way. Texans left in droves to join the Confederates, but no battles were ever fought on its ground." Creede picked up a pebble and tossed it into the woods. "The Yanks tried to blockade us, but they didn't succeed."

"Did you ever feel it was your duty to join the army?"

"No," he replied without hesitation. "I wasn't keen on the Northern states dictating to us, but I never believed one man had the right to own another, either." He shrugged. "It was a stupid war fought for stupid reasons."

"Many folks didn't believe the reasons were stupid ones."

Creede eyed her closely. "Were you one of them?"

Laurel brushed some dust from her skirt. "My husband was. Robert didn't like the businessmen in the North setting the prices for tobacco and cotton. He thought the South was doing all the work and the North was reaping all the rewards."

Creede had heard that argument among his fellow Texans, too. But she hadn't answered his question. "That was your husband. What about you?"

She shrugged. "I believed in Robert."

"So you became a nurse to follow him?"

"I'd already been trained as a nurse, much to my parents' eternal mortification." A wry smile played across her lips. "Then I merely used my talents, much to my husband's disapproval."

Creede frowned. "Why didn't he forbid you from working as a nurse?"

She laughed, startling him since he'd never heard her laugh before. It was a nice sound, musical and feminine with a touch of mischief in it. He couldn't help but smile in return.

"I'm sorry for laughing, Mr.—Creede. If you knew me better, you'd know that if I was forbidden something, I would try that much harder to do it."

Creede could easily see this woman—the one with sparkling eyes and bright expression—defy her parents and husband. And anyone else who dared tell her she couldn't do something. "You're right. I don't know you that well, but I have a feeling we'll know each other a whole lot better by the time we get to Texas."

In a matter of moments, her features lost their animation and somberness returned.

"Be careful, Creede. You may not like what you find." She jumped off the rock. "We've been here long enough."

Baffled by her comment, Creede gathered his horse's reins and pulled himself into the saddle. Laurel did the same but when she grabbed Dickens's lead rope, the mule refused to budge. She jerked the rope, but the jackass dug his hooves into the earth.

"Come on, Dickens. We don't have time for your stubborn antics," Laurel said with more than a shred of impatience.

Creede shook his head in exasperation and steered his mare around the mule's hindquarters. He slapped the mule's rump and only the reflexes of Red saved him from being struck by flailing hooves.

"Stay back," Laurel said belatedly. "I can usually get him to move."

After five minutes of cajoling and threatening, Laurel succeeded in getting Dickens to follow. Sweat sheened her red face and her lips puckered like a sour lemon had passed them. Creede opened his mouth to speak, but after another glance at her set features, he closed it. Laurel obviously didn't want to talk about Dickens or anything else.

Adjusting his hat brim, Creede sighed in exasperation and kept his thoughts on their surroundings rather than the perplexing Laurel Covey.

$\mathcal{F}$IVE

May 14, 1864. Private Luther Donovan of Fordingham, Tennessee. Red hair, green eyes, freckles across nose and cheeks, seventeen years old. Wounded at the Battle of the Wilderness on May 6th. Cause of death: putrefaction of back wound. "Tell Ma I tried my hardest. Tell her I loved her even though I hated what she was." (Picture of boy and mother.)

LAUREL tried to be unobtrusive as she glanced behind them, checking the trail. She didn't want the cat following them, but she couldn't help worrying that he might try. In its near-starved condition, it wouldn't last long. It would probably become so weak a fox or owl would find it easy prey. *Stupid cat.*

"I haven't seen it either."

Laurel stiffened and met Creede's gaze. "What are you talking about?"

"The cat. That's what you've been looking for, right?"

Laurel straightened her backbone and stared ahead. "Why would I be worried about a stray cat?"

"Didn't say you were worried, only that you were looking."

She could hear the smile in his voice and defensiveness made her reply, "Well, I'm not looking and I'm not worried."

He chuckled. "Yes, ma'am."

Laurel bit back a retort, knowing she'd just be giving Creede more ammunition against her. Maybe she was a tad bit worried about the cat, but then she'd been the one to give the animal some food, so it was her fault if it followed them.

She was relieved when they topped a hill and spotted Fordingham only a couple of miles away. Suddenly exhausted, Laurel urged Jeanie down the road's gentle slope.

As they entered the small but bustling town, Laurel wasn't surprised when they garnered the attention of those on the boardwalks. She doubted they had many visitors, and by the unfriendly looks on the faces, those they'd had since the War's end were probably unwelcome ones.

"Looks to be a boardinghouse down there," Creede said.

Laurel followed his line of sight and spotted the peeling sign that simply read ROOMS FOR RENT. She looked around, hoping there might be a hotel or something more reputable looking, but was disappointed.

"Let's see if they have any rooms available," she said without enthusiasm.

They dismounted by the hitching post that stood in front of the large, wood-frame house. The building, like the sign, needed fresh paint but otherwise it appeared tidy and well kept.

Creede knocked on the door, which was opened almost immediately. A middle-aged man with a soft, doughy face, who wore shabby but clean trousers and a neatly pressed shirt, gazed at them. "Can I help you?"

"We're looking for a place to spend a night or two," Laurel said.

"Please, come in." He swept open the door and motioned them inside.

Laurel stepped in and was surprised by the spotless,

homey interior. Creede removed his hat and stood behind her.

The boardinghouse owner's eyes displayed his delight at the possibility of guests and his hands fluttered about as he spoke. "I have just the room for you. It's my largest with a comfortable bed and I recently put up new curtains, very bright and cheery."

Although Laurel's face heated, she couldn't help but smile at his pleasant disposition. "It sounds lovely, but we'd each like our own room."

The man glanced down at the ring on her left hand and Laurel reflexively touched her wedding band. "I'm a widow."

His expression fell. "I'm sorry for your loss. Too many have lost loved ones. Perhaps you'd like that room anyhow, and your, uh, friend can have the one across the hall?"

"Does it cost more?"

"Not for you," he said gallantly.

Laurel fought a smile. "Thank you, Mr.—"

"Floyd Preston, but you must call me Floyd. Rooms are fifty cents a night. If you'd like meals, it'll be an extra fifty cents a day."

"Does your wife do the cooking?" Creede asked.

Floyd waved a pudgy hand. "I'm not married but I assure you I can cook a decent meal."

"I'm sure you can," Laurel said before Creede could utter a rude remark. "I'm Laurel Covey and this is Creede Forrester."

She shook his hand, which was soft like a woman's. Then Creede shook his hand. Hiding a smile with a cough, she tried not to notice that Floyd held Creede's hand a few moments longer than necessary.

"We'll be staying one night, maybe two," Laurel said, pulling Floyd's attention from Creede. "And I'd like to take my meals here, too."

"Same," Creede said with a touch of reluctance.

"That'll be a dollar each—coin, not paper. If you decide to stay another day, you can pay then," Floyd said.

Laurel and Creede each gave him a silver dollar.

"Let me show you to your rooms," he said.

Laurel followed him up the steep staircase and down a narrow hall.

Floyd opened a door on the right. "This will be yours, Mrs. Covey."

Laurel peeked inside and nearly gasped. Vibrantly colored curtains covered the windows and the four-poster bed gleamed, as did the matching dresser. A rug covered most of the shiny wood floor. "It's beautiful."

Floyd shrugged, but she could tell he was pleased. "Like I said, I just finished fixing it up. I made the curtains myself." He looked up at Creede. "I'm afraid yours isn't quite as nice." He opened the door across the hallway.

"It'll be fine," Creede murmured.

Laurel peeked over Floyd's shoulder at the simple but orderly room that would be Creede's. Even though it was smaller, it also displayed a bright, homey touch. It was obvious Floyd took pride in the house's interior.

"I'll check on the horses," Creede said.

"There's a livery around the corner," Floyd called after him.

"Thanks." Creede headed downstairs.

"I hope I didn't insult him with his room," Floyd said in a low undertone.

Laurel patted his arm. "You didn't. He's naturally ill-mannered."

Floyd sighed. "I suppose that's a relief." He shook his head. "Do you need some assistance in getting your things in?"

"No, thank you. I can get them."

"Then I'll get dinner started. It will be ready about six."

"That'll be fine."

Laurel followed him down and went outside to get her bags, while Floyd veered into the kitchen.

"You sure you want to stay here?" Creede asked gruffly from the other side of his horse.

"Why wouldn't I? It's the cleanest place I've seen in a long time."

"Yeah, and he's pretty handy with a needle and thread."

Laurel laughed at his disgusted tone. "So? He's a very nice man."

Creede ducked under his horse's neck to stand next to her. "He's a sissy."

She had recognized Floyd's nature almost immediately, but didn't harbor any aversion. She shrugged. "I've known other men like him. The last one was a soldier who'd been beaten within an inch of his life by his own comrades." Anger made her shake her head. "He fought the enemy beside those men for weeks, then they found out his secret and nearly beat him to death. It's one thing to be hurt or killed by your enemy, but when it's your fellow soldiers, men you thought were your friends . . ." Her stomach twisted. "That's madness."

Creede sighed. "When you put it like that, it doesn't make a whole lot of sense, does it?"

Melancholy caught Laurel unaware. "A lot of things don't make much sense, Creede."

He patted her shoulder, startling her. "I've got a spare hand to help carry in your things," he offered.

Grateful, she handed him her bag from Dickens's back. "Thank you."

"When I come back down, I'll take the horses and your mule to the livery."

She watched him walk back to the house with a long-legged stride. Perhaps having Creede Forrester for the long journey wouldn't be as bad as she imagined. On the other hand, she'd have to ensure she didn't become too comfortable in his company either. That could lead to far more intimacy than she could afford.

CREEDE had to admit Floyd definitely knew how to cook. Although it was nothing fancy—venison, potatoes, fried okra, bread, and apple butter—it tasted mighty good and filled his belly.

Floyd had joined them, making Creede uncomfortable for a few moments until Laurel filled the awkward silence. Soon she and Floyd were conversing like old friends.

As they talked, Creede found his gaze straying to Laurel more often than not. She'd taken time to wash and change into clean clothes before their meal. Her hair, usually pinned back and hidden beneath her floppy hat, was loose and flowing down her back, like waves of wheat in a summer field. It softened her face and made Creede uncomfortably aware of her as a handsome woman.

Floyd stood and refilled their coffee cups then rejoined them.

"How has the War affected Fordingham?" Creede asked curiously.

Their host's perpetual smile faded. "How hasn't it? We lost many men, leaving widows and orphans penniless. Then the Yankee tax collectors came and demanded their share. But last I heard you can only get nothing from nothing. Still they insisted." He motioned to their surroundings. "It broke my heart to sell some of my mother's heirlooms, but I managed to pay their taxes. There was just enough left to fix up a room or two."

"How's business been?" Laurel asked.

"Not so good. As much as I hate the collectors, I do get some income from them since I'm the only place in town to stay." He shrugged. "I get by."

Creede traced the rim of his coffee cup. "Have you ever thought of moving on?"

"Where would I go, Mr. Forrester? I hear a lot of folks are pulling up stakes and heading for Texas, but as you can tell, I'm not of pioneer stock." He shook his head. "No, this is my home, for better or for worse. So what brings you two through Fordingham?"

Creede glanced at Laurel, letting her answer.

"I'm actually here to speak with Luther Donovan's mother," Laurel said, her voice returning to cool courtesy.

Floyd's face immediately reddened and he took a long drink of water. "Why do you want to talk to her?"

"I was with her son when he died in a Confederate hospital."

"But your voice—aren't you from the North?"

"My husband was from Virginia."

"He died in the War?"

Laurel nodded, her expression steady. "As did many other men. Can you tell me where I can find Mrs. Donovan?"

Floyd's round face flushed as he squirmed uncomfortably. "Actually, it's Miss Donovan, Miss Fancy Donovan."

Creede straightened in his chair. He had a feeling the boy's mother wasn't what Laurel expected.

"She has a house about three blocks from here. Go up a block then east for two. You can't miss it—it's the biggest house around," Floyd said.

"Thank you," Laurel replied.

"I didn't realize her boy was killed. I knew Luther. He was a bit of a bully—broke one of my windows one time. But I suppose I shouldn't speak ill of the dead."

Creede noticed Floyd's gaze didn't meet theirs. He figured Luther might have done more than merely break Floyd's window.

"Death doesn't care if a person is a bully or a saint," Laurel said softly. "And what a person did while alive is remembered, whether it's good or bad."

Floyd patted the back of Laurel's hand. "I'd say you've seen your share of both kinds, yet I have a feeling you didn't care one way or another while they were under your care."

Laurel gave Floyd a sweet smile that made Creede's breath catch in his throat. "Thank you, Floyd, but I just did what I had to."

"I've heard heroes say the same."

For a moment, Creede thought Laurel might cry, but she surprised him with a laugh.

"I'm no hero." She dabbed her lips with a napkin and

set it by her empty plate. "I'll help you with the dishes then pay a visit to Miss Donovan."

Floyd stood and said sternly, "You're a guest, Mrs. Covey, and guests don't help with the menial labor."

Laurel smiled. "Thank you."

Floyd paused with his hands filled with stacked plates. Worry lines etched his brow. "I think you should have Mr. Forrester escort you to Miss Donovan's place."

"That's a good idea," Creede said before Laurel could argue.

He'd already decided to do so, since he had a suspicion he knew why Miss Fancy Donovan had the most impressive house in town. In fact, he would've preferred to have Laurel forget about delivering her message altogether, but figured he didn't have a prayer of convincing her.

Laurel frowned at him. "I'm sure I can find the place on my own."

"I'm sure you can, but I still think it's a good idea to take a man with you," Floyd said firmly.

"Fine."

But Creede could tell it wasn't fine. Laurel was merely being courteous by not arguing with Floyd, who'd disappeared into the kitchen.

She looked at Creede. "Shall we go in half an hour?"

"Sure."

"Meet me in the foyer then."

Laurel rose and gracefully exited, but Creede wasn't fooled by her easy capitulation.

"She's an admirable woman," Floyd said as he returned.

Creede couldn't hide his surprise.

Floyd chuckled. "Just because I wouldn't marry a woman doesn't mean I can't admire one."

Despite his lingering discomfort, Creede grinned. "Guess I never thought of it that way." He stood. "Thanks for dinner. It was good."

"Now that wasn't so difficult, was it?"

Shaking his head in wry amusement, Creede left the dining room and went out onto the porch to sit on a warped chair. He slid a cigar out of his breast pocket, lit it with a flaring match and sat down to wait.

LAUREL reread the journal entry of Luther Donovan's last words.

"Tell Ma I tried my hardest. Tell her I loved her even though I hated what she was."

She tried to reconcile the boy's words with Floyd's description of Luther as a bully, but all she could see was a boy's pain-wracked face as infection had spread throughout his body.

She placed the ribbon bookmark between the pages and closed the journal with sweat-dampened hands. Although she'd done this numerous times already, it didn't make it any easier. Each time she expected to see accusation in the family's eyes for letting their son or husband die, but each time she'd only been met with renewed grief. Maybe Creede was right. Maybe she shouldn't reopen barely healed wounds. Maybe the family was better off not hearing their loved one's final message.

No. Despite Creede's objection, she knew he wished his son had left him some last words. But he'd been robbed of that, just as his son had been robbed of life at such a young age.

She gathered her long hair and twisted it into a bun at the back of her neck and pinned it up. The bonnet she'd unpacked earlier lay on the bed and she donned it, tying the ribbon beneath her chin.

She stared at the pale woman in the mirror and a sense of unfamiliarity swam through her. Who was this stranger she'd become? How much of Laurel Monteille Covey remained? It seemed so little of late that she could've been another person, a stranger even to herself.

She blinked and took a deep breath. Only ten minutes had passed since she'd left the dining room, saying she'd meet Creede in thirty minutes. However, she didn't want his company. This was her mission, not his.

Squaring her shoulders, she picked up her journal and left her room on tiptoe. She moved as quietly as she could, straining to hear Creede in his room. At the bottom of the stairs, she stopped and glanced up but his door remained closed. Sighing in relief, she walked to the front door and opened it.

"Going somewhere, Laurel?"

She jumped at the sound of Creede's voice.

"What are you doing out here?" she demanded.

"Enjoying a cigar." He turned to look at her. "And waiting for you to sneak off without me."

Laurel glared at him. Although he was right, she didn't want to give him any satisfaction. "I was merely going to wait for you on the porch."

Creede snorted. "I never took you for a liar before."

Her face grew hot with the truth of his words, but her pride wouldn't let her apologize. "You don't have to go with me. I'm perfectly capable of finding Miss Donovan by myself."

"I'm certain you are." Creede stood and ground his cigar out on the porch's sagging railing. "Are you ready?"

Laurel wanted to stamp her foot in frustration but the gravity of her task stopped her. "Suit yourself."

"I always do."

She squelched her aggravation and lifted her head to stride past him. With his long legs, Creede had no trouble catching up to her. At first, she ignored him, but after they turned east, the town's character changed. Where there'd been stores and offices with sedate men and women, now there were saloons, gaming halls, and raucous laughter.

Laurel could hear curses and drunken laughter from smoke-filled bars and she shifted closer to Creede. And she was strangely comforted when he put his arm around her shoulders so she was tucked into his side. His solid warmth and clean masculine scent was a welcome sanctuary.

They found the house easily. It was a three-story white-frame house with two red lanterns lit on either side of the door. Laurel's mouth grew cottony as she recognized what the red lights meant. Her steps faltered then halted altogether.

"You don't have to do this." Creede's hat brim brushed her bonnet and his warm, moist breath cascaded across her cheek.

As she studied the imposing house with lights shining in almost every window, the door opened and a man stumbled out onto the expansive porch. He was singing a bawdy song about a woman's attributes. Laurel's feet urged her to turn around and return to the boardinghouse, but her heart insisted on completing her task.

"No, I don't have to do this, but I will." Laurel drew out of Creede's sheltering arm. "You don't have to go inside with me."

"The hell I don't," he muttered.

She breathed a sigh of relief but didn't admit her gratitude. With reluctant footsteps, Laurel climbed the steps onto the porch.

The man who'd stumbled out moments before stared at her with a gimlet-eyed gaze. "You must be the new girl," he said in a drunken slur. He sidled close and cupped her bottom.

Laurel jerked away but before she could retaliate, the drunk tumbled off the porch. Creede's furious expression and his fisted hand told Laurel he'd taken care of the rude man.

"I could've handled him," she said, glaring at him.

"Probably. But I *wanted* to."

Despite Laurel's dislike of violence, she couldn't stop a tendril of warmth at his protectiveness. Flustered by her reaction, Laurel knocked on the wide door.

Feminine giggles preceded the open door, revealing a young woman wearing only her underclothes, and those left little to the imagination. The girl's gaze skipped over Laurel and immediately settled on Creede. The approval in her eyes started a burn in Laurel's chest.

She stepped in front of Creede, blocking the prostitute's view of him. "I'm here to see Miss Fancy Donovan."

The girl laughed, a braying sound that didn't seem to fit her petite but large-breasted figure. "Well, la-di-da. What would a lady like you want with Miss Fancy?"

"She has business to discuss with her," Creede said.

The girl tipped her head to the side and eyed Creede like he was a thick, juicy steak. "I tell you what, while she does her business with Miss Fancy, you and I can do some business of our own."

Suddenly another woman appeared behind the barely clad girl. She was a tall, full-figured redhead who wore a faded red dress with a plunging neckline that barely restrained her nipples. "What's going on here, Lacy?"

"This here lady wants to talk to you," Lacy replied, twirling a strand of blond hair around her finger as she gave Creede a come-hither look.

"Get back to work. I'll take care of this."

With obvious reluctance, Lacy left.

"Are you Miss Fancy Donovan?" Laurel asked.

She nodded warily. "Who are you?"

"My name's Laurel Covey and I'd like to speak with you about your son Luther."

Miss Fancy's cheeks lost all color except for the two splotches of rouge. "He's dead."

"Yes, I know. I was with him when he died."

Despite her pallor, Miss Fancy's voice was harsh. "Good for you. So what's there to talk about?"

Nonplussed, Laurel glanced around. "I'd rather talk in private."

Miss Fancy narrowed her eyes then opened the door wide. "Sure, honey. Come on in, and bring the handsome stud with you."

Confused by the woman's attitude, Laurel stepped inside and her attention was immediately captured by the scene of debauchery. Three girls wearing as much—or as little—as Lacy were entertaining the men. One girl was sitting on a lap, her hand inside the man's shirt. Another was having her bare breast fondled and the last was dancing,

her body moving sensuously beneath the skimpy undergarments, as three men stared in rapt attention.

Sweat beaded Laurel's brow as her stomach tightened
and her nipples hardened in response to the erotic scene.

"You sure it's talking you want to do?" Miss Fancy
asked Laurel, a pencil-thin eyebrow arched knowingly.

Startled, Laurel quickly averted her gaze. "Yes."

Miss Fancy shrugged as if she could care less. She
spoke to Creede. "Why don't you make yourself comfortable? I'm sure my girls will make you feel welcome."

A mixture of jealousy and humiliation seared though
Laurel.

"If you don't mind, I'd rather stay with Mrs. Covey,"
Creede said.

Though Laurel didn't want him around Miss Fancy's
girls, she didn't want him to be with her when she delivered her message either. "It's all right, Creede. I'll be fine."

For a moment, Creede looked like an animal caught in a
trap, then he nodded curtly. "I'll be waiting for you."

Miss Fancy motioned for Laurel to follow her and they
passed closed doors. Behind one, Laurel thought she heard
the sounds of coupling, but firmly set the image out of her
mind. Besides, this wasn't the first time she'd been privy to
the goings-on of soiled doves. Laurel had felt sorry for the
camp followers, who were oftentimes widows of soldiers
who had no other option but to sell their bodies. She'd been
the one the women sought out when they were sick or had
the clap.

Miss Fancy led her into a room that was both office and
boudoir and settled herself on a worn chair. She motioned
for Laurel to sit on the matching one. Laurel perched on
the edge, keeping her gaze away from the mussed bed in
the corner.

"I'm waiting, Mrs. Covey."

Laurel brought her chaotic thoughts back to her task. "I
was a nurse with the Confederacy. I was working in the
hospital tent where your son died."

"Are you looking for a medal?"

"No. I-I was with Luther when he died."

Miss Fancy lifted a cheroot out of a carved box and lit it. Her fingers trembled slightly. "You already told me that. If you've got nothing else to say, you're wasting my time."

Disturbed by her indifference, Laurel said sharply, "He was your son."

Miss Fancy exhaled a stream of smoke. "He was my *bastard* son, Mrs. Covey."

"But surely you must've loved him."

She laughed, but it was a hollow sound. "Love? Tell me, Mrs. Covey, what the hell is love? From what I've seen, it's a commodity bought and sold like flour or beef."

Laurel leaned back in her chair, eyeing the woman's garish make-up and timeworn dress. "You loved Luther's father, didn't you?"

Anguish flashed through Miss Fancy's flinty eyes. "Luther's father took my virginity with the promise of marrying me. A month later he was gone and I had his bastard growing in my belly. My folks didn't take too kindly to their fifteen-year-old daughter getting knocked up, so they tossed me out on my ass."

"And you've been selling 'love' ever since," Laurel finished softly.

Miss Fancy shrugged. "I'm damned good at it. So good that I got this place."

"If this is what makes you happy, then I'm glad."

"You really mean that, don't you?"

"After what I saw during the War, I've learned that a person has to find happiness wherever they can. It's not for me to judge."

Miss Fancy glanced away and continued to smoke her cheroot. However, her jaded expression faded to reluctant curiosity. "How did Luther die?"

Laurel took a deep breath and opened her journal that was marked with the blue ribbon and a picture. "He received a wound that putrefied." She looked up at Miss Fancy and realized the madam wouldn't appreciate the watered-down version. "He was in terrible pain the last few days of his life. I tried to sit with him whenever I could. All he wanted was to hold my hand. It was little enough. He asked me to give you this." Laurel handed her the picture of Luther as a young boy with his mother.

Miss Fancy studied the picture, her expression blank.

"And he asked me to give you a message." Laurel took a deep breath and read from the journal. " 'Tell Ma I tried my hardest. Tell her I loved her even though I hated what she was.' "

Laurel kept her gaze aimed at her handwriting, giving Miss Fancy time to absorb her son's message.

"He wasn't a good boy," Miss Fancy finally said, her coarse voice amazingly gentle. "He used to beat up other boys, weaker boys, but he never hurt a girl. I did teach him that."

Laurel remained silent.

"I know growing up in a whorehouse wasn't good for a boy, but I didn't have any choice. When he asked me if he could join the army, I gave him my blessing. Fact is, I was glad to see him go. He was getting too old to be around the girls." Miss Fancy's forgotten cheroot burned out. "I'll never forget how ugly he was when he was born. And the crying and carrying on, like he couldn't wait to get out." She chuckled, but it was a watery, teary sound. "If he'd have known his mother was a whore, I doubt he would've been so eager to join the world." She visibly roused herself and the vulnerability faded. She set the picture aside. "Thank you for bringing me the picture and his final words."

"You're welcome." Laurel rose, instinctively knowing Miss Fancy was embarrassed by her candidness.

Without another word, Miss Fancy led Laurel back to the parlor. Laurel's gaze flew to Creede who sat in a chair, with Lacy sitting on his lap.

"Maybe your friend would like to stay and sample the goods," Miss Fancy said, reverting back to the coarse madam.

Laurel forced herself to shrug. "He can do whatever he pleases."

Creede suddenly noticed them and clambered to his feet, nearly dumping Lacy on the floor. He steadied the girl then joined Laurel.

"Is your business done?" he asked her.

She nodded. "Is yours?"

Creede's face reddened. "I didn't ask for her company."

"I doubt someone like you ever needs to ask a girl for company," Miss Fancy said, winking at Laurel.

Discomfited, Laurel crossed to the door. When she heard Creede's footsteps following, she couldn't help but feel relieved.

Miss Fancy beat them to the door and opened it. As Laurel went out, the madam caught her arm and said in a low voice, "I loved my son, Mrs. Covey. He was the only person in this world I ever gave a damn about."

Laurel gazed at her, seeing the woman—the mother—Miss Fancy could have been if circumstances had been different. "He knows that now."

As the madam closed the door, Laurel spotted one tear rolling down her painted cheek.

$\mathcal{S}$IX

CREEDE hoped like hell the trip to the bawdyhouse had been worth it for Laurel. Although Lacy was young enough to be his daughter, her charms were mature enough to fire his blood. Combined with months of abstinence, Lacy was temptation personified. Only the appearance of Laurel had cooled his body enough to allow reason to take control once more.

Besides, if he had his druthers, he'd prefer taking someone like Laurel to his bed. Of course, that was a hell of a thing to admit to himself when they'd be spending weeks alone on the trail to Texas.

"You could've stayed," Laurel said, drawing Creede out of his musings.

Creede couldn't tell if she'd wanted him to stay or to leave with her. Surely she knew what he'd end up doing if he remained. "No reason to."

Laurel's lips twitched. "Lacy seemed to be a pretty good reason."

"She thought so."

Laurel's smile broke through this time, but it faded a

few moments later. "Miss Fancy was younger than Lacy when she started selling her body."

Creede wasn't certain talking about loose women with a lady was proper, but Laurel wasn't a typical lady. "Did she say why she did it?"

"She didn't have a choice with a child on the way and no husband."

Creede suspected that was the case. He'd seen more than one child around a whorehouse in his time and although he felt sorry for the children, it never stopped him from enjoying a prostitute's body. But now guilt niggled at him for using women whose circumstances placed them in that position.

From one of the saloons a gunshot exploded followed by rough laughter. Laurel shifted closer to Creede and he instinctively put his arm around her slender shoulders just as he had earlier. He tried to ignore his body's reaction to her soft curves, but after Lacy's priming his body wasn't so easily dissuaded.

He focused on what Laurel had said. "Tough break."

"For her, but not the man who abandoned her. Who knows, maybe if he'd married her, their son wouldn't have gone off to war to die."

Impatience washed away Creede's lingering lust. "Just because a boy has a father doesn't mean he'll be able to talk his son out of joining the army."

Laurel's eyes widened. "I didn't mean it that way."

He knew she hadn't meant to be cruel, but the wound was still too fresh. He swallowed back the burgeoning grief, hiding it behind a veil of indifference. "Was Miss Fancy glad to hear her son's last words?"

Laurel seemed surprised by the question. Perhaps she'd expected him to talk about his son, but Creede couldn't. Not yet.

"I think so," Laurel replied. "She's a hard woman. She's had to be to survive as long as she has in her business." She paused. "But I think now she'll finally be able to cry for him."

A block filled Creede's throat and he swallowed back the emotion. He'd needed a bottle of whiskey to allow himself to cry for his son, but now the tears welled within him without invitation.

They walked silently back to the safety of the main street and Creede removed his arm from Laurel's shoulders. Without her tucked close to his side, he felt the loneliness more keenly. It'd been years since he'd been alone. Even when he and Austin were arguing, he could count on his son being there. But now he, too, was gone.

At the boardinghouse Creede opened the door for Laurel. "I'll see you in the morning."

"Aren't you coming in?"

He shook his head. "I need to take a walk, clear my head."

Her muscles stiffened and her lips pressed in a thin line. "I hope that walk won't take you to the nearest bottle of whiskey."

Her holier-than-thou attitude angered him and he smiled without warmth. "My ma's been dead for over twenty years and I reckon it's a little late for you to take over."

A flush crept across her face and she dropped her gaze. Before she could say anything he spun around and strode away toward the edge of town. He didn't want whiskey or a woman. All he wanted was peace, but he knew there'd be precious little of that.

UNABLE to fall back to sleep despite having a real bed instead of a blanket on the hard ground, Laurel stared up at the ceiling. She'd heard Creede return from his walk a couple of hours ago and was more relieved than she wanted to admit when he didn't stumble or curse.

She'd chastised herself numerous times for being so inconsiderate with her earlier comment about sons and fathers. She suspected he'd gone back to Miss Fancy's to forget his troubles for a little while with Lacy's willing body. Laurel felt the same rush of heat and jealousy when she imagined the two of them together. But it was no business of hers whom Creede Forrester bedded. It surely wouldn't be her so there was absolutely no reason to experience envy.

But it wasn't her head that had trouble accepting the explanation . . .

Knowing she'd not fall asleep soon, Laurel rose and pulled her skirt on over her nightgown and threw a shawl around her shoulders. She decided not to slip on her shoes since she didn't plan on leaving the porch.

She tiptoed downstairs and out the door, closing it quietly behind her. The air was still warm and damp, but it was cooler than the day had been and Laurel breathed deeply of the crispness. The town was silent; even the east side, which housed the saloons and Miss Fancy's bordello, slept.

She leaned a shoulder against a porch post and stared into the darkness. In the peace and quiet of the night she could almost believe the last few years were all a nightmare, and when she returned to her bed Robert would be waiting for her.

Robert. She tried to picture his face and although she could make out the shape, the details were fuzzy. He'd had brown eyes. She remembered that. But his mouth, nose, chin, and jaw were all a blur.

Closing her eyes, she concentrated on the man who'd been her husband for three years, but whom she'd lived with for little more than one. So little time to get to know a man. She thought she'd had a lifetime, only Robert's lifetime had been shorter than either one of them had imagined. And her lifetime stretched out before her, bleak and indistinct. She had a goal for now, but what then? She could see nothing beyond delivering the messages.

Her thoughts strayed to Creede, first a widower, then losing his only child. What gave him a reason to continue? Was it his home in Texas? Or did he simply possess more courage than she?

A horse neighed shrilly from the livery. The sickening

stench of rotting meat suddenly assailed Laurel's nostrils and her stomach lurched. The darkness evaporated, leaving the vision of dead and dying horses and mules scattered across a battlefield drenched in blood of both man and beast.

Part of her knew it wasn't real and she tried to draw away from the onslaught but couldn't escape. Looking down, she saw mud covering her feet, but it was mud made of blood and dirt. She opened her mouth to scream but it stuck in her throat, choking her.

"Laurel?"

The voice, low and gentle, drew her out of the hideous waking nightmare. The rotting carcasses disappeared and the reek drifted away, replaced by the heavy scents of damp earth and green trees.

Creede touched her shoulder. "Laurel, are you all right?"

Regaining her composure, Laurel turned and lifted her gaze to his shadowed face. "I'm fine."

He brushed his fingertips across her cheek and held up his damp fingers. "You're crying."

Was she? She didn't remember crying. "It's nothing."

Neither one moved and an expectant hush rose between them.

"What's wrong?" Creede asked, his voice full of concern. "Why were you crying?"

She couldn't tell him, couldn't confess her deepest fear. But his tender solicitude made her feel guilty for having to deceive him. "I-I was thinking about my husband, Robert."

Creede drew back. "I'm sorry. I didn't mean to intrude."

Unable to bear his remorse, she reached for his hand so he couldn't leave her. "No. It's all right. I'm glad you did." More than glad that he'd chased away the ghosts.

Creede glanced down. "After I lost Anna, I had trouble sleeping. I'd wake up in the middle of the night and reach for her but she wouldn't be there. Then I would remember she was dead, and it was like having to say good-bye to her again."

"How long did it go on?"

"A long time."

Laurel wondered if he was aware he was stroking her knuckles with his thumb. It had been a long time since a man had held her hand, and the intimate touch played havoc with her heart.

She cleared her throat. "I should get back—"

A meow interrupted her and Laurel peered into the darkness.

"Do you think it's the same cat?" Creede asked, also searching.

"It doesn't seem possible."

She drew away from Creede and went down the porch steps, flinching slightly when she stepped on a stone with her bare foot. "Kitty, kitty," she called softly.

The next meow was closer.

"Come here, kitty, kitty."

A shadowed movement caught her eye and she strained to make out the shape. It was a cat, but it couldn't be the same one. She squatted down and held out her hand. "Come here, kitty."

The thin animal butted its head against her hand, and Laurel leaned closer and gasped. It *was* the stray she'd left fifteen miles back. How had it walked so far? Didn't the stupid cat know she had no home to give it?

"Damn. It's a stubborn little thing," Creede murmured.

Despite herself, Laurel picked up the scrawny cat and cuddled it close to her chest. The animal purred contentedly even though she knew it had to be tired and hungry.

"So what're you going to do with it?" Creede asked.

"I shouldn't do anything."

"But you can't do nothing." There was a tenderness in Creede's voice she hadn't heard before, but she didn't want his understanding.

She scowled and tried to stand without releasing the cat. Creede grasped her elbow and helped her rise.

"I'm sure Floyd wouldn't mind if you gave it some leftovers," Creede said.

Although Laurel knew feeding it was the last thing she should do, she couldn't let it starve either. The stupid cat trusted her.

Laurel grunted her assent and they made their way to the kitchen. Creede found the lantern and matches and lit the kerosene wick. Soft light flooded the kitchen.

Despite Creede's seeming indifference to the stray cat, he found two bowls. One he filled with water and set on the floor. Laurel put the cat beside it then tore a piece of leftover venison into small chunks, which she placed in the other bowl. The stray wolfed down the meat.

Creede leaned against a wall, his arms and ankles crossed. And Laurel suddenly realized his shirt was unbuttoned and he wore only stockings on his feet. No gunbelt adorned his hips, but it didn't detract her gaze from the snug fit of his trousers.

She shivered and tugged her shawl tighter about her, too aware of the thin gown that couldn't hide her hard nipples. For so long, she'd only looked at men as patients. But Creede Forrester wasn't one of those wounded men. He was virile, strong yet tender, and her reaction to him was far from professional.

"Why aren't you sleeping?" she asked, anxious to detract her body's response.

He shrugged. "Couldn't. What about you?"

"Same."

Creede shook his head, chuckling. "We finally have a real bed and neither of us can get a good night's rest." He sobered. "Course, I don't think a soft mattress had anything to do with it."

Laurel grimaced at the truth of his words. "Nights are always the worst."

"It does get better, Laurel. One day you'll be able to think about him and smile."

Although Laurel was referring to her nightmares, she didn't correct him. Let him think it was only a wife's grief for her dead husband, not insanity drawing nearer and nearer.

The cat rubbed across her ankles, then Creede's.

"Floyd might want it," Creede said.

Although Laurel didn't want the cat, her first reaction was to object. Fortunately, common sense intervened. "I'll ask him in the morning."

"So what're you going to do with him until then?"

Laurel worried her lower lip. "I'll put him out. He's used to finding a place to sleep."

She picked up the purring cat and carried him onto the porch. Creede followed but stood back while she set him on the ground.

Surprisingly, the cat immediately dashed off into the night.

Feeling betrayed by the animal's eager flight, Laurel remained standing on the porch.

"Are we leaving tomorrow?" Creede asked.

"Yes. It's time to move on to the next one."

"Why are you doing this, Laurel?" he asked, his voice intense but low.

A hundred reasons came to mind, but there was only one real reason. "I have to."

"No, you don't. No one will know the difference."

She pivoted slowly, the wood cool against her bare soles. "I'll know."

Creede muttered a curse. "You're a stubborn woman, Laurel Covey."

It wasn't stubbornness that drove her, but guilt. And there was the gnawing fear that her mind would break before the messages were all delivered. However, that was her burden to bear.

Suddenly it was difficult to keep her eyes open. "I'm going to bed."

Creede raked a hand through his already tousled hair, making him look younger. "Good idea. There's only a couple of hours left before dawn."

With a hand at her back, Creede guided Laurel through the door and up the stairs. Only when they stood by their bedroom doors did he draw his hand away. Cold invaded the spot where his palm had warmed her.

"I'll see you in a few hours," he said.

Laurel nodded and when he closed the door behind him, she finally entered her own room. Without removing her skirt or shawl, she lay down on the bed and closed her eyes. No visions leapt out to haunt her and she fell asleep with only the memory of Creede's warm, steady hand on her waist.

THE stray cat didn't return the next morning and Laurel forced herself not to search for it. Obviously, the cat had found a home or moved on. Either way, she should be relieved.

Laurel waited on the porch with her bags. Creede had gone to retrieve the horses and mule from the livery. Floyd stood outside with her.

"I'm sorry to see you leave so soon, Mrs. Covey," he said, his words sincere.

"I accomplished what I came here to do."

"Where are you going now?"

Laurel tightened her hold on her journal. "Lefsburg, Mississippi."

"Why?"

"I have another message to deliver."

He frowned. "I don't pretend to understand, but good luck with your mission."

Maybe he didn't understand, but he did know that her journey had become a mission. The words locked on the journal pages had to be freed before she lost what remained of reason and sanity. It was a small enough task, compared to those who'd given their lives.

She grasped his hands and squeezed them. "Thank you, Floyd. We're grateful for your hospitality and clean rooms."

Floyd blushed and she released him. She glanced past

him to see Creede riding his sorrel mare and leading Jeanie. Dickens was nowhere in sight. Frowning, she picked up her two bags and went out to meet him.

"Your damned mule won't budge," Creede said before Laurel could ask. "I don't know why you don't just shoot him and put him out of *our* misery."

Laurel rolled her eyes. "Really, Creede. He's only a dumb animal. He doesn't do it on purpose."

"He may be a dumb animal, but he knows exactly what he's doing."

Laurel didn't deign to reply. She handed Creede her bags then climbed into Jeanie's saddle. He gave her back the smaller bag and hung unto the larger.

"Bye, Floyd," Creede said, touching the brim of his hat.

"Good-bye, Mr. Forrester."

Laurel doubted if Creede heard the wistfulness in Floyd's voice and she figured it wouldn't be prudent to tell him. Let Floyd have his dreams. Too often that was all a person had in this life.

Creede led the way back to the livery and dismounted outside by the corral. He took Laurel's bag from her so she could climb down from Jeanie's back. Once inside the livery, Laurel definitely knew Dickens was having one of those days. He sat in the middle of the barn, giving everyone the evil eye.

She stifled a sigh. Maybe she should sell the insufferable mule, but doubted his next owner would be so patient and he would end up as dinner. She couldn't do that to him. He'd pulled the wagons bearing wounded and dead soldiers back to the tent hospitals. He'd never balked when he was needed, but on the days he wasn't required to pull an ambulance, he'd earned his name, in spades.

"What the dickens are you up to?" Laurel scolded the mule. "It's time to go."

Dickens merely brayed at her.

Shaking her head, Laurel ignored his cussedness and got his frame pack in place. She pinched the skin behind his front leg and the mule scrambled to his feet. Prepared,

Laurel stepped back so she wasn't knocked over by his swift upsurge.

"How'd you do that?" Creede asked.

"That's our little secret."

Creede scowled but handed her the two bags, which she lashed to the frame with practiced efficiency. Laurel took Dickens's lead rope and the mule docilely followed her out of the livery.

As Laurel neared Jeanie, she spotted the stray cat sitting patiently a few feet away.

"What are you doing here?" she asked.

The cat meowed.

Creede shook his head. "Something tells me he wants to go with you."

Laurel shook her head. "No. He's got a warm barn and I'll bet folks around here will leave food out for him."

"Yep. The cat would be stupid to leave."

Laurel glanced at Creede, unable to tell if he was making fun of her. Then she ignored the stray and mounted Jeanie. With a firm hold on Dickens's rope, she led the way out of town, refusing to look back to see if the cat followed.

She heard Creede ride up beside her but kept her gaze aimed straight ahead.

A mile out of town Creede looked back. "Your friend is back."

Laurel twisted around and spotted the skinny cat trotting behind them. "Doesn't he have any sense of self-preservation?" she asked in disgust.

Creede chuckled. "Sure he does. He knows a softie when he sees one."

Unable to vent her frustration on the cat, she glared at Creede. "Now what?"

"It's your cat."

"It's not my—" She broke off with a growl and halted her horse. She dismounted, handed Creede Jeanie's reins and waited for the cat to catch up to them. She picked up the creature and set it on the bags on Dickens's back. "If you knew what was good for you, you would've stayed in town where you'd have your choice of warm barns. This way, you're going to have to make do."

He meowed and curled into a ball.

Dickens brayed.

Jeanie whinnied.

Creede chuckled.

And Laurel was stuck with another uninvited traveling companion.

$\mathcal{S}$EVEN

MOSQUITOES buzzed around Creede's head and he swatted the back of his neck as one stung him. His hand came away bloody and he cursed the bothersome insects for the umpteenth time that day. Since leaving Fordingham, he and Laurel had traveled nearly a hundred miles, and most of the distance had been seething with biting flies and mosquitoes. He had counted fifteen welts on his arms and neck that morning. Laurel had given him some ointment from her bag, which had helped the swelling, but the new bites were now irritating him.

He glanced at his silent companion, noticing her fixed gaze on the horizon. In some ways she was the perfect traveling companion—quiet and asking nothing of him. Yet Creede couldn't help but wonder about her uncommon silences and what chased through her thoughts.

"We should be in Lefsburg tomorrow," he said, his voice unusually loud amid the buzzing insects and rustling grass.

She seemed to rouse herself and nodded after a moment. "Good."

"Who is it this time?"

She turned to look at him. "William Gaddsen. His friends called him Will."

Although her voice was flat, he caught the flash of anguish in her eyes. "Did you know him?"

"Not really. After he died, one of the men from his company told me about him. He said Will used to play the fiddle and tell terrible jokes." She smiled wanly. "But he had an eagle eye and a steady hand on the battlefield."

Creede's grip on the reins tightened. So many men and boys gone, and Laurel had seen more than her share pass to the next life. "That's important when you're depending on the person standing next to you," he said lamely.

Laurel nodded, but he could tell her thoughts were locked in the past.

"I remember a soldier who was brought in covered with blood and gore," she began. "He was screaming like the devil himself was after him and would hardly sit still long enough for a doctor to look at him. It turned out he wasn't hurt at all and the blood was from his best friend who'd been standing right next to him when he was shredded by grapeshot." She glanced down, her floppy brim covering her expression. "He never got over it and was sent home. I doubt he'll ever be in his right mind again."

How many friends had seen Austin die? What about the neighbor boy he'd run off with? Had they been fighting side by side when Austin had received his fatal wound?

The crashing of brush to his right brought Creede's hand to his revolver and a moment later a pig burst out of the undergrowth in front of them. Creede's horse whinnied and tried to rear, but he held tight to the reins. Laurel's mare did the same and nearly unseated her, but she managed to get the dun back under control.

The pig raced around them, keeping the horses on edge, but Dickens flattened his ears and kicked at the runaway pig. He managed to catch the sow's shoulder and it squealed and rolled across the grass, but rebounded to its feet immediately.

Amid the chaos, two men dressed in ragged overalls ran

onto the road following the pig. One man chased after the sow while the other aimed an ancient shotgun at Creede.

"We found him first so he's ours," the one with the shotgun drawled.

Creede eyed him, noting his skinny frame, bare feet, and unshaved, grimy face. He could smell the man, too—a mixture of old sweat, pig manure, and tobacco. He could've been anywhere from twenty to sixty years old.

"We don't want any trouble," Creede said evenly.

"And you won't get none iffen you don't touch our pig." His shifty gaze slid to Laurel and his eyes widened. "Well, look-ee there, Delbert."

The one named Delbert struggled to hang onto the shrieking pig by its hind legs as he stared at Laurel like she was an angel. "It's a lady."

"Course it's a lady. I knew you wasn't as dumb as you looked."

"She's purty, Rufus."

Rufus, the man with the shotgun, swept his gaze up and down Laurel. "We could get us a bundle of money for her."

Creede stiffened. "You're not touching her."

Rufus cackled. "You ain't got no say with this here shotgun aimed at yer noggin."

Laurel spoke up for the first time. "You have your pig so why don't you just leave?"

Rufus grinned, revealing wide gaps between tobacco-stained teeth. "She even talks purty, don't she, Delbert?"

The man holding the pig bobbed his head, his entranced gaze fixed on Laurel.

Creede inched his hand toward his revolver. Torn between amusement and irritation, he preferred to be prepared if the situation got ugly.

"Maybe we could keep her, huh, Rufus?" Delbert asked tentatively, still clinging to the pig, which had stopped its efforts to escape. "I ain't seen a woman like her afore."

Rufus spat a stream of brown juice, barely missing his own foot. "Ma wouldn't take too kindly to her livin' with us. She'd want a proper weddin' first."

"Then I want to marry her," Delbert said, his enthrall-ment changing to stubbornness.

Creede shook his head, wondering if Rufus and Del-bert were as addle-brained as they appeared. He couldn't believe any man with an ounce of brains or decency would be considering stealing a woman and taking her home to meet his mother or arguing about who'd get to marry her.

"She's already married," Creede spoke up, hoping he was doing the right thing. "I'm taking her back home to her husband and if we don't arrive, he'll send out a hundred men from his regiment to look for her."

Delbert's thick eyebrows drew together and he looked like he was about to cry. "She already hitched?"

Laurel held out her left hand. "To Major Robert Covey."

"He a soldier?"

"Yes. He was in the Confederate Army," Laurel said.

Rufus stared at her a moment then lowered the shotgun and sighed heavily. "Damn, don't seem right stealin' a Johnny Reb's wife."

Delbert shook his big head sadly. "Nope. Wouldn't be right t'all."

Creede exchanged a bewildered look with Laurel. He'd hoped his ploy might throw them off a bit, but he hadn't expected such an easy capitulation. However, it appeared that although the two men were thieves and not all that bright, they had their own sense of right and wrong.

"Why don't you come with us to meet Ma? She'd be right pleased to have another woman's company, even if it ain't for long," Rufus said.

Creede was thinking of some way to answer that wouldn't insult their ma when Laurel replied.

"Thank you, but I'm afraid my escort and I have to be on our way," she said, affecting a drawl. "We're already behind schedule and I'm certain Robert is growing quite concerned."

His mouth gaping, Delbert stared at her while Rufus finally remembered his hat and doffed the greasy, floppy thing.

"I'm right sorry to hear that, but I don't want to be givin' your man any call to worry," Rufus said gallantly.

"Thank you," Laurel said in a genteel voice. "Enjoy your pig."

"Yes, ma'am, we will."

Creede allowed Laurel to move ahead of him and he kept himself between her and the two pig thieves. Although they now seemed harmless enough, he didn't want to take a chance with Laurel's well-being.

"Do you think they'll follow us?" Laurel asked Creede once they were far enough away they couldn't be overheard.

"I think they'll have their hands full with the pig."

"Especially if the real owner shows up to claim it." She shuddered. "I can't believe they actually thought I'd marry one of them."

Creede removed his hat and mopped his brow with a damp handkerchief. "I don't think they would've actually gone through with it. Besides, I have a feeling even they'll be able to find wives with so many men killed in the War."

Laurel nodded somberly. She glanced back to where the stray cat still lay nestled in the middle of the mule's pack frame, between the two bags. The incident hadn't even woken the cat. "That was some fast thinking on your part," she said.

Creede shrugged. "I was hoping they were loyal to the Confederacy, which meant they'd respect one of their officers."

"I'm merely glad it worked. I didn't relish the thought of being introduced to Ma."

"I don't plan on letting anything happen to you, Laurel."

She appeared startled but quickly looked away. "Plans often have a way of changing, whether we want them to or not." Then she turned back to him and caught his gaze, her eyes clear and determined. "*I* made the decision to deliver the messages. If anything happens to me, I don't want you blaming yourself. I need you to promise you won't feel guilty."

Irritation made Creede's voice sharp. "I can't make a promise like that any more than you can stop delivering those damned messages."

Laurel glared at him. "You're more stubborn than Dickens."

Creede's annoyance dropped and he grinned. "Thanks."

She rolled her eyes heavenward.

Creede laughed at her expression and she joined in after a few moments. He couldn't draw his gaze away from her bright expression and his chest tightened unexpectedly. His mirth faded and he looked away, troubled by his reaction. To be attracted to her like any man was attracted to a pretty woman was expected, but this was more— something he didn't have the courage to examine too closely.

As they rode through the battle-scarred land and crossed paths with the poverty-stricken folks, he was thankful for Laurel's company. When he'd left Texas all those months ago to search for his son, he'd hoped to travel home with Austin. He never expected to be escorting a former Confederate nurse to Texas instead.

Creede and Laurel continued their travels in silence. The wind picked up as increasingly gray clouds moved overhead. On the western horizon, a bluish-black wall heralded a storm.

Despite the heat of the day, a shiver sliced through him. "We should make an early camp."

"I was thinking the same thing." She swatted a fly on Jeanie's neck. "The flies are biting worse."

Creede nodded.

As they rode, the clouds overtook the sun and turned daylight into early evening. The air grew heavy and cool. Electricity sparked, giving the darkness a greenish hue.

Creede's mare twitched her ears, which glowed with a greenish-blue light. Creede had seen the same odd phenomenon a few times before, and each time a violent storm had followed. They had to find shelter, and soon.

Creede halted.

"What is it?" Laurel asked.

"Looks to be a place about a quarter of a mile away."

Laurel squinted through the dimness. "They might let us use their barn."

"If it's Rufus and Delbert's, they'll probably let you share the cabin with Ma," Creede teased.

She wrinkled her nose. "I'd rather share the barn with Jeanie and Dickens."

"And me?" The husky question was out before Creede could stop himself.

Laurel's expression didn't change, but her cheeks flushed pink. "If it's a choice between you or Delbert or Rufus, then yes, I'd rather sleep with you."

Creede was relieved she'd made light of his question and continued in kind. "I think I've been insulted."

She reached out and laid her gloved hand on his arm then smiled sweetly. "Think of yourself as the lesser of three evils."

Creede chuckled, finding Laurel's burgeoning humor a welcome and altogether too-attractive part of her personality.

Lightning streaked across the clouds and the horses pawed the ground, shifting restlessly. The still air was charged with expectancy and the hairs on Creede's arms tingled. They needed to get to shelter. "Come on."

Laurel, too, grew serious and followed him. He could hear her murmuring to her horse and the mule, trying to keep them calm amid the spectacular light show behind the heavy gray clouds. St. Elmo's fire continued to dance between the horses' ears and produced a faint glow around their manes and tails.

Approaching the homestead, Creede realized it was abandoned, and the house had suffered a fire, leaving nothing but a black shell. The barn, however, was still standing, although the roof sagged and there were undoubtedly holes in it. But it would be better than nothing once the storm began in earnest.

He dismounted in front of the barn door, which hung by a single hinge. Peering inside through the grayness, he saw some stalls and old hay. It was more than he'd hoped.

"Is it safe in there?" Laurel asked, startling him by her closeness. He hadn't realized she, too, had gotten off her horse.

He shrugged. "Hard to say, but I'd rather take that chance than staying out here when that storm comes."

"Me, too."

She started forward but Creede placed his hand on her wrist. "Wait. Let me go in first and see if there's a lantern."

Laurel nodded and accepted his horse's reins then watched him enter the barn. In the distance lightning zigzagged from the clouds to the ground, catching her attention. Five seconds later, thunder rolled like a cattle stampede. The storm was closing fast.

She could feel the electricity buzzing around her, like the incessant bugs that had plagued them earlier. Jeanie danced and her eyes rolled, the whites showing. Creede's usually steady mare also pranced nervously. The cat twitched his tail. Only Dickens appeared bored by the entire affair.

Creede lit a lantern inside the barn, illuminating a six-foot circle around him. "It looks safe enough," he called out.

Laurel half led, half tugged the animals into the barn, her nerves suddenly chittering like sparrows. Creede took his mare's reins from her and went to work unsaddling the horse.

Laurel followed his example and stripped Jeanie of her gear then led her into a decent stall before removing her bridle. Lightning flashed, lighting up the corners of the barn and leaving an eerie afterglow in its wake.

Ignoring her internal trembling, she turned her attention to Dickens but found Creede already there.

"I'll take care of him . . . if he lets me," he said.

Dickens swung his head toward Creede and showed his teeth in a caricature of a smile. But the mule stood placidly as if proving to Creede he could behave.

Before Laurel could lift the stray cat from the mule's back, he meowed and leapt down, landing on his four paws with a grace that defied his scruffy appearance. The hair along the cat's back stood up.

Laurel squatted down to pick him up, but lightning followed closely by resounding thunder sent the cat into a frenzy. He dashed out of the barn just as heavy raindrops fell, sounding like rapid hammer strikes against the roof.

Laurel didn't hesitate but dashed outside after the stupid cat.

"Laurel!"

She barely heard Creede's holler above the storm's intensity. The rain lashed at her face and the wind, which had been dormant only minutes earlier, bowed the trees. Leaves were ripped from branches and shunted away by the wind's force.

Holding an arm in front of her face to ward off the driving rain, she searched for the stray cat. Her clothing became soaked in seconds, but she hardly noticed. She focused on finding the cat, afraid if it remained outside it would be drowned or get sick from the cold rain.

A movement caught her eye and she turned to squint through the rain's curtain. She made out the dim shape of something about the size of the cat and leaned into the wind to trudge toward it.

Getting closer, she could make out the skinny animal, looking even thinner with the water flattening his fur. She picked up the cat and he curled into her arms, burrowing his head beneath her chin.

She soothed the trembling cat in low tones, ignoring nature's temper tantrum swirling around her. As she staggered toward the barn, lightning flashed and thunder cracked so close that she stumbled back, falling on her backside.

And found herself in another storm.

The cannon's fire was too close. She could almost feel the whisper of heat across her face when it sent another cannonball into the camp. Man and beast unlucky enough to simply be wounded screamed in pain and horror.

She helped another patient into one of the wagons and turned back to the tent to help another man. The cannon exploded again and she was flung forward by the percussion of the blast. She lay there, listening, but there was unholy silence, and she pushed herself to her knees on bloody palms. Turning her head, she spotted a crater where the ambulance wagon had been. Around the crater were parts of bodies half buried by dirt.

Bile fought with the scream to climb out of her throat and the scream won, except she couldn't hear it. The only way she could tell she was hollering was that her throat ached and her lungs burned. And there was nothing else she could do to hold on to her sanity.

A hand on her arm shocked Laurel back to the present.

"You've got to get back in the barn," Creede said, tugging her to her feet.

Dazed, Laurel allowed herself to be pulled along. She glanced behind her, through the rain, and saw the split trunk of an ancient oak tree. Smoke curled from the burnt slash that cut through bark and wood.

She stumbled behind Creede, her hands filled with the quivering stray cat. Only she wasn't certain anymore if it was her or the cat shivering.

The shift from pelting rain to dryness made her gasp in shock. Unable to move on her own, Laurel stood where Creede had stopped. Her teeth chattered and the cat clawed at her arms and chest to jump down. She opened her hands, although they didn't feel like hers, and the stray hopped down and disappeared into Dickens's stall.

"That was a crazy thing to do," Creede said, anger resonating in his voice. "The cat would've been fine, but you almost got hit by lightning. When I saw it strike . . ." He ran a shaking hand through his dripping hair. "Damn it,

Laurel, I thought you didn't even care about that cat."

She stared at him, hearing his words but barely able to comprehend them, much less reply. Then she was aware of his silence and the furious gaze that turned to concern.

He stepped up to her and grasped her shoulders. "Laurel, are you all right?"

She peered at his lips, seeing them move and an inkling of understanding filtered through her. He was frightened . . . for her.

Lifting a trembling hand, she pressed two fingers to his lips. They were warm and supple, kindling heat in her fingertips, like the fire that danced between the horses' ears before the storm.

"I-I'm all r-right," she stuttered.

He grasped her wrist gently and lowered her hand from his mouth. "No, you're not. You're nearly blue and you're shaking like cotton in the breeze."

He placed his palm against her cheek and she leaned into it, closing her eyes.

"You have to get out of those wet clothes," he said gently.

Wet. That's why I'm so cold.

Her fingers fumbled with her buttons.

"Will you let me help you?" Creede asked.

Frustrated with her clumsy attempt and desperately cold, she nodded.

She watched him unbutton her blouse with long, tapered fingers that captivated her. So gentle, but she'd seen those same hands draw a revolver with the swiftness of a rattlesnake strike. Of course, he'd loved a wife and a son with those hands, too. Strong, caressing, assuring, confident, hardworking—his hands were all that and more.

"I'm going to take off your shirt now."

Laurel blinked and lifted her gaze to his face, only to find it inches from her own. "A . . . all right."

She felt his hands move across her arms and back, his touch warm against her cold skin.

"Do you think you can take your skirt off?"

Laurel nodded and although her motions weren't quite coordinated, she was able to undo the catch at her waist and step out of the skirt. Standing in her chemise and drawers, she thought she should be embarrassed, but all she could do was shiver.

Creede held up a blanket and looked away. "Get out of those wet things and wrap the blanket around you."

With the feeling returning to her limbs, Laurel removed the soaked undergarments then took the blanket from Creede and wrapped it around her shoulders. It overlapped and swathed her from neck to toe, although she was more grateful for the warmth seeping back into her chilled body than the covering.

"Do you think you can stay there while I start a fire?" Creede asked.

Laurel's scattered thoughts were becoming less jumbled. "Yes." She managed a weak smile. "I won't even chase after the cat if he runs outside again."

A smile with more relief than amusement teased his lips. "Glad to hear it."

Laurel became aware of the storm again, of the lightning and thunder. There were only single beats between one and the other, but inside the barn, she didn't feel its fury as intensely as when she'd been surrounded by it outside.

The flashback to the War skated along her awareness but she shied away from it. The thunder must have made her remember it so vividly. Another memory that would've been better left as a nightmare.

She tugged the blanket closer and buried her chin in the rough wool. Although she didn't want to dwell on the memory, she couldn't help but remember the gory scene and the bubble of silence that had surrounded her. Fortunately, one of the doctors had managed to get her to stop screaming and her hearing had returned soon after. Then she'd gone right back to helping transfer those still alive in the hospital tents to another wagon. She hadn't thought about it again . . . until the thunder had yanked out the memory.

"Sit by the fire," Creede said.

Laurel glanced up to see the cheery blaze he'd started near the door of the barn so most of the smoke would be drawn out. He guided her to the fire and motioned for her to sit on an upturned pail.

Her gaze followed him and her cheeks heated when she saw him hang her chemise and drawers near the fire to dry. She reminded herself he'd been married, so women's undergarments weren't unknown to him.

He returned and hunkered down on the other side of the fire. "Warming up?"

She nodded, knotting her fingers within the blanket, and attempted a smile. "I guess it was foolish of me to go after the cat."

Creede scratched his jaw. "It wasn't the brightest idea. Why'd you do it?"

Laurel gazed into the fire's crackling flames, shuddering slightly with every crack of thunder and bolt of lightning. "Maybe for the same reason I remained a nurse after Robert was killed." She raised her head, meeting his puzzled look. "It simply seemed the right thing to do."

Thunder shook the ground and the horses shuffled in their stalls.

Creede tossed some old hay into the fire. "Austin used the same argument before he ran off to join the army. I didn't agree with him."

Laurel noticed the gleam of moisture in his eyes and said softly, "Maybe he didn't want your agreement, only your understanding."

"And my blessing." Creede's voice wavered. "I never gave him either."

"But you did give him your love."

Creede clenched his jaw and glanced away. "It wasn't enough, was it?"

$\mathcal{E}$IGHT

THE sagging walls of the barn closed in on Creede, but the storm cut off any escape. Unable to remain still, he went to Red and patted her neck, easing the sorrel's nervous trembling.

"Tell me about yourself," Laurel suddenly said.

Creede's hand froze in mid-stroke. "Why?"

She shrugged. "Why not? We aren't going anywhere until tomorrow morning and neither one of us is tired enough to sleep."

He couldn't imagine anyone wanting to hear about his luckless life. Keeping his head averted, he gave her an abbreviated version. "I was married, we had a son, my wife died, and now my son's dead."

Her impatient sigh overrode the rain's clatter. "What of your own parents? Are you from Texas or did you settle there? What did you do before you were married? What were your wife and son like?"

Her questions unlocked memories he'd left behind years ago, but he was surprised to find he wanted to talk about the bittersweet recollections. However, he'd done things in his life he wasn't certain she'd understand.

He gave his mare one final rub and moved back to the fire to squat across from Laurel. "I'm not sure you're going to like what I have to say."

"I learned a long time ago we all have good and bad in us. It's how much we have of each that determines what kind of person we become."

Creede studied her a moment, attempting to determine if she was serious or merely trying to set him at ease. Either way, he'd warned her. "My folks had a small ranch in the Colorado Territory, raised a few head of cattle, some pigs and chickens. There was enough to feed me and my two younger brothers."

He stared into the flames, seeing the small but neat cabin where he'd spent his childhood. "Pa died when I was fourteen. The night before he died he gave me his revolver, and made me promise to take care of Ma and my brothers. I promised I would."

The memories of his family were so clear he could hear his mother's soft singing and his younger brothers arguing over their chores. He swallowed hard and rubbed his jaw, hoping to rub away the too-real pictures.

"A year later two men came and stole our cattle and hurt Ma." He flinched, hearing his mother's screams after the first man had taken her into the cabin while the second had made him and his brothers stay outside. When the first man came out and the second went in, his mother hadn't screamed anymore.

"She died about a week later. Doc said it was a fever that took her. I always figured she just gave up." He clenched his hands into fists. "But I'd broken my promise to my pa."

"You were only fifteen," Laurel said, her expressive eyes filled with sympathy and compassion.

"I was a man," he said sharply, then waved an apologetic hand. "Not long after Ma died we lost the place and my brothers—Slater and Rye—were taken away to the orphan home."

"I'm sorry, Creede."

"It was a long time ago."

"Not to you."

Startled, he realized she was right. *Like yesterday . . .*

"So what did you do?" Laurel asked.

Creede held his chilled hands over the fire, but even the flame's heat couldn't dispel the cold. "I tracked down the men who murdered Ma and killed them."

Laurel's sharp gasp didn't surprise him. She was a woman who saved lives and wouldn't condone a man who'd taken them without remorse. Her opinion mattered more to him than he'd expected, and he wished he hadn't been so free with his words. "I told you that you probably wouldn't like what you heard."

"Did you kill them in cold blood?" she asked, her gaze flicking to his gunbelt.

The two arrogant rapists had been so certain they could take a kid, but Creede had shown them otherwise. He'd started practicing with the Colt revolver the day after his father died, and the two men had paid for their cockiness with their lives, which was a fair price after what they'd done.

"I gave them more of a chance than they gave Ma," he said unapologetically.

"Then I'm glad."

Her unexpected comment brought a brittle smile to Creede's lips. "Me, too."

She didn't ask him to continue with his story and for that, he was grateful. Those years between gunning down the outlaws and meeting Anna were filled with regrets.

The seconds between lightning and thunder increased, until the thunder was only a faint percussive roll. The rain, too, lessened and left only a damp mist as the dark clouds drifted away. Sunset had come and gone during the storm and only a hint of orange on the western horizon remained.

Laurel stood, keeping the blanket clutched tight about her. In the firelight, her face was cast in light and shadows, and her damp unbound hair gleamed, giving her an ethereal appearance.

The knowledge that she wore nothing beneath the blanket caused an instinctive stir in his groin. But there was more to his attraction than simple physical need—he admired her understanding and ability to listen and not judge. When he'd first met Laurel, he thought she was simply a do-gooder, but there were layers to her that he hadn't anticipated.

"Where are my bags?" she asked.

Creede cleared his throat. "In front of Dickens's stall."

"If you don't mind, I'd like to put on some dry clothing."

I do mind.

Instead Creede only nodded. "Go ahead. I won't peek."

Husky laughter spilled from her lips. "If you wanted to peek, I doubt I could stop you."

His blood heated rapidly. "Is that an invitation?"

Her eyes darkened with passion and she licked her lips, leaving a glossy trail. Expectancy crackled between them.

Never taking his gaze off her, Creede rose and stepped in front of her. He framed her face in his hands. Laurel's eyelids fluttered shut and she sighed wistfully.

She was a widow. She knew what she was asking for and Creede knew what he wanted. He yearned to bury himself in Laurel's heat—lose himself in their shared passion. But his head and heart fought his body's response. There was a fragility about Laurel that invoked his protective instincts. Hell, he even wanted to protect her from himself.

Creede pressed a chaste kiss to Laurel's forehead.

She opened her eyes, which reflected sultry passion. "I want more, Creede. I want you."

"You do now, but tomorrow you'd regret it," he said, sweeping his thumbs across her velvety cheeks.

She lowered her gaze but not before Creede caught her recognition of the truth. But there was also hunger and disappointment to match his own.

Unable to stay close without craving what she offered so freely, he forced himself to step back and his hands fell to his sides. "Put on some dry clothes while I fix something to eat."

He could see the effort it cost her to smile.

"I've eaten your meals, so you just sit down and relax," she said with forced lightness. "I'll fix something after I'm decent."

She turned but Creede caught her arm and the blanket slipped off a creamy, smooth shoulder. He stifled a groan and focused on her startled features. "Even wearing only a blanket, you're decent, Laurel, and because you are, I can't do something we'll both be sorry for later."

Laurel slipped a hand out of her blanket and pressed her palm to the shirt covering his chest. "Thank you." A hint of mischief entered her eyes. "Your clothes are still damp. Maybe you should change." She winked. "Don't worry, if I peek, I won't be seeing anything I haven't seen before."

She spun away with the jauntiness of a young girl and Creede laughed. One moment solemn and thoughtful, and the next playful and teasing. He hoped her husband had appreciated her for everything she was, and not simply for her beauty.

He kept his gaze averted but could hear cloth pulled over skin and his mind conjured images which he dispelled with difficulty. The swish of air warned him a moment before the blanket fell across his shoulder.

"Your turn," Laurel said.

Grinning, he went to an empty stall, stripped and wrapped the blanket around him. He inhaled deeply of her sweet scent held within the folds before digging out dry clothes from his saddlebags. He drew on his pants and shirt and hung his damp clothing over a stall rail. After giving the horses and mule some water, he rejoined Laurel by the fire. Side pork crackled in the frying pan and he barely suppressed a groan. "Tomorrow I'll see if I can get a rabbit."

"You don't like pork?" she asked sharply.

Puzzled by her abrupt tone, he held up his hands. "I didn't say that. But it would be nice to have some fresh meat."

Impatience tightened her mouth.

"I didn't mean to make you mad," Creede tried again.

Her eyes sparked with annoyance. "I'm not mad."

Creede frowned, recognizing "mad" when he saw it. Why was she so upset about something so slight? "Did I say something wrong?"

She blinked and the irritation trickled away, replaced by sheepishness. "You didn't say or do anything, Creede. I'm just tired."

He nodded, accepting her excuse, but there was a ring of untruth to it. What was she hiding? Or was he only imagining things?

The stray cat joined them and sat down on his haunches. The feline had dried from his dash into the storm. He licked his front paw to clean his face and whiskers.

Creede studied the damned fur ball that had nearly gotten Laurel killed. His heart had nearly stopped when the lightning had struck less than twenty feet from her. When he could see again after the bright flash and she was still alive, his heart started beating again.

He shouldn't have been shocked when Laurel had followed the stray into the storm. That was simply part of who she was, yet she denied she held any affection for the cat.

He recalled Laurel's blank face when he'd called to her. It was the same look she'd had when the cat had showed up at their camp. She'd scrambled away from Creede then, too, like she hadn't even recognized him. She had insisted she was fine, but even then he suspected something was wrong.

What made her change like that? Was something amiss with her mind? He shied away from that thought, not wanting to imagine the intelligent woman with vacant eyes and a slack expression. He'd seen a man like that once, a long time ago. A bullet to the head should've killed him, but instead it had turned him into something less than a human being.

Creede vowed to keep a closer watch on Laurel. If she had another one of those bouts, he wouldn't let her lie about it. Traveling with her, he had a right to know what was wrong.

"The food's ready, if you can stomach more side pork and biscuits," Laurel said coolly.

Creede didn't bother to argue, but accepted the plate with a murmured "thanks."

Gazing at the silent, almost belligerent woman, Creede couldn't help but wonder where the other Laurel had gone—the Laurel who teased and smiled, the Laurel who attracted him like no other woman, even his late wife Anna.

He ate the food without tasting it and noticed Laurel wasn't too keen on it either, but she cleaned off her plate. Creede took their dishes outside to the barrel he'd noticed when they'd arrived and cleaned them in the fresh rainwater.

The mist had stopped, but the air was damp and heavy. It was hard to fill his lungs, worse even than the air back home.

Homesickness caught him unaware as he thought of his cotton farm in Texas. Since learning Austin was dead, Creede wasn't certain he wanted to return to the farm that held so many memories. Yet those cotton fields and the warm summer days drew him.

But the revolver he wore on his hip called to the man he had once been. Powerful people had hired him to take care of their problems and they'd paid him well for his skill with the revolver. That Creede Forrester had been proud of his abilities, but four years later Anna convinced him it wasn't something to take pride in.

Now his father's Colt was cleaned and oiled and back in the holster he'd worn nearly two decades ago. Maybe it wasn't as fancy as the new revolvers, but Creede had no doubt it was just as deadly, especially in his hand. Age and disuse hadn't dulled him or the revolver.

His skill with the Colt revolver might keep Laurel alive long enough to deliver her messages. Then he would move on and find out who needed someone with his specific skills. He could lose himself in the company of men like himself, who had nobody to mourn their passing.

And what of Laurel? Where would she go after she completed the obligation she felt she owed the dead soldiers? Would she find another husband and settle down to a life she should've had five years earlier? Or would she go back to nursing and live alone the rest of her life? It seemed odd that she never spoke of the future, of what she might do after she'd fulfilled her promises.

Shaking himself free of his somber musings, Creede returned to the barn. The fire had burned down and Laurel was stretched out on her bedroll.

Creede placed the clean dishes back in their place and crept into his blanket. As the cicadas' chorus grew, he stared out into the darkness until sleep finally overtook him.

LAUREL gasped and bolted upright. With wide eyes, she searched her dim surroundings and listened to the eerie silence. Where were the sounds of men moaning and muttering in feverish delirium? Why hadn't anyone awakened her for her shift?

However, she wasn't on a cot in a hospital tent. Soft fur brushed her cheek and everything fell into place. Careful of the stray cat, she dropped back onto her bedroll and drew a hand across her damp brow.

"Laurel?"

She jerked slightly. "Yes?"

"You're awake," Creede said.

It wasn't a question, but she replied, "Now I am."

"Another nightmare?"

"Yes." Laurel sat up, bracing herself on her bent arms. "How did you know?"

He shifted. "I didn't, until you told me."

Her muscles stiffened. He'd taken advantage of her half-awake state.

"You want to talk about it?" Creede asked.

"No." *Merely thinking about the nightmares is difficult enough.*

They lay in silence and Laurel suspected Creede was waiting for her to speak. He'd wait until Hades froze over.

"You must have seen a lot of horrible things during the War," Creede finally said, his gentle tone inviting her confidence.

Laurel pressed her lips together and tried to shut out his voice.

"I can't even imagine what it must've been like for you," he continued. "To watch them die and knowing you couldn't do anything to help."

Her stomach twisted and sourness rose in her throat. She placed a hand on the cat's warm, vibrating body and concentrated on the tickling against her palm.

Creede's voice cut through the cat's purring. "I've seen a few men die of bullet wounds and it's not something I can stomach. But you must've seen a lot worse, what with bullets and bayonets and cannons."

Red visions swam through Laurel's mind. She saw blood covering her hands and vile green oozing from putrefied wounds. They were men and boys but all of them screamed when the pain became too intense. Before the war, Laurel had never heard a man scream. Now all she could hear in her nightmares were those horrific cries.

"It's done and in the past. No reason to talk about it," Laurel said, barely able to speak in her normal voice.

"My wife Anna liked to talk. Said it helped her think things through better."

Annoyance threaded through her. "Maybe it helped her. It doesn't help me."

"How do you know?"

"Talking about something doesn't change it. You're escorting me to Texas against my wishes. I've accepted that, but that doesn't mean I have to confide in you."

"You asked me about my past and I told you."

"That doesn't give you the right to demand the same of me." Laurel turned on to her side, giving her back to Creede.

If he spoke again, she didn't hear him over the furious pounding of her heart. She wanted to curl up into a ball and hide from Creede, from the surviving families for whom she carried messages, and from all the ghosts of dead and crippled soldiers. She wished she could take Jeanie and Dickens and simply disappear, but that option was past. Creede would hound her until she made it to Texas safely, even if she tried to escape him. And the damned cat would probably follow her, too. Not to mention the ghosts who didn't need a trail to follow—they'd just wait until she slept to find her.

Tears burned her eyes but she blinked them back. She had no reason to feel sorry for herself. She was alive and whole. So why couldn't she be grateful she wasn't lying in a cold grave?

"I'm sorry. You're right. You don't have to tell me anything. I guess, I just want you to know, well, that I'm not a bad listener," Creede said. "At least that's what Anna used to say."

The awkward contrition in his voice doused Laurel's anger, but her tight throat made it impossible to speak. Robert had been a good husband, but his formal upbringing had left him stiff and courteous, even with his own wife. She'd started to make slight inroads into his tightly reined personality, but the War had taken him before she'd been able to unearth his true character. Would she have heard the same endearing self-consciousness in Robert's voice one day?

She doubted it. The two men were worlds apart, yet she found herself drawn to Creede just as she'd been attracted to Robert. However, she'd married Robert before learning the cruel realties of life. Now she was too familiar with death. A possible future would forever be clouded by its specter.

Laurel managed to clear her throat. "I appreciate the offer, Creede. Truly I do. But we aren't going to be together for more than a month or so. Once we get to Texas, we'll go our separate ways."

"That doesn't mean we can't be friends."

"I-I don't think that's a good idea."

"Why not?"

Laurel's hair-trigger temper soared again. "It just isn't."

When had she become so easily riled? She prided herself on her ability to remain calm even in the worst conditions, so why couldn't she control herself with Creede?

"If that's the way you want it." His curt tone bespoke his frustration.

Laurel's emotions seesawed again and her eyes filled with moisture. She hadn't meant to vex him. At times like this, she recognized how closely insanity lurked.

No, it wasn't the way she wanted it, but it was the way things had to be.

$\mathcal{N}$INE

December 23, 1864. Private William Gaddsen from Lefsburg, Mississippi. Fatally wounded during the battle at Petersburg on December 21. Light brown hair, eye color unknown, twenty-two years old. Cause of death: head wound. "Don't let my son forget me. And tell Katy I'll always remember how pretty the sun shone on her gold hair the day we got hitched."

LAUREL was relieved when they rode away from the barn the next morning. She'd spent too much time in close quarters with Creede and had become too much at ease. Her cheeks burned as she recalled how she'd offered her body to him in shameless abandon. More dangerous, however, was allowing herself to learn more about him, his life, and the kind of man he was. That tempted a different—deeper—kind of intimacy and she didn't dare surrender to it. She couldn't afford to grow close to anyone ever again.

Creede remained pensive as they rode abreast, their stirrups occasionally brushing. Perhaps he was finally regretting his hasty decision to accompany her to Texas. That should've relieved her, but Laurel found her throat constricting with the painful realization that she didn't want him to leave.

Being a nurse, she'd learned to set her feelings aside and remain detached from her patients. Surely she could do the same with Creede Forrester.

She focused on the land and noticed people working in a meager field, perhaps a quarter mile away. Squinting, she could tell most of the workers were dark skinned. With the end of the conflict, slavery was abolished, yet Laurel wondered how many farms continued to use ex-slaves.

She swallowed her revulsion, just as she'd done for the past four years. Although Robert hadn't fought for the Confederacy because of the slavery issue, it had been difficult for Laurel to remain on the side that condoned it. Yet most of the Confederate soldiers who'd died had never owned a slave in their short lives, which was how Laurel was able to live with her conscience.

It was shortly before noon when they entered Lefsburg. There was little activity, but the people who were on the boardwalks stopped to watch them. Their expressions ranged from weary to suspicious, and sometimes belligerent. Clothes were patched and threadbare, and very few wore shoes. The war had obviously struck close to this town and its people had suffered worse than others.

"Do you know where the family lives?" Creede broke their long silence.

She shook her head. "I'll have to ask around."

Creede adjusted the brim of his wide-brimmed hat. "You'll have to do it careful-like. I get the feeling these folks don't take too kindly to strangers."

Recognizing the truth of his words, she didn't bother to reply, but glanced back to check on Dickens and the curious cat that peered out from his perch atop the mule's pack. By the covetous attention the horses, mule, and cat garnered, she suspected there might be some who wouldn't see anything wrong in stealing from a stranger.

"We'll have to pay extra for the livery to keep an eye on our stock," she said in a low voice.

"Yep. Already figured on it."

She should've realized he'd be thinking ahead, weighing and measuring the possible risks. He and Robert would've gotten along brilliantly with their similar strategy skills.

The hotel was located close to the bank and a decent restaurant, while the boardinghouse had saloons on either side of it. They reined in their horses at the hotel's hitching post.

"You go in and get a room," Creede said in a low voice. "I'll stay out here with the horses."

"Where will you sleep?"

Creede's lips thinned. "With you." His hooded eyes surveyed the town and the people who went about their business in eerie silence. "I got a bad feeling about this place."

Laurel glanced around and a shiver skittered down her spine. She didn't want Creede sleeping in the same room, but she, too, felt the desperate pall that hung over the town.

She was aware of Creede's gaze on her back until the hotel door closed between them. After the sun's warmth, she took a moment to savor the cooler air inside the building. Then, keeping her back straight, she marched to the front desk where the clerk ogled her.

"Can I help you, ma'am?" His drawled tone was just as slick as his hair.

Laurel affected a Virginia accent, suspecting a Massachusetts inflection would create even more mistrust. "I'd like a room." She paused. "For my husband and myself."

The clerk's gaze lost some of its ardor. "That'll be a dollar—and we don't take any worthless paper."

Fortunately Laurel had exchanged her Confederate money for coin before leaving Virginia, but not without a significant loss. She dropped a silver dollar on the counter and, glad for her wedding band, signed the register as Mr. and Mrs. Creede Forrester.

"Your room is up the stairs and down the hall to the left. Number 112." The clerk handed her a key, his fingers lingering in her palm.

She closed her hand around the key and stepped back, repressing a shudder. "Thank you."

He didn't seem to notice her frosty tone. "You're welcome, Mrs. Forrester."

Laurel hurried back outside to Creede.

"Any problems?" he asked.

"No. I registered as Mr. and Mrs. Creede Forrester."

His eyebrows shot up. "I thought you'd use your husband's name."

Laurel hadn't even thought of it and she shifted her feet restlessly. "I figured it would be less complicated using yours."

He inclined his head. "There's a livery down the block."

She took Jeanie's reins and Dickens's lead rope and followed Creede down the street. Stares followed them and the skin between her shoulder blades crawled. Once in the barn, Laurel stayed back while Creede dealt with the shrewd-eyed owner. After the liveryman promised to keep a close eye on the stock for an added fee, Laurel and Creede removed their bags from the animals. The cat darted off, but Laurel suspected he'd be back when they were ready to leave town.

Dickens made his displeasure at being left there known with laid-back ears and loud brays. Laurel set down her belongings and grasped his ears, one in each hand. "Behave yourself, Dickens, or I may not come back for you."

As if he understood, the mule quieted and meekly followed the liveryman into an open stall.

"How did you do that?" Creede asked, reaching for Laurel's bag.

She let him take it and said with a smile, "We have an understanding."

Creede grinned and walked out of the barn with Laurel beside him. They returned to the hotel, where a large-bellied man wearing a suit and vest sat in a chair beside the door. A gold chain stretched across his vest, revealing a prosperity nobody else in Lefsburg possessed.

"New in town?" he asked, scratching his thick neck.

Creede stepped in front of Laurel. "Just passing through."

"We don't get many folks just passing through." His oily gaze slid across Laurel. "Most men around here died fighting the Yanks. Left a lot of womenfolk behind."

Laurel looked around, seeing only very young and old men, but none in their prime. The women kept their gaze lowered as they hurried to carry out their errands. She turned her attention back to the suited man, who looked to be slightly older than Creede.

"Yep. Left a lot of widows behind, they did," the man said. He stood and hitched up his trousers.

"So why didn't you join up?" Creede asked.

"Bad back." He eyed Laurel one more time then nodded and sauntered away.

Laurel stared after him, her heart pounding, although she wasn't certain why, since the man hadn't made any threats.

"Let's get inside," Creede urged, his head close to hers.

He ushered her into the hotel with a steady hand on her waist and she relaxed into his touch. Even the clerk's prurient look didn't bother her with Creede beside her. Upstairs, he took the key and unlocked their door.

A double bed dominated the small room, with a straight-backed chair in one corner and a battered pitcher and basin stand in another.

"Cozy," Creede said dryly.

Laurel lifted the yellowed coverlet and wrinkled her nose at the crumpled sheets. She doubted they'd been changed since the last occupant. Fortunately, they had their own bedrolls to lie on the mattress. God willing, there weren't any nits or other pests lying in wait on the bedclothes.

"We could stay with the horses," Creede suggested, reading her thoughts.

Despite being tempted, Laurel shook her head. "I've already paid for the room and we do have water and privacy to wash up."

After they piled their meager belongings in the room, Laurel had to make a trip to the privy. Much to her chagrin Creede insisted on accompanying her. He waited outside the smelly outhouse while she quickly used the necessary. Her face burning, she hurried back to their room without meeting Creede's eyes. Yet she couldn't deny the spark of gratitude for his comforting presence. There was an ominous feeling about the town.

They took turns cleaning up in the room with lukewarm water from the pitcher. Laurel had Creede wait outside as she changed into a clean but wrinkled skirt and shirtwaist to wear to the restaurant. Creede escorted her as if they were man and wife, and Laurel leaned into him, enjoying the deception far more than she should have.

As they waited for their lunch, she studied the five other diners. All were men and four were gray-haired.

"I wonder how many towns are like this one," Laurel commented.

"Like this how?" Creede asked.

"Inhabited by old men and young widows with children."

Creede raked a hand through his thick dark hair. "I reckon there's a lot of them. Damned near a whole generation of men lost for no good reason."

Laurel speared him with a sharp glare. "Each of those men who died had a reason. We may not have agreed with it, but it's not our place to say their reason wasn't good enough."

He leaned back in his chair, affecting a nonchalant pose, but she knew she'd touched a raw nerve.

Laurel leaned forward to clasp his fisted hand. "I didn't know him, but I do know his father, and I'm sure Austin believed in his heart that he was doing the right thing."

"When I was Austin's age, I'd already killed two men. I thought it was the right thing to do, too."

"And now?"

He shrugged and sat up, forcing Laurel to draw away. "And now I don't know a damned thing."

She didn't know what to say so gave him the dignity of looking away from his naked anguish.

The homely waitress, appearing harried despite the few customers, brought their plates and set them on the table. She swooped back seconds later with the coffeepot to refill their cups. "Is there anything else you wanted?"

Creede shook his head, but Laurel spoke up. "I'm looking for someone. Katy Gaddsen. Her husband's name was William."

"What're you wanting Katy for?" she asked suspiciously.

"I have a message for her." When the waitress began to shake her head, Laurel added, "From her husband."

The woman's plain face paled until only two red splotches stained her cheeks. "He's dead."

"That's right. I was a nurse. I was with him at the last."

The waitress leaned close enough that Laurel could see the nervous twitch at the corner of her left eye. "Katy loved William."

"And William loved her, which is why his last words were for her."

"I can give Katy the message."

Laurel shook her head. "No. I'll deliver the words personally."

"You can't." She glanced around as if fearful someone might overhear her. "She don't like strangers coming to call."

"Where does she live?" Creede asked in a steely voice.

One look at Creede and the waitress gave them directions to a place three miles out of town. "Go during the day, not in the evening."

"Why?" Laurel asked.

"Jest do like I said."

The woman scurried away.

"What do you think that was about?" Creede asked.

"She's scared, like most of the women around here."

"Why?"

"I don't know, but I'd like to find out."

Creede's jaw muscle clenched.

"We should eat before the food gets any colder," Laurel said.

It looked unappetizing but she forced herself to eat the watery potatoes and tough meat. She refused to ponder if it was beef or mule. Creede, too, ate with decidedly less enthusiasm but cleaned his plate.

The waitress steered clear of their table, increasing Laurel's frustration. She wanted to ask her more questions about the town, and especially how many of the women were widowed and how they got by.

"You done?" Creede asked, motioning to her plate.

She nodded.

"Let's go then." He dropped some coins on the table and ushered Laurel out of the restaurant.

She glanced back into the restaurant to try to discover a reason for their abrupt departure, and her gaze collided with the suited man who'd been sitting outside the hotel earlier. Was he the reason Creede wanted to leave so quickly?

"You don't like him," she said.

For a moment, Creede looked puzzled then he narrowed his eyes. "I've seen men like him before."

Their footsteps echoed on the wood as they walked back to the hotel under the early afternoon sun.

"He's a bully. All bark and no bite," Laurel said, although not believing her own words.

"Only when he's sure he can win." His gaze drilled into hers. "Women, children, old men."

The very same makeup of Lefsburg. But could one man control an entire town? Remembering the man's cunning eyes, Laurel reluctantly answered her own question. The sooner she could conduct her business, the sooner they could move on.

"I want to see Mrs. Gaddsen now," Laurel said.

"The horses need to rest for a day," Creede said.

"I'll have Dickens hitched to a wagon."

Creede grunted. "He won't be happy about that."

"I know, but I don't want to spend any more time in this town than necessary."

"Gotta agree with you there," he said grudgingly. "I'll take you back to our room, then get the wagon and bring it over to the hotel."

Laurel opened her mouth to tell him she could find the way herself, but abruptly changed her mind. The town gave her the creeps. "All right."

"No argument?" Creede's expression was filled with deigned surprise.

She rolled her eyes and smiled.

Like a proper husband, he clasped her hand, which rested on his arm. She curved her fingers around his forearm, enjoying the play of his muscles against her skin. With guilty delight, she breathed in the scent she'd come to associate with him—shaving soap, leather, and a hint of male muskiness. It gave her a sense of being harbored, protected, and in her deepest recesses, cherished. Yet she knew it was an illusion. Even if she'd been an old hag, Creede would protect her all the way to Texas.

She was startled out of her reverie to find herself in their room.

"Come down in fifteen minutes. I'll be out front." Creede closed the door behind him.

Laurel retrieved the bag with her journal and dashed some cool water on her face then patted it dry with the thin towel. After twisting her hair tightly into a bun at the back of her neck and donning her good bonnet, she left the room with her journal tucked under her arm.

Dickens brayed when she came out of the hotel. No, he was definitely not happy to be out of his straw-lined stall and hitched to a wagon. Laurel patted his neck and the mule's flattened ears perked up.

Creede hopped down from the seat and limped over to Laurel.

"What happened?" she asked.

Creede glared at Dickens. "Your damned mule kicked me."

Laurel grimaced. "I'm sorry. At least he didn't break your leg."

"He got me in the shin. I'll be lucky if I can get my boot off."

Creede assisted her into the wagon and she settled on the seat, which had little spring left. He pulled himself up to sit beside her, huffing a groan.

"I can examine your leg for you," she offered.

"Not much you can do for a bruise."

He managed to get Dickens to move and the town disappeared behind them. Laurel curled her fingers around the journal and her thoughts shifted to delivering the next message. She usually reread the note before meeting with the family, but she hadn't had any time alone to do so this time.

Her stomach churned and sourness rose in her throat. She hated doing this, but she had no choice. She'd made a promise to each of the soldiers who'd entrusted her with messages.

After delivering seventeen of the twenty-one messages, it wasn't any easier to deliver the eighteenth. In fact, it had grown more difficult with every delivery.

"I'll go in with you, if you'd like," Creede suddenly said.

"No. This is something I have to do alone."

"Why?"

She frowned. "Because I was the one with them when they died."

"It wasn't your fault they died."

Tears burned her eyes and she turned her gaze so he couldn't see the moisture. "Minie balls and sabers and grapeshot killed them. So did diphtheria and a dozen other illnesses," she said, her throat raw and full.

"Other soldiers—men—killed them."

Creede might try to ease her guilt, but she knew the truth. Many of those wounded soldiers would have lived if she'd been able to help them. Because she was the most experienced nurse, oftentimes her job was to determine who the doctor would tend first. Men who might have lived had been left to die because other lives were more readily saved and it was up to Laurel to separate them.

She'd played God . . . and she'd hated every moment of it.

The wagon slowed and she spotted a fairly well-to-do cabin. Two horses pranced in the corral and colorful flowers bloomed along the front of the house. It wasn't what Laurel had expected after witnessing the poverty in town. Had William Gaddsen come from a well-to-do family?

"Are you certain this is the right place?" she asked.

Creede shrugged. "It's what the waitress told us."

The cabin door opened and a boy about four years old scampered out.

"Willie, you get in here right now," a woman called after him.

Creede jumped down from the wagon and caught the boy, swinging him high in the air before holding him against his side. "What's your hurry, son?"

Laurel smiled at Creede's easy way with the boy. He must've been a wonderful father.

"Thank you for catchin' him."

Laurel turned to see a beautiful blonde woman with a shy smile approach them. However, it was her rounded belly that caught Laurel's attention.

"No problem, ma'am. He must be quite a handful for you," Creede said easily.

"I don't know what I'd do without him," she said softly.

"He's William's son, isn't he?" Laurel asked.

Alarm swept across Mrs. Gaddsen's face and she reached for her son, who wound his arms around her neck and his thin legs around her thick waist. "Who are you?"

Creede assisted Laurel down from the wagon and stepped back.

"My name is Laurel Covey and I was a Confederate nurse. Your husband died in the hospital where I worked."

The woman's face went milk white and Creede reached out to steady her.

"Mama, what's wrong?" the boy asked fearfully.

"She's fine," Creede assured. "She just needs to sit down out of the sun." He gave Laurel a quick nod toward the house.

"May we go inside?" Laurel asked her. "My friend, Creede Forrester, will look after Willie out here if that's all right with you."

"Why are you here?" she asked, her wary gaze moving between Laurel and Creede.

"Your husband gave me a message to give you."

Joy coupled with apprehension lit Katy Gaddsen's face. "Would you like to play with Mr. Forrester, Willie?" she asked her son.

"I promise I won't bite," Creede said.

The boy giggled and his mother set him down. Creede took the boy's hand. "Why don't you tell me about your horses?"

Creede led the chattering boy away.

"He's good with children," Mrs. Gaddsen said.

"He had a son." At the woman's questioning look, Laurel added, "He died fighting for the Confederacy, too."

Mrs. Gaddsen's eyes clouded with sympathy that was left unspoken. She led Laurel into the house, her advanced pregnancy making her slow and awkward.

"You can't stay long," Mrs. Gaddsen said, placing her hands on the curve of her belly.

Laurel did some quick subtraction in her mind. William must've gotten his wife with child not long before he was killed. But how had he been to Mississippi and back to Virginia in a matter of a week or two? "Did William know you were expecting another child?"

Katy Gaddsen flinched as if struck. "No. He left a year ago and I never saw him again." She lifted her chin. "What did you have to tell me?"

Puzzled, but realizing it wasn't any of her business, Laurel pulled her journal out of the bag and out of habit, caressed the cover with a reverent hand. She opened it to the place the ribbon marked. "Your husband died on December 23. Before he died, he gave me these words to pass on to you." Laurel took a deep breath and pressed a finger to the page, following the lines as she read. " 'Don't let my son forget me. And tell Katy I'll always remember how pretty the sun shone on her gold hair the day we got hitched.' "

Katy's sob broke the silence and Laurel laid a hand on the young woman's arm. "You were on his mind at the last."

The widow broke down, crying in earnest as she laid her head on her folded arms. Laurel went to her knees beside her, patted her shoulder and uttered soothing words.

After a few minutes, Katy pulled herself together and lifted her head. She used a handkerchief from her blouse sleeve to wipe her tear-stained face.

"I'm sorry," Katy whispered. "I thought I was done grieving for him."

"There's no need to apologize." Laurel returned to her chair. "Women in your condition tend to be weepy."

"You must think I'm terrible."

"Why would I think that?"

"Because you know my sin." Her tone was filled with self-recrimination.

Laurel shifted uncomfortably. "It's not my place to judge."

Katy dabbed her eyes and blew her nose then pushed to her feet clumsily. She waddled to the window and gazed outward, giving Laurel her profile. "Will was gone less than a month when Jasper Thomas started coming around. At first he pretended to be worried about me and Willie, but I assured him Ethan, our hired man, could take care of the place.

"Then one day Ethan up and disappears. Willie and me tried to take care of everything that needed doing, but it was a losing battle. Between the bills and the cost of food-stuffs, we were getting more and more in debt, until no-body would give us credit no more."

Katy dashed a hand across her furrowed brow. "Mr.

Thomas said he'd take care of me and Willie if I—" She swallowed hard. "If I signed this place over to him. I told him no. This was Will's folks' home. I couldn't just hand it over. But then Willie got sick. I went to Mr. Thomas, begged him to loan me some money to pay the doctor. The only way he said he'd help is if I did what he asked, so I signed Will's place over to him. But that wasn't enough." A tear rolled unheeded down her cheek and dripped onto the front of her blouse. "It was either whore myself or lose my son.

"When I got word that Will was dead, I was already carrying Jasper Thomas's bastard." She turned and faced Laurel. "God forgive me, but there was a part of me that was glad he'd never know what I'd become."

Laurel rose and moved to her side. "You did what you had to in order to keep your son alive."

"Jasper owns this place and me, but he won't marry me." Her gaze dropped. "And I'm not the only woman."

Laurel swallowed her revulsion and was grateful Jasper Thomas wasn't standing in front of her.

Suddenly Katy gasped and pressed her hands to her belly.

"What's wrong?" Laurel asked, alarmed.

"The b-baby. It's coming."

$\mathcal{T}$EN

"CREEDE!"

He jerked his head up to see Laurel framed in the cabin's doorway. Even from across the yard, he could see the panic in her features. Keeping his own apprehension tempered so he wouldn't frighten the boy, he left Willie playing with the kittens near the barn and hurried to the house.

"What is it?" he demanded.

"Katy's going to have her baby. You'll have to watch Willie."

He looked past her, into the cabin. "Have you ever delivered a baby?"

"I've helped with a few."

Her brave words couldn't hide the tremor lurking behind them.

"Should I go into town and see if they have a midwife or a doctor?"

Laurel shook her head. "I don't think she wants anyone else here." She paused as if trying to make a decision. "The baby isn't her husband's and she isn't remarried."

Creede narrowed his eyes. There was a lot she wasn't

telling him, but a woman's cry from the cabin stopped him from pressing for more. "If you need help, let me know. I was with Anna when Austin was born."

Laurel blinked in surprise and a soft smile played on her lips. "You're a surprising man, Creede."

He shrugged it off, embarrassed. "Who's the father?"

Her expression changed to anger. "A bastard by the name of Jasper Thomas."

Shocked by her profanity, Creede wished there was time to learn more about Thomas. The woman cried out again. "Go to her. I'll keep an eye on Willie."

Laurel reached out to snag his wrist. "Thank you."

Creede gave in to the temptation to cup her warm, silky cheek in his palm. "You're welcome."

He hurried back to the boy, grateful Willie hadn't noticed anything amiss. As he stood just inside the barn in the shade, Creede tried to come up with something to keep the boy busy without straying too far from the cabin.

The kittens scampered away and Willie hopped to his feet. "Wanna go play in the crick."

"Where is it?" Creede asked.

Willie pointed beyond the back of the house. "Over yonder."

"Does your ma let you play there?"

He stubbed his bare toe in the dirt. "She don't care."

Somehow Creede doubted that. "Why don't you take me there and we won't tell her?"

Willie's face lit with a mischievous grin. "Okay."

The familiar grin, so much like the one on another boy's face twelve years earlier, robbed Creede of his next breath. He blinked, fighting the unexpected gut-wrenching pain.

A small hand tugged at his larger one. "C'mon, Mr. Creede."

He let himself be dragged along by the boy, allowing his thoughts to be caught up in memory's undercurrent. He pictured Austin's third birthday when Anna had made a chocolate cake. More of the frosting had ended up on Austin's face than in his mouth. The first time Austin had ridden a horse, Creede had stayed close to his side, but the boy had urged the mare into a trot. He'd left Creede behind, but Austin had a natural riding ability and he'd only laughed with joy. Then the darker memories came, of Anna's death and dealing with Austin's grief and anger, as well as his own. The last argument he'd had with his son had been riddled with accusations and anger—Austin had called him a coward and blamed him for not saving his mother's life. But Creede had stayed true to his vow to Anna and hadn't used his revolver. Instead, he'd used his fists but he'd been too late to save her.

Creede wiped at the tickling sensation on his cheek and was shocked to find moisture. He'd tried to tell Austin that violence only begat violence, and guns never solved anything. But Austin had joined the army and Creede again wore his revolver on his hip.

The creek wasn't far from the house and Creede roused himself from his bleak musings to watch Willie. The boy squatted down beside the shallow brook. Water riffled over rocks, creating a soothing backdrop to cover the faint sounds from the cabin. Willie found a stick and dipped it into the creek to turn over some rocks. He laughed in delight and Creede hunkered beside him to see what was so funny.

"Crawfish," Willie said, pointing to one about three inches long. "Me and Ma like to eat 'em."

"And I'll bet you like to catch them," Creede said with a forced smile.

"Uh-huh, but we don't got a pail."

"Let's go back and get one."

Back in the yard, Creede sent Willie to fetch a pail from the barn while he went to the cabin. Sticking his head in the door, he spotted Laurel with her arms filled with sheets. "Willie and I will be at the creek that runs about a couple hundred feet behind the house."

Laurel nodded, her cheeks flushed. "I think the baby's going to come quickly."

"That's good. Better for the baby and the mother." He took a step back. "You know where I'll be."

Mrs. Gaddsen cried out from the bedroom and Laurel hurried to her. Creede wished he could do more to help, but knew the baby would come whether he was here or keeping Willie out from underfoot.

As Willie came racing toward him with a pail nearly as big as he was bumping against his leg, Creede wasn't certain whose job was more difficult—his or Laurel's.

LAUREL barely had the baby cleaned of blood and mucus when the child let out a wail. Laurel grimaced at the ear-splitting sound but it didn't stop the satisfaction flowing through her.

She quickly severed the cord between mother and daughter, tying off the ends of both with thread she'd barely had time enough to boil in water. The birth had taken a little over an hour and had been relatively easy for the mother.

As air swirled through the infant girl's veins, a healthy red color displaced the bluish caste of her skin. Laurel took a moment to count the toes and fingers, and found everything perfect.

"She sounds healthy," Katie said, eyeing the tiny bundle lying on her chest with love and affection.

Laurel smiled. "Healthy, and mad at being forced out into the world."

Katie's smile wavered. "I can't blame her. She won't have an easy time of it."

Laurel wrapped the newborn in a clean blanket and set her in the crook of Katie's arm. She couldn't help but brush the baby's cheek with the backs of her fingers. "I know it'll be difficult, but you have to remember, it wasn't yours or your daughter's fault that she was born."

Katie stared into the baby's wrinkled face. "By assigning fault, I'm as much as saying I'm sorry she was born." A tear trickled down the side of her face into her sweat-dampened hair. "And looking at her, I can't ever be sorry for that."

"I'm glad. A child shouldn't be punished for the sins of her father."

"And mother."

"No," Laurel said firmly. "You have nothing to be ashamed of. You committed no sin and did nothing wrong. You did what you had to in order to save yourself and your son."

"My, isn't this a touching scene?"

Laurel whirled around, shocked by the man's voice. Her eyes widened at the sight of the suited man who'd been sitting in front of the hotel.

"What are you doing here?" Laurel demanded.

Katy grasped her hand and whispered hoarsely, "That's him. Jasper."

Laurel should have realized it by the man's arrogance and the asides he'd made about the War widows. He'd used the War and families' hardships to create his own empire as good men died on bloody battlefields.

"You loathsome bastard," Laurel said in a voice quivering with rage.

"Seems to me there's only one bastard in this room." Jasper Thomas's gaze fell on the innocent infant.

Laurel flung herself at Thomas, only to be thrown aside like a rag doll. Her shoulder struck the wall but the pain did little to dim her anger. Holding her injured arm, she glared at the revolting man.

Suddenly Thomas was yanked around and punched in the jaw. He stumbled back and Creede rushed in, fists held at his sides.

"Laurel, are you all right?" he asked, his rugged face filled with concern.

She nodded. "That's Jasper Thomas. He-he's the father of Katy's child."

Creede's gaze darted to the blonde woman in the bed, her blue eyes wide and frightened.

"He used her," Laurel said in a voice only he could hear. "Just like he's used a lot of other women in town."

Creede's expression went from solicitous to murderous

as he turned his gaze to Thomas, who was standing hunched over with a hand to his cheek.

"Not so brave when it's not a woman, are you?" Creede taunted. "In fact, I'd be willing to bet you're nothing but a chickenshit coward when it comes to facing a man."

Thomas's eyes glittered with hatred. "Who the hell do you think you are, coming into my town and insulting me?"

Creede's laughter chilled Laurel and she moved closer to Katy and her baby. This was a side of Creede Forrester she'd never seen before, and she wasn't certain how she felt about it.

"You have no right to use the women of this town," Creede said, his cold humor replaced by scalding fury. "You're a sorry excuse for a man and I think it's time everyone knew it." He leaned down and pulled a knife from inside his boot. His gaze fell to Thomas's crotch, his meaning obvious.

Laurel swallowed her aversion to Creede's implied threat, yet she couldn't find it in herself to argue against it. Thomas had forced Katy Gaddsen while her husband fought for their way of life, a way of life that didn't include stealing from and despoiling women.

"Y-you can't do that," Thomas sputtered.

Creede's smile sent an icy chill down Laurel's spine. "Oh, I think I can. I've castrated some calves in my time. Can't be much different. Course, I haven't sharpened my knife lately."

Thomas's face became a pasty white. "You'll kill me."

Creede shrugged. "Maybe, but then maybe I won't. Which would you prefer?"

Suddenly Willie rushed into the bedroom and Creede scooped him up before he could get close to Thomas.

The boy's eyes were wide and frantic as he stared at his mother. "Ma!"

"It's okay, Willie," Katy said, her trembling voice barely above a whisper. "I'm all right."

Then the baby started crying, proving her lungs were more than healthy, and Willie struggled to escape Creede's hold. Creede released him, but kept himself between the boy and Thomas.

"Now what are you going to do, mister?" Thomas asked, his bravado returning. "Going to cut me in front of the boy?"

Creede growled and Laurel knew he was tempted.

"Get the hell out of here," Creede said.

Thomas eyed Katy and the baby. "I'll be back later to see my daughter."

Katy inhaled sharply and Laurel laid a calming hand on her arm even though she, too, was distressed by Thomas's assertion.

Creede followed Thomas out and for a moment, Laurel wondered if he wouldn't make do on his threat to emasculate the man when they were out of sight. The possibility made her stomach queasy but didn't rouse her conscience. Jasper Thomas was worse than a rattlesnake. A snake only bit when it was threatened or disturbed, but Thomas preyed on his victims out of greed and lust.

She glanced down to see Katy trying to get her baby to suckle. Willie watched in fascination as he kept murmuring, "My little sister."

Luckily the infant was as quick in figuring out how to get her mother's milk as she was in coming into the world.

"Laurel," Creede called from the front part of the cabin.

She smiled reassuringly at Katy and hurried out to Creede. "Is he gone?"

Creede clenched his teeth. "Yes, but he's going to be trouble."

"He's already been trouble. The man has to be stopped. Isn't there some law officer in town?"

"Probably, but what would he arrest Thomas for? Do you think the women will admit to being used by him? And even if some step forward, who will the lawman believe, them or an upstanding citizen like Thomas?"

"We have to do something. We can't let him continue doing what he's been doing."

"Short of shooting Thomas down like a mad dog, I don't see how we can stop him."

Laurel shook with anger. "But he'll just keep terrorizing Katy and others like her. He's just like the men who hurt your mother."

"So you want me to call him out then shoot him?" he asked flatly, his cold gaze drilling into her.

Startled out of her anger, she shook her head. "I don't know. Maybe. Would that be so bad?"

Creede turned away. "You want me to do your dirty work."

She didn't know if the cutting sarcasm was directed at her or himself. "It would be justice."

"With you as judge and jury?"

"You were judge and jury for your mother's rapists."

"And my wife's killer, except I used my hands that time." He turned and faced her. "So, which do you want me to use, Laurel, a gun or my fists?"

The matter-of-fact words punched her, stealing the air from her lungs. She was again playing God, deciding who lived and who died. Only this time she was using Creede as the executioner.

Suddenly feeling sick, she pressed her hands to her belly. "I-I'm sorry, Creede. I had no right."

Creede's tense shoulders slumped but his expression remained unreadable. "You're right about one thing. If someone doesn't stop him, he'll keep getting away with it."

Laurel latched onto his wrist, feeling the warmth of his skin over firm sinew and bone. "But it's not your job to stop him. You wouldn't even be in this town if not for me."

Creede laid his large hand over hers. "What if you were in Katy's position? What would you want?"

Laurel couldn't hold his compassionate gaze and stared past him. "I'd be living in fear, knowing Thomas would be back and take his anger out on me. Or my children." She closed her eyes as sickness churned through her. "I'd kill him before he hurt my children."

Creede tilted her chin up and she opened her eyes to find his face close to hers. "Then she'd have to live with the guilt of killing another human being, even if he was a son of a bitch."

His breath wafted across her cheeks and his blue eyes caressed her face, making it difficult to think. "So what can we do?" she asked, her voice barely above a whisper.

He studied her and she lifted her hand and placed it in the middle of his chest, feeling his heart beat against her palm. She became aware of one of his legs between hers, touching her skirt and teasing her with his closeness. Her gaze fell on his lips and hunger exploded, urging her to taste him.

Abruptly, as if guessing her thoughts, he stepped away. "I have an idea."

Although her body crackled with tension, she regained some semblance of control. "What is it?"

As Creede explained, Laurel's desire faded, replaced by equal doses of anticipation and apprehension.

EVERY bone in Creede's body urged him to return to the cabin, but this had been his idea—an idea he was fast beginning to dislike. Leaving Laurel, Mrs. Gaddsen, and her two children alone for even an hour didn't set right with him. Maybe Jasper Thomas was watching from near the cabin instead of having returned to town.

Sweat rolled down the side of his face and he wiped it away with an impatient hand. No, what he knew of Thomas told him he'd gone back to town to fortify himself with a drink or two while he watched for them to return. Once he knew he'd only have women and children to face, he'd go back to the Gaddsen cabin. But what would he do when he got there?

Dickens drew the wagon down the main street as Creede unobtrusively searched for Jasper Thomas. There were few people about so it would've been easy enough to spot him, if Thomas was outside. But Creede suspected the coward was watching from a saloon window.

Creede halted Dickens outside the livery and patted the mule's withers, giving him more time to look for Thomas. But Creede didn't see him and had to hope Thomas spotted him.

The liveryman took care of Dickens and the wagon while Creede headed back to the hotel. He wanted to hurry, but forced himself to stroll down the street. Pausing by the restaurant, he poked his head in and motioned to the waitress. It was the same one who'd told them how to find Katy Gaddsen. She approached Creede warily.

"Since you're a friend of Katy's, I just wanted to let you know she delivered a little girl this afternoon," Creede said in a voice pitched low enough that only she could hear. "Both Katy and the baby are doing fine."

The waitress smiled, but it was tempered by the sorrow in her eyes. "Thank you for telling me."

"You're a friend of hers, right?"

She nodded, again with suspicion.

"How many more women are there like Katy—women that Jasper Thomas has used?"

The waitress's plain face paled, but after a moment, she stiffened her spine. "Seven that I know of. He's taken possession of their land and turned three of them into his mistresses." She bit her lower lip. "The others either had to leave town or go to work in one of the saloons."

She didn't have to say what they did in the saloons—Creede could see it in her expression.

"Are you one of them?" Creede asked gently.

She glanced up, startled. "No. I'm not married so I didn't have anything he wanted."

"Thanks for the information."

He turned to leave, but she caught his arm.

"Tell Katy I'll be over to see her as soon as I can."

Creede nodded. Knowing he probably shouldn't have spent those precious minutes talking to the waitress, he strode to the hotel and paused a moment, unobtrusively turning in a half circle. If Thomas was watching for him, Creede wanted to make sure he saw him entering the hotel.

Not wanting to waste another second, he went inside and nodded at the clerk then climbed the stairs as if he had all the time in the world. In case the clerk was listening, Creede unlocked the room and entered it, but stepped right back out.

Fortunately the hotel had back stairs and he went down them quietly, not wanting to alert anyone to his leaving. He opened the door and cringed when it creaked, then stepped out into the alley. He only had a split second of warning before the world went black.

LAUREL listened to Willie chatter about Rachel, his new sister, while she warmed the leftover stew. Her shoulder throbbed from where it had struck the wall when Thomas had shoved her. She hadn't really noticed it until after Creede had gone. Nothing was broken, but she was certain it was bruised.

Willie tiptoed to his mother's room and peered inside. "Ma and Rachel are sleeping," he said in a loud whisper.

"We'll let them nap until dinner is ready."

He tipped his head back to look at her quizzically. "We ate dinner before. This is supper."

She couldn't help but smile. "Where I grew up, this meal was called dinner."

"Then what was dinner called?"

"Lunch."

Willie's brow puckered up as he thought about that.

Laurel ruffled his fine hair. "Why don't you go lie down with them? I'll call you when it's time to eat."

The boy seemed torn for a moment then scampered into the bedroom to lie beside his mother. He extended his arm over her and his fingers rested protectively on his sister.

Feeling the sting of dreams unrealized, Laurel turned away.

She stirred the stew while she gazed out the window. Dusk fell and she hadn't seen a sign of Creede or Thomas. She wasn't surprised about Creede since the plan was for him to stay out of sight until Thomas showed his hand.

She knew it was risky. When Creede had outlined his plan, she'd agreed with it, but wanted Katy's approval since she would be in the middle of it all. Katy hadn't even hesitated. She wanted Jasper Thomas out of their lives for good.

Laurel lit a lantern and turned just as the door was thrown open. She froze, shocked to see Thomas standing in the entrance, even though she'd been expecting him.

"Nice to see you again, Mrs. Forrester."

Laurel blinked at the unfamiliar title. Thomas must have checked with the hotel clerk to learn their names.

"The feeling isn't mutual, Mr. Thomas." Acid dripped from her voice.

Thomas made a show of looking around. "Where is your husband?" Then he deigned surprise. "Oh, that's right, he's busy right now."

Laurel had counted on Creede being nearby but Thomas's tone inferred he knew something she didn't. "What do you mean?"

Thomas approached her, his eyes lit with unholy glee. "He thought he was being so clever by sneaking out the back door, but I was waiting for him."

Her heart compressed with fear. "Wh-what did you do?"

"He's been taken care of so I can take care of . . . loose ends here." He laughed at his own gallows humor. He took another step toward her. "Starting with you."

Laurel took a step back and bumped into the stove. She jumped away, but only far enough that she wouldn't set her skirt on fire. "I don't have any land and my husband isn't in the army so I don't see why I'm of any interest to you."

"You have other things I'm interested in." He motioned to the bedroom where Katy and her children slept. "Now that Katy won't be able to perform her duties for a little while, I'll have you."

Fear spiked in Laurel and as quickly as it came, it disappeared. A strange calm spread through her. She was well acquainted with death and wasn't afraid of it. Before

Thomas could use her, she'd find some way to kill him or herself.

His eyes glittering with lust, Thomas neared her. Laurel automatically backed away and encountered the stove . . . and the pot of hot stew.

ELEVEN

CONSCIOUSNESS prodded at Creede and his body resisted, wanting to remain in the comfort of floating darkness. However, unease nagged at him, urging him awake. He opened his eyes and blinked his dim surroundings into focus. Trying to remember where he was and how he ended up here proved more difficult.

The memories slammed back and he shot to a sitting position, making his head and stomach roll. He swallowed back the nausea and lifted a hand to the base of his throbbing skull. Sharp pain stabbed him and he hissed through clenched teeth as he pulled his hand away. Blood stained his fingertips.

Surprisingly, he still had his revolver. Obviously Thomas didn't know who he was up against. Creede grinned ferally. Thomas's cockiness would be his downfall.

Spotting his hat nearby, he picked it up and placed it on his head gingerly. He forced himself to his feet, moving with deliberate motions. Taking a good look around, he realized he was by the hotel's back door. Whoever had struck him had left him where he'd fallen.

How long had he been unconscious? The dusky light

told him it hadn't been any longer than half an hour, but that was time enough for Thomas to ride over to Gaddsen's. And Creede had no doubt it was Thomas who'd waylaid him.

Ignoring his pounding head and roiling gut, he half staggered, half ran to the livery. The liveryman wasn't in sight and he saddled Red with as much haste as he could muster.

Creede leaned over his mare's neck as he spurred her out of the barn and down the dark street. The horse stretched into a gallop. Creede's head thundered with the hoof beats, but he didn't dare travel any slower. He might already be too late.

Although he was worried about Katy Gaddsen and her children, he was more concerned for Laurel. Thomas didn't have her under his thumb and knowing Laurel, if he tried anything she'd fight like a wildcat. With nothing to lose, Thomas might hurt or even kill her. Determination shoved aside his headache and churning gut.

Creede spotted Thomas's horse at the same time he saw the lights from the cabin windows. Fear for Laurel tightened his muscles. He considered rushing inside, but Thomas wouldn't think twice about using a woman or child as a shield.

Making a wide circle around the cabin so he wouldn't be seen, he stopped at the creek where he and Willie had played earlier. He dismounted and dropped his horse's reins, knowing Red wouldn't stray far with abundant grass and water. His fingers curled around the revolver's handle, the smooth indents as familiar as his own hand.

He crept with measured stealth toward the house. At the edge of the brush, he searched the fifty feet of open ground between him and the door. Nothing moved but the milk cow and the scratching chickens. But, more disturbing, he didn't hear anything—no voices, no baby's squalls. Nothing.

Despite the sweat gliding down his back and soaking his shirt, a chill swept through him. Had Thomas killed them?

A bellow ripped through the air, shocking Creede. Cold dread snapped through him and he sprinted across the yard, not bothering to keep down. The roar had come from a man and the only man inside was Jasper Thomas.

He dashed around the corner of the cabin and shouldered aside the closed door, exploding inside. The smell of food hit him immediately. And it appeared the food was all over Thomas, from his head to his feet. Creede would've laughed, except Thomas had a stew-covered arm wrapped around Laurel's throat.

"Come any closer and I'll snap her neck," Thomas said, his arm squeezing to demonstrate his threat.

Creede expected to see terror in Laurel's face, but calm acceptance shown instead, despite her reddening cheeks from the lack of air. He didn't have time to ponder her odd reaction, but slipped his revolver into the holster and held up his hands. "Let her go."

Thomas's gaze bounced around the room before settling on Creede. Hatred blazed from the depths of his eyes. "You two spoiled everything. We had a nice arrangement—I took care of the widows and they took care of me."

"Did you ask the widows what they thought of your 'arrangement'?" Creede asked with a twist of derision.

"They needed me."

"You *made* them need you so you could get your hands on their land and them." Creede struggled to keep his voice steady. He didn't know how close Thomas was to breaking Laurel's neck.

"No one complained."

"Because you played on their emotions," Laurel said, her tone raspy. "You turned them into your own personal whores."

"Only the prettiest," Thomas admitted. "The rest had to find their own man." His cruel laughter made Creede flinch. "Or men."

His reference to those who'd had no choice but to work in upstairs saloon rooms ignited Creede's temper. He took a step forward, but Thomas jerked Laurel hard against him.

"Don't come any closer, Forrester," Thomas warned.

"Let her go, Jasper Thomas."

Creede spun around to see Katy Gaddsen standing in the bedroom doorway, wearing a nightgown and holding a double barrel shotgun. Even though her gaze was directed at Thomas, Creede felt a chill at the loathing in her eyes.

"Katy, no!" Laurel cried weakly.

"I won't let you die for my mistakes, Laurel."

"You won't shoot me," Thomas said with bravado. "You had a hundred chances before and you never did."

"Things are different now," Katy declared.

Although he'd never had control of the situation, Creede felt it spinning onto dangerous ground. "Put the shotgun down, Mrs. Gaddsen," he said softly. "You don't want him to hurt Laurel."

"Or Rachel or Willie," Katy added not taking her gaze off of Thomas.

"Let her be, Creede," Laurel said. "Even if I'm killed, she'll be rid of Thomas."

There was resignation in her voice and expression. It reminded Creede of a badly beaten horse that had given up fighting back.

Suddenly Laurel sank her teeth into Thomas's forearm. With a bellow of rage, Thomas shoved her away. An explosion filled the room and Thomas fell back, blood pouring from dozens of pellet wounds in his chest and neck. The man's breath rattled once, twice, then stopped altogether.

Thick smoke filled the hushed room and Creede coughed, breaking the brittle silence. The baby began to cry, bringing back a sense of normalcy.

Laurel crossed to Katy's side and gently took the shotgun from her unresisting hands. "Go and take care of Rachel and Willie. Creede and I will clean up in here."

Katy weaved slightly and comprehension seeped back into her blank expression. She nodded and shuffled into the bedroom.

Laurel leaned the shotgun against the wall, not thinking about how close she'd come to being killed. She turned to

Creede. When he'd charged into the cabin, she'd nearly fainted in relief. She hadn't cared about her own safety, only that he was alive and whole. How could she live with another death on her conscience, especially his?

"Are you all right?" he asked.

"He didn't hurt me." She spotted dried blood on his shirt collar. "What happened to you?"

Creede placed his hand at the back of his head and winced. "He got me when I came out the back door of the hotel. I didn't expect him to be waiting for me."

Laurel moved behind him. Her heart hammered at the sight of his blood-encrusted hair and for a moment, she thought she'd be sick. She reminded herself this was nothing compared to the wounds she'd dealt with during the War. She examined the wound carefully. "There's no fresh blood."

"I was out for less than an hour."

Irrational anger seized Laurel. "Head injuries aren't to be trifled with."

"My head hurts some but I'll be fine." He motioned to Thomas's body. "I'll get him out of here."

"I'll help."

"No. I can handle it."

"I've seen more dead men than you ever will."

Creede's stubborn expression eased. "That's why I don't want you to have to take care of another one." He turned her toward the bedroom. "Go check on Katy and the children."

Like a lamp being blown out, Laurel's annoyance fled, replaced by deep, lingering exhaustion. Not possessing the strength to argue, she did as he said.

Katy was sitting on the bed, her bare feet flat on the floor. She rocked Rachel in her arms as Willie pressed close to her side, his young face wan.

"How're Rachel and Willie?" Laurel asked.

"They're fine," Katy replied, not meeting her gaze.

Laurel eased down beside her and studied the baby's

perfect button nose and tiny pursed lips. She lifted her gaze
to Katy. "Thank you for saving my life."

"It was as much for me and Willie and Rachel."

"I know, but that doesn't make my gratitude any less."
Laurel gathered her thoughts. "Will would've been proud
of you."

Katy shook her head vehemently. "No. He would've
been shamed."

"You survived, and that's what counts."

"Then why'd you give up?" Her eyes blazed challeng-
ingly.

Laurel's heart slammed against her ribs. "What do you
mean?"

"I saw it in your face. You didn't care if Jasper killed
you or not."

Laurel couldn't meet her gaze. As Thomas had begun
to squeeze and her body began its involuntary battle for
air, she'd welcomed the numbness. There were no memories there. No accusing ghosts. For a few moments, she'd
been free.

Katy set the now sleeping baby on the bed and Willie
lay down beside his sister. She sat sideways, her knees
touching Laurel, and took her hands in her own.

"You gave me hope again," Katy said in a low voice.
"You convinced me it was all right to do what I had to in
order to survive. Why is it right for me and not for you?"

Laurel's mouth lost all moisture. "Your children need
you."

"You have Mr. Forrester. He needs you."

Laurel stifled the insane urge to laugh. "He doesn't
need me."

"He cares about you. I could see it in his eyes. He looks
at you like my Will used to look at me. It made me feel safe
but all excited, too, inside here." She pressed her hand to
the middle of her chest.

Laurel knew that feeling. She'd had the same fluttery
sensation when Robert had looked at her a certain way, but

he'd been her husband. With Creede, it was different—the nervous excitement was more powerful. Or maybe it was simply because it had been three long years since she'd been touched as a man touches a woman.

She stood to escape that feeling. Afraid to feel too much again. "You're wrong, Katy. I didn't let Thomas kill me. I got away from him, didn't I?" The walls closed in on her and she couldn't catch her breath. "Rest. I'll call you when dinner is ready."

Katy looked like she wanted to argue but as easy as Rachel's birth had been, she needed sleep to regain her strength.

As soon as Laurel was out of the bedroom, she leaned against a wall and tipped her head back. She concentrated on regulating her breathing, hearing her own words as she'd helped a patient do the same.

That's right. Take slow, easy breaths. You're safe now.

Finally, her heart didn't feel like it was going to explode out of her chest.

Keeping her gaze averted from the bloodstained floor, she filled a pail with water then got down on her hands and knees to scrub. The thick, coppery scent reminded her of other places reeking with the stench of blood. She focused on dipping the brush in the water, scrubbing the wood then rinsing again.

Surprisingly clear images of Katy's husband William played across her mind. When he'd been brought in, his face was covered with blood and where his eyes had been was a gaping wound. Laurel hadn't expected him to be alive, but he'd moaned and she'd gone to his side. He was lucid despite the pain. Although morphine supplies were low, she'd given him some to ease his agony. He'd survived for a day and had even managed to give Laurel the message for his wife.

What if he'd lived? Blinded, he would've been dependent on the charity of strangers. He'd never see his son grow to be a man. He'd never see his wife's gold hair shining in the sun again. And he'd never be able to give Katy that look, the one that filled her with love.

The water in her bucket changed to red and when Laurel lifted out the brush, her hand was covered with reddish water. She stared at it a moment, then dunked her hand and the brush back in the water and lifted them out again. Pale red glistened on her skin. She dropped the brush in the pail and rose, moving to the kitchen pump. After washing her hands with soap, she ran fresh water over them, but the red remained. Why wouldn't it come off?

Frantic, she found a small scrub brush and attempted to scour her hands clean with it using more soap. Her fingers and palms tingled painfully from the scrubbing but the blood clung to her. Her heart thudded in her chest and her breath grew short and raspy. She had to remove the stain.

"What're you doing?" Big hands closed around hers.

"I have to wash it off." Laurel struggled to escape his grasp but he was too strong. "Let me go."

"You're hurting yourself," Creede said, drawing her away from the sink with his arms wrapped around her from behind.

"I have to get the blood off."

Creede froze but didn't release her. "What blood?"

"It's all over my hands." She spread her fingers wide. "Can't you see it?"

"They're just red from being scrubbed so hard. There's no blood on them, Laurel," Creede said gently.

She blinked and, like magic, the blood was gone. She could see only irritated skin. Creede studied her for a moment and she glanced away, afraid he'd see the encroaching insanity in her eyes. "I'm all right. I just need a towel," she said, her voice shaky.

After another moment, Creede let her go and passed her a towel. She dried her hands with it, careful not to chafe the skin any more.

"Are you all right now?" Creede asked.

Despite her sore throat from Thomas's treatment and the dread humming along her nerves, she managed a nod.

"Thomas is dead. He won't hurt anyone else ever again," he reassured.

Was that what was bothering her? Or was it the reminder that death and blood went hand in hand? Yet as she'd told Creede, she'd seen too much death to be afraid of it. Why had she been so certain her hands were blood-covered?

Realizing he expected her to say something, she simply said, "I know."

He frowned at her, as if suspecting she was holding something back.

Please don't ask me any more questions.

"I'll get rid of the dirty water," he volunteered.

"I'm not done. There's still blood on the floor."

"It's stained. You can't get rid of it all."

Stained. Like my soul.

Creede guided her to a chair, setting her down firmly.

"Stay here. I'll be right back," he said.

She wanted to argue but it was easier to let him have his way. She leaned back and closed her eyes. She'd just sit here for five minutes then find something for dinner.

CREEDE carried the bloody water some distance away from the house and dumped it. His nose wrinkled at the odor. How had Laurel managed to clean the mess without being sick?

I've seen more dead men than you ever will.

Because she'd seen—and cleaned—far worse messes while she'd been a nurse. Although he knew what she'd faced during the war, he hadn't really *known*. How had she lived through the horror?

Unease coiled in his belly. How long could even a strong woman like Laurel continue to work under battle conditions and not have it affect her? She'd managed to make it through the war, but something was happening to her now. Something Creede didn't understand.

His head ached but it wasn't all from the bump he'd received. He'd put himself in this position by volunteering to see her safely to Texas. He could just as easily part trails, leaving her alone again. Yet he rebelled against doing that. He may not agree with her task, but he admired her for her determination and for respecting the soldiers' last wishes. And if he wasn't damned to hell already, he surely would be if he allowed Laurel to continue her journey alone.

He stopped by the barn before heading back to the cabin. Just inside the barn lay a dark lump that was Thomas's body rolled up in an old blanket. Although the moon was up, he planned to take the body into town tonight. He didn't want Laurel with him when he did, and he'd bring Dickens and the wagon back to carry them to town come morning.

Unable to stall any longer, he stepped into the cabin and stopped short. Laurel had fallen asleep in the chair with her neck slightly bent and her head tilted back. So strong in the face of adversity, she now appeared vulnerable and fragile. A surge of protectiveness made his breath catch in his throat.

He found a blanket in the trunk to cover her. Careful to not wake her, he draped the blanket across her. Her lips parted and she sighed noiselessly.

He allowed himself to simply study her, his gaze following the arch of her brow, the curve of her cheek, and the bow of her lips. Noticing the smudges beneath her eyes, he frowned. Had those always been there?

Troubled, he looked away and set his mind on other tasks.

LAUREL sat on the top step of the porch. Although she watched Willie play a game of tag with imaginary friends, her mind was elsewhere. That morning she'd awakened lying on a pile of blankets on the floor beside the fireplace and had only a vague recollection of how she'd gotten there. The last thing she remembered with any clarity was sitting down while Creede went to take care of Thomas's body.

Through a fog of sleep, she barely recalled being urged to her feet by Creede's gentle hands and gentler voice. Then she was lying on a bed of blankets that smelled of cedar and soap. For some reason, she thought Creede had lain beside her, but this morning she'd been alone. Rising, she found a note from him saying he'd taken Thomas's body into town and would return soon.

Her gaze drifted to the empty road and she wondered if Creede had taken the opportunity to continue to Texas alone. She wouldn't blame him. The possibility filled her with a sense of loss that she savagely thrust aside. She didn't need his help to deliver the last three messages. Besides, she hadn't wanted him with her in the first place. She'd already allowed him to get too close.

Movement caught her attention and she stood, then shaded her eyes against the bright morning sun. There was a wagon being pulled by a mule.

Relief made her lightheaded. He hadn't abandoned her.

A second wagon followed, and a single rider. Who was returning with Creede?

Willie halted his game and ran back to Laurel's side. "Is that Mr. Creede?"

Laurel put an arm around his slender shoulders. "Yes. Do you know the other two people?"

Willie squinted then jumped up and down. "It's Miss Sally."

The woman looked familiar, but Laurel couldn't place her. The older man, however, was a stranger, but the metal badge pinned to his chest told her he was a lawman.

They all stopped by the corral and Laurel and Willie joined them. The boy skipped over and greeted the woman with a hug.

Laurel rubbed Dickens's forehead as Creede jumped down. He had taken time to change his shirt, as well as wash, making Laurel self-conscious of how she must look in the clothes she'd slept in.

"What's going on?" she asked him in a low voice.

He canted his head toward the heavy-set lawman. "Sheriff Beller decided to come along to make sure I didn't make up the story about Thomas."

"He didn't know what Thomas was doing to Katy and the others?"

"According to him, Jasper Thomas was an upstanding citizen," Creede said dryly. "He was going to throw me in jail, but Miss Franklin came to my rescue."

Laurel eyed the woman who held Willie's hand as they walked to the cabin. "I've seen her before."

"Sally Franklin. She's the waitress who told us how to find this place. She's a friend of Katy's and knew all about Thomas. With the bastard gone, she wasn't afraid to tell the sheriff all she knew. But Beller wanted to hear it from Katy."

Sheriff Beller shambled over to them, puffing slightly. "This Mrs. Covey?"

"Laurel Monteille Covey," she said before Creede could reply.

"She don't look like she's been hurt."

Angry at his offhanded tone, Laurel undid the top two buttons of her blouse and moved the collar aside. Both the sheriff's and Creede's eyes widened at the bruise across her neck that she'd seen in the mirror that morning. "Your *upstanding* citizen did this to me. And if you need more proof, I've got another one on my shoulder."

Beller's round face reddened but she could tell his wrath wasn't directed at her. "I'll go talk to Mrs. Gaddsen."

He shambled to the house.

"I should've known he'd leave marks," Creede said between gritted teeth.

Laurel's face heated beneath his intense scrutiny and she buttoned her blouse. "It looks worse than it is." Her black-and-blue shoulder, however, ached, but Creede didn't need to know that. "Katy is feeling much better."

"Good. Miss Franklin plans on staying here with her."

"That means we can leave today."

"If Sheriff Beller doesn't arrest me for murder."

"You didn't kill Thomas."

Creede shrugged. "Beller isn't convinced."

Laurel glanced at Creede's narrow hips. "Where's your gun?"

"Beller took it. He said he'd give it back once I was cleared. I'm just damned glad he didn't throw me in jail."

"You wouldn't be in this mess if it weren't for me."

Creede chuckled. "Believe me, I used to get into a lot worse messes on my own." He sobered. "I'm glad I was here. Who knows what Thomas would've done to you or Katy and the kids?"

Laurel shivered, having some clear ideas that didn't bear thinking about.

Creede took her arm and they walked to the cabin but stayed outside on the porch. They heard the sheriff questioning Katy and her replying, although Laurel couldn't make out the words.

Ten minutes later Sheriff Beller came out, his expression grim.

"Did you get what you needed?" Creede asked.

Beller looked like he was going to be sick. "The son of a bitch had me believing he was helping out the widows out of the goodness of his goddamned heart." He touched the brim of his hat. "Pardon, ma'am."

Laurel nodded, having heard far worse cursing.

"I want my gun back," Creede said.

"Come see me when you get back to town." Beller strode across the yard to his horse.

"I'll say good-bye to Katy and Willie."

Before she could go into the cabin, Creede clasped her sore arm and she flinched slightly. He abruptly released her. "How bad is it?" he asked gently, motioning to her shoulder.

She didn't meet his gaze. "It's nothing."

"We can stay here another day if you'd like."

She thought of the bloodstained floor and worse, her

bloodstained hands. "Katy and Rachel are doing fine. I'd just be in the way with her friend here."

"All right. We'll stay at the hotel tonight then leave tomorrow."

"We can leave today—"

"No," Creede said firmly. "Riding a horse most of the day isn't going to help your shoulder."

Although Laurel wanted to leave Lefsburg and the memories of Jasper Thomas behind, she wouldn't mind resting another day. Sleeping on a mattress instead of the hard ground would be less painful, too.

"All right," she conceded.

Creede seemed surprised by her capitulation. When they entered the bedroom, Sally excused herself. Creede said his good-bye to Mrs. Gaddsen then took Willie outside, leaving Laurel and Katy alone.

Laurel sat on the edge of the bed and gazed down into Rachel's innocent face. After seeing so much suffering and death, the sight of the healthy infant made Laurel's breath catch in her throat. "She's beautiful."

Katy nodded proudly. "She is." Her smile faded and she clasped Laurel's hand. "Thank you for everything. Now that Jasper is gone, I have a chance to start over."

"Will you stay here?"

Katy turned and stared out the window. "I don't know. This place is all tied up with Jasper Thomas, but me and Will made a lot of good memories here, too."

"You don't have to decide right now."

Katy nodded and a tear rolled down her cheek, although she was smiling. "I think Will would've wanted his son to grow up here, in the same place he did."

Laurel squeezed Katy's thin hand gently. "I think he would, too."

Laurel's gaze strayed to the nightstand where a photograph that hadn't been there before now sat. She picked up the black-and-white likeness and gazed at the serious young man who was gazing at Katy.

"That's Will and me right after our wedding," Katy said. She took the framed picture from Laurel and traced Will's face. "He was the handsomest man I ever saw."

Laurel's throat tightened, remembering Will's ravaged face. "What color were his eyes?" At Katy's questioning look, she quickly added, "I can't recall."

"Green like the grass in springtime. I'll always remember how he used to look at me with his beautiful green eyes." Katy sniffed and set the frame back on the table. "Thank you, Laurel, for being with my Will at the end and for helping me get free."

"You're welcome. Good-bye, Katy."

Laurel glanced down once more at the picture, and imagined Will whole and healthy and with beautiful green eyes.

$\mathcal{T}$WELVE

LAUREL remained in the bathtub until the water cooled, then reluctantly stepped out, using one of the hotel's rough, worn towels to dry herself. The bath cost almost as much as the room, but she needed the soothing embrace of hot water after the last twenty-four hours.

Dusk had fallen and she lit a lamp before donning her wrinkled clothing. As she dressed, much of her peace of mind acquired by the leisurely soak melted away. Creede had been a gentleman and gone out, so she'd had the room and tub to herself. Now, however, the walls pressed in on her, along with the phantoms.

She twisted her hair into a knot at the nape of her neck and left the room to find someone to take care of the bathtub. At the top of the stairs, she spotted Creede entering the hotel's shabby lobby. He didn't see her so she took a moment to simply observe him—the way his shirt stretched taut over his shoulders, the glide of muscle beneath his snug trousers, and the intensity in his hawklike features. His long-legged stride reminded Laurel of the predatory pace of a lion she'd seen at the zoo when she was a child.

She figured Creede was at least ten years her senior, yet

from a distance he appeared closer to her age. However, up close, she'd seen the creases in his brow and the lines at the corners of his eyes—badges of the sorrow he'd endured.

As if sensing her, he glanced up sharply and caught her gaze. Laurel should've looked away, but his eyes held her in thrall as he climbed the stairs. The first thing she noticed was his clean scent and smooth-shaven cheeks and jaw. Beneath his wide-brimmed hat, his hair was damp and markedly shorter than when he'd left two hours earlier.

"I went to the barber and bathhouse," Creede said, guessing her thoughts.

Laurel cleared her throat. "You look nice."

With an amused smile, Creede cast his gaze up and down her figure and his lips tipped upward. "So do you."

Although they were in full view at the top of the stairs, Laurel couldn't make herself move. The air between them crackled with bridled passion, unspoken and unacknowledged, but as tangible as the dark lashes framing Creede's blue eyes. Her body swayed toward his, shocking Laurel out of her daze.

She stepped away, not realizing she was so close to the edge of the steps. She fought for balance even as a firm hand caught her, drawing her away from the precipice. She latched onto Creede's arms, her heart battering her ribs.

"I've got you, Laurel," he assured.

"Th-thank you," she whispered.

She continued to cling to him until self-consciousness intervened and she drew away.

"Where were you going?" Creede asked.

"Down to let the clerk know I was done with the tub."

"I'll tell him. You go back to the room."

Her backbone stiffened at his command. "No. I'll do it."

"Why do you fight me all the time?" Impatience twined through his tone.

Laurel glanced away and noticed the clerk standing with his back to the stairs, but she knew he was listening. "We'll talk about this later," she said in a low voice.

Creede's eyes glittered dangerously but after following

her gaze, he nodded curtly. "Fine." He strode down the hall to their room.

Laurel pressed her lips together and descended the stairs, careful that she didn't stumble.

The clerk turned and his expression lit with feigned surprise. "Mrs. Forrester. You startled me."

Laurel didn't bother to call him a liar. "I'm done with the bath. Could you have someone remove the tub?"

"I'll send Tommy up right away to take care of it." He sidled closer. "I heard your husband killed Jasper Thomas."

She glared at him. "You heard wrong."

Anger drumming through her, she marched back up the steps and to the room. She froze in the doorway at the sight of Creede lounging on the bed. His arms were behind his head and his stocking feet were crossed at the ankles. His hat hung on a bedpost, as did his holster, and his boots sat upright on the floor.

Her gaze traveled down his lean figure, detecting the slight prominence below his belt buckle. Heat invaded her cheeks, reminding her of her own needs—needs she'd had to bury along with all her other emotions simply to survive. She'd ignored those needs for three years; she could do so again.

Turning away from the tempting sight, she found the only place to sit was the straight-backed chair. Sidling around the tub, she perched on the hard seat, her backbone straight and her hands clasped in her lap.

"You can lie beside me," Creede suggested.

She nearly gasped at his challenging note with a hint of sensual dare. Had he read her mind?

She held herself still and concentrated on controlling her breathing and relaxing her suddenly taut muscles— anything to help maintain her distance. "No, thank you. I'm fine right here."

"You want to talk about it?"

"If you're referring to joining you, sleeping on the same bed at night is a matter of necessity, but lying beside you now is another matter. In fact, you can get your own room now that Jasper Thomas is gone."

He shrugged. "I could." He turned his head to look at her. "But there's no reason to, unless you don't trust yourself around me."

A tendril of alarm licked at her nerves. "Don't be absurd."

"How long has it been since you let someone get close to you?"

"How many times have I told you that I don't need anyone?"

"Like you didn't need anyone the first time we met? Or when you didn't need anyone last night with Jasper Thomas?"

He struck too close, fueling her fears. "I can take care of myself," she shot back.

Creede sprang off the bed, nearly pouncing on her. Startled, Laurel pressed back against the chair, away from his thunderous expression.

He leaned in, his face inches from hers. "You're making it awfully damned hard for me to help you when you won't tell me what's going on in that stubborn head of yours."

The warm moistness of his breath against her cheek and the smell of the shaving soap the barber had used played havoc with her tenuous control. Her pulse skittered erratically and her vision tunneled, fixing on his hypnotic blue eyes. Pinned by his stare, she couldn't think, couldn't move. The air became viscous, too thick to breathe. She gasped, searching for air that should've been there.

"Laurel," Creede's voice cut through her panic. "Laurel, breathe. Listen to me. Just breathe."

She became aware of his tight grip on her shoulders and the sound of knocking at the door. Her lungs suddenly expanded, sucking in air and irritating her bruised throat. She coughed. "I-I'm all right." She waved him aside. "Someone's . . . at the door."

Creede opened it but it was clear he was frustrated and annoyed by the interruption. "Yes?"

"I'm here to take care of the bath," a black-haired boy about ten years old said.

For a moment, Laurel thought he'd slam the door on the boy. Then Creede nodded and opened the door wide. "Go on."

Laurel considered leaving the room but knew her weak legs wouldn't support her. She tipped her head back and closed her eyes.

What was wrong with her? Was it merely exhaustion after everything that had happened since riding into Lefsburg? Or did it have to do with her dreams, both waking and nighttime? Was her insanity growing, taking over her thoughts more and more?

Creede returned to his position on the bed while the boy made numerous trips carrying buckets to empty the bathtub. Finally, the tub was empty and he lugged it out. Creede tossed the boy a coin, bringing a gap-toothed grin to the kid's dark-skinned face.

The door closed behind him, leaving brittle silence in his wake.

Creede sat up and tugged on his boots. "Let's get something to eat."

"I'm not hungry," Laurel said.

He propped his elbows on his thighs. "You haven't eaten anything all day."

"I had breakfast at Katy's." She didn't say that had been only a slice of bread with some molasses.

"You're a nurse, Laurel. I thought it was important to eat to keep up your strength."

A spark of rebellion sliced through her apathy. "I'm well aware that I'm a nurse. I'm also aware that missing a meal or two won't hurt anyone."

Creede stood and stared down at her, but there was no anger this time. In truth, there was little at all in his expression.

He strapped on his gunbelt and plucked his hat from the bedpost. "Don't wait up for me."

As the door shut behind him, Laurel couldn't help but

wonder if his tone had been mocking or regretful. Or which she preferred.

CREEDE eased the door open, taking care that he made as little noise as possible. The murky light from the hallway lamps seeped in, illuminating Laurel, who slept curled up on the bed facing the doorway. For a moment, Creede didn't recognize her soft, vulnerable features, so different than when he'd left earlier that evening.

He closed the door behind him and the cat burrowed against his side squirmed. He petted its head and the animal settled back in the crook of his arm. While he'd been checking on the horses the cat had found him. At first he'd tried to shoo it away, but the stupid cat kept following him. Finally, Creede had given in and smuggled it in past the dozing hotel clerk. Hell, the cat was probably cleaner than most of the hotel's clientele.

Inside the room, he leaned over to set the cat on the rug and whispered, "No using the floor for your business."

The cat simply meowed, lifted its nose, and turned away. It took the animal only a few moments to find the most comfortable place in the room—curled up on the bed beside Laurel.

Envious of the cat's position, Creede merely sighed. He'd slept with Laurel last night, holding her in his arms, but had risen before she'd awakened. It was the first time since Anna had died that he'd slept with a woman through the night. Laurel had been exhausted, mentally and physically, but he didn't dare risk lying beside her again. She would undoubtedly be angry and upset if she awakened in the middle of the night to find him beside her.

He removed everything but his pants and unrolled his bedroll on the floor, then lay down, using his shirt as a pillow. The September night was warm so he didn't need a blanket.

Staring up at the ceiling, he crossed his arms and listened to the cat's purring. For such a small critter, he sure was loud. Shocked to find he was growing fond of the scrawny furball, he smiled wryly in the dark.

A low moan came from the bed and Laurel shifted restlessly. She echoed the sound and cried out something Creede didn't understand. Should he wake her? Or simply shut his ears to her nightmare?

"No, please, I'm sorry," she murmured.

Her thrashing startled the cat and, with a protesting meow, he jumped down and crawled under the bed.

Unable to ignore Laurel's distress, Creede sat up and knelt beside the bed. Laurel's mouth gaped and her expression was one of horror. Even in the sparse light, he could see sweat glistening her brow.

His stomach clenched in empathy at her obvious anguish. He touched her shoulder. "Laurel, wake up. It's only a dream."

"Leave me alone. I'm sorry," she yelled.

For a moment, Creede thought she'd awakened but her tightly closed eyes dispelled him of that notion. "Laurel, it's Creede. Come on, wake up."

He shook her harder and she gasped and bolted upright, her eyes wide. He remained silent, letting her figure out where she was. She held her hands out in front of her face and her frantic gaze inspected them.

Creede had no trouble guessing her thoughts. He took hold of her slender wrists. "There's no blood on them, Laurel. It was only a nightmare." He kept whispering the words over and over again.

Finally, the terror in her eyes abated and she curled her fingers into her palms. Creede released her wrists, and she pressed her forehead against her clenched hands. "I-I'm sorry I woke you."

Creede rubbed circles on her back. "I wasn't asleep. Would you like to talk about it?"

Laurel's muscles went rigid, but with her face hidden, he couldn't see her expression.

"It's all right. Talking can't hurt you," he said.

She remained still for a long moment, then raised her head and met his gaze. "Why are you on the floor?"

The unexpected question made him pause. "I didn't want to wake you."

"It wouldn't have mattered."

Her dull voice alarmed him. "What do you mean?"

Her shrug was his only answer.

His knees protested kneeling on the hard floor. "Would you mind if I sat on the bed?"

With one hand still on her back, he felt her tense slightly. "I promise to behave," he said with forced levity.

A slight nod.

He climbed to his feet and eased down a foot from her. "Was your dream about the War?" Laurel's sharp glance told him he'd guessed correctly. "Austin used to have nightmares after his mother was killed." He swallowed, finding it harder to talk about than he'd expected. "She was standing right beside him when she was shot."

"I'm sorry."

"At first he didn't want to talk about his nightmares, but after more than a week of them, he finally told me he dreamed about his ma's blood splashing on him." Creede paused, his throat suddenly full and tight. "After that, there were fewer and fewer nightmares, until he eventually slept through the night."

Laurel stared down at her tightly clenched hands.

A plaintive meow from the floor brought her puzzled gaze to him. "What's that?"

The cat leapt onto the bed, giving Laurel her answer. He rubbed his arched back against her, his tail held straight up.

Her pinched face lightened. Picking up the cat, she cuddled it close to her chest. "Where did you come from?"

Creede cleared his throat. "I brought him in. Hope you don't mind, but he just didn't want to be left outside."

Laurel buried her nose in the cat's fur. "I don't mind."

"Maybe he'll help you sleep."

"Maybe." She didn't sound hopeful.

Creede ached to pull her in his arms just as she held the cat in hers, but he wouldn't risk their tenuous truce. "Lie down. I won't be far away."

She lay down with the cat, which snuggled up against her and immediately started purring again.

Creede crawled back to his bedroll and stretched out on his back. He focused on getting his body to relax, but his senses centered on Laurel, from the sound of her quiet breathing to the scent of her clean skin to the sight of her pale face in the relative darkness. Acutely aware of her, Creede's body answered with sharp arousal. Although his trousers grew snug, he couldn't ease the discomfort with Laurel so near.

Two gunshots followed by men's coarse laughter startled him. Just like any other town, men sometimes drank too much and let off steam.

"Will you sleep with me tonight?"

Laurel's unexpected question sent a bolt of lust to his crotch. He cleared his throat, hoping his voice wouldn't fail him. "Are you sure?"

"I-I might sleep better with you beside me."

Christ, here he was thinking with the thing between his legs when all Laurel wanted was someone to hold her. Yet how could he do it? She wasn't a naïve virgin. She'd feel the evidence of his arousal. He opened his mouth to give some excuse, but when he brought his gaze back to her strained face, he couldn't deny her. Maybe if he kept the blanket between their bodies . . .

"If you move over some, I'll spread my bedroll beside yours," he said.

She did so, and as she and the cat settled in their new position, he smoothed his blanket over the yellowed coverlet, just as Laurel had done with hers. He gingerly lay down, close to the edge of the bed. "Is this all right?"

"Are you afraid of me?"

He was surprised to hear a smile in her voice.

"Should I be?" Instead of the teasing note he'd intended, his voice came out husky.

She remained silent for a minute. "Maybe we should both be afraid," she whispered.

"Maybe."

Creede forced himself to breathe evenly as he watched Laurel's silhouette, backlit by the moonlight coming in the window. He was afraid to say anything, afraid to shatter the fragile connection between them.

After what seemed like hours but was closer to five minutes, Laurel shifted closer. Her breath wafted across his bare chest and her gown brushed his arm, bringing him to full hardness again.

"I'm afraid to sleep."

Creede's breath caught in his throat at her childlike whisper. "Maybe it'll be all right now that you're not alone."

"My father used to check the closets and under my bed before I went to sleep at night. He'd always make sure there were no ghosts hiding there."

"If you'd like, I could do that," Creede volunteered. It would also put some distance between them to get his body back under control.

"It won't do any good. The ghosts don't hide in easy places like closets and under the bed anymore."

It seemed the cover of darkness made it easier for Laurel to talk and Creede wasn't above using that to his advantage. "Where do they hide now?"

Her arm moved and he realized she was petting the cat. "Places where my father—and you—can't find them."

Creede suddenly understood. "Places where only *you* can find them and chase them away?"

"Unless they don't want to be chased away."

"There's always some way to get rid of them."

She made a sound like a hiccough, then he realized it was a dry chuckle. "Not always. Sometimes they pretend they're gone, but I know they're not. I know they're always there, waiting."

A chill swept down Creede's spine. "Waiting for what? Nighttime?"

"Not always. Sometimes they visit during the day, too. They wait and come out when you least expect them."

Like when you were cleaning the blood off the floor yesterday? He couldn't voice the question.

The night sounds—the wind sifting through the leaves, crickets chirping, and nightwings skirling as they soared high above them—filled the void.

"I thought I'd never stop hearing cannon fire and men and horses screaming, but this quiet reminds me that wars aren't forever," Laurel said, her voice barely audible.

"And life continues," Creede added.

"For most."

A foreboding slid through him like a sharp knife. "What do you mean?"

"A few of those men who fought will never be able to forget what they saw or what they did. For them, the War will never end."

Creede relaxed minutely. She was talking about the soldiers. "Is there anything that can help them?"

"Pray for them and hope death will bring them peace."

His arousal vanquished by their somber conversation, Creede closed his eyes. What if Austin had returned in body but not spirit? Was it more merciful for him to die than be lost in an endless war?

And what of Laurel? Although she hadn't fought the Yankees, she'd fought another kind of war, one against death. One where the odds were stacked against her.

Perhaps by bringing the dying soldiers' messages to living people, Laurel was still fighting the battle against death in her own way. Where would that leave her when all her messages were delivered?

Creede reminded himself that Laurel was strong, the strongest woman he'd ever met. She would survive and use her skills in another hospital, helping more people.

"Good night, Creede," Laurel said softly.

"Good night."

The cat meowed, chiming in with his good night.

ᎢHIRTEEN

CREEDE was glad to leave Lefsburg behind the following morning. Their next destination lay a little over a hundred miles to the southwest and he hoped Rounder had fared better than the town they'd just left. However, as they traveled through the war-torn area, he suspected it might be worse off than Lefsburg.

They saw former slaves with everything they owned on their backs, walking northward. Most appeared lost and bewildered. After living in one place all their lives and having every decision made for them, now they were faced with freedom. Creede could imagine the prospect was both frightening and exhilarating. It also meant more hungry people without work or a home.

It was almost dark when he found a decent campsite. Since it was so late, he suggested Laurel prepare supper while he took care of the animals. She didn't argue, which told him how tired she was.

The cat hopped down from Dickens's back and followed Laurel. Smiling at the cat's devotion to the woman, Creede removed Jeanie's tack then rubbed her down with the saddle blanket. By the time he took care of Red and removed Dickens's pack frame, night had fallen.

A bright fire led him to Laurel, who was mixing together a batch of biscuits. Side pork already sizzled in the frying pan.

Creede lowered himself to the ground, sitting with his back against a tree and an arm resting on a bent knee. "I managed to get away without a bruise from Dickens."

She glanced up. "I think he's starting to like you."

Creede snorted. "I think he's starting to learn I'm meaner than he is."

"You're both too much alike," she teased.

He grinned, enjoying her banter. However, his amusement faded as he thought about all the ex-slaves they'd seen. He'd grown up in the Colorado Territory where slavery wasn't practiced, but after moving to Texas he'd come to see firsthand how debasing it was for one person to own another. It was the main reason he hadn't supported the Confederacy, despite Texas's secession from the Union.

"Did it ever bother you knowing you were helping the side that bought and sold people?" he asked.

Laurel's movements faltered. "Yes. I never believed one person had the right to own another, even though my husband's family owned slaves."

"So why did you help the Confederacy?"

"I was a nurse and it was my duty."

"But you didn't believe in their cause."

"Those soldiers weren't rich landowners. Most were poor farmers who believed they'd be subjugated by the rich merchants in the North if they lost the War." Her tone was rife with cynicism.

"Confederate claptrap."

She shrugged one shoulder. "The North had their share of claptrap, too."

He'd known few people, man or woman, who had Laurel's intelligence and perceptiveness. She also possessed generosity and compassion, which were scarce these days, and he wondered how Laurel, who'd lost so much, could still cling to those values.

"This is the last of the meat," Laurel said. "We'll have to restock our supplies in Rounder."

"If they have any to buy. It might be better to keep an eye out for a rabbit or possum."

She wrinkled her nose. "If you get a possum, it's all yours."

Creede chuckled, pleased to see a glint of humor in her usually somber eyes. "All right, maybe not a possum. You eat squirrel?"

"I've eaten it."

Her guarded tone made him pause. "I swear we ate squirrel every day when I was a kid," he said. "We didn't have much so we made do. What about you?"

She brushed a strand of hair back from her forehead, leaving a streak of flour on her brow. It was a picture Creede took pleasure in, knowing she didn't often allow herself to appear less than self-possessed.

"We had a cook named Maurice who made these meals I couldn't pronounce," she replied with a wry smile. "I doubt a squirrel ever passed through his kitchen. I do remember having rabbit, though. Maurice said it was a delicacy in Europe."

Creede barked a laugh. "You mean we were eating like the high and mighty in Europe?"

"He made it with a special sauce that tasted like raspberry jam."

"Jam on rabbit? Now that's something we never had."

He watched her form the biscuits and place them in the sizzling grease. "How did you learn to cook when you never had to do it yourself?"

"The hard way." She smirked. "When I trained to be a nurse, I rented a room in a house close to the hospital. My landlady taught me how to cook, beginning with how to boil water. She had the patience of a saint. I can't tell you how many times I nearly set her kitchen on fire."

Creede chuckled as he gazed at Laurel's face, which reflected the orange flames. "If you picked up nursing as well as you picked up cooking, you must've been one helluva nurse."

She glanced up, but didn't seem shocked by his cuss word. Instead, she appeared embarrassed. "All I ever wanted to do was help people."

"I would've thought a girl growing up with money would be too busy going to dances and buying new dresses."

"Oh, I did my share of that, too," she admitted. "It just wasn't enough for me." She flipped the biscuits and pork. "I got my share of trying to help people during the War, although sometimes I wonder if I did more harm than good."

Startled, Creede shook his head. "I don't see how you could've. You were there to put the pieces back together."

"For all the good that did. They were just thrown back into the War to return in more pieces, if they came back at all."

Creede shivered at the self-recrimination in her voice and was grateful for the stray cat's reappearance. Laurel automatically petted the animal even as she kept watch on their sizzling meal.

"Did you have a pet when you were a child?" he asked, changing the subject to something less somber.

His tactic worked and her face lit up. "My parents gave us a spaniel when I was five. We taught it how to dance."

"Don't tell me you put a dress on it, too."

"Bright red."

Creede groaned, although he was enjoying her childhood stories. "At least it wasn't a dancing pony."

"We had one of those, too."

"With a dress?"

"Don't be ridiculous. It was a skirt." Her eyes glowed with laughter. She leaned forward and said in a conspiratorial tone, "The rest of that pony was buck naked."

Creede laughed aloud. "You must've been a terror for your parents."

Laurel used a cloth to wrap around the frying pan han-

dle and removed their meal from the fire. After she filled
two plates, she handed one to Creede then tossed the cat a
piece of meat.

"We had a nanny. Actually we had more than one. We
used to scare them off," she said.

Creede didn't have any trouble imagining this Laurel as
an impish child. "We?"

"My sister and brother." She placed a piece of pork between a split biscuit and took a bite. When she was done
chewing, she continued. "The first thing we tried with a
new nanny was putting a frog in her bed. That night we'd
wait for her scream. If she stayed on after that, the next
night we tried a snake. If that didn't do it, we hid her
corsets."

"You didn't."

Laurel's eyes glittered with amusement. "Oh, yes. Usually one of those worked, but we finally got a nanny who I
swear wasn't afraid of anything. When she found the frog,
she carried it to our room as calm as could be and asked us
if we'd lost something. Same with the snake. After we hid
her corsets, she wouldn't let us outside to play until we returned them. We lasted less than a day." Laurel shook her
head, the memories obviously fond ones. "She ended up
being the best nanny. We couldn't pull the wool over her
eyes, but she was fair and she cared for us in her own way.
She was the one I talked to about becoming a nurse."

"What about your parents?"

Her expression shifted to reticence. "Father and Mother
believed that children should be seen and not heard. I
think the first time they actually heard me was when I told
them I was going to become a nurse, whether they ap-
proved or not."

Creede wiped his plate clean with a biscuit and popped
it in his mouth. It was difficult to imagine that kind of
childhood, with parents who weren't around. "I suppose
they didn't think too highly of your decision."

"That's being kind. Father forbade it, but I didn't let that stop me. It took me a year to get him to change his mind. He still didn't like the idea but he decided it would be easier to let me do it and come to realize on my own that it had been a foolish notion."

"Only you liked it."

She glanced at him, an eyebrow angled upward. "Yes. Then I met Robert and the War started. Because I was loyal to my husband, my father disowned me." Her eyes glimmered, and she blinked and turned away.

"Have you tried to contact him since the War ended?"

She shook her head, keeping her face averted. "It wouldn't do any good. Jonathan Monteille is a very stubborn man and his word is law."

Creede wondered, however, if her father might have had a change of heart. After losing Austin, Creede couldn't imagine a father washing his hands of his child.

A twig snapped in the darkness and Creede froze. The cat was calmly washing its face beside Laurel and the horses grazed unperturbed.

"It was probably a rabbit or squirrel," Laurel said, but her voice wasn't convinced.

Creede rose. "Stay here. I'll check it out."

Laurel's eyes widened and panic flicked through them. Her lips pressed into a thin line, but she nodded.

Creede palmed his revolver and crept into the brush.

Laurel gathered the cat in her arms and tried to slow her galloping heartbeat. A month ago she wouldn't have been afraid, but that was before she'd run into men like Jasper Thomas and the odd duo of Delbert and Rufus.

The cat squirmed, wanting to be set free, and she reluctantly let it jump down. It disappeared, leaving her alone. Refusing to allow her fear to dictate to her, Laurel wrapped the leftover food in a cloth, then added an inch of water to the frying pan and set it over the fire. The water heated quickly and she washed the two dishes and the frying pan.

Creede hadn't returned yet and Laurel tried to rein in her wild imagination. She hadn't heard any shooting or the sounds of a scuffle. He was only being thorough in his search. She hoped.

"It's just me," Creede called out as he entered the fire's circle of light minutes later.

Relief eddied through Laurel, making her dizzy. "Did you find anything?"

Creede slid his hat back off his forehead and his dark hair fell across his brow. "Nope. And I didn't hear anything either, but it wasn't a normal silence. No crickets, no birds, no nothing."

His worried expression did nothing to assuage Laurel's own apprehension. "So, what do you think it was?"

He shrugged. "If it was a larger animal, the horses would've been spooked and I think Dickens would kick up a fuss if anything got near them. Could've been a person, but if it was, he's long gone."

"Probably, but it doesn't hurt to bring the animals in closer." Laurel finished tidying their camp and glanced nervously at the darkness. She needed to make her nightly ablutions before turning in.

"Don't go far," Creede said, guessing her thoughts.

With her heart in her throat, Laurel moved only far enough away to maintain propriety. She quickly took care of her business and returned to the fire.

"Go to sleep. I'm going to sit up for a while longer," Creede said.

Laurel held his gaze for a moment then gave in and spread her bedroll. She removed her shoes and lay down. The familiar night sounds, which had returned, should've calmed her, but a tingle along her spine unnerved her. She turned on her side and pillowed her head on her forearms to watch Creede. The firelight flickered across his rugged features as he cleaned his revolver with practiced ease.

"You've done that before," she commented.

He glanced up and a wry grin touched his lips. "A time or two."

"Is that the gun that you used—" She broke off, unable to articulate the rest of her question.

His motions slowed and he nodded reluctantly. She searched his face, trying to interpret his expression.

"I promised Anna, my wife, that I'd never touch it again," he said in a barely audible voice.

Laurel frowned. "Why?"

"She didn't believe in violence and I'd had more than my share." He picked up an oiled rag and wiped the barrel. "Those two men who hurt Ma weren't the only people I killed with this gun."

Laurel's heart stumbled and her mouth grew dry.

"I sold my gun hand to the highest bidder." Bitterness twisted his features. "Anna loved me enough to forgive me as long as I promised to hang up my gun. And I loved her enough to leave that part of my life behind and become a cotton farmer."

"But not enough to keep your promise after she died," Laurel said.

He stabbed her with a sharp look. "I kept my word until I came east looking for my son. When I found out he was dead, I figured there was no reason anymore."

"No reason to keep your promise?"

He pressed his lips together and shook his head. Whether that was his answer or he was merely unwilling to talk about it, Laurel didn't know. She continued to study him, trying to figure out what kind of man Creede Forrester was. No matter how hard she tried, she couldn't see him as a cold-blooded killer. Yet hadn't he insinuated that?

"Anna was right," Creede said a few minutes later. "Guns and violence never solved anything. I tried to teach that to Austin, but he never understood." He gave his gun one more wipe then slid it into his holster. His gaze was steady but his voice trembled ever so slightly. "The night before he ran away to join the army, he called me a coward."

Laurel closed her eyes, unable to bear the anguish in Creede's expression.

*   *   *

THE following morning, Laurel reached into her saddle-bag to dig out the leftover biscuits and pork for breakfast. The cloth holding the food wasn't there. Frowning, she opened the other side but didn't find it there, either.

"Creede, have you seen the food left over from last night?" she called.

He turned, wiping his fresh-shaven face. "Didn't we eat it all?"

She shook her head impatiently. "I know there was some left."

He shrugged. "Maybe the cat ate it."

The cat couldn't have gotten into her saddlebag and she was certain she'd wrapped three biscuits and four pieces of pork to save for the morning.

"It'll turn up," Creede assured. "We'll just have some coffee and jerky then get on the road."

Frustrated, Laurel wanted to tear everything apart to find the food, but Creede was right. They had to continue on to Rounder if they wanted to reach the town tomorrow. She poured fresh coffee into two tin cups and they ate their meager breakfast in silence.

Fifteen minutes later, they rode away, heading south. They kept their pace slow so they wouldn't exhaust the horses. Dickens plodded along without throwing a single temper tantrum.

Laurel considered asking Creede more questions about his past, but each time she opened her mouth, she closed it again. Creede hadn't pushed her for the details of her life. The least she could do was treat him with the same courtesy.

Clouds drifted in by mid-afternoon and spit rain, enough to make riding uncomfortable, but not enough to seek shelter. They continued to travel down the road that was little more than two nearly invisible ruts. By late afternoon, Laurel and Creede were soaked to the skin. Fortunately, the day's heat remained.

Creede reined in and squinted through the mist.

"There's a farm up ahead. We might be able to sleep in their barn."

Laurel nodded. A mattress of straw with a roof would definitely be more agreeable than the wet ground.

They rode up to the tiny but well-kept house, scattering a half dozen chickens. A pig wallowed in a muddy pen, looking fat and contented.

"Don't come any closer." A double-barrel shotgun poked out of the home's cracked-open door.

"We're looking for a dry place to spend the night," Creede said, keeping his hands in plain sight.

"We ain't got room," the man yelled.

"Could we stay in your barn?" Laurel asked, remembering to inject a drawl into her voice.

There was a long pause but the shotgun didn't waver. "Where you headed?"

"Rounder," Creede replied.

"What kinda business you got there?"

"Personal. My name's Creede Forrester and this is my wife Laurel. All we want is a dry place to spend the night."

She heard murmured voices in the house then the door opened fully. A man about Creede's age stepped onto the porch, the shotgun cradled in his arms. "Afore the War we'd invite you in for a meal, but times ain't been good."

"We understand," Creede said soberly. "We can only give you our word we don't mean you or your family any harm."

The man shifted his gaze to Laurel, who nodded, rain dripping from her nose and chin.

"All right. You can stay in the barn," he said.

Laurel sagged in her saddle. "Thank you."

"I'll be sleepin' with my shotgun close," the man warned.

Creede nodded.

Laurel and Creede dismounted and led their animals to the barn. As soon as they were inside, the cat leaped down from Dickens's back and began to explore. Like the house, the barn wasn't large, but it was dry and didn't appear to have any leaks. It smelled of dust, animal, and straw. There were four stalls but only one was occupied—by a mule.

Creede handed Laurel his horse's reins. "I'm going to check out the hayloft."

She watched him climb the ladder, trying not to notice his backside as he ascended the steps. Although wet and uncomfortable, she couldn't deny her body's response to him. Part of it was three years of abstinence, but it wasn't merely physical. Although handsome, Creede was someone she wouldn't have looked at twice five years ago, but after everything she'd gone through, she'd learned to see beyond a man's appearance. And she'd come to respect and appreciate Creede's kindness and integrity.

"It looks dry and comfortable," he reported.

They took care of the animals and put them in the empty stalls. Creede carried a bag up to the loft and Laurel handed him the rest of their things, then climbed the ladder. At the top, Creede took hold of her arm and helped her into the spacious area.

It was growing dark, so they quickly mounded up straw in two separate piles and lay their respective bedrolls on them.

"Mr. Forrester," their host called up.

After exchanging a glance with Laurel, Creede went down to join him. Laurel lay on her belly and looked over the edge.

"The missus had me bring this out," he said, giving Creede a kettle and something wrapped in cloth. "She made some stew and figgered y'all would like some hot food."

"Tell her thanks," Creede said.

He glanced around, clearly uncomfortable. "It's hard on her. She don't like not trustin' folks."

"It's hard on everyone. You're luckier than most we've seen."

"I heard 'bout folks gettin' burned out. It ain't right." He took a deep breath. "Name's Daniel Overby."

Creede shook his hand. "Nice to meet you."

Overby shifted his weight from one worn shoe to the

other. "I'd best get back inside. We ain't usually so un-neighborly, but times is bad. A person don't know who's friend and who's gonna rob you blind."

"We understand," Creede assured. "Thanks again for letting us sleep here."

Clearly embarrassed, Overby left the barn.

Creede brought the food up to the loft and the smell of the stew made Laurel's stomach growl.

"Even as hungry as I am, I'd like to put on some dry clothes first," she said.

"Go ahead. I won't look," Creede said with a wink.

Flustered, Laurel dug some clothes out of her bag and glanced at Creede. True to his word, his back was to her and it appeared he was doing the same thing. Turning away quickly, she changed out of her wet garments.

By the time she was done, Creede had donned a dry shirt and pants. Laurel sat cross-legged on the straw, one knee almost touching Creede. The cat sat on her lap, his nose twitching as he stared at the kettle.

Creede unrolled the cloth from Overby and in it were two spoons and some warm bread. Steam rolled from the stew when he removed the pot's lid. Creede's stomach took its turn to growl even louder than Laurel's had. They laughed and dug into the tasty meal, both eating from the kettle and sharing with the cat.

After Laurel finished, she leaned back against the wall. She was pleasantly full and comfortably tired. The rain was coming down harder and the patter had become a steady rhythm that soothed her. If she wasn't so afraid of her nightmares, she'd lie down and go to sleep now.

She looked at Creede and caught him studying her. "What?"

"Your husband was a lucky man."

Discomfited, Laurel cast her gaze downward and picked up a piece of straw, which she twirled between two fingers. "I'm sure he didn't think so."

"That wasn't what I meant. I meant it as a compliment to you."

"Don't." She couldn't afford to let anyone inside again.

A warm, callused hand caught her chin and tipped her face upward. Creede gazed at her, and the lantern's glow reflected in his dark eyes. "Why? You're a beautiful woman."

"Who's lost everyone she's cared for. I won't let that happen again. I *can't* let that happen again." Sickness welled up in her throat.

"You can't cut yourself off from ever feeling again, Laurel."

"Yes, I can."

His gaze moved across her cheeks and down to her lips. He leaned toward her, his mouth searching for hers. Laurel wanted to escape, but her muscles wouldn't obey. His breath caressed her, then his lips brushed hers. She forgot how to breathe, forgot everything but the sweet touch of his mouth. She raised a hand and laid it behind his neck. His soft hair tickled her fingers and sent spasms of longing straight to her middle. She pulled his face close, this time initiating the kiss herself.

Sometimes soft, sometimes hard, the press of his lips against hers stirred the long-denied heat of passion. It radiated to her limbs and into her belly, making her body sing with sensations almost forgotten.

Creede drew away. His face was flushed, his eyes half-closed with desire. "We have to stop, Laurel," he whispered hoarsely.

His voice brought reality crashing down around her. The pain of losing someone she cared about could never be offset by a few stolen moments of pleasure.

She dropped her arms to her sides. "You're right. I'm sorry."

He brushed his thumb across her lower lip. "Don't be. I was the one who wanted to prove something."

"What?"

"That no matter how hard you try, you can't cut yourself off from feeling."

He'd proved his point. And Laurel was more frightened than ever.

$\mathscr{F}$OURTEEN

CREEDE awakened with a start. He lay still, trying to determine what had pulled him from a deep sleep. Laurel, who dozed about ten feet away, shifted restlessly. She moaned, and tossed and turned on her bed of straw.

She was obviously having a nightmare and he debated whether to wake her. Maybe if he woke her, he could get her to tell him about it. However, knowing Laurel's stubborn nature, she'd more than likely refuse.

Although he couldn't understand what she was murmuring, her tone was one of pain and suffering. She cried out and he closed his hands into fists as he forced himself to remain still. Finally, she grew silent and her breathing evened out.

Creede loosened his tense muscles and rolled onto his side. It was still an hour before dawn, long enough to try to catch some more sleep.

From below, one of the horses snorted and bumped into its stall. More hooves fidgeted on the floor, alerting Creede to the presence of something—or someone. He tugged on his boots and reached for his revolver, then soundlessly crept across the straw-covered loft. Keeping low, he peered over the edge and searched the darkness, but saw nothing except shadows.

The animals snuffled and stirred restlessly, telling him whatever had disturbed them was still there. Frowning, Creede carefully swung a leg over the ladder and climbed down. He stood in the middle of the barn, his head tipped to the side as he listened.

A scuffle to his right, away from the animals, made him spin around. Out of the corner of his eye, he spotted a flash of movement—a dark shadow against lighter shadows.

Creede considered calling out, but that would only give away his position. Walking on the balls of his feet, he moved in that direction. He spotted motion to his left and heard the unmistakable sound of running feet. He charged after the person. The horses neighed and one of the mules brayed, but he didn't know which one.

The barn door burst open and Creede saw a slight figure duck through the opening. He hurried after the person, his gun in his hand. In the predawn light, he could make out a short person running across the yard.

"Hold it," Creede shouted.

The pig oinked and the chickens clucked and scattered. The thief didn't stop. Creede pointed his gun in the air and fired once.

The figure stumbled and fell. Creede quickly caught up and aimed his revolver at the intruder, who turned out to be a child. The whites of his eyes were set in a dark face surrounded by a mop of curly black hair. His tan shirt and trousers were streaked with dirt and his feet were bare.

Self-consciously, Creede lowered his revolver and stared at the kid.

"What's goin' on out there?" Overby shouted from the cabin's porch. His overalls were hooked at one shoulder and in his hands was his trusty shotgun.

"Come take a look," Creede called back.

Overby cautiously joined him, unsure of whom he should be aiming his shotgun at. "It's a darkie."

Creede bit back a retort. "It's a boy."

"He's a damned thief."

"We don't know that."

"What's that in his hand?"

Creede looked down at the boy whose wide-eyed gaze darted back and forth between him and Overby. "What do you have, kid?"

The boy narrowed his eyes. "Nuthin'."

"That doesn't look like nothing," Creede said, pointing at the bag in his hand.

He clutched it close to his chest. "Mine."

Overby leaned over and grabbed the sack, but the kid clung to it and he was jerked to his feet.

"Let go," Overby said.

The boy shook his head. Overby raised his hand to strike him and Creede caught his arm.

"There's no need for that," Creede growled.

"He's a damned thief."

Creede reined in his temper. "Let me talk to him."

Overby swore under his breath but released the boy, who tried to flee. Creede caught his shoulder.

"Tell me what's in the bag, son," Creede said gently.

The boy's gaze flicked away.

"I'm not going to hurt you. I'd just like to see what you have."

The tension in the kid's body leached away and he opened the bag but didn't release it. Creede put his hand inside and came up with something wrapped in cloth. He unrolled it and a biscuit and two pieces of meat tumbled into his hand.

"Creede?"

Laurel's voice startled him and he glanced up to see her coming toward them, a shawl around her shoulders.

"I think I found the leftovers from the other night," he said dryly.

"Who is he?" she asked.

"A thievin' bastard," Overby said.

"He didn't steal from you," Creede growled.

"How do ya know?"

Creede restrained an impatient sigh. "Where would he hide it?"

Overby grumbled but held his tongue.

Laurel knelt in front of the boy, putting their heads at the same height. "What's your name?"

The kid shuffled his bare feet. "Seb." He lifted his chin. "I ain't no runaway. I's free."

Laurel smiled. "Yes, you are. Where's your family?"

He looked at her like she'd asked him to move a mountain. "Ain't got none."

"No mother or father?"

Seb shook his head. "Didn't never know 'em."

Creede felt a stab of sympathy.

"How old are you?" Laurel asked.

"They told me I was eight."

"They?"

"The master and the others."

"Where do you live now?" Laurel asked.

"Nowheres."

Laurel glanced up at Creede and he could plainly see her compassion. "We can't just leave him out here on his own."

"What do you think we should do?"

"Turn 'im in to the law," Overby interjected.

"And what will they do with him?" Laurel asked.

"They'll make sure he don't steal from law-abidin' folks again."

Seb's eyes widened in fear.

Creede suspected Seb would be better off on his own than handed over to a lawman. "Maybe we can find someone in Rounder willing to give him a job," he said in a low voice to Laurel.

She nodded and asked Seb softly, "Would you like to come with us?"

"Why?"

"Maybe we can find you a place to live."

"I ain't no slave no more," he said stubbornly.

"No, you're not. You're free—free to decide if you want to come with us or not."

Seb stared at her, as if trying to determine if this was a trick. "Iffen I wanna leave, I can?"

"Yes," Laurel said solemnly. "I promise."

Finally, he nodded.

"Crazy as a flea-bitten coonhound," Overby muttered. He turned around and strode back to the house.

Dawn cast an orange glow across the eastern sky.

Creede took hold of Laurel's arm and helped her to her feet. "I doubt anyone will sleep anymore. We might as well get organized and head out."

He didn't get any argument from Laurel. Or Seb.

LAUREL glanced back at Dickens, amazed anew at how the mule had taken to Seb. The cat wasn't too happy to share his perch with the boy, but he didn't hop down either. Seb seemed more relaxed now than when they'd started traveling. Laurel could only imagine how ingrained distrust was in the boy.

"Town should be just up ahead," Creede announced.

"Maybe we can find someone willing to take Seb in." She kept her voice low so the boy wouldn't hear.

"It's not going to be easy. I doubt any white folks will want him."

"We won't know until we ask," she said, unwilling to believe the War had turned everyone bitter.

Creede merely grunted in reply.

Entering Rounder, they noticed a handful of people moving about the town. Most glanced curiously at the newcomers, but even with Seb's presence, they didn't garner the same looks of deep suspicion that greeted them in Lefsburg.

They reined in by the livery and dismounted. Creede swung Seb down from Dickens's back. The cat leapt gracefully to the ground and dashed off to find a hiding place. Laurel didn't doubt he'd find them when they left town.

She spotted two men playing checkers on a barrel just inside the barn door. One was old and grizzled, and the other, who was half-hidden in the shadows, was younger, maybe twenty or so.

The older man stood and straightened his coverall straps as he walked out to join them. He eyed Seb but didn't make any comment. "Afternoon. Looks like ya'll have ridden a ways."

"We have," Creede said. "Got room for a couple of tired horses and a mule?"

The whipcord-thin man's laugh was surprisingly low-pitched. "All we got is room, mister. Two bits a day for each animal."

"Oats?"

"Can't help ya there. We ain't had no oats for two years now. All they growed 'round here went to General Lee and his soldiers." He spit to the side. "And now they done decided we ain't sec-ceded no more."

The younger man, who was still sitting, glared at them but Laurel couldn't figure out if it was aimed at her or Creede. Or perhaps Seb.

"What do you mean?" Laurel asked the older man.

He leveled a gimlet-eyed gaze on her. "Well, missy, it means that them politicians figured since we lost the war, we'd best get on the good side of them Yanks. Voted to get rid of slaves, too." His glance slid to Seb again, but there wasn't any overt hostility in his expression.

"How long ago was that?" Creede asked.

The liveryman scrubbed his whiskered jaw. "Over a month ago, middle of August, it was."

Laurel realized the former slaves they'd seen on the road had probably been traveling since the Mississippi congress voted to emancipate them.

"Give them a good rubdown," Creede said, flipping the man a dollar.

The man caught the coin and examined it. Satisfied, he slipped it in his pocket. "Robbie, come take care of their stock."

The younger man swore and rose awkwardly as he

reached for a crutch. As he hobbled over, Laurel saw one pants leg hung limp. Her belly clenched. She'd seen too many like him during the war, with arms or legs shattered by rifle balls and nothing to do but cut off the limb or let the patient die a slow painful death.

"What you starin' at, lady?" the boy growled.

Laurel flinched as if struck and shook her head. "I-I'm sorry." Flustered, she grabbed her two bags but then realized she didn't know where to go.

"He didn't mean anything, Laurel," Creede said quietly.

She swallowed back a hysterical laugh. "No, I'm sure he didn't."

Remembered images swarmed through her mind, triggered by the crippled boy's appearance. Her head pounded and her skin was both hot and cold, clammy and dry. "Let's find a room."

Keeping his concerned gaze on her, Creede asked the liveryman, "There a hotel in town?"

He shook his head. "Only a roomin' house. Don't s'pect she'll let the boy in, though."

Anger flared in Laurel, nearly obliterating the nausea. "Why?"

He looked at her like she was lacking sense. "Look at him."

Seb stood close to Laurel, his gaze aimed at the ground. His subservient posture angered her further.

"He's a boy," she said.

The liveryman shrugged his bony shoulders. "Don't make no never mind to me, but don't be s'prised if she don't give you a room." He motioned with his chin to a building across the street. "There's the roomin' house."

Creede seized one of Laurel's bags, and with her free hand, she clasped Seb's hand. They walked across the street to a large house with a sign that read ROOMS.

The proprietor, a stout woman with her hair pulled in a severe bun, met them on the porch. "Can I help you?" Her tone was cool.

"We'd like a room for the night," Creede said.

She crossed her arms over her large bosom. "You and your missus can have one, but the darkie's gotta sleep someplace else."

Laurel didn't correct her assumption that they were married, but she couldn't overlook her slur against Seb. "The boy's name is Seb and he's with us."

"He your slave?"

"No. And even if he had been, he wouldn't be anymore. Haven't you heard—slavery is against the law now," Laurel said.

The woman's round face reddened. "This is my place and I says who can stay here."

"Business has been that good that you can turn away folks with good money?" Creede asked.

Flustered, she stared at him, and Laurel could tell she was weighing her greed with her aversion. Finally, the woman nodded curtly. "As long as the . . . the boy sleeps on the floor, you can have a room."

Creede paid her and she led them to a room on the main floor. Laurel pulled Seb along, knowing he was reluctant, but she refused to give in to the landlady's prejudice.

Once the woman left them, Laurel examined their room. A davenport and chair were positioned in front of a fireplace, and an armoire stood against the wall to the right. The bed itself was large enough for four people and the coverlet appeared clean.

She glanced at Seb, who was standing in the same place she'd left him. His eyes were wide and he drew a finger along the sofa's cushion then jerked his hand back as if he'd be punished for stroking it. She doubted he'd ever been allowed in a room like this, much less touched the furniture.

"It's better than the hotel in Lefsburg," Creede said.

She shuddered. "Don't remind me."

She sank onto the bed and her encounter with the crippled young man at the livery came back to haunt her.

"You should lie down," Creede suggested. "You look like you're going to swoon."

"I've never swooned in my life," she tossed back, but without any weight.

Seb looked around like he didn't know what to do.

"You can sit down," Laurel said gently.

After a moment, Seb sank down onto the floor.

"You don't have to sit on the floor."

Seb shrugged and curled up on the rug, his eyes closing.

Before Laurel could say something more, Creede said, "Leave him be. This is all new to him."

Laurel studied the boy for a minute, then nodded. "I guess it's better than the ground."

"Why don't you rest, too?" Creede suggested softly.

She thought she should argue since it was only late afternoon, but she was tired. She lay back on the bed and closed her eyes. Horrific images from the hospital camps and the amputation tents ambushed her and her eyes flashed open, her heart pounding.

"What is it?"

She focused on Creede, who was studying her with concern. "Nothing."

His lips curled into a scowl, obviously recognizing her lie. "The boy at the livery brought back memories."

She glanced at him, not surprised he'd guessed. "Too many."

His irritation gone, he swept back a strand of hair from her damp forehead and his fingers brushed her brow. Awareness rippled through her.

"But he's alive," Creede said.

"He's bitter. A lot of them were." The ghosts scuttled closer, pressing against her.

"You aren't to blame for that. A person makes his own decisions."

"Most of them weren't given the chance to decide if they wanted to lose a limb."

Creede bent closer. "Stop it, Laurel. *You* didn't force a gun into their hands and make them fight."

How many times had she been told that by other nurses, doctors, and even herself?

"I'm tired. I think I will take a nap." She knew she was taking the coward's way out, but at the moment all she wanted was to be alone.

Creede sighed. "I think I'll look around the town. What's the name of the folks you're looking for?"

Laurel struggled to remember, even though she'd just read the journal entry the night before. "Smith. Their son was Nathan."

"I'll see what I can find out. You get some rest."

"Thank you." She turned her head, fearful of what she'd see in his eyes.

But more fearful of what he'd see in hers.

CREEDE kicked a stone and watched it skitter into the street. He glanced back at the rooming house, torn between staying close to Laurel and giving her the time she needed to gather her composure. The urge to wrap her in his arms and comfort her still gnawed at him. He wanted to take away some of her pain, but understood how some hurt was just too deep to make go away with an embrace and some soothing words.

Uncertain where to go, he just started walking and found himself back at the livery. Robbie and the older man were back to their checkers game.

"Come to check on your horses?" the older man asked in between puffs on a corncob pipe.

"Just stretching my legs. Name's Creede Forrester."

"Bill Cutter, and this here's my nephew Robbie," the old man introduced.

Creede shook Bill's hand, but Robbie didn't offer his.

"Mary rent you a room?" Bill asked.

Creede grinned wryly. "After I pointed out she would be losing money if she turned us away."

"Don't be too hard on her. Son was killed in the War."

Although Creede couldn't excuse her intolerance, he empathized with her loss. "Quiet little town you have."

"Wasn't as quiet afore the War. Lost about two dozen

men." Bill motioned to his nephew with his pipe stem. "But Robbie here made it back."

"I'm a damned cripple," Robbie said bitterly.

"You're alive," Creede said.

Robbie glared at him. "What the hell do you know, mister?"

"I know that if my son had come back with one leg, I'd be thanking God."

Bill's eyes narrowed. "You lose your boy?"

Creede swallowed hard and looked away. "Sixteen years old."

"Well maybe *he* wouldn't a been very happy 'bout comin' back less than a man," Robbie snarled.

"Maybe, maybe not. But I wouldn't have let him sit around feeling sorry for himself."

Robbie launched himself at Creede, knocking him down and falling on top of him. The boy swung his fist but Creede stuck up his arm, blocking his punch. He didn't want to hurt Robbie, but he wasn't afraid to defend himself either.

"Hold your horses there, boy," Bill ordered, pulling Robbie up by the back of his shirt. "Forrester was just talkin'. No need for you to be gettin' all riled up."

Creede pushed himself to his feet and held up his hands. "Your uncle's right. I didn't mean anything."

Robbie's eyes blazed with anger. "Don't you be tellin' me how I should be feelin'. You got two good legs."

"Go find someplace to get rid of your mad, Robbie." Bill handed his nephew his crutch.

The boy snatched it from him and hobbled away.

"Sorry 'bout that, Forrester. He always was a prideful boy. It don't set right with him that he only got one leg now."

"Laurel was a nurse," Creede said. "She said she saw a lot of boys like him."

Bill shoved his hands in his pockets. "Wanna play some checkers?"

"Sure."

He took Robbie's former place and Bill relit his pipe.

"You got black. Your turn," Bill said.

Creede studied the pieces a minute before making his move. "Where'd Robbie lose his leg?"

"Shiloh, back in '62. He was only eighteen. Only been in the army three months. What about your son?"

"Petersburg, Virginia. March of this year. I didn't find out until June." Creede kept his voice steady.

"You fight?"

Creede glanced up, expecting to see censure, but there was only curiosity. "No. Didn't believe in it."

"S'prised you admitted it."

"What about you?"

"Too old. They wouldn't take me."

"You were lucky."

"Didn't think so then, but after seein' Robbie I figured maybe I was." Bill puffed on his pipe and took his turn. "I'm right sorry Robbie upset your wife."

Creede shifted, uncomfortable with lying to the older man but not wanting to hurt Laurel's reputation. "She'll be all right."

"Where'd the darkie come from?"

"We found Seb this morning." Creede didn't figure Bill needed to know the circumstances. "He was by himself. No family, no one to look out for him."

"What do you figger on doin' with him?"

Irritation prickled Creede. "We told him we'd try to find someone to take him in, but he's free to leave whenever he wants."

Bill merely grunted. It was obvious he didn't share Laurel and Creede's view of former slaves.

He jumped one of Bill's checkers and picked it up.

"So where you headed?" Bill asked.

"Texas."

"I figured you was from there. The missus, too?"

"No. She's delivering some last words from soldiers she was with at the end."

"Don't seem like somethin' many folks would do."

"Laurel isn't like most folks. Say, you wouldn't happen to know a family by the name of Smith, would you?"

"More'n one."

"They had a son named Nathan."

Bill's eyes widened. "He and Robbie joined up together. He leave some last words?"

Creede nodded. "Laurel wants to give them to his folks."

He rubbed his grizzled jaw. "Nathan's pa's heart gave out when they got the news he was killed in the War. His ma runs the roomin' house you're stayin' in."

Startled, Creede frowned. "I'd best let Laurel know. Will Robbie be all right?"

Bill shrugged and sadness shadowed his creased face. "Don't know if he ever will be."

Creede didn't know how to answer so he merely nodded and headed back to the rooming house. He didn't want Laurel finding out from the landlady that she was Nathan Smith's mother.

$\mathcal{F}$IFTEEN

May 11, 1864. Private Nathan Smith from Rounder, Mississippi. Mortally wounded at Yellow Tavern. Twenty years old. Cause of death: saber through his chest. "Tell my folks I didn't mean to be contrary, but I did what I had to do. Just like I done when I climbed that apple tree and broke my arm. Just had to do it."

TO divert her downward spiraling thoughts, Laurel focused on Seb, who was snoring quietly. The boy had to have followed them the day after he'd stolen the biscuits and pork, and they'd traveled a good thirty miles that day, half of it in the rain. It was no wonder Seb was tired. Laurel hoped he didn't get sick on top of his exhaustion.

Unable to sleep, she sat up, careful to remain quiet lest she waken him. Studying the boy, she figured he wasn't much more than eight or nine years old. The leathery soles of his feet told her he'd rarely, if ever, worn shoes. One of his hands was outstretched and calluses covered his fingertips and some of his small palm. Although she'd known children were also slaves, the evidence of Seb's labor brought home the reality of that fact.

An invisible band constricted her chest. She'd nursed the soldiers who'd fought to keep children like Seb bound as slaves. She'd justified her actions by telling herself most of the soldiers were poor and didn't own slaves, and they'd fought for other reasons. Yet that wouldn't have made a difference if the South had won. Seb and all the children like him would've never known freedom.

Restlessness seized her and she stood, impatient to do something, anything to make her mind stop swirling. But she wouldn't leave Seb here alone, especially with a landlady who'd made her repugnance of "darkies" clear.

The door opened and Laurel's gaze leaped to Creede. His gaze lit on her then moved over to Seb. With deliberate stealth, he entered the room and crossed to Laurel.

"I found out where Nathan Smith's mother lives," he said in a low voice. Before Laurel could ask, Creede continued. "She owns this rooming house."

Laurel's anxiety was quickly masked by disappointment.

"It explains why she doesn't like Seb," Creede said.

She scowled and shook her head. "No, it doesn't. You lost your son and you don't take it out on innocents."

"She grew up in the South. I didn't."

"Don't make excuses for her." Laurel's irritation for all those like Mrs. Smith fanned her temper.

Creede studied her with an unfathomable expression. "So you aren't going to deliver her son's message because you don't agree with her?"

She flinched as if struck. Would she withhold Nathan Smith's last words because she didn't like who was to receive the message? She'd made a promise to Nathan and all the others and that vow couldn't be altered by her personal biases. It wasn't her place to judge, only to bear witness to the words left behind. "I didn't say that." She stiffened her spine, suddenly eager to fulfill her obligation. "I'm going to tell her now."

"Maybe you should wait until the morning when you're more rested."

Laurel shook her head, stubbornness dousing her earlier tiredness. "I won't feel right if I wait."

Creede searched her eyes and he must've seen her determination. "All right, but I'm going with you."

She opened her mouth to argue, but he held up his hand. "Please, Laurel."

Bewildered, she asked, "Why?"

"You have to be strong for them. Let me be strong for you." His solemn eyes held empathy.

A lump the size of an apple filled her throat and tears burned her eyes. A chaotic mix of gratitude, relief, and some unnamable emotion rocked through her. Unable to speak, she nodded.

Creede motioned to the loveseat. "I'll wait until you're ready."

He'd been with her long enough to know she spent some time organizing her thoughts and preparing for her visits to the surviving families. While he waited, she retrieved her journal and sat on the edge of the bed to re-read the entry from Nathan Smith. One hand curled into a fist as her thoughts traveled back to Nathan's death, just as she recalled each and every soldier before passing on their final message. The saber had gone clear through his chest, from front to back. He'd lived less than two hours after he'd been brought to the hospital. It was a miracle he'd been coherent enough to give her a message for his family.

She could envision the scene so clearly. The sun had been merciless that day, heating the tent's interior and exacerbating the stench of blood and excrement. There was the never-ending sound of men in pain—moans, crying, and sometimes screams. Nathan was one of those who'd occasionally scream.

Her brow grew damp with sweat and her stomach churned, as if smelling those same odors and feeling that same heat all over again. Her ears rang with the sounds of battle and the overflowing tent hospital. She stood abruptly, intent on escaping the sensory assault.

"Laurel," Creede said.

She blinked his concerned features into focus and she realized she'd had another waking nightmare. Hiding her panic, she said, "Yes?"

"What were you saying?"

She'd been talking aloud? A cold chill swept through her at another sign of her weakening mind. "It was nothing."

She set the journal on the bed and poured some water from the pitcher into the basin. Cupping water into her hands, she splashed it on her face, removing the sweat and too-real memories.

After drying herself, she picked up her journal and hugged it to her chest to cover the remnants of her trembling. "I'm ready. Will Seb be all right?"

"He looks like he'd sleep through a locomotive whistle." Creede swept a tendril of hair back from her brow. "It's you I'm worried about."

She fought the urge to lean against him. "There's no need to worry about me. We'll probably find Mrs. Smith in the kitchen this time of day."

They left the room, shutting the door softly behind them. Laurel, her knees shaky, led the way to the kitchen where Mrs. Smith was bustling around the hot stove. Creede stayed near the doorway, leaning against the jamb with his hat in hand.

"Meal won't be ready for another hour," the woman said curtly.

Laurel glanced at Creede, who gave her a nod of encouragement. Suddenly nervous, she wished she hadn't agreed to Creede's presence. The messages represented her failures—her failure to save another life. Nobody but the families had ever heard them. Yet as much as she wanted Creede gone, she wanted his solid presence even more.

"We're not here about dinner," she began. "We didn't introduce ourselves earlier. This is Creede Forrester and I'm Laurel. I was a nurse with the Confederate army."

Mrs. Smith froze in mid-stir and turned around slowly. Her lips compressed in a thin line and her eyes narrowed. "I'm Mrs. Mary Smith."

"Yes, I know." Laurel licked her dry lips. "I have a message from your son."

The older woman's pink cheeks paled but anger flared in her eyes. "My son is dead."

Laurel took a step closer to her. "I was with him when he died. Maybe you should sit down."

Mrs. Smith turned back to the pots on the stove. "I have work to do. Jus' tell me."

Laurel could feel Creede's sympathetic gaze on her back but refused to look at him. She would handle this like she'd handled all the other messages—alone.

She opened the journal, noting her hands were amazingly steady. Moving aside the blue ribbon that marked her entry, she cleared her throat. "From Private Nathan Smith, who was mortally wounded at Yellow Tavern on May 11, 1864. 'Tell my folks I didn't mean to be contrary, but I did what I had to do. Just like I done when I climbed that apple tree and broke my arm. Just had to do it.'"

Mrs. Smith didn't pause in her cooking tasks. "You come all this way for that?" Derision resonated in her voice.

Shocked, Laurel nodded then realized Mrs. Smith couldn't see her. "Yes, that's all."

"You done your good deed, now leave me be."

She didn't like Mrs. Smith, but she'd believed the woman would have some maternal feelings toward her son. "Are you all right?"

Mrs. Smith turned around. Her eyes were dry and a fierce frown tugged at her thin lips. The truth was there in her expression—her son's words hadn't even stirred her.

"Nathan never was real bright. He died a fool and killed his own pa as sure as if he shot him dead. Now I ain't got no one and nothin' 'cept this here place, so don't be judgin' me for not fallin' down and thankin' you for bringin' me Nathan's last words." Resentment burned in her eyes.

Angered by the woman's callousness, Laurel raised her chin. "The last hour of your son's life, the pain was so intense he cried out for you. At the time, I would've given anything to be able to give him his mother but now I'm glad you weren't there."

Mrs. Smith's nostrils flared and she raised her hand. But before she could strike, Creede caught her arm. The woman stared at Laurel, hatred flashing in her narrowed eyes. Finally, she blinked and he released her. Mrs. Smith returned to her cooking.

Laurel felt a warm hand at her back.

"Come on," Creede said.

She allowed him to steer her out of the kitchen and up the stairs. Halfway back to the room, the headache struck. Sharp pain stabbed her temples and she gasped. Although she was growing accustomed to the headaches, this one was the worst. Her stomach tossed and she had to squint against the light coming in the windows.

Creede wrapped an arm around her waist and helped her into their room and to the bed. She lay down and closed her eyes, but reopened them immediately when colors spun behind her eyelids.

She hated her malady, and she saw with terror that her mind, which had once been so sharp, was slowly being destroyed. And she hated that Creede was witnessing her decline.

Creede laid a cool, damp cloth on her brow. "I can't understand how a mother could feel that way about her son."

"She blames him for her being alone. No one likes having nobody to care for them."

"Who cares for you, Laurel?"

His husky voice caressed her, sending a shiver down her spine. She gazed into his eyes and floundered in their compassionate depths. Her pain made her reply less guarded than usual. "You do."

A slow smile curled his lips. "Is there anyone else?"

Unable to lie, even by omission, she shook her head. "No."

He rested his palm against the side of her face and brushed her cheek with his thumb. There was sadness in his expression. "You cared for so many during the War."

His gentle touch soothed her headache, bringing it down to a tolerable thudding. "But they all died anyway."

His thumb stilled for a moment, then he continued stroking her face. "Not all of them. What about those you saved?"

"Too few. More died."

"That wasn't your fault."

They were back to that. He couldn't understand why she took responsibility for those who died just as he would never know what it was like to determine who lived and who didn't.

"Is Seb still asleep?" she asked, changing the subject.

He glanced at the boy. "Yes. He was tuckered out. You should sleep, too. I'll wake you when it's time to eat."

Although the thought of food made her queasy, she nodded and closed her eyes. A moment later, the mattress shifted and Creede settled beside her. He gathered her in his arms and she didn't possess the will to fight him. Besides, lying in his embrace was the only place she truly felt like the woman she had been before the War.

He kissed her crown and laid his chin on the top of her head. "I'll be right here."

Laurel curled into him, her forehead pressed against his chest. She savored his masculine scent and the security of his arms. For the first time in months, she might sleep without ghosts visiting her.

THE following morning Creede and Seb walked down to the livery to gather the horses and Dickens. Seb wore the new trousers and shirt they'd bought for him earlier, but he refused to wear shoes. After having been barefoot most of his life, forcing him to wear shoes would seem like a punishment.

Bill sat outside the livery, his chair tipped back on two legs and leaning against the barn. He sipped coffee from a tin cup as he observed the town's lackluster activity. When he spotted Creede, he let the chair legs thump to the ground and stood. "Reckon you're headin' out."

"That's right," Creede said. "Robbie around?"

Bill shrugged. "Ain't seen him this mornin'."

Creede had wanted to apologize to the younger man, although he still believed Robbie should've been grateful to be alive. But if the young man was determined to be bitter, Creede couldn't do anything to change his mind. Shrugging to himself, he followed the liveryman into the barn.

Seb tagged along and while Creede and Bill saddled the two horses, the boy brushed Dickens's mangy coat.

"Get what ya needed done?" Bill asked Creede.

"Laurel did." He leaned against his mare's broad side. "Mrs. Smith's a bitter woman."

"She ain't the only one. Hard on the womenfolk left behind."

Creede thought of Laurel and how she, too, was a widow because of the War. Yet she wasn't bitter. Instead, she seemed driven—driven to deliver the words uttered by dying soldiers. What would drive her when all the messages were delivered?

Troubled, Creede placed the packframe on Dickens. He was conscious of Seb talking softly to the mule and was surprised to see Dickens appeared to be listening. It seemed the stubborn jackass actually liked someone.

Creede attached the lead rope to the mule's halter and handed it to Seb. "You mind walking Dickens to the rooming house?"

"No, sir," Seb said, smiling widely.

Creede exchanged a firm handshake with Bill. "When you see Robbie, tell him I'm sorry about what happened."

"I'll tell 'im, but it won't make no never mind. Boy makes himself miserable."

"Guess nobody can change how he feels but it's a damned shame."

Bill shrugged. "I'll keep workin' on him."

Creede managed a smile.

Just as he and Seb were leaving the livery with the animals in tow, the cat bounced out after them. Delighted, Seb bent down to pet the stray.

"Is he gonna come with us?" Seb asked.

"I don't think we can stop him," Creede replied with a rueful grin. He lifted the cat onto its customary place on Dickens's back and the stray curled up into a ball.

They left the animals at the rooming house hitching post and went inside to get Laurel. Creede's heart quickened as he remembered what she'd looked like that morning. With her hair tousled and her face flushed, she'd given him a smile that had gone straight south of his belt buckle. He'd slept on the floor overnight, although sleep had been scarce. Her soft breathing and the memory of holding her yesterday while she'd napped had kept him hard and aching. The temptation to join her on the bed under the cover of darkness had nearly overwhelmed him, but having Seb in the room helped curtail his passion.

Shaking the enticing thoughts away, Creede led Seb down the hall to their room. Laurel opened the door just as they were approaching. She glanced up, startled, and quickly looked away.

"This is everything," she said.

Creede took her two bags and Seb carried one of the saddlebags, leaving Laurel with the other.

"Did you tell Mrs. Smith we were leaving?" Creede asked.

Laurel shook her head. "I'm sure she knows." She smiled at Seb. "We'll find a home for you. Don't you worry."

"I ain't worried, Miz Laurel," he said with all the bravado of a young boy. "I knows how to take care of myself."

She sighed and ruffled his tight curls. "It won't come to that, Seb. I promise."

The boy didn't appear convinced. It would take a lot longer than two days and Laurel's word to get him to believe.

They left Rounder and traveled throughout the day,

speaking little and giving the animals a rest every few hours. Laurel had told Creede their next destination—a town in Arkansas—and had an approximate location on the map she carried. As they drew closer, they would get better directions from folks in the area.

That night when they made camp, Laurel cooked supper from the supplies they'd bought in Rounder. Seb ate quickly, as if afraid the food would be stolen before he could finish. Laurel offered him more, and he eagerly accepted, wolfing it down as fast as he had the first helping. Her heart went out to the waif and she couldn't help but wonder what his life had been like. He'd never volunteered any information and she hadn't asked. Perhaps it was because she hadn't wanted to face any more harsh truths—a coward's way of seeing the world.

"What did you do when you were a slave?" she asked the boy.

Startled, he set his empty plate down and shrugged. "What they tol' me."

"Like what?"

"Cleanin' the barn, hoein' the garden, gatherin' nuts, and pickin' apples." Another shrug. "Done whatever needed doin'."

"Did you have to do things you didn't like?"

Seb squirmed. "Didn't matter. Had to do what they tol' me."

She glanced at Creede, who frowned at her, obviously disliking her interrogation of the boy. Laurel herself wasn't certain why she needed to know.

"Why don't you get some sleep, Seb?" Creede suggested.

Seb eagerly moved to the blanket they'd bought for him along with the clothes.

"Do you think we'll find him a home?" Laurel asked, troubled by her growing affection for the boy.

"I don't know," he answered. "I doubt you'll find a white family who'll take him in, and those who used to be slaves have enough trouble finding food without adding another mouth."

"I'm afraid you're probably right." Although her goal was to find him a home, a part of her wanted to care for him herself. But if she'd learned one thing during the War, it was that she couldn't let herself care, or she wouldn't survive.

"He could stay with you," Creede said.

"No!" Her explosive answer shocked her as much as Creede. "No," she repeated more calmly. "I don't have a place to live and I won't do that to a young boy. He needs some place stable, a home with other children."

"Someone who'll care for him," Creede interjected.

She hated that he could read her so easily, but she wouldn't give him the satisfaction of knowing how close his comments struck. "That's right." She gave her attention to the task of washing their dishes.

Thankfully, Creede allowed the subject to drop. How could she explain what she was feeling when she was so confused about everything herself?

Sixteen

THE following day, with the sun high, Creede led them off the road to a burbling creek. It was so clear they could see the rocks below. Laurel and Seb dismounted and allowed Dickens and Jeanie to drink their fill. Once they seemed satisfied, she had Seb ground-tie them next to Creede's horse so the animals could forage in the knee-high green grass. Taking her canteens, she refilled them from the shallow brook. She gave one to the boy and urged him to drink, and kept the other one with her, its strap looped over her shoulder.

She and Seb joined Creede, who gave them each a piece of dried meat. With only a slight wrinkle of her nose, she accepted it and leaned against a nearby tree. She noticed Seb seemed more than happy for the food, and guilt assailed her. She should be grateful for what they had instead of irritated about what they did not.

She waved her free hand in front of her face, dispersing a cloud of gnats. She froze for a moment, remembering the episode at the Gaddsen's cabin when she'd been so certain her hand was covered with blood. If Creede hadn't stopped her, who knew how badly she would've hurt herself trying to remove a stain that wasn't there. That incident was just another reminder that she had little time to spare in delivering the last two messages.

She bit off a piece of the tough, salty meat and chewed until it was soft enough to chase down with a long draw from her canteen. The sun's heat and the steady drone of insects made her eyelids grow heavy. Sometimes she wondered what it would be like to fall asleep and not wake up. No more nightmares and no more too-real memories. But then she thought of Creede and all he'd lost. She couldn't imagine him giving up without a fight. Yet how long should a person have to fight?

Creede suddenly tensed. "We've got company."

She followed his line of sight and spotted a group of a half dozen former slaves by the looks of their ragged clothing and bare, dusty feet. There was a man and a woman, and four children ranging in age from perhaps six to twelve. Each of them carried a rope slung across his or her chest that was tied to a rolled-up blanket.

Laurel looked over at Seb, who watched them with suspicion glinting in his coal black eyes.

"What should we do?" she asked Creede in a low voice.

"With children, I doubt they're looking for trouble. They probably just want some water."

Laurel stepped away from the tree and went to stand beside Seb, putting a hand on his shoulder.

"Howdy," Creede greeted the family.

The tall black man nodded suspiciously. He had an expansive chest and large, work-roughened hands. A black beard covered the lower half of his face except for where a puckered scar cut from the left corner of his mouth to his jaw. The woman was about Laurel's height but thinner, almost to the point of emaciation, but her gaze was direct and her chin raised. The children huddled together, but their gazes kept shifting to Seb.

"We just come to get some water," the man said, his voice a deep rumble.

"Help yourselves," Creede said, motioning to the creek. "We were just getting ready to leave."

"Go on, now." The woman waved her arms, urging the children to the water. "Drink up."

Laurel watched them do as they were told. One of the middle ones, a girl, limped and her teeth were clenched together.

"What happened to her?" Laurel asked the woman as she motioned to the girl.

"Cut herself on a rock a coupla days ago," she replied curtly. "She be fine."

"Would you mind if I looked at her foot?"

Both the man and woman stared at her, their gazes shifting to Seb and growing more wary. Laurel didn't blame them for being distrustful. She had a feeling folks didn't look too kindly on former slaves in this part of the country. They were a reminder of all the South had lost.

"This is Seb," she introduced. "He's been traveling with us for a few days now. He said he doesn't have any family."

"That true?" the big man asked Seb.

The boy nodded. "They been good to me. Said I didn't have to stay iffen I don' want to."

The man and woman studied him for a moment, then they relaxed slightly.

"If you don't mind, I'd like to look at your daughter's foot. I'm a nurse," Laurel said.

"Ada," the woman called. The girl turned toward them, water dripping from her face and cupped hands. "Let the lady look at yer foot."

Ada's enormous brown eyes telegraphed her mistrust, but she sat back on the bank, pulling her simple flour-sack shift down over her knobby knees. Numerous scratches covered her thin legs, telling Laurel they'd traveled a fair number of miles.

"My name's Laurel and I just want to examine that cut to make sure it's healing. Is that all right?"

The girl, who was probably the same age as Seb, nodded slowly. "Yes, Miz Laurel."

Laurel checked her foot, cleaning it first in the cool running water. The cut wasn't long but it was deep, and the skin around it was reddish and warm.

"Seb, could you get my saddlebag?" she asked.

The boy bounded over to Jeanie and stood on his tiptoes to retrieve it. He brought it back to Laurel.

"Thank you, Seb." She dug some things out and held up a bottle and a roll of bandages for Ada and her parents to see. "I'm going to clean the cut then wrap your foot so it doesn't get dirty. All right?"

Ada glanced at her mother, who nodded, and said to Laurel, "Yes, ma'am."

As Laurel worked, she listened to Creede speak with the girl's father.

"Name's Creede Forrester," he said.

"I'm Ezekial Wollings, and this is Sarie Wollings." He motioned to the woman.

"Where you from?"

Ezekial motioned to the southeast. "Thataways. We was slaves for Mr. Wollings." He pressed back his shoulders. "Now we's free."

Laurel was startled to hear that they'd taken the last name of their previous owner. Of course, it made sense since most slaves didn't have one of their own.

"Where you headed?" Creede asked.

The ex-slave's expression fell. "Lookin' for work. Mr. Wollings couldn't keep us all on as hired help."

"You would've stayed working for him?"

Ezekial shrugged. "He never beat us and we always had enough to eat, until the last, that is. But that weren't his fault. I ain't sorry we're free but we don't got no place to go. Thought we'd head north and hope we find somethin'."

"Don't you fret about us, Mr. Forrester. We get by," the woman said proudly.

Just barely, Laurel thought with more than a twinge of sympathy. These were only six ex-slaves, plus Seb. How many more were there who didn't have a roof over their heads or food to eat? After the South's battering, it was going to take a long time for the former slaves to find paying jobs.

She finished bandaging Ada's foot. "I'm all done."

The girl scrambled up and after testing the injured foot, she smiled shyly. "Thank you, Miz Laurel."

"You're welcome, Ada. Now you be careful and make sure to wash it every day, you hear?"

"Yes'm." She joined her siblings who had gathered around Dickens.

Laurel opened her mouth to warn the children to be careful, but she abruptly closed it. Seb was in the middle of the group, watching them closely even as he told them about "his" mule. She smiled, enjoying the pride in the boy's voice.

Creede extended her a hand and, after a moment of surprised hesitation, Laurel took it and he pulled her to her feet. The warmth and strength of his grasp stirred Laurel's suppressed desire and she reluctantly released him.

Ezekial and Sarie had moved some distance away to slake their thirsts from the stream.

"How's her foot?" Creede asked.

"There was some swelling and heat around the cut. It might've taken care of itself or it might've gone septic." She shrugged. "But I think it'll be fine. I have to tell her mother to make sure it's cleaned every day."

"She already knows," Creede said. "She was listening to every word you said."

Laurel wasn't surprised. Sarie Wollings had been watching her like a hawk, making Laurel wonder if they'd already had some bad encounters with white folks.

Dickens brayed and Laurel turned to see the mule being petted by five pairs of young hands. His ears were up and he stood calmly, with more tolerance than Laurel had seen since he'd pulled the ambulance wagons. His back quarters swayed back and forth under the children's rubbing, eliciting laughter from the youngsters.

Ezekial returned to stand by Creede and Laurel. "Thank you for takin' care of Ada's foot." He shuffled his feet. "We ain't got nothin' to pay ya—"

Laurel held up her hand. "The only thing I want is for Ada to be able to run around and play without limping." She glanced again at the girl who was smiling and giggling while the children lavished attention on the mule.

"What you gonna do with him?" Ezekial asked, motioning to Seb.

"I hope to find a home for him," Laurel replied.

Ezekial and Sarie exchanged a look.

"He ought to be with those like him," Sarie said.

Laurel understood the meaning behind her words. "I agree but we haven't found anyone willing."

"One more ain't gonna be noticed," Ezekial said.

"You'd be taking on another mouth to feed," Creede cut in.

"I knows how to trap rabbits and squirrels. We ain't gone hungry yet."

Laurel hadn't imagined a family this large would want another child. Still, it was the perfect solution for Seb. So why was she reluctant to agree to it? "It's not our decision to make," she said. "It's Seb's."

After a moment of startled hesitation, Ezekial and Sarie nodded in agreement.

"Seb," Laurel called. "Come over here, please."

The boy relinquished his dominion over Dickens and came to stand by Laurel's side.

"This is Ezekial and Sarie Wollings," Laurel said. "They were slaves just like you and they'd like to ask you something."

Seb nodded shyly.

Sarie knelt down in front of him and took his small hands in hers. "Do you have a ma or pa?"

Seb shook his head.

"Ezekial and me was wonderin' iffen you'd like us to be your folks. And them other children would be your brothers and sisters."

Seb shot a yearning glance at the youngsters, but long-honed survival instincts made him cautious. "Why you want me?"

Ezekial hunkered down by Sarie. "Because family takes care of each other and we'd like to take care of you."

Still the boy wasn't convinced. "But you don't need me. You already got them."

"Love ain't somethin' that can be made smaller or taken away. It only gets bigger and bigger."

Seb tilted his head back to look at Laurel. "That true, Miz Laurel?"

Her throat tightened, but she managed to speak. "That's right, Seb. Ezekial and Sarie want you to be part of their family."

His gaze flitted back to the other children and this time there was no mistaking the longing in his eyes. "It'd be nice to have brothers and sisters."

"They'd like that, too," Sarie said with a smile. She stood. "What do you say, Seb?"

After a moment, he nodded.

"Children, come and meet your new brother," Sarie called.

Laurel and Creede were forced back as the four youngsters gathered around Seb. Dickens brayed, diverting Laurel's attention. An idea blossomed.

"Ezekial, would you like a mule?" she asked.

The big former slave blinked in confusion. "We can't afford no mule. Hardly nobody got them no more. Most of Mr. Wollings' was used for eatin'."

"Would you like that one?"

Laurel couldn't tell who was more surprised by her offer, Creede or Ezekial.

The ex-slave shook his head firmly. "We ain't gonna take no charity."

The color of a man's skin didn't matter when it came to pride.

"You'd be doing me a favor," Laurel said. "I really don't have any need for him, but I don't want to sell him to someone just so they can use him for meat. You'd have to promise me you'll treat him well and not butcher him. That's my price. Do we have a deal?"

The man's gaze darted between her and Dickens. "It don't seem right."

"It's my mule and I can name my own price. Besides, it'd be good for Ada to ride until her foot heals. Do you want him or not?" Laurel pressed, afraid she'd change her mind if she didn't get him to agree quickly.

Ezekial glanced at Sarie, who gave a slight nod. He turned back to Laurel and squared his shoulders. "We'd be right proud to take him, Miz Laurel, and we'll take good care of him, too."

Laurel swallowed the lump in her throat. She and Dickens had been through a lot together, but she'd never planned on keeping him. It's just that she hadn't expected to feel so miserable when she got rid of him. She forced a smile. "Let me get my things, then he's all yours."

Creede went with her to remove her bags from the mule's packframe. The cat was nowhere in sight. Laurel figured he wasn't as fond of children as the mule.

"You don't have to do this," Creede said in a voice that wouldn't be overheard.

"Do *you* want Dickens?" she asked, arching an eyebrow.

"Hell, no."

His immediate and vehement reply made Laurel chuckle, easing some of her misery.

"But I thought *you* wanted him," he said.

If things were different, Laurel probably would've kept him. But once she delivered the rest of the messages, she'd have no reason to keep him, and she had no home for the stubborn mule. To divert her melancholy, she asked Creede, "Did I ever tell you how Dickens got his name?"

He shook his head.

"Whenever Dickens was hitched to the ambulance wagon, he was an angel. But the rest of the time, he acted like the devil. The men used to ask him what in dickens got into him. One day somebody just started calling him Dickens and it stuck." She shrugged. "If I hadn't taken him after the War, he would've been butchered for meat. After he had served so well, I couldn't let that happen to his ornery hide."

Shaking his head, Creede set the two bags from Dickens's back on the ground. "You sure about this?"

No she wasn't. But she was relieved to give him to someone who would care for him. And Seb would be happy to keep his newfound friend. All in all, it was the best solution, especially since she had no intention of becoming attached to anyone or anything again.

"I wanted to find the right home for him, and I did that." She dug out her journal and tore out an empty page from the back of the book. With a blunt pencil, she wrote on the paper.

Creede rested his arms on the mule's back and said in a low tone to Laurel, "They get hungry enough and they might eat Dickens steaks."

Laurel kept her attention on the paper. "No. Ezekial will keep his word."

"How can you be so sure?"

Laurel paused and gazed at the former slave, trying to imagine what his life had been like. But just as with Seb, she couldn't fathom belonging to someone or having everything she did dictated to her. "He's a free man now and that means more to him than you and I can ever understand. And as a free man, he gave us his word. He'll keep it."

Although Creede didn't appear convinced, Laurel was certain she'd made the right decision. She finished writing then stood in front of the ugly, temperamental mule. She gently clasped his big ears and leaned close.

"You saved a lot of soldiers during the war and now it's time for you to take it easy." She rested her forehead against the mule's. "These folks will treat you well, so you behave for them, you hear me? And watch out for Seb."

With a quiet sniff, she straightened and led Dickens over to Seb, who stood in the midst of Ezekial and his family. She held out the rope to him, then handed the older man the paper. "He's yours. And here's the bill of sale proving you own him."

Ezekial stood there, looking stunned for a long moment. "Thank you," he finally said. "We ain't never gonna be able to repay you."

"Just take care of Seb and the rest of your family."

"Yes, ma'am." He adjusted his makeshift haversack across his wide chest. "None of us is blood-related, least-ways, not that we know. But when all of us was set free by Mr. Wollings, we made us our own family." He gazed at Seb. "And Seb's just as much kin as the rest of us."

Laurel was struck by his simple but sincere declaration. The defeat of the South had freed them, but their victory was a double-edged sword. There was no work and no food, but now they had the freedom to choose whom to love.

"Godspeed," the former slave said.

"Godspeed," Creede echoed.

Laurel hugged Seb but wasn't surprised he didn't recip-rocate. She hoped he'd get more comfortable with his new family. "Take care of yourself and Dickens," she whispered to the boy, tears thickening her voice.

"I will, Miz Laurel," he assured her in a grown-up voice.

Laurel released the boy and stepped back to stand be-side Creede, who put an arm around her shoulders. Grate-ful for his support, she leaned against his side.

Ezekial lifted Ada with her sore foot onto Dickens's back and let Seb lead the mule up the road.

"They won't have an easy time of it," Creede said.

"No, but at least they have each other."

Creede smiled. "And Dickens."

As if hearing his name, the mule turned to look back at them one last time. He brayed once, then he, Seb, and their new family disappeared around the bend.

$\mathcal{S}$EVENTEEN

FOUR days later found Laurel, Creede, and the cat across the Mississippi River traveling through Arkansas. Setting up camp the night before they reached Pine Hill, Laurel fell into their usual routine. Creede took care of the horses while she gathered wood for a fire and started their meal.

Living in such close proximity to Creede continued to play havoc with her emotions. On one hand, she found his company comforting and his concern for her heartwarming. However, those same traits combined with his masculine appeal kept her body pining for his touch.

She thought of the few kisses they'd shared and her face flamed hotter than the cookfire. The nights, which had been difficult because of her nightmares, were doubly so with the attraction that sizzled between them. She'd seen his hungry looks and recognized them for what they were—he wanted her as she wanted him.

"Smells good," Creede commented.

She glanced up, following his long, lean legs to his trim hips and waist, and higher to a well-proportioned chest hidden by a tan shirt. Although she knew he was at least thirty-five, he appeared younger and more fit than men ten years his junior. The only evidence of the tragedies he'd endured lay in his eyes and the creases in his brow. However, instead of detracting from his appearance, the etched lines only increased her attraction to him.

Flustered, she returned her attention to dishing up their supper, which was a rabbit Creede had shot earlier that afternoon. She gave the cat a small chunk of meat.

"I'm surprised you haven't named him," Creede said, motioning to the cat.

Laurel had been on the verge of giving him a name more than once, but each time she'd bitten back the inclination. If she gave the cat a name, it implied she planned on keeping him as a pet and she had no intention of doing so.

Don't let anyone get close or you won't survive.

It wasn't long after Robert's death that she'd learned that important lesson. Caring meant pain, and caring too much meant too much pain, so she'd buried her feelings so deep that most of the time all she'd felt was numb. Now, with the War over, that numbness was wearing away, leaving an aching pain in her soul.

"Why should I name him? He'll disappear one day, just like he appeared, and we'll never see him again."

Creede eyed her for a minute then shrugged. "He's your cat."

She opened her mouth to deny it, but realized she was petting the animal and his purr was soothing her in a way she hadn't even consciously recognized. Drawing her hand away, she concentrated on her meal and tried to ignore the cat as he butted his head against her arm.

However, when she lay down on her bedroll some time later, she wrapped an arm around the animal and held him close. His purring lulled her to sleep, and although she slept restlessly, his small comforting presence kept her from crying out during her nightmares.

CREEDE glanced over at Laurel, who rode stirrup to stirrup with him, as had become their habit over the past weeks. Her back was straight and she held the reins in her gloved hands with familiar ease. Her aloof gaze kept him at a distance as effectively as a stone wall between them.

What was going on behind her cool exterior? Even as long as they'd been traveling together, he had yet to figure out her silences. She'd allowed him glimpses of her soul, yet never more than brief insights. Although he respected her privacy, he grew frustrated with trying to determine what motivated Laurel Monteille Covey. Compassion? Honor? Guilt? All of the above . . . ?

He frowned to himself, knowing he'd never learn what drove Laurel unless she told him. And the chance of that happening was pretty damned small.

Focusing on their peaceful surroundings, Creede listened to the clopping of their horses' hooves and the occasional swish of a tail. The buzzing insects created a steady background drone and birdsong would occasionally arise from the trees. His head drooped in the sun's warmth.

A rifle shot broke the tranquility. Creede's drowsiness snapped under the harsh hammering of his heart. He yanked his reins, drawing Red to an abrupt stop, and listened for a second blast.

Laurel halted, too. Her eyes were wide as she searched the area around them. "That was close. Do you think it was a hunter?"

Creede considered her guess. "Since there was only the one shot, probably." He sent another probing look around them but didn't see anything. "Let's keep moving."

His senses attuned to every little nuance in the woods, Creede led the way down the narrow road. Even if it was a hunter, that didn't mean they were out of danger. Laurel's dun-colored horse could easily be mistaken for a deer. His blood ran cold at the thought of Laurel being hurt.

A quarter of a mile later the sound of something crashing through the brush brought Creede to another stop. Instinct made him draw his revolver.

A person burst out onto the road. It took a moment for

Creede to realize it was a boy about fourteen years old. His clothing and hands were covered with blood.

"Help me," the boy said frantically. "Please, you gotta help."

"What happened?" Laurel asked.

"My grandda. I-I shot him." Tears trailed down his cheeks. "I d-didn't mean to."

Creede holstered his gun and dismounted. He took hold of the kid's shaking shoulders. "Tell us what happened."

He gulped visibly and drew a bloody hand across his face, leaving a red mark behind. "We were huntin'. We ain't g-got hardly no meat left. I-I saw something and lifted my rifle." Fresh tears coursed down. "It went off. I k-killed my grandfather."

"Are you certain he's dead?" Creede asked, keeping his voice firm to offset the kid's hysteria.

He blinked and shook his head. "I d-don't know."

"Take us to him," Laurel ordered.

The boy nodded and took off back into the trees and Laurel followed. Swearing under his breath at her impulsiveness, Creede climbed back onto his horse and hurried after them. Branches snatched at him and scratched his arms and face, but he barely noticed them. He caught up to Laurel and stayed close, so close he almost collided with her mare when Jeanie stopped abruptly.

Laurel was off her horse before Creede could settle his own mare. One look at the prone body on the ground told him the boy hadn't made up the story. Creede jumped down and joined Laurel, who had already opened her saddlebag. She pressed a cloth against the older man's oozing shoulder wound then took Creede's hand and placed it on the makeshift bandage.

"Keep pressure on it to stop the bleeding," she ordered.

He did it without question. Laurel carefully rolled the older man onto his side so she could check his front. She swore softly, using words Creede was surprised she knew.

"The bullet is still inside," she said.

"Is he goin' to die?" the boy asked fearfully.

Laurel's determined expression softened. "Not if I can help it. How far away do you live?"

He pointed to the west. "'Bout two miles that way."

"Do you have a wagon?"

He nodded. "But we had to sell our mule."

Laurel was afraid the wounded man would lose too much blood in the time it took to get him back to their home. "All right." She forced a smile. "What's your name?"

"Todd."

"Okay, Todd, I'm going to have to get the bullet out so I'll need you to build a fire. Can you do that?"

"Yes, ma'am."

"Go on then," she urged.

With one more look at his grandfather, Todd began to gather twigs and branches.

"He can ride double with me to his place and I can hitch my horse to their wagon," Creede suggested. "We can get a doctor to get the bullet out."

"We don't have enough time."

The wounded man's face was pale, almost waxen.

"Can you remove the bullet?" Creede asked.

She kept her gaze averted. "I don't have a choice. If I don't get it out he's going to die. Even if I do, I'm not sure he'll survive."

Disturbed for some reason he couldn't pin down, Creede watched Laurel work. He realized he was getting an idea of what she'd been like working as a nurse. Her sole concentration was on the injured man as she cut away his shirt, while Creede continued to press down on the bandage to stop the bleeding. She spread two blankets on the ground and he helped maneuver the injured man onto them.

Once Todd had a fire going, Laurel had him heat water until it was steaming. She washed her hands and immersed a razor-sharp knife and some cloths in the hot water.

"Todd, I'm going to need you to talk to your grandfather. Even though he's unconscious, I believe he can still hear you. You need to keep him calm and tell him we're helping him," Laurel said.

His young face grave, Todd nodded. He started speaking in a quiet voice to his grandfather, first apologizing for what he'd done then reassuring him he was being taken care of.

"Creede, I'll need your assistance while I'm looking for the bullet. Just do as I say." Confidence exuded from her voice and echoed in her actions.

"All right." He removed his hat and gnashed his teeth. He wasn't a stranger to gunshot wounds, but he'd never helped anyone dig out a bullet.

The first cut Laurel made with the knife sent Creede's stomach into a slow roll and he swallowed back the rise of bile. He forced himself to observe her steady hands and sure movements, and to ignore the oozing blood and stringy tissue beneath the skin.

"Dab the blood away," she said.

Startled, Creede reached for a large cloth, but Laurel motioned to the smaller squares. "Use those."

Stifling his queasiness, he cleaned the blood from around the wound. It didn't take him long to become engrossed in the surgery and he soon recognized when the wound needed the blood cleared away so Laurel could see what she was doing.

Sweat rolled down Creede's face. He noticed Laurel, too, was perspiring, and without being asked, he patted her forehead and chin with a clean dry cloth. Her startled look and quick nod thanked him, but she didn't spare him any more attention. Her entire absorption was on her patient, as if by will alone she could save him.

In what felt like days later, Laurel finally fished out a misshapen piece of metal. She held it up with her forceps then set it on the makeshift tray.

Creede retrieved the needle and thread from the pot of hot water and passed it to Laurel. Fifteen minutes later she tied a knot in the thread, effectively closing the wound. Creede helped her place a clean bandage on it then tied it on with another cloth around the old man's chest and back.

"We'll have to check the bandage every hour or so," Laurel said.

"Is he gonna be all right?" Todd asked with a raspy voice.

"I've done all I can. Now it's up to your grandfather."

Creede pushed himself to his feet, barely stifling a groan. He was getting too damned old to be kneeling on the ground for two hours. Noticing Laurel's less-than-graceful motions, he hooked a hand beneath her elbow and helped her up. She planted her hands on her lower back and stretched, producing more than one pop.

"I'm getting old," she said wryly.

"Not from where I stand," Creede said with a smile that left no doubt as to his meaning.

She blushed, which he found endearing after her self-assurance during the surgery.

"If you'd like to take Todd back home and bring back the wagon, I think it's safe to move his grandfather, as long as we use a lot of blankets to cushion him," she said.

"I don't like the idea of you staying out here by yourself. Why don't you go with the boy? I'll keep an eye on the old man."

She propped her hands on her waist. "Will you know what to do if he starts bleeding again? Or has trouble breathing?"

Creede shook his head reluctantly. "But you don't know something will happen."

"And you don't know something won't. No, I'll stay here and you take Todd back to get their wagon. Take Jeanie, too. She can help pull the wagon."

"If you stay, your horse stays," he stated with no room for argument.

Stubbornness glinted in Laurel's eyes but Creede knew his own expression matched hers. He didn't like leaving her out here alone with a wounded man, but he sure as hell wasn't going to leave her without a means to escape if someone happened upon them.

She looked away first and surrendered gracelessly. "All right, but I won't leave him."

It was all Creede could do to restrain the urge to shake some sense into her. "Damn it, Laurel. Don't risk your life for someone who might not even survive."

"It's my life to risk."

Frustration made Creede spin on his heel and stalk back to his horse. He leaned against Red's back, resting his forehead on his saddle seat. Why did he bother? What was Laurel to him besides someone to escort to Texas? Yes, she'd seen his son at the last but she had nothing to give him—none of those precious words she gifted other families. If he had an ounce of brains, he'd ride off and leave her to her fate.

So why didn't he? Because she would attract every ruffian in a fifty-mile radius. Because Laurel Covey was too damned compassionate for her own good. Because against all common sense, he was falling in love with the frustrating, exasperating, beautiful woman.

Sighing in resignation, he straightened and walked back to the boy, who remained by his grandfather's side. Laurel was cleaning up the things she'd used to retrieve the bullet, but he kept his gaze away from her.

"Let's go and get your wagon, Todd," Creede said.

"But—"

"You'll ride double with me, then we'll hitch my horse to the wagon and bring it back."

Todd's face lit up and he said a few more quiet words to his grandfather then joined Creede.

"We'll be back in an hour, two at the most," Creede said to Laurel.

"Remember to bring blankets so we can make him as comfortable as possible," she said, not looking at him.

Creede nodded and strode back to Red with Todd on his heels.

*   *   *

LAUREL stretched and rubbed eyes that felt like someone had poured a pail of sand in them. Heavens, she was
tired. Too many nights of disturbed sleep and too many
days filled with long hours of travel.

Restless, she checked the old man's wound for the third
time in less than two hours. There was only a small spot of
blood that had already dried on the bandage. He'd remained unconscious the entire time and she was starting to
worry that perhaps he had a head injury she couldn't de-
tect. However, he was older and his body was probably
having a difficult time dealing with the strain.

Annoyed by how long it was taking Creede to return
with the wagon, she paced the small area, but never going
so far that she couldn't see her patient. With nothing to do
but wait, Laurel found her thoughts spinning with memories she'd worked hard to bury. The faint call of a bugle's
retreat floated through her and she found herself looking
around to assure herself it was only in her mind.

But a few moments later, the woods disappeared, to be
replaced by a tent surrounded by stretchers, each one bearing a wounded soldier. She shook her head to rid it of the
too-real pictures and fought down the panic that accompa-
nied her loss of control.

"Laurel!"

Creede's call was a welcome diversion and she turned
toward it. He walked through the brush, leading Todd, a
woman who looked to be his mother, and a girl younger
than Todd by a year or two.

"Where's the wagon?" Laurel demanded, unable to curb
her irritation.

"On the road. The trail was too narrow to bring it
through."

Laurel should've realized that. Jeanie had barely made
it through the brush and trees when she'd followed Todd.

"We'll have to carry the old man out to it," Creede said
in a low voice. He pointed to the strangers who'd returned
with him. "That's Todd's mother Elizabeth and his sister

Jane. The old man is Henry, Elizabeth's husband's father. Her husband died in the War."

She nodded absently, watching the family gather around the patriarch. After checking her father-in-law, Elizabeth joined them. Although she was probably younger than Creede, the lines in her face added ten years.

"Thank you for savin' his life," she said in a surprisingly genteel voice. "I don't know what we'd a done if we lost him, too."

"He's not out of danger yet," Laurel warned. "The wound will have to be watched closely until it's healing properly."

"If you can help us get him home and show me what I need to do, I'll make sure he gets the care he needs."

Laurel was impressed by the woman's mettle. "I'd be more than happy to show you."

Between the five of them, they carried Henry the hundred feet to the wagon and got him settled on the blanket-covered floor. Creede drove the wagon while everybody else walked beside it, including Laurel, who led Jeanie. Elizabeth fell back beside her to speak.

"You're not from the South," Elizabeth said, but there was no condemnation in her tone.

"That's right," Laurel admitted. She'd forgotten to use a drawl. "I'm originally from Massachusetts. My husband was from Virginia."

Elizabeth's gaze traveled to Creede. "He doesn't sound like a Virginian."

"Oh, no, my first husband," Laurel corrected then realized she was insinuating she and Creede were married. She mentally shrugged. "He was an officer in the Confederate army."

"He's dead?"

"That's right. Three years now."

"I lost my husband two years ago at Chancellorsville. I wasn't certain I'd be able to go on without him, but his father and the children gave me strength." Elizabeth glanced at her father-in-law in the wagon. "Henry was devastated by his only son's death, but he's raisin' Todd like he was his own." Her expression crumpled. "Then this happens. I know it was an accident, but sometimes it seems like God has cursed us."

Laurel grasped Elizabeth's hand with her free one. "God doesn't curse folks. I think things happen for a reason, even if we don't know what it is at the time."

"You sound like a good God-fearin' woman."

Laurel tried to remember the last time she'd prayed, and failed. She managed a smile. "We each do what we have to."

They walked behind the wagon in companionable silence, although it was made tense by Henry's uncertain condition. For all those she hadn't been able to save during the War, she hoped she could give this family, who'd already lost a husband and father, the life of their loved one.

Thirty minutes of walking brought them to a respectable farm, complete with a milk cow and some chickens. After Laurel checked Henry to ensure his wound hadn't broken open during the trip home, they carried the old man into the house. Elizabeth directed them to a bed in a corner of the main room and they laid him there.

As soon as he was settled, Henry groaned and his eyelids flickered open. Elizabeth leaned over him and spoke in a quiet, soothing voice.

Suddenly the interior seemed too close, too dark, and too much like the inside of a hospital tent. Laurel's heart tripped into her throat and she fought to keep the panic from surging forth. She hurried out of the house. The late afternoon sun slanted down and she breathed deeply of the fresh air.

She heard footsteps behind her and knew Creede had followed her outside.

"Mrs. Hudson asked us to supper," Creede said.

Laurel froze. "What's her name?"

"Elizabeth Hudson."

Bethie.

"Do you know her?" Creede asked.

She shook her head. "No. But I knew her husband."

$\mathcal{E}$IGHTEEN

May 7, 1863. Corporal Hank Hudson from Pine Hill, Arkansas. Wounded by a rifle ball at Chancellorsville on May 3. Thirty-four years old, brown hair, hazel eyes, missing middle finger on left hand. Cause of death: hemorrhaging after right leg was amputated. "I wished to God I hadn't signed up and I'm damned sorry I ain't gonna make it home. Don't you take any guff, Bethie, but then you never did, not even from old man McConnell. The place is yours free and clear so our boy can have it once he's old enough. Take care of yourself and the young'uns." (Necklace with locket.)

CREEDE leaned against a porch post, facing Laurel. How did she know? The answer came in a flash. "His is the next message."

"We must not be far from Pine Hill," she said by way of a reply and her entire body sagged. "I should've suspected it was her when she said her husband was killed at Chancellorsville."

"How could you have known? Besides, does it matter? The important thing is you've found her."

She straightened but he could see the effort it took for her to do so, and he admired her all the more for it.

"Remember what you said about maybe it was better not to reopen old wounds?" she asked. "That what I'm doing might be hurting rather than helping the families?"

Creede stirred restlessly. "I remember. I was wrong."

Puzzled, she tipped her head. "How can you say that? You saw Mrs. Smith's reaction."

"What about the other folks?"

She recalled each visit, remembering the tears more than anything. "Some were grateful, others weren't. But I brought grief to all of them."

"So you think they might've been better off not knowing their husbands and sons were thinking of them at the last?"

She flinched. "I don't know."

Creede took a deep breath and laid his hands on Laurel's taut shoulders. "I know that if Austin had left me a message, I'd want to hear it." His chest felt battered and torn. "Yeah, it'd hurt, but it'd be worth it to know Austin's last thoughts before he passed."

She studied him with anguished eyes. "I wish I could give you that."

His throat grew tight and he glanced away, not wanting her to witness his despair. She carried enough burdens on her slim shoulders. "You can't stop, Laurel." He brought his gaze back to her. "In a way you're like my wife, Anna. She had more faith than ten men."

Laurel looked past him. "I'm not anything like her. I lost my faith a long time ago."

"No. If you had, you wouldn't be risking your life to deliver those messages you carry in that book of yours."

She laughed, but it was a bitter, painful sound. "That's not faith. That's having nothing left to live for."

Creede's heart missed a beat. "You're still a young woman, Laurel. You can remarry and have children." Although it hurt him to think of her with another man, her unexpected comment triggered protective instincts that ran deeper than jealousy.

She pressed her palm to the center of her chest and whispered, "There's nothing left in here." Then she returned to the house.

Stunned, Creede remained rooted to the porch. How could she think she had nothing to give a man? How many times had he barely restrained himself from taking her in his arms? It was only the cold hard fact that she deserved someone who had more to offer that kept him from loving her.

Todd came out of the small house, swiping his arm across his face. Suddenly he noticed Creede and his cheeks turned beet red.

"How's your grandfather?" Creede asked.

"Right enough, considerin' I shot him."

"It was an accident."

"It was stupid," he said, his voice filled with self-reproach. "Didn't listen to Grandda."

Creede managed a smile. "Seems to me I did a lot of stupid things, too, when I was your age. You learn and move on."

"Bet you never shot your grandda."

He hadn't, but then he'd killed two men intentionally. He'd shot other men, too, simply because he'd been paid to do so. That was before he'd realized that life wasn't cheap and nobody had the right to take another person's.

"No, but I did other things I'm not proud of." He paused. "What would your pa say if he was here?"

Todd thrust his fists into his overall pockets. "Don't matter since he ain't." Anger vibrated in the kid's voice and body.

"Let's get the horses rubbed down," Creede said, diverting Todd's attention.

The boy didn't reply but plodded after Creede, who led Red, still hitched to the wagon, down to the run-down barn.

"Why don't you take care of Miss Laurel's horse?" Creede suggested.

They worked on their individual animals in companionable silence. Creede removed the traces from Red, who tossed her head indignantly when he led her into the corral.

He joined Todd, who had unsaddled Jeanie and was now brushing her. The boy pointed to another brush on a post and Creede nodded his thanks then began to curry his own sorrel mare.

"You know your way around horses," Creede commented, keeping his tone light.

Todd grunted and Creede waited. His patience was rewarded a few minutes later.

"Pa used to train horses for folks. He was teachin' me how to do it afore—" Todd's voice broke. "Afore he went off to fight."

"Did he grow any crop?"

"Some corn and cotton. Grandda helps in the fields, but he's gettin' old. And now he's gonna be laid up." Todd sniffed but Creede couldn't see his face. "Guess that leaves me to take care of it."

Creede flashed back to the time when he was a year or two older than Todd and had taken on a man's responsibility. It hadn't been easy and, like he'd told the boy, he'd made mistakes. "You just do what your pa would've done and you'll be fine."

He wondered what message Todd's father had left for his family. If Creede had been given a chance to leave a message for his son, what would he have said? How did someone put a lifetime of words into a final note?

"I used to get mad at Pa, always talkin' about treatin' other folks right even when they treated us like we was no good," Todd said. "I don't think he wanted to go off to fight, but he figgered it was his duty. I only seen Ma cry twice—first time was when Pa left."

"When was the second time?"

Todd stroked Jeanie's neck. "When she got word Pa was dead." Vulnerable bravado filled the boy's eyes. "I never cried."

A lump filled Creede's throat and he swallowed it back. "There isn't any shame in crying. Fact is, when I heard my son was killed, I cried." He didn't tell him he needed to get drunk to do so.

Todd stared at Creede in disbelief. "Men don't cry."

"Who told you that?"

He shrugged. "Other boys."

Creede went around his horse to face the boy. "They're wrong, Todd. Crying doesn't make you less of a man. It makes you more of a human being."

Todd drew his arm across his overly bright eyes. "I miss him, Mr. Forrester."

"I know," he said softly.

Todd's shoulders shook and he leaned against him. Creede closed his eyes against his own renewed pain and put his arms around the boy, letting him grieve.

Once the boy's sorrow was spent, he pulled away from Creede. He kept his gaze downcast as he wiped his face with his hands.

Knowing Todd was embarrassed, Creede gathered the two curry brushes. "Why don't you put these away? I think the horses have been spoiled enough for a day."

Todd took them and hurried into the barn. Creede left the corral, closing the gate behind him.

Todd rejoined him as he started to the house. "You stayin' on for a while?"

"We'll probably head out tomorrow unless Laurel thinks we should stay longer."

"I never knew me a woman doctor before."

"She's not a doctor. She nursed soldiers during the War."

"I wonder if she knew my pa."

Creede glanced down, unwilling to lie but knowing it wasn't his place to tell the boy about the message Laurel carried. "You'll have to ask her."

At the door Todd dragged his feet. "What if Grandda's gone?"

"Somebody would've come out to tell us." Creede gave him a nudge. "Go on. Maybe he woke up."

"He's gonna be mad."

"I think he'll be more worried than mad." If Austin had accidentally shot him, Creede would've been more concerned for his son's feelings than his own injury. He hoped Henry felt the same way.

Laurel stepped out of the cabin, wiping her hands on a towel. Her bright expression told Creede the older man was faring better.

"I was just coming to look for you," she said, gazing at Todd. "Your grandfather wants to see you."

"Is he—" Todd began.

She smiled reassuringly. "He's going to be fine, but don't talk long. He needs his rest."

"Yes, ma'am."

The relieved boy hurried inside.

"Glad to hear the old man will be all right," Creede said.

"I wasn't sure, but he's a tough old coot." A smile tempered her words, but faded away. "His son Hank was a fighter, too."

"You remember him?"

Haunted eyes caught his. "I remember all of them." She shook her head, as if she could physically remove the memories. "I told Elizabeth we'd spend the night."

"When are you going to give her the message?"

"This evening, after dinner."

After their earlier conversation, he was relieved she decided to do so.

"How many are left after this?"

"One."

Startled, Creede hadn't realized how close to the end they were. "The last one's in Texas?"

She nodded.

Creede's palms dampened. He was headed home, yet was that what he wanted? Or did the revolver at his hip hold his future? And what about Laurel? His vow to lead her safely to Texas would be fulfilled, but what would she do then?

"Creede?"

Her tone told him she'd been trying to get his attention. "What?"

"I asked if that was all right with you."

"It's your decision, Laurel."

She frowned. "I thought you'd be excited to be going home."

Funny how she could guess his thoughts, even if she couldn't sense the accompanying mixed feelings. "I have fifty acres of cotton ready for harvest, but it just doesn't seem worth it anymore."

"But it's your home."

He didn't have an explanation for her so he lapsed into silence.

"Have you seen the cat?" she asked after some minutes of quiet.

"Not since we ran into Todd and his grandfather."

She crossed her arms, holding them snug against her waist. "Do you think he'll find us?"

Creede noted the worry in her tone. "He hasn't lost us yet."

Laurel's apprehension didn't abate and there was forced nonchalance in her shrug. "Or he's gone. It doesn't matter."

Her words said she didn't care, but her actions told him otherwise. How many other times had her words and actions been at odds?

"I'd best show Elizabeth what she needs to do for Henry."

Laurel returned to the cabin, leaving Creede alone with his thoughts.

AT dinner, Elizabeth suggested that Laurel and Creede sleep in her bedroom. However, it gave Laurel the colly-wobbles to think of sleeping in the same bed where a soldier she'd watched die had lain with his wife. Perhaps she was being foolish, but her stomach wouldn't let her accept Elizabeth's offer.

The barn was out of the question with its sagging roof and leaning walls. So, since the night was so balmy, Laurel and Creede decided to sleep outside.

While Elizabeth fed her father-in-law, Laurel helped

Jane wash the dishes and Creede took Todd outside to check on the horses and set up a campsite.

Jane was a painfully shy girl of twelve years old who gazed up at Laurel like she was some kind of heroine. It made Laurel uncomfortable but she didn't know how to dissuade the girl from her awe.

Finally, the long silence ended when the last dish was put away. Jane immediately disappeared into the loft where Laurel assumed her bed was located.

Elizabeth came away from the bed in the corner and set Henry's empty bowl in the basin. "I swear being shot didn't hurt his appetite any."

Laurel smiled. "That's a good sign. If he eats, rests, and drinks what he's supposed to, he'll be up and around in no time."

Elizabeth's plain round face lit with gratitude. "We were blessed that you and your husband were close by when it happened."

"It was fortuitous," she said awkwardly. The reason Laurel had been in that location weighed heavily on her mind.

"Henry has been a godsend since Hank's been gone. Without him, I don't know what we would have done."

"It helps that you own the place free and clear."

Elizabeth froze in mid-nod and her gratitude was replaced by wariness. "How'd you know that?"

Laurel cursed her loose tongue. She brushed a wavy tendril back from her brow and swept it behind her ear. "I told you I was a Confederate nurse."

"Yes." Elizabeth's suspicion didn't lessen.

"I saw many soldiers die." Laurel took a deep breath. "Including your husband."

Elizabeth pressed a palm to her mouth. "You knew Hank?"

"Not well." She worried her lower lip. "He asked me to give you a message before he died. I wrote it in my journal."

"You've known all along?"

"Since we brought Henry back in the wagon," Laurel admitted. "I didn't think that was the time to tell you."

"So you came here to find us?"

"Yes. Your husband was one of twenty-one soldiers who asked me to give their families final messages." Laurel's stomach cramped and she was glad she hadn't eaten much for dinner. "I didn't mean to upset you."

Elizabeth clenched her hands together, but not before Laurel noticed they were shaking . . . almost as badly as her own. "Do you know what the hardest thing was for me when I learned he was gone?"

Laurel shook her head.

"Not knowin' about his last minutes." She stared out the window into the growing dusk. "I prayed he went fast but I couldn't stop the nightmares. I'd wake in the middle of the night after dreamin' of seein' him die slow and painful-like."

Laurel kept her expression blank. The last thing she wanted was for Elizabeth to know how close to the truth her nightmares were. "I'll get my journal."

She forced herself to walk, not run, out the door as the terrible memories assailed her once more. Her trembling increased and she frantically searched for a place where no one could see her.

Crossing the yard at a faster pace, she went around the corner of the old barn and sank down to the ground. She drew her knees up and wrapped her arms around them, burying her face.

As with the others, she could clearly see Private Hank Hudson. He'd been one of the older soldiers and he'd been more pragmatic than those barely out of boyhood. He knew he was dying, but didn't dwell on it. Instead, he'd talked about his family and how proud he was of his Bethie and his two children. He'd even told her a story or two about his father.

Laurel wrinkled her nostrils at the stench of putrefied flesh and blood. Why did she smell it now? It was in the past—the past she tried so hard to forget but couldn't. Yet it was so real that her belly lurched and she fought back the rise of vomit.

No, she couldn't let the madness take her yet. Just two more messages . . . She pushed herself to her feet and forced herself to breathe deeply. After the first few breaths, the vile smell disappeared, replaced by the earthy scents of damp ground and green plants.

Stiffening her backbone, she went in search of her journal and found it a few minutes later with her things at the campsite. Also in the bag was a necklace, which Hank had asked Laurel to give to his wife. Creede and Todd were creating a sleeping area by clearing away rocks and sticks. Creede kept the boy's attention away from her, which she appreciated.

With the journal and necklace clutched in her hand, she trudged back to the house. Although she wanted to get this done, she found anger and regret swirling through her in equal measures. What if she'd done something different— would Hank Hudson be alive today? Or would he have been like the embittered young man in Rounder who'd lost his leg?

She entered the house and smelled fresh coffee.

Elizabeth poured two cups and set them on the table. Holding herself stiffly, she sat down and motioned for Laurel to take the chair across from her. "I thought you might like some chicory. Lord knows I need it." She attempted a smile but failed.

Laurel perched on the edge of her seat and set the journal on the table. She held out her hand with the necklace nestled in the center of her palm. "He asked me to return this to you."

"That's the locket I gave him," Elizabeth whispered. She reached out, her hand trembling, and picked up the necklace. She opened the heart-shaped locket. "My parents gave this to me when I was sixteen. It has my picture and a lock of my hair in it. I-I thought it would . . . comfort Hank."

"It did. He had it in his hand all the time. He didn't give it to me—" Laurel cleared her full throat. "Until right before he died."

Elizabeth closed her hand around the locket and pressed it to her breast. Her gaze shifted to the journal. "Is that it?"

"Yes." Laurel laid her hand on the cover, gaining strength from the familiar leather binding.

"What did he say?"

Laurel took a deep breath and opened her journal to the blue ribbon. Her heartbeat echoed in her ears and she wondered if Elizabeth could hear it. She kept her voice low, so she wouldn't awaken Henry or allow Jane in the loft to overhear. " 'I wished to God I hadn't signed up and I'm damned sorry I ain't gonna make it home. Don't you take any guff, Bethie, but then you never did, not even from old man McConnell. The place is yours free and clear so our boy can have it once he's old enough. Take care of yourself and the young'uns.' "

Elizabeth turned to gaze out a window, giving Laurel her profile. A tear slid down her cheek. "Tell me, what did he die for?"

Her unexpected question gave Laurel pause. She'd tried many times to answer the same question, had discussed it with Creede, yet she still didn't have the answer. "For the South? For his beliefs? For you and the children?"

Elizabeth's attention shot back to Laurel and wrath burned in her eyes. "Don't you tell me that he died for me and the children."

Laurel drew back, startled by her outburst and even more shocked by the vehemence behind it. "I didn't mean to imply—"

"Then what did you mean? You were there. You saw hurt and dyin' men. Why did you keep nursin' them? What kept you from leavin'?" The woman's southern drawl was exaggerated in her anger.

The images bombarded Laurel anew, pictures of the battlefield hospital conditions—the grime and blood-covered men, the pile of amputated limbs, the woeful cries of the wounded. Every day she'd prayed it would end, but when it did, there was nothing left. And the reasons she'd remained were no longer clear.

"I wish I had an answer for you, Elizabeth, but I don't," Laurel said, her voice barely above a whisper. "Maybe I could've answered your question two years ago, but not now."

Most of Elizabeth's anger drained away. "Hank thought he knew, too, when he signed up. I tried to talk him out of it, told him it wasn't our war. That it didn't matter which politician was president—they all sat on their high and mighty thrones and declared a war they didn't have to fight. But Hank wouldn't listen."

"Maybe, but that doesn't make your husband's death meaningless."

Elizabeth leaned across the table. "How can you say that? You know what the War did to men like my Hank."

Because if their deaths were meaningless, then what I did was also without meaning.

"It doesn't matter if it was right or wrong, you have to respect what he did," Laurel said softly. "Maybe that's all Hank wanted."

Elizabeth pulled a handkerchief out of her apron pocket and blew her nose. "I loved my husband, Laurel, but I don't know if I can respect what he did."

Suddenly feeling exhausted, Laurel wondered anew if she'd done the right thing in giving Elizabeth the message. She'd obviously dredged up embittered feelings that hadn't been laid to rest with Hank's remains. She closed the journal and rose. "I did as your late husband asked and brought you his message. I'm sorry I caused you pain."

Elizabeth blinked rapidly. "I'm sorry, too."

Laurel retreated, leaving the woman with her renewed sorrow. Instead of helping, she'd hurt someone again. Did she have the strength for the final message? Or had she finally learned her lesson?

$\mathcal{N}$INETEEN

CREEDE awakened instantly and lay motionless in the dark, trying to determine what had brought him out of a deep slumber. Familiar night sounds—an owl hooting, insects trilling, and leaves fluttering—filtered through the layered stillness. Everything seemed normal. He turned his head to check on Laurel, whose bedroll was a tempting four feet away. The bed was empty, with no sign of the woman. Her shoes lay by her blanket, as did her neatly folded skirt and blouse where the cat lay curled, so she couldn't have gone far.

He sat up and searched for her among the shadows. Had she only gone off to relieve herself? He counted to one hundred slowly, but she didn't reappear.

"Laurel," he called, throwing back his blanket. "Where are you?"

No answer.

He tugged on his boots and put on his shirt, not bothering to button it, and stood. "Laurel," he shouted.

Still no reply.

Both concerned and angry, he strapped on his gunbelt and went in search of her. He called out her name and listened intently. After fifteen endless minutes, he heard the rustle of brush and followed the sound.

Laurel stood in the middle of a moonlit clearing, wearing only the undergarments she'd slept in. Her hair was unpinned, trailing down her back to her waist in thick waves. Creede's breath caught in his lungs at the silver glow that formed a nimbus around her figure.

"What are you doing, Laurel?" he asked, unable to hide the lust that thickened his tone.

She turned and surprise followed by confusion swept across her face. "Creede, what are you doing here?"

He frowned. "What are *you* doing here?"

"I work here," she replied.

Unease rippled through him. "What do you mean?"

She turned in a slow circle, gesturing outward. "All these men. So many hurt." Her voice broke. "The stretcher bearers are bringing more in. There are so many casualties. Can you help me get those we can save into the tent?"

Creede's heart hammered in his ears as he looked around, seeing nothing but the silhouettes of trees, grass, and bushes. "There isn't anybody here but you and me."

Laurel's brow creased and she frowned impatiently. "How can you not see them? They're all around us."

Fear brought sweat to his palms. He'd seen this type of thing one other time, after a man had lost his wife and children in a fire. The man had spoken to his family as if they were beside him. He'd taken his own life the next day.

"The War is over. There are no more injured soldiers." He inched closer to her.

"Can't you smell the blood? Hear them crying?" A tear rolled down her cheek, leaving a glistening silver trail in its wake. "We have to help them."

Creede reached for Laurel and his hands closed on cool flesh. She tugged, trying to escape, as her gaze skipped around them.

"Look at me, Laurel." She continued to struggle and looked everywhere but at him.

Using one hand, he gripped her chin and forced her to

face him. "Look at me, Laurel. The War is over. You're delivering messages to families of dead soldiers. Do you remember?"

The blankness in her eyes frightened him. He wrapped both arms around her and hugged her stiff body close to his chest, hoping the contact would draw her out of the delusion. "The War is over. There's no more killing."

She struggled against him, hands and feet lashing out, and he tightened his hold on her. He didn't want to hurt her, but he didn't want a flailing limb to strike him in a sensitive place either.

Suddenly her body sagged. He scooped her into his arms and her head lolled against his chest, where his shirt gaped open. Her warm breath puckered his nipple and he stifled a moan. "Are you back with me now?" he asked softly.

He felt her nod and relief poured through him. He couldn't see her expression, but at least she wasn't ranting about wounded soldiers. After he carried her back to their camp, he eased her down on her bedroll. She remained sitting up, but her neck was bent, her face hidden by a cascade of thick hair.

"Want to tell me what that was about?" he asked, fear making him curt.

She didn't speak and Creede tamped down his rising irritation. She obviously didn't even realize what was happening. To give her time to gather her composure—and his own—he built a fire. The cat had disappeared, leaving a depression in Laurel's folded clothing.

Creede removed his gunbelt and set it aside, then knelt beside her. He noticed her toes curling and wrapped his hands around her cold foot, intending to warm it. She jerked, but didn't try to draw away, and he massaged her sole and the velvety softness of her upper foot. When that one was warmed, he switched to the other foot, rubbing heat back into it.

Although Laurel didn't speak, he detected the gradual

relaxation of her muscles. Creede continued to caress her feet, one in each hand now. They were long and slender, a reflection of her tall, willowy figure. He grew hard at the intimate contact but ignored his body's insistence. Laurel needed a friend, not a man pawing at her.

"It was so real," she whispered.

Creede didn't push her. She'd continue if she trusted him.

She raised her head and swept her hair back from her face. "I thought I was back at the hospital. I could hear and smell and see everything, just like it used to be." A visible shiver passed through her.

"Has this happened before?" he asked gently.

She nodded. "I-I've been having nightmares for weeks, and a few times I woke up to find myself out of bed. But this time was the worst. I've never wandered so far before." Her breath hitched and a small sob escaped. "Why can't I forget?"

The aching vulnerability in her voice brought a lump to his throat. "You saw horrible things, Laurel, things most people can't even imagine. Your mind just can't forget so easily."

Her expression became distant. "I saw soldiers who couldn't forget. Some would just sit and stare for days on end. We had to force them to eat and drink. Others would lose their temper at the smallest thing. The doctors thought it was because of what they'd seen and done on the battle-field." Her eyes swam with tears. "But I wasn't a soldier. I didn't have to kill others or watch friends die."

Creede freed her feet and moved up to sit beside her. "No, but you saw other terrible things, including men dying painful deaths. Personally, I don't know how you were able work in those conditions."

She managed a small, watery laugh. "Obviously, I didn't handle it well or I wouldn't be going crazy."

"You're *not* going crazy."

She studied him, her eyes softening, and rested her hand against his cheek. "You're a good man, Creede Forrester."

He recalled the lives he'd taken, not caring if those men had mothers, fathers, wives, or children waiting for them. "No, I'm not."

"You're not the same man you were then."

Her words did little to ease his conscience, but the tenderness in her expression and the womanly curves revealed by her thin undergarments brought other thoughts to the fore. "Maybe not, but what I'm thinking right now isn't exactly what a good man should be thinking on."

She tipped her head to the side. "And what are you thinking?"

"That I want to kiss you."

Her eyes widened and the dark circles within them reflected the firelight. Then she leaned forward and pressed her pliant lips to his. Unable to stop himself, Creede wound his arms around her and deepened the kiss. He swept his tongue across her mouth and she opened, allowing him to enter her warm depths.

Laurel placed her palm on the center of his chest, reminding Creede he hadn't buttoned his shirt. However, he felt no repentance when her touch sent sparks racing through his body. The fire settled in his groin, in the erection that pressed against his trousers.

Although he'd known her for only a month, he'd wanted her for most of that time. But the want was different than the relief he craved from the few women he'd paid since he lost his wife. No, he wanted every part of Laurel that she was willing to share with him, and, greedy bastard that he was, even that which she didn't want to share.

He leaned back to catch his breath and she followed him, like a flower seeking the sun. Wanting to draw out the pleasure, he took control gently. He eased her down on the bedroll and lay over her, his legs straddling hers. Laurel pushed his shirt off his shoulders and he shrugged out of it, letting it fall to the ground.

"I've dreamed of this," Laurel confessed as she splayed her fingers across his chest. "Of me loving you. You loving me."

The knowledge that she desired him made him throb in response. She smiled and thrust her hips upward, obviously detecting his interest. Suddenly uncertain, he raised his body, his weight balanced on his hands and knees.

"What is it?" Laurel asked.

"Do you know what you're doing?"

"I know that I want you." Blunt honesty shown in her face and in her voice's husky timber.

"Are you sure?" He glanced away. "Or is it only because of the nightmare?"

She considered his question. It was true that if she hadn't had the nightmare, they wouldn't be lying face to face, their denied desire and lust straining to be set free. Yet she'd been fighting the attraction since the beginning, and all the reasons she'd done so seemed empty now. "I'm certain, Creede."

With one last probing look, he made his decision. He leaned down to kiss her brow, her cheek, and ended up nuzzling her jaw. She squirmed, shocked by the sensitivity beneath her ear. Her body felt like a stranger, striving to meet Creede's kisses, begging to be touched . . . and to touch.

She slid her hands up his chest, reveling in the coarse hairs sprinkled sparingly across it, then slipped around to his back. His muscles rippled beneath the smooth skin.

Suddenly she was aware of his hand cupping her breast. Although the camisole's sheer material was little barrier for the fingers that played with her nipple, she wanted the undergarment gone . . . wanted Creede's hand on bare skin. She nipped at his whiskery jaw.

"Let me up," she whispered.

Creede drew back onto his knees, panting slightly. His expression was puzzled until he saw her reach for the hem of her camisole. Smiling, he pushed away her hands and tugged the garment off over her head.

His admiring gaze settled on her breasts and Laurel fought the urge to cover them. During the time she'd been married to Robert, he'd never seen her this way. He'd al-

ways sought release under the cover of darkness, as if seeing her nakedness was a sin. She wondered if she should be
ashamed by her wantonness, but Creede's fiery expression
melted away the shame.

He leaned down and flicked his tongue across her nipple. She sucked in her breath while arching upward, seeking his mouth. Skimming his hands down her torso, Creede
laved first one breast then the other. Laurel bit her lower lip
to stifle a passionate cry.

Untying the ribbon at the waist of her drawers, he slid
his hands inside them and pushed them down to her ankles.
He traced the bend of her leg, where it met her hips, and
she shivered at the contact. Need pulsed through her,
coursing through her veins and gathering at the juncture of
her thighs. She had forgotten how good it felt, had forgotten the all-consuming desire that demanded completion.

She gazed at the top of Creede's head as he dropped
kisses on her belly and lower, to the center of her passion.
When he swept his tongue inside her, Laurel's hips
bucked upward. Not even her husband had been bold
enough to do such a thing. The mind-robbing sensation
stole away any thoughts of the past and she buried her fingers in Creede's thick dark hair, urging him to continue
the exquisite torment.

He continued to lick her in the most intimate—and
exciting—manner she'd ever experienced. He was giving
her a gift, something she would never forget. Her passion
rose swiftly and overtook her without warning. She
screamed hoarsely, everything forgotten but the intensity
of pleasure.

Before she could regain her breath, she felt the drawers
tugged off her ankles. Through a kaleidoscope of colors,
she watched Creede remove the rest of his clothing. His
masculinity curved upward, hard and glistening in the
fire's light.

Creede settled between her legs and framed her face in
his large palms. "You don't have to do this."

She placed her own hands on his. "Make me feel alive, Creede."

He kissed her and she opened to him. As their tongues met, Creede shifted and entered her, moaning in his throat at the snug fit. He wasn't surprised when she thrust up to meet him. She wasn't a woman who did things halfway.

She gently bit his lower lip then soothed it with her tongue. "I won't break," she whispered.

"Like a willow, bending never breaking." He withdrew and thrust his full length into her. She raised her legs, fitted them around his waist, and pulled him in even deeper. The sensation made him harder, more eager to love her as she deserved to be loved.

"Please, Creede. I need you."

Her words shattered whatever remnants of self-control he possessed and he moved with her, falling into an exhilarating rhythm he'd never found with anyone, not even Anna. The inescapable caught him earlier than he'd anticipated and he buried himself deep as he emptied himself within her wet heat. She cried out again and pulsed around him, signaling her second release.

He gasped for air, pleased to see Laurel panting with him. After his heart settled to a slower pace, Creede lay down by her side. Curving his arm around her waist, he pulled her supple body close to his. Sweat sheened their skin and Creede couldn't resist tasting a droplet above her breast. A tremor skated through her.

"I need more than a minute to regain my strength," Laurel said.

He raised his head and saw a teasing smile on her swollen lips. He grinned in return. "Usually I do, too, but with you, I seem to be more than ready."

She lifted her head and glanced down the length of his body. Meeting his gaze, she arched an eyebrow. "Didn't you know men your age aren't supposed to be so randy?"

Creede nearly choked on her blunt question. He'd never met another woman as brash as Laurel, yet he found her sassiness intoxicating. Just as he found the rest of her impossible to resist.

He proceeded to show her what a man his age was more than capable of doing . . . again.

LAUREL awakened early the following morning. For a moment, confusion reigned as she tried to recall why she was so stiff and sore. Then she realized her head was pillowed by a muscular chest and her legs were entwined with masculine ones.

Her pulse shimmied with the memory of making love with Creede. Being a married woman as well as a nurse, she thought she'd known everything about sexual relations there was to know. However, Creede had shown her things she'd never known could be done between a man and a woman.

Remembering those things, she squeezed her thighs together. But that only rekindled the desire and she shifted again.

Creede moved and she raised her head to meet his half-lidded eyes. His crooked smile brought a mirroring one to her lips. "Morning."

"Good morning, sleepyhead."

He eyed the sun, which had already cleared the horizon. "Guess I am later than usual."

"We had a busy night."

He stirred and his morning erection brushed her thigh, making her inhale sharply.

"How are you feeling?" he asked.

The question held a number of meanings with an equal number of responses. "Fine," she simply replied.

"Do you remember the nightmare?"

Her burgeoning passion evaporated and she sat up, careful to keep her breasts covered by the blanket. "Parts of it."

Creede rose up to sit beside her. "I found you about a hundred yards from the camp. You thought you were back in the War taking care of wounded soldiers."

Restlessness seized Laurel, but she wasn't sure how to extricate herself from the blanket . . . and Creede. "That wasn't the first time I've dreamt about it."

"But it was the first time I've seen you walk in your sleep." He scrubbed a hand through his sleep-tousled hair. "You scared me, Laurel."

I scare myself.

"I'm sorry. I'll try not to let it happen again."

He cursed under his breath. "I don't want an apology."

She turned to face him. "Then what do you want?"

"I want to help you."

His plaintive reply misted Laurel's eyes and she glanced away. "And how can you stop *my* nightmares?"

"I don't know, but there's got to be something . . ."

Laurel sighed, suddenly tired even though she'd slept soundly—without nightmares—after making love. "Don't you think I've tried? They've only been getting more frequent and more real."

Creede seemed at a loss. "Isn't there somebody—some doctor—who might be able to help?"

She smiled without warmth. "I tried that, too. Do you know what he told me? He said that women shouldn't have been allowed to work so closely with the wounded soldiers since our nature is too sensitive. If my 'condition' worsened, he said he could remove my uterus. Do you know what that is?"

Creede shook his head.

"It's my ability to have children. What does a woman's uterus have to do with having nightmares?" she demanded although she wasn't expecting a reply.

He appeared stunned. "Is there anything else that could be done?"

Laurel liked the doctor's second option even less, although she suspected it was her eventuality. She kept her voice free of fear. "I could be put in a sanitarium for the rest of my life."

There, she'd told him. Now he knew why she couldn't marry or have a family.

Feeling sick, she grabbed her undergarments and pulled them on. Picking up her folded clothing, she donned those and her shoes, all the while keeping her back to Creede.

She wondered if he was revolted, knowing he'd made love to a crazy woman. If only she'd had more willpower. If only she'd been strong enough to resist him.

If only she could be normal and dream of a future with him.

"I won't let that happen."

Creede's low voice shocked Laurel into motionlessness. She swallowed and turned to look at him. "What?"

He stood and the blanket fell to the ground. Despite herself, she couldn't help but admire his body. Her heart missed a beat and reawakened passion surged through her blood.

"I won't let them put you into one of those places. You're not crazy," Creede said.

She focused on his words instead of the tempting expanse of his chest and the hair arrowing down the center of his torso to his groin. "You have no say in what happens to me."

He stepped toward her, his hands outstretched, and she retreated hastily.

"I would if you were my wife," he said softly.

Panicked fear shoved aside her growing desire. As noble as his offer sounded, she wasn't going to destroy his life along with her own. "I have no intention of becoming your wife."

"I can protect you, Laurel."

Although she wanted to shout, she kept her voice calm and steady. "No you can't. Nobody can." She held up her trembling hands. "We both wanted what happened last night, but that doesn't mean you owe me anything. In fact, you can leave this morning. I can find my way to Texas alone." She quaked at the thought of him leaving her, but she'd never expected him to stay with her this long.

Creede's jaw muscle flexed. "I said I'd get you safely to Texas, and I won't go back on my word."

Unable to show her gratitude, she nodded tersely. "Fine. But I don't expect anything else from you."

She spun around and marched toward the privy, ignoring the temptation to take one last look at Creede's exposed charms.

TWENTY

THE cool morning breeze reminded Creede to dress before one of the Hudsons came through the trees and spotted him. Grumbling under his breath at Laurel's
stubbornness, he donned his clothing. By the time he buckled on his gunbelt, his annoyance with her had faded to
concern.

Did she really believe she was going crazy? He hadn't
spent any time around crazy people, but she didn't strike
him as the type to lose her mind. She was too strong, her
will too formidable. Surely her nightmares were only
memories of what she'd seen during the War. Reliving
them at night didn't make her crazy, did it?

The thought of her in an asylum surrounded by insane
people brought a ball of ice to his gut. As sure as he was
that his name was Forrester, he was certain Laurel didn't
belong there.

She hadn't actually told him that was what would happen to her, but he saw the belief in her haunted eyes and
haggard features. She'd disappear into one of those places
and nobody would be the wiser. Her family didn't care, and

all those families she visited would remember the final words she brought them, but would forget her.

What about me? Would he be too busy selling his gun to the highest bidder . . . until the other side's hired gun was faster?

Disgust boiled in him and he balled his hand into a fist, striking a nearby tree. Pain radiated in his hand and up his arm. His knuckles stung and blood welled up where the bark had scraped off the skin. He held the throbbing hand in his other one, grateful to have something to take his mind off Laurel.

He wrapped the injured hand with a bandanna from his saddlebag and took care of his morning tasks. Just as he finished shaving, Todd entered the camp.

"Mornin'," the boy said.

"Morning." Creede wiped his face free of the remaining soap.

"What happened to your hand?"

"Me and a tree had a disagreement." He smiled ruefully. "The tree won."

Todd seemed puzzled, but didn't ask anything more. "Ma says breakfast is almost on."

"Thanks. How's your grandfather this morning?"

Todd grinned. "Miz Laurel says he's on the mend. She said Grandda has the constitution of a mule."

"That's good news, son. So, Miss Laurel is at the house?"

"Yes, sir. She's helpin' Ma with breakfast and Grandda."

That sounded like Laurel, always putting others first. "I'll be up as soon as I'm done here."

"I'll tell Ma." Todd disappeared through the trees.

Five minutes later, Creede entered the cabin and Laurel glanced at him, her gaze dashing to his wrapped hand. But other than a tightening of her mouth, she didn't acknowledge him. He knew her well enough by now to recognize her damned stubborn pride.

Breakfast turned out to be grits, hotcakes with butter and molasses, and fried eggs. Creede remained subdued throughout the meal as he observed Laurel and noticed how she kept her attention on Elizabeth, Jane, and Todd. She could ignore him now, but once they were traveling again, it would be difficult. Creede had until Texas to change her mind about marrying him.

His decision made, he finished eating, thanked Elizabeth, then went to get their gear loaded onto the horses. With a twinge of satisfaction, he noticed Laurel's confusion at *his* avoidance of *her*.

Todd helped gather their things from the campsite and saddled Jeanie. Creede enjoyed his company, but it bothered him that he didn't know if it was only because Todd reminded him of his own son. Anxious to have Laurel to himself and to leave behind the confusion Todd evoked, he went to retrieve her as soon as the horses were ready to travel.

In the house she was giving Elizabeth last minute instructions on how to care for Henry and what to watch for. However, when she spotted Creede she didn't waste any time saying good-bye to the family.

Creede tried not to notice the disappointment in Todd's eyes when he shook the boy's hand. "You take care of your ma and sister."

"And Grandda until he's all healed," he said solemnly.

His throat tight, Creede clapped him on the back and turned to Elizabeth. "Good luck, Mrs. Hudson."

"Thank you for savin' Henry's life," she said.

Although it was Laurel's experience that had saved him, Creede only nodded. Jane stayed back but she did give him a shy smile.

The cat waited patiently by the horses and once Laurel was mounted on her dun mare, Creede lifted the cat onto the back of her saddle. Then he climbed atop his horse for the final leg of their journey. There was only one more message, one more destination, one more chance to prove to Laurel she wasn't going crazy.

*　*　*

LAUREL knew Creede would continue the disagreement begun that morning, but refused to be drawn into it. She had experience in ignoring what she didn't want to acknowledge and used that skill to disregard his words. She also knew he grew more and more frustrated, but she didn't dare give voice to her dark thoughts. She'd already confessed too much.

After saying no more than a dozen words to him all day, Laurel prepared herself for another round of persuasive arguments that evening. However, silence hung between them. She cast furtive glances at him, but his expression was blank, his gaze locked on the flames. She knew she was being ridiculous, but she was disappointed when he remained mute.

With nothing to distract her, Laurel found her thoughts straying to the previous night. That she wanted a repeat of their lovemaking went without question, but what her body demanded, her mind denied. Her only comfort was that with the turmoil his nearness caused, the ghosts were kept at bay.

Without exchanging a word, Laurel and Creede settled into their respective bedrolls. The cat, which had filled out due to the food scraps he received, curled up beside her. The long day had taken a toll on Laurel and she fell asleep immediately, only to awaken a few hours later with a cry caught in her throat. The cat's eyes reflected the moon's light as he stared at Laurel, as if asking what was so important as to disturb his sleep. She petted the cat absently then wiped a hand across her damp brow and stood, intending to take a walk to clear the remnants of the nightmare. After last night's sleepwalking, she hadn't stripped to her underclothing despite the evening's warmth.

"Laurel?" Creede's voice was clear, not sluggish with sleep.

He'd obviously been waiting until her slumber was disturbed by nightmares. That he knew her so well irritated her, although she was more annoyed at herself for appreciating his concern.

"I'm going to take a walk. I won't go far," she said.

The fire had burned down, so she couldn't make out his face but suspected his gaze was on her dim figure. She didn't wait for a reply and crossed to where the horses were tied, her eyes adjusted enough to the darkness that she didn't stumble.

She hadn't intended to make a confession last night. But she was tired of fighting the demons and her exhaustion had made her vulnerable. Yet despite that, her burden seemed lighter today. Creede hadn't abandoned her like she'd expected. He hadn't even treated her any differently. He'd said she wasn't going crazy. Although she didn't agree, he'd placed a kernel of doubt in her mind.

She felt more than saw Creede join her, and was upset that her heart did a pirouette. After being independent for so long, it had taken her little time to come to rely on him.

"Another nightmare?" he asked quietly.

"It wasn't as bad as last night's."

He drew his hand along his mare's neck. "Want to talk about it?"

"No, but maybe I should." She laughed without humor. "Since you've already seen me in one."

"I saw a woman trying to cope with what she experienced during the War."

She eyed him, trying to discern his expression in the inky shadows. "How do you know so much about it?"

"You aren't the only one who has nightmares."

"You dream of what you did to those men who hurt your mother?"

"No. I dream of what *they* did to *her*, and of my wife being shot. And I dream of the men I killed after I started hiring out my gun."

The remorse in his voice brought moisture to her eyes that she blinked back. "So why did you start wearing your gun again?"

"What else do I have left?"

"Your farm. Your memories of your wife and son." She paused. "Your self-respect."

He remained silent and she sensed she'd struck a nerve.

"This wasn't supposed to be about me," he finally said. "We were talking about you."

"No, we were talking about nightmares." For some reason, they didn't seem as horrifying now. "Mine are always the same. I'm surrounded by wounded men and there's blood everywhere. I can hear them groaning and I can hear the flies buzzing. The smell is terrible—blood and rotting animal carcasses and decaying flesh. It's like I'm right there again."

"Maybe you were too busy to think about it then, but now it's all coming back to you."

"I have nightmares while I'm awake, too," she admitted in a low voice. "Everything will fade away and I'm in the hospital again."

"Those happen during the day?"

"Yes. Usually when I'm alone, though."

"Then I have to make sure you're never alone." His voice was husky, reminiscent of the previous night.

The thought of spending every day—and night—with Creede tempted her far more than it had before they'd made love. But doubts for her sanity remained and she refused to burden him.

"Why don't we try to get some sleep?" Creede suggested.

The lingering unease from her nightmare had faded and she nodded. "I think I might be able to do that now."

Creede guided her back to their camp with a hand at her waist. When they got there, he moved his bedroll next to hers.

"I'll be able to wake you if you have a nightmare," he said.

She didn't know if that was his sole reason, but her spirit was too battered to argue. She simply returned to her bedroll and Creede lay next to her, his body stretched out inches from hers. Without speaking, she curled against his side and with his familiar scent surrounding her, she fell asleep within minutes.

THE days passed in a blur of greens as they moved southwestward through the wilderness. Creede supplemented their dwindling food supply with an occasional rabbit. One afternoon they stopped early to camp beside a river. They feasted on fresh fish that evening. They also took advantage of the water and bathed and washed their clothes.

At night she and Creede placed their bedrolls close but there wasn't a repeat of their lovemaking. Laurel was grateful for his comforting presence, but found it increasingly difficult to set aside the passion his nearness evoked. In spite of Creede's assurances, she suspected their sleeping arrangements were just as taxing for him.

Six days after they left the Hudsons, they stumbled across their first town in Texas. As they rode down the main street, Laurel read the signs on the building fronts.

"Have you ever been to Colson?" she asked Creede.

He reined in by a hitching post in front of a small hotel and dismounted. "Once."

Laurel frowned at the curtness of the single-word reply. She wrapped Jeanie's reins around the post and stepped on the boardwalk. "When was that?"

"A lifetime ago."

The reason for his reticence became clear and she looked around, trying to see the town through his eyes. "Did you, uh, shoot someone here?"

He didn't reply. Obviously it was a touchy subject. Yet Laurel couldn't help but feel slighted that he wouldn't talk to her when she'd told him things she hadn't planned to share with another living soul. She bit down on her tongue to keep from venting her childish frustration.

"One room or two?" he asked as they entered the hotel.

Annoyed, she almost said two, but realized she didn't want to sleep alone. Although she still had nightmares, they weren't as bad when she slept with him, or maybe Creede woke her before they caused her to sleepwalk again.

"One." Because she was impatient with her growing reliance on him, her tone came out surly.

He gave her a questioning look that she ignored. If he couldn't figure out why she was upset, she certainly wasn't going to tell him. Of course, she knew she was being illogical, but her emotions continued to seesaw as they had for the past months—another symptom of what she assumed was encroaching insanity.

She stayed back while he acquired a room.

"Upstairs, two-seventeen," Creede said, holding up a key.

After carrying their things to the room, Creede volunteered to find a livery barn for the horses. Laurel was grateful for the time alone, which she used to sort through her things. In her saddlebag, she pulled out the cloth sack that held her journal and the last personal item to return to a family member. She withdrew the pocket watch and snapped it open for the first time since she'd taken it from the dead soldier's pocket. Inside was a tiny photograph of a man and a woman taken on their wedding day. The man was tall and lean and the woman slender and petite. She was unable to make out any facial details—they could be anybody.

Laurel heard the door open and slid the watch back into her bag.

"We should get our supplies now since we'll be leaving early in the morning," Creede said from the doorway.

"All right." Laurel found the reticule that held her money.

They walked to the mercantile, the silence between them strained. Once at the store, Laurel and Creede gathered the goods they'd need on the trail.

"What town are we headed to?" Creede asked.

Laurel searched her memory. "Robles."

Creede's sharp inhalation sent her gaze to his face, which had gone stony.

"Have you been there?" she asked.

"My farm's near there," he replied, his voice gravelly. "Who is it?"

"Private Lyman Eaton." She'd read the names often enough to have them memorized.

His tanned face paled. "Goddammit." Although his voice was quiet, vehemence twined through it.

She didn't need to ask him if he knew the name. "Who is he?"

He turned and stumbled out of the store. Laurel started to follow him.

"What should I do with all this?" the clerk asked, motioning to the supplies spread across his counter.

Torn, Laurel wavered between leaving and staying. Knowing they needed the staples, she returned to the counter. "How much do I owe you?"

He gave her the total and, without hesitating at the exorbitant amount, she paid him.

"That man you're with. He looks familiar," he began.

"He has a farm here in Texas," Laurel replied.

The clerk cackled. "Texas is a big state, ma'am. What's his name?"

She considered not telling him, but he could easily get the information from the hotel. "Creede Forrester."

"Forrester? You sure?"

"Yes, I'm certain," she said with more than a hint of impatience.

"Been some time since I heard that name."

"What do you mean?"

"Quite a few years ago Orville Standish was having some problems. Hired Forrester to take care of them."

A chill swept through her. "That was a long time ago."

"That it was and it's a good thing Ben ain't around no more."

"Who?"

"Ben Larson. He was the one Standish was havin' problems with."

Despite herself, Laurel wanted the details. "What did Mr. Forrester do?"

"Killed Larson's oldest boy," he replied matter-of-factly. "Old Ben swore he'd get Forrester someday, but his heart gave out not long after his son passed."

Creede had told her about his sordid past, yet hearing about it from someone else made it more real, more . . . deplorable.

"Didn't know that, eh?" The clerk seemed smug that he'd been able to pass on a juicy piece of gossip.

Laurel composed her features. "Mr. Forrester told me what he'd done as a younger man. He's changed."

The older man shrugged. "Maybe so, but it don't change the fact that he killed an eighteen-year-old boy."

Her stomach heaved but she managed to maintain her composure. "I want these things delivered to the hotel, room 217."

"That'll cost ya a dollar," he replied.

Her patience frayed, Laurel gave her temper free rein. "If you don't deliver these items—for which I paid three times the normal price—for free, I want my money back and you can take these supplies and ram them up your rectum." She leaned across the counter. "Which would you prefer?"

His Adam's apple bobbed up and down and sweat pearled his brow. "No problem, ma'am. I'll have a boy bring them to the hotel this afternoon."

Feeling only a small measure of satisfaction, she nodded but kept her flinty gaze aimed at him. Only when he looked away did she leave.

She dashed onto the boardwalk but Creede was nowhere in sight. With her shoulders slumped, she trudged back to the hotel. Fortunately, he'd given her the key, so she'd be able to get into their room.

At the top of the stairs she looked down the hall and spotted Creede leaning against the wall beside their door. Relieved to see him, but discomfited by what the clerk had told her, she joined him. He glanced at her and she was glad to see his face had lost its pallor. She entered the room and Creede closed the door behind them.

Laurel kept her questions bottled up inside and returned her reticule to her saddlebag. Looking for things to occupy her, she checked the bed sheets and was pleased to see they were clean. She walked around the room and ran a finger across the windowsill, the bureau, and the chair, noting the layer of dust. However, she was overly aware of Creede's presence and knew when he removed his gunbelt and when he perched on the edge of the bed, even though she wasn't looking at him.

Creede broke the silence. "He was Austin's friend, the one he ran away with to join the army."

Laurel suspected as much after she'd seen his reaction to the name. She recalled the date she recorded Austin's death and knew it was the same day Lyman had died. She'd been right all those months ago—the boys had been friends who ended up dying together. Her stomach clenched at the tragic loss of the two young men.

"I'm sorry."

"Me, too." Creede threw his hat across the room in a fit of rage. "Lyman's folks were the ones who were all-fired up about him joining the army. Austin and Lyman were best friends most of their lives, so it was easy for Lyman to talk my son into joining up with him. Hell, when you're sixteen you think you know everything and you won't ever die."

Laurel sat beside Creede and grasped his fisted hand that pressed into his thigh. "He could've just as easily joined the army on his own. I didn't know Austin but he might have thought he had something to prove."

"What did he have to prove? He was my son, for God's sake."

"Why did you kill those men who hurt your mother?"

He fixed his fiery gaze on her. "What does that have to do with Austin?"

Laurel ignored the question. "When those men hurt your mother, you thought you disappointed your father."

"He was dead."

"It didn't matter. You still had to prove to him that you were a man. By killing them, you figured you did that. Maybe Austin wanted to prove to you he was a man, too."

"I didn't want him to join the army."

"No, but it was probably the easiest way to prove himself."

Creede laughed harshly. "So easy it killed him."

Laurel didn't know what else to say so she lapsed into silence and held his hand. She remained beside him, trying not to think about how their thighs touched or how large his hand was within her smaller one or how that same hand had touched her so intimately.

A knock on the door sounded and Laurel was grateful for the interruption. She brushed a hand across her warm cheeks and rose to open it. A boy stood there holding several packages. "Mr. Dobbins told me I was to bring these things here."

"Just set them over there." Laurel pointed to a spot on the floor by her bags.

The boy did as she asked, then waited.

Creede withdrew a coin from his pocket and tossed it to him. "Thanks, kid."

The boy grinned and scooted out, slamming the door behind him.

"Sorry about leaving you with the supplies," Creede said with a wry smile.

Laurel crossed her arms. "That's all right." Curiosity got the better of her discretion. "The clerk—Mr. Dobbins—recognized you. He said you took care of a problem for someone named Orville Standish a long time ago."

Creede's face lost all color.

Again.

$\mathcal{T}$WENTY-ONE

THE past rushed back to Creede with the force of a locomotive. When he'd realized what town they were in, he
wondered if anyone would remember him. Just his luck
Laurel would run into the one person who did. "I told you
what I used to be."

She continued to study him, like she didn't know
him . . . like she hadn't lain beneath him, her face flushed
with passion, less than a week ago.

"I know. I just never expected to meet someone—" she
finally glanced away. "Someone who knew you then."

Despite his disappointment with her reaction, he
shrugged nonchalantly. "It was bound to happen sooner or
later once we hit Texas."

"Do you remember the bo—man you killed?"

"It was a long time ago. I tried to forget that time."

"So why are you thinking about becoming that man
again?" Her challenge was delivered with a lift of her chin.

For the first time, he truly realized what he'd done when
he buckled on his gunbelt again. He'd taken a step back to
the man he'd once been—a man he didn't even like, much
less respect. If he took another step back and hired out his

gun again, the man who'd been Anna's husband and
Austin's father would no longer exist. There would be nobody to lay flowers by their crosses.

Sick with the thought, Creede snatched his hat from the
floor and strode out of the room. His vision blurred and he
could barely make out the walls and stairs. Halfway down
the steps, he realized he'd left his gunbelt in the room. He
also realized he didn't need it. Laurel was right. He had the
memories of his family and he had his cotton farm. And
more important, he had his self-respect.

He scrubbed his face with his palms and continued out
onto the boardwalk. With no destination in mind he simply
walked and thought about the tattered remnants of his life.
He could see things clearer now, not distorted by grief and
anger. No longer did he want to sell his gun or make a
woman a widow. He wanted the peace and quiet of his farm.

And he wanted Laurel with him.

Now all he had to do was convince her.

LAUREL paced their room, counting the steps even
though she knew how many there were after the first fifty
times. Shadows stretched across the scuffed floor from the
single window. What could Creede be doing that took so
long in this small town?

Her face burned with the obvious answer and she
dropped onto the bed. No doubt he'd found a saloon and a
friendly, willing woman. Although jealousy surged through
her, she couldn't blame him. Creede had done nothing to
inspire fear, nor had he hidden what he'd been. So why had
she behaved like some blushing virgin when confronted
with his past—the past he himself had told her about?

A sharp rapping startled Laurel and she hurried to the
door, expecting Creede. Instead, a woman maybe ten years
older than herself stood in the hallway. Although her dress
was clean and neat, it was faded from too much wear. Her
face, however, was smooth except for laugh lines at the
corners of her eyes, but she wasn't smiling now.

"I'm looking for Creede Forrester," she said.

Laurel frowned, wondering how she knew Creede. And how she'd known to come here to find him. "He's not here."

"Who are you?"

"Laurel Covey. And you?"

"Felicia Dunn."

The name didn't mean anything to her. "Why are you looking for Mr. Forrester?"

"That's between him and me." Although the words were terse, her voice shook. "When will he return?"

"I don't know."

"May I wait for him?"

Curiosity impelled Laurel to invite her into the room. "Why don't you sit down?"

Mrs. Dunn perched on the edge of the chair. It seemed she would've preferred to be anywhere but here, so why had she come?

Laurel eased down onto the edge of the mattress as her mind puzzled over the woman and managed to put some pieces together. "Which one did you know, Orville Standish or Ben Larson?"

Mrs. Dunn blinked, clearly startled. "Did he tell you?"

So Laurel was correct in her assumption. "No. The store clerk did. I didn't know Cre—I only met Mr. Forrester a month ago."

"Mr. Forrester killed my fiancé."

Laurel's heart clenched. "Your fiancé was Ben Larson's son?"

"Jeffrey. We were supposed to get married the Saturday after Mr. Forrester shot him."

"I'm sorry." Laurel wondered anew why a woman, after nearly twenty years, would seek out her fiancé's . . . killer. She glanced down to see a wedding band on the woman's left hand. "But you're married now?"

The older woman nodded and some of her tension was replaced by pride and love. "Yes. For nearly seventeen years. We have four children."

"So why do you wish to see Mr. Forrester?"

Mrs. Dunn's gaze faltered and dropped. "I-I made a promise to someone."

Laurel understood promises.

The door opened and Creede stood silhouetted in the opening.

"Laurel, what's—" He broke off when he spotted the woman. "I didn't realize you had company."

Mrs. Dunn stood, her stare locked on Creede. "You're older than I remember."

Creede stepped inside and closed the door. "Do I know you?"

"Not really. I remember seeing you around town." The woman blushed. "At the time I thought you were handsome and exciting. Until you killed Jeffrey Larson."

Recognition flooded Creede's features and he nodded woodenly. "You were engaged to marry him."

"Yes."

"He tried to shoot me in the back. He missed. I didn't."

So Creede hadn't killed in cold blood. Why had he let Laurel believe he had?

Mrs. Dunn bowed her head. "I know. His father died a month later. He made me promise . . ." She reached into her purse and pulled out a derringer, which she aimed at Creede.

Laurel's hand flew to her mouth. Even though it was a small gun, at such close range Mrs. Dunn could easily kill him. However, Creede's expression didn't falter.

"Promise what? That you'd kill me?" he asked.

"You were all Mr. Larson talked about from the time you shot Jeffrey until his heart stopped. He hated you."

"I can't say I'm sorry the old man is dead. He was full of mean and Jeffrey was the same. You knew how they were." His expression gentled. "That bruise you had on your face wasn't from running into a post."

Mrs. Dunn closed her eyes briefly. "You're right. He used to hit me." She straightened her shoulders. "I know this makes me a bad person, but I was glad you shot him."

"Then why kill Creede?" Laurel demanded.

"You didn't see Mr. Larson at the end. I think he would've fought with the devil himself if I hadn't promised to do this."

"It's in the past. You don't owe Ben Larson anything," Creede said.

That Mrs. Dunn didn't want to kill Creede was obvious, but a deathbed promise was a hard one to break.

"Do you want your children to grow up without their mother?" Laurel asked. "Or your husband to grow old with someone else?"

She flinched. "No."

"Then forget about the promise you made. A decent person wouldn't make another person commit murder."

"The Larsons weren't worth it then, and they aren't worth it now," Creede added, his tone oddly gentle.

The woman bowed her head and her arm fell to her side, the derringer slipping from her limp fingers. Creede leaned over to pick up the small weapon and opened it up, only to discover the chamber was empty.

"You weren't going to kill me," he said.

She raised her gaze to him and smiled feebly. "I can't even kill a mouse."

Relief made Laurel lightheaded.

"If I ever thought I'd see you again, I wouldn't have agreed to Ben's demand." Mrs. Dunn's smile was shaky. "When I went into the store, Mr. Dobbins couldn't wait to tell me about you."

"He always was a gossipy bastard." Creede sighed. "For what it's worth, I wish I could change what I did. I was young and stupid, and didn't understand that life wasn't cheap."

Mrs. Dunn laid her gloved hand on his arm. "We all did things we're not proud of, Mr. Forrester. I'm ashamed I wasn't strong enough to refuse making such a promise to Mr. Larson, and I'm even more ashamed I came here. Long ago, I realized I was much better off than if I'd married Jeffrey."

Laurel stood and was surprised her knees didn't wobble. She'd faced situations more dangerous than this, but never had she cared so much for the outcome. If Creede had been shot and killed . . . She shoved the fear aside.

"You're a strong woman to be able to admit that," she said to Mrs. Dunn.

The older woman faced her. "No. It's just that I'm not as weak as I was then. I have to leave. My husband is probably at wit's end waiting for me."

Creede held out his hand with the derringer nestled in his palm. "This is yours."

She grimaced. "No, it was Ben Larson's. I never wanted it."

"I'll take care of it." He opened the door for her and Felicia Dunn departed.

A vacuum of silence was left in her wake.

"Are you all right?" Creede asked.

"Fine. It wasn't me she wanted to kill."

"You heard her. She didn't want to kill anyone. It was all because of a foolish promise she made."

Laurel nodded. "Have you ever had someone else come after you because of your past?"

His eyes became opaque. "Once."

"What happened?"

"They killed Anna instead of me."

Laurel gasped.

"That's the reason Austin believed I was a coward," Creede confessed. "He said if I'd been wearing my gun, she'd still be alive. Maybe he was right, but if I'd done that, I would've gone against what Anna wanted." The furrows in his brow became more evident, making him appear older.

Laurel wanted to hold him and soothe the lines from his face. She wanted to make things right for him, but as for herself, nothing could ever be the way it used to be.

"I made a decision," he said.

Startled, she glanced up. "What?"

"I'm going back to my farm. I should get there in time for the cotton harvest, and with any luck I'll make enough to get by until next year."

Laurel's gaze strayed to his gunbelt hanging from the hook. "What about that?"

He sighed and weariness added to his haggardness. "Austin thought I was a coward for packing away my gun, but Anna had convinced me it was the braver man who fought his battles without weapons. Maybe there's a middle point in there."

"If there is, you'll find it."

Laurel's stomach growled and Creede grinned. "Would you like to get something to eat?"

After the stress of the day, Laurel was startled to find she was starving. She smiled. "I'd like that."

Creede escorted Laurel out of their room, and she noticed he didn't even glance at his gunbelt hanging on the hook.

THE third morning after they left Colson, the skies filled with bloated storm clouds. Despite the muggy heat, Laurel pulled on her slicker before they rode out of camp. The cat didn't seem to mind being covered by it as he rode curled on the back of her saddle.

"We only have about ten miles to my place," Creede said at mid-morning.

The excitement in his voice brought a bittersweet lump to Laurel's throat. Both their journeys would end—he would return home and she would . . . do what?

"How far is it from there to the Eaton home?" she asked, unwilling to think beyond the final message.

"Only four or five miles."

They rode in silence for nearly an hour.

"So what will you do after you deliver Eaton's message?" Creede asked.

"I haven't thought about it," she lied.

"Yes, you have. You're still planning on putting yourself in one of those asylums, aren't you?"

She glanced away. "I don't know."

"You didn't have a nightmare last night."

Ever since she'd talked about the nightmares, they had lost some of their terror. She hadn't had a spell in days, either.

"You're not going crazy, Laurel."

It didn't surprise her that he knew what she was thinking. "The brain is a complicated thing," she began quietly. "There was a soldier who had a minie ball lodged in his head. Everyone thought he'd either die or be unable to do anything for himself. He healed without any problems." She threaded Jeanie's reins through her gloved fingers. "But there were others who didn't appear seriously wounded who either died or became raving lunatics." She frowned. "Then there were those who didn't have a single wound but who lost their minds because of something they saw or experienced."

"You're not losing your mind."

Laurel smiled. "You've almost convinced me."

He appeared pleased, but puzzled. "So what will you do after you've visited the Eatons?"

"I don't know," she repeated. "But I can tell you I won't work as a nurse again."

"Why?"

The horror of choosing who lived and who died sent a shiver through her. That was the one secret she'd shared with no one. How could she confess that it was her decision that brought death to some soldiers, including a few of those for whom she'd delivered messages?

"It would bring back too many memories," she finally said.

Creede lapsed into silence. Laurel's own thoughts remained murky as they rode.

The lightning in the distance drew nearer, and the rolling thunder rippled through her, increasing in volume and fury. Then the first raindrops fell and it didn't take long to become a deluge.

"My place is only a mile away," Creede shouted above the storm.

Laurel wiped a hand across her wet face and nodded.

Although she knew Creede well after the weeks of traveling together, she was nervous about seeing his home—the place he'd been a husband and father.

It wasn't long before a gathering of buildings came into view. Her heart hammering against her ribs, Laurel followed Creede to his home. He stopped in front of a barn and opened a door, then led his chestnut horse inside. Laurel followed, riding Jeanie into the building. Creede lit a lantern and slid the door shut.

The air inside was musty after being closed up for so long, but Laurel was grateful for the dry refuge. The rain pounded on the roof, but the barn was solid and no wetness leaked in. She dismounted and quickly set to work taking care of her horse. Creede took Jeanie's saddle from her and showed her to the tack room. She hung the bridle from a hook and turned to see Creede standing motionless, his gaze on a small, well-worn saddle.

"Was it your son's?" she asked quietly.

Creede nodded. "His first one. I had hoped Anna and I would have more children, but . . ."

The anguish in his tone brought mist to Laurel's eyes. "I suppose coming back here is difficult," she said awkwardly.

He finally turned to her. "I knew it would be. When I left here all I knew was that Austin had been injured. I thought I'd be bringing him home. Instead, I have nothing, not even his body."

Laurel was glad she'd never had children. To lose one would be an agony she never wanted to experience. However, another part of her ached for a child of her own. If she and Robert had been able to conceive, perhaps she wouldn't have spent the past three years surrounded by death. Instead, she would've been raising a daughter or son and experiencing life rather than death.

They walked back into the main part of the barn and brushed their horses, then picked up their bags. The thunderstorm hadn't abated and they ran across the yard, skirting the worst of the puddles. Laurel removed her dripping slicker, left it on the porch, and followed Creede inside.

Laurel's first impression of his home was one of comfortable warmth. In front of the fireplace sat two wooden rocking chairs draped with colorful blankets. On the mantel a carved rearing horse stood, obviously made by young hands, and a framed picture of two people. Above the mantel hung a needlepoint of a house with a verse stitched in cursive beside it, but she couldn't read it from across the room.

"I know it isn't much, not what you're used to," Creede said awkwardly.

She turned and smiled. "I've spent the last few years either in a tent or in a dormitory with other women. This is by far the nicest place I've been in a long time."

Whether he believed her or not, he seemed to appreciate the compliment.

"It's pretty dusty," he said with a grimace.

"Nothing some water and soap won't take care of." She set her bags against a wall and rolled up her sleeves. Cleaning was something she had control over. "We've got half the day left to get things in order."

The afternoon passed quickly as they worked together to rid the home of the months of accumulated dust and dirt. That evening after everything was done, including their meal, they each sat down on a rocking chair. The rain continued to patter on the roof, providing a lulling background. Laurel was exhausted from the physical labor, but it was a satisfying tired.

"This could be your home, too," Creede said softly.

She wasn't prepared to argue with him now. "No. It's yours and Anna's and Austin's."

"Anna and Austin are gone and this place will be damned lonely by myself."

"Then find another wife."

"I found the one I want."

Laurel's head suddenly pounded. "We've already gone over this, Creede."

He leaned forward, his elbows on his knees. "You're not going crazy, you have nobody to go home to, and you'll fulfill your promise when you deliver the last message. What else is there?"

"I still have nightmares. I don't know if those will ever go away." She clenched her hands. "It hurts to care for people. I had to teach myself to keep from growing fond of my patients. I lost my husband and family. I don't want to feel that kind of pain ever again."

"And you think I don't know what that's like?"

Irritated and chagrined, Laurel could deal easier with the irritation. "I didn't say you didn't. But you and I are different. I can't forget."

"I can't either, but that doesn't mean I can't move forward. I don't want to grow old alone."

Annoyance flared to anger. "Then get a dog, or find another woman. I can't marry you."

"Can't or won't?"

"It doesn't matter." Laurel's anger drained away. "I'm tired. Where should I sleep? I think it's better if we discontinue our traveling sleeping arrangements." Embarrassment made her stiffly formal.

He stared at her and she had to look away from his too-perceptive eyes. She heard him sigh and he rose.

"You can have my room. I'll sleep in Austin's."

"Thank you."

As they each made up their beds with fresh linens, the only sound in the cabin was the falling rain.

CREEDE rocked gently in the chair he'd made for Anna over seventeen years ago when she'd been expecting Austin. He recalled watching her nurse their son at her breast and the awe he'd felt at the tiny child they'd created. It seemed that was another life he'd lived, when he'd been a different man. Just as he'd been a different man before he'd married Anna. And just as he was a different man now.

He'd been unable to sleep in Austin's bed, surrounded by the boy's things—his slingshot, a rabbit's foot, carved animals in various stages. Everything but Austin himself.

So he'd come out to sit only to have memories ambush him here, too. Laurel had been right—it was difficult to return.

Knowing she was in his bed made it hard in other ways, too. He imagined her hair fanned out across his pillow and the moonlight shining upon her face. There was no doubt he loved her. His love was no more and no less than what he'd had for Anna, but it was different.

A muffled groan from his bedroom caught his attention and he was moving to the door before he'd even made the decision to do so. Laurel hadn't closed it and he pushed it farther open to check on her. Just as he'd imagined, her hair was spread out around her and the moonlight gilded her skin, but her wretched expression was one he never wanted to see again.

He sat on the edge of the bed and placed his hand on her shoulder. "Wake up, Laurel. It's only a dream." She thrashed back and forth and he spoke louder to break the nightmare's hold. "Laurel! You're dreaming. Wake up."

Her eyes widened and it took a few moments for comprehension to seep back into her features. She wiped her damp brow with a shaking hand. "Another nightmare." It wasn't a question, merely a statement of fact, delivered with impatience.

"I heard you," Creede said.

"Were you even sleeping?"

He frowned at the brusque question. "No. I was sitting in the front room."

"Waiting for me to have a nightmare again?" Her sarcastic tone cut deep.

Creede shook his head, his own temper flaring. "I hate to tell you this, but you're not the only person I think about." He reined in his anger. "I was thinking about Austin and Anna."

Laurel's expression crumpled. "I'm sorry. I-I just wish these nightmares would go away."

Creede brushed her cheek with his fingertips. "You said they weren't as bad when you slept with me."

"I can't sleep with you the rest of my life."

Yes, you can. Creede bit the words back. "While you're here, you can."

Her gaze fell to his chest and he suddenly remembered he was bare from the waist up. "I'll put a shirt on."

He stood, but she clasped his wrist. "Don't." She drew her tongue along her lower lip, leaving it glistening in the silvery light.

He groaned and joined her on the bed.

CREEDE awakened before Laurel. In the early dawn light, he studied her swollen lips and lax features, so different than the terror during her nightmares. They'd made love long into the early morning hours and had fallen asleep as the rain tapered to a gentle patter. The light along the eastern horizon told him the clouds were gone, taking the rain with them.

Reluctantly he rose to take care of nature's call. After tugging on his pants and boots, he hurried out to the privy and returned, hoping to lie with Laurel for another hour or two. As he took off his boots, he spotted a pocket watch spilling out of her saddlebag on the dresser. Curious, he picked it up, and an odd sense of familiarity filled him. With a shaking hand, he popped open the spring to reveal the watch face and a small photograph. It was too dark to make out the image, so he carried it to the window and held it up to the weak light.

His heart skipped a beat then pounded in his chest. He recognized himself and Anna. She'd gifted him with the watch on their wedding day and had put their picture in it later. Creede had given the pocket watch to Austin on his sixteenth birthday and he had taken it with him when he'd joined the army.

His gaze jumped to Laurel. She must've taken it from Austin after his body had been brought to the hospital. Why had she hidden it from him?

Her journal. Maybe the answer was in there. Keeping

quiet, he opened her saddlebag and found the cloth sack he'd seen her carry the journal. He paused, his conscience prodding him. He had no right delving into her private thoughts. However, she had no right withholding Austin's watch from him.

His resentment overcame his conscience and he carried the journal outside to the porch. Wearing only his trousers, he sat down on the top step and with the pocket watch in one hand, he opened Laurel's journal with the other.

TWENTY-TWO

March 25, 1865. Private Lyman Eaton from Robles, Texas. Mortally wounded at Fort Stedman. Dark brown hair, blue eyes, sixteen years old. Cause of death: grapeshot in the abdominal area. "My pa was right about killing . . . the War. Tell him that he's the bravest man I know." (Pocket watch with picture in it.)

CREEDE reread his son's—not Lyman Eaton's—words over and over until Laurel's writing blurred. He raised his head, oblivious to the tears that trailed down his cheeks. He stared at the horizon, at the orange and pink and gold behind the trees that heralded a new day.

What was the last thing Austin had seen? Had it been Laurel? Or maybe a blue sky with white fluffy clouds? When Austin was young, he and Creede used to lie on the ground and find shapes in the clouds. Austin's imagination had been vivid and his excitement contagious. Some of Creede's most treasured memories were those stolen moments during a busy day.

Austin understood. In the end, he'd finally seen what

Anna had taught Creede, who in turn had tried to pass it on to their son. There was no glory in war and killing, no matter how noble the cause.

Yet Creede owed it to Austin to honor his life and his death. If he didn't, his son would have died for nothing and he could never do that to his memory.

A mourning dove cooed, its plaintive call echoing Creede's pain, the pain that came with the first strains of healing.

Light footsteps alerted him to Laurel's presence but he couldn't look at her. Her mistake had nearly stolen these precious last words from his son.

"What are you doing?" she asked.

Creede cleared his tight throat. "I'm reading my son's deathbed message."

She moved into his side vision. "Your son was dead when he was brought in."

"Lyman had light-colored hair, not dark." He opened the hand that held the pocket watch, the hand closest to Laurel. "And the picture in here is of Anna and me on our wedding day."

Laurel gasped. "But the ration card . . ."

Creede wiped his damp cheeks with a shaking hand and turned to look up at her. He recognized the blanket wrapped around her as one from the bed. "What ration card?"

Her face was the color of a sun-bleached bone. "I used the soldiers' ration cards to determine their names. It was always in their jacket or pants pocket."

"You mixed them up," he said flatly.

"I-I don't understand."

He stood and stared down at her. "If I hadn't seen the watch, you would've taken my son's message to Eaton. You would've read the words to the wrong man."

A frantic note crept into her voice. "But I remember. The ration card was in his jacket and the watch in his trouser pocket."

"Then the boys must have been wearing each other's

coat," Creede stated flatly. Although he was upset with Laurel, he couldn't imagine she would purposely switch the boys' names.

"How many others did I get wrong?" she asked, her voice filled with self-loathing and her eyes glistening.

He wanted to reassure her, but the wound in his heart was too raw. He closed Laurel's journal and held it out to her. She took it with a hand that trembled as much as his and enfolded it close to her chest.

"I'll put on some coffee," Creede said and walked into the house.

Laurel couldn't face him, not after she'd nearly given away the one thing he wanted most, even if her mistake had been an honest one. She heard him using the hand pump in the kitchen and sank down onto the step he'd vacated. Staring unseeingly into the distance, Laurel invited the ghosts to visit.

She recalled the boys' deaths with sharp clarity, how the sky was dark with smoke from cannons and guns like so many other mornings. The mule-drawn wagons started coming in early with injured soldiers. Austin and Lyman had been brought in with the second group of casualties. Austin—no, Lyman—had been dead, but Creede's son had lived long enough to give her his message.

She saw the gaping belly wound and smelled the nauseating stench of Austin's perforated stomach and intestines. Could he have been saved if she'd gotten him to the doctor right away? Her mind told her no, but her heart wasn't so certain. Even if her mind was right, there were others she'd condemned to death because she'd had to choose. The doctors only wanted those whom they had the best chance of saving. If they spent too much time on the badly wounded soldiers who would probably die anyhow, less severely injured men would also die. Laurel understood the reasons, but it hadn't hurt any less.

How could she even consider a future with Creede when Austin might have been saved if she'd picked him? Striking blue eyes stared accusingly at her . . .

She blinked and returned to the Texas morning. Father and son had the same crystal blue eyes. She'd thought Creede's looked familiar when she'd met him, but she'd ignored the feeling. But there'd been other clues, too, as Creede had told her more and more about himself and his son. Why hadn't she put them together?

Opening the journal to Austin's entry, she read aloud the final words to his father. "My pa was right about killing . . . the War. Tell him that he's the bravest man I know."

She bowed her head and closed her eyes. Creede's wish had been granted and she was more than grateful that he could find peace. But now there was nothing left for her to do. All twenty-one promises had been carried out.

Feeling heavy as lead, Laurel pushed herself upright and went into the bedroom. As she dressed, she wondered how she could even face Creede. She'd made a horrible mistake. Perhaps she'd mixed up more names. How many families had been given messages not from a loved one, but from a stranger?

What if she hadn't fulfilled her promises after all?

Methodically, she made up the bed then stuffed her things into her bags, including the journal Creede had read. Although she was upset he'd done so, she couldn't muster any real anger. He'd righted her wrong. However, she was grateful he hadn't read the other journal—the one where she'd recorded her own personal thoughts and confessions. That one she kept buried under her extra clothing, hidden from all but herself.

Unable to find anything else to delay her facing Creede, she straightened her spine and walked out to the kitchen. He sat by the table, a cup in one hand, the pocket watch in the other. She found the cup he left her and filled it from the pot.

Remaining by the stove, she sipped the steaming coffee. She glanced over to see Creede's gaze locked on her, but there was no expression in his eyes, eyes the identical shade of blue as his son's. Struggling with her guilt, she looked away.

"He finally understood," Creede said softly.

Laurel nodded. "Your son had courage."

"How—" He cleared his throat. "Was he in a lot of pain?"

She raised her head. "There's no reason for you—"

Creede struck the table with his fist and coffee sloshed over the cup rim. "Damn it, Laurel. I have a right to know what his last minutes were like."

She didn't want to add to his sorrow, but she couldn't deny his request either. "Abdominal wounds are painful and your son was conscious right up to the end. I held his hand. His grip was so tight, like if he hung on hard enough, the pain would go away." Laurel paused, feeling phantom fingers like vises around hers. "He asked me if he was going to die. I wanted to lie, but I couldn't. That's when he gave me his last words to pass on to his father—to you."

She expected to see tears on Creede's sun-darkened face, but there was only poignant sadness.

"Are you going to visit the Eatons?" he asked.

The unanticipated question threw her for a moment. "Why would I do that? The message was for you."

He shrugged. "I thought I might go over there today."

The last thing she wanted to do was deal with more parents who lost a child in the War. "Fine. They're your neighbors. I'll be leaving as soon as I finish my coffee."

He narrowed his eyes. "What's your hurry?"

"There's no reason for me to stay."

"Jeanie could use a rest and I'd be willing to bet the cat wouldn't mind getting rid of the mice in the barn."

"I'll leave the cat with you so he can have all the mice he wants." Even if she didn't end up in an asylum, she had no reason to keep the stupid cat.

Creede laid the pocket watch on the table and stood. "He'll follow you."

"Lock him in the barn so he can't."

He studied her, making her uncomfortable with his scrutiny. "Come with me to the Eatons. You won't have to say a thing. After that you can leave. I won't try to stop you."

"Why is it so important that I go with you?"

He tilted his head back and gazed up at the ceiling. "The last time I saw them was right after Austin ran away with their son. I said some things I regret. I'm not even sure if they'll talk to me."

"But if I'm with you, they might be more agreeable?"

He chuckled. "Agreeable isn't a word I'd use for Eaton, but it's close enough." He sobered. "You owe me, Laurel."

He used the one argument her conscience couldn't counter. "I'll go, but you do the talking," she said firmly.

"Promise?"

Promises had brought her to this point and given her a reason to live. Did Creede know that or was he merely ensuring she would accompany him? "I promise." Her voice shook with the vow.

He studied her as if judging her sincerity and finally nodded. "We'll go after we eat."

Since there were no supplies left in the house, Laurel used the food from their bags to make breakfast. Although they'd spent numerous mornings together on the trail, there was an intimacy to being alone in the cabin. That they'd made love less than twelve hours ago added to the awareness simmering just beneath the surface. She tried to ignore it, but Creede's deliberate touches and gentle looks kept her on edge. She would've preferred him being angry with her—anger was easier to deal with than kindness.

After they'd eaten, Laurel volunteered to wash the dishes while Creede saddled their horses. She placed a bonnet on her head and joined him outside. Without the journal, Laurel felt adrift and empty. If this was what her future held, she didn't want it.

Creede gave her a leg up onto her mare and she nodded her thanks, unable to trust her voice. She was afraid that if she opened her mouth, she'd scream until only an empty husk remained. Just like all those dead soldiers who left behind nothing but their broken shells.

Laurel clung to the reins as Jeanie followed Creede's horse. Her heart beat like the hooves of a charging cavalry, and the urge to turn around and ride away was almost overwhelming. But she'd promised him, and Laurel Monteille Covey took her promises seriously.

It took them nearly an hour to ride to the Eaton homestead. It was similar to Creede's, although it was obvious no one had left this place alone for months. The buildings and corral were in good repair and it appeared the house had been whitewashed not too long ago.

A man carrying a rifle came out onto the porch. He was shorter and stockier than Creede, and his face deeply creased from the wind and sun.

Creede halted his mare and Laurel stopped beside him.

"What do you want, Forrester?" the man Laurel assumed was Lyman Eaton's father called out.

"To talk."

"'Bout what?"

Creede glanced down then met Eaton's angry gaze. "Our sons."

Pain flashed across the older man's face. "Seems to me we done talked 'nough about them last time you was here."

"I want to apologize."

Startled silence met Creede's words.

"We're neighbors and our sons were best friends. I thought—" Creede took a deep, shaky breath. "I think we owe them to try'n get along."

Eaton continued to scrutinize him with narrowed eyes and his gaze darted to Laurel. She held her breath, wondering what his decision would be.

Finally, Eaton lowered his rifle and leaned it up against the cabin. His shoulders slumped and he seemed to age before their eyes. "C'mon in. Betsy's got coffee on."

Creede glanced at Laurel and motioned ahead. She followed him and dismounted by the hitching rail.

"Who's she?" Eaton asked, nodding at Laurel.

"Laurel Covey. I met her when I went looking for Austin. He's dead."

"Lyman's dead, too," Eaton said, his voice weary.

"They died the same day," Creede said quietly.

Eaton didn't look surprised and led them into the cabin where an older woman bustled around getting coffee cups filled. The couple didn't strike Laurel as being as fanatical about the Confederacy as Creede had described them. Or maybe the loss of their son had dulled their fervor.

Creede and Laurel sat down with Eaton, and his wife joined them after she set a plate of molasses cookies on the table.

"So you been back East?" Eaton asked.

Creede nodded. "Virginia. That's where I got word Austin was dead. Mrs. Covey here was a Confederate nurse."

Betsy laid a hand on Laurel's, startling her. "God bless you."

Embarrassed, Laurel shook her head. "I didn't do that much."

"She's being modest," Creede said to the Eatons, although his piercing gaze remained on Laurel. "She just spent the last four months delivering soldiers' last words to their families. I don't know of any other person—man or woman—who would do something as selfless."

Laurel glared at Creede, willing him to stop talking about her. He didn't know the truth. Nobody knew the truth.

"What of your husband?" Betsy asked.

"He's dead," she replied curtly.

"What was it like back there?" Eaton asked.

Laurel concentrated on sipping her coffee as Creede described the depressing conditions of the postwar areas. When her cup was empty, she fisted her hands and pressed them into her lap. She stared at the scarred wooden table-top and imagined their son Lyman sitting in the very same chair she was in.

A familiar hand settled on hers and Lyman's specter disappeared. Creede continued to speak to the Eatons without interruption, but his comforting touch remained. Even after her horrible mistake, Creede protected her. In fact, his manner seemed more solicitous and understanding. It made no sense.

Betsy refilled the coffee cups and the cookies were passed around. Laurel relaxed slightly as the talk turned to the cotton crop, and when Eaton offered to help Creede with his harvest, it seemed the two men finally buried their antagonism.

The door opened and a young man entered, his cheeks flushed from the warm autumn sun. There was a friendly smile on his face. "Didn't know we got company. Good to see you, Mr. Forrester."

Creede stood and when the younger man extended his left hand, Laurel noticed his right arm was missing from above the elbow. Her stomach caved.

"I didn't know you were back home, Augustus," Creede greeted him with hardly a pause of surprise.

Augustus smiled wryly. "Lost my arm 'bout a year ago. Took some time to heal, then the army mustered me out." His grin became genuine. "I'm grateful to be alive, Mr. Forrester."

"And he's been a big help 'round here, too," old man Eaton said proudly. "Don't know what I woulda done without him."

Augustus's fair face flushed and Laurel could tell he was pleased by his father's words.

The young man approached Laurel, studying her face. "Mrs. Covey?"

Shocked, Laurel nodded. "Do I know you?"

"I'm sorry, ma'am. You probably don't remember me with me bein' only one of the soldiers you helped. After my arm was cut off, you talked with me, held my hand." His face reddened like a ripe tomato. "I used to watch you walk around talkin' to the other men. You never treated us like cripples. You talked to everyone like we was, well, normal."

A lump filled Laurel's throat, making it hard to breathe.

"I meant to thank you but you wasn't in the day they came and took me to the big hospital. I never figgered I'd see you again and have a chance to thank you for savin' my life." Augustus shifted his weight from one foot to the other. "Thank you, Mrs. Covey, and 'tweren't just me that owes you thanks. I know a lot of soldiers who would say the same iffen they was standin' here."

Laurel blinked against stinging moisture. She couldn't remember Augustus, but that hadn't made his gratitude any less heartfelt. It was strange how she could remember few of those who lived yet recall every one who'd died.

"I'm glad you're doing well," she said with a husky voice. "If you'll excuse me."

She hurried out of the stifling cabin and climbed up onto Jeanie's saddle. Wheeling her mare around, she urged the horse into a gallop. Her tears spilled over and the wind stole them away.

It didn't take long to return to Creede's cabin and retrieve her bags from inside. She tied them to the saddle, hoping to escape before he returned. However, luck wasn't on her side and Creede rode into the yard, his expression furious.

He dismounted before his horse even came to a full stop. "What're you doing?"

She kept her attention on her hands, on the leather saddle string she knotted. "I'm leaving."

"Where are you going?"

She faltered, but came up with a name. "Houston."

He grabbed her arm and pulled her around to face him. "Why are you leaving?"

She struggled to come up with a reason he'd accept but her mind went blank.

"I'll tell you why you're leaving," Creede said, his face close to hers. "You're afraid. I never thought I'd see the day when Laurel Monteille Covey was a coward."

She slapped him and was shocked by her reaction.

Creede smiled thinly. "Prove to me you're not a coward. Stay here and marry me."

Panic raced through her and she tried to pull out of his grasp, but he was too strong, too determined. "You don't love me."

"I love you."

"You don't know me," she shouted.

"Then let me know you. Let me decide if I can love you."

Frustration and fear bubbled up within her. She had to prove to him that nobody could love her. She sagged. "Let me go and I'll introduce you to the real Laurel Monteille Covey." Her tone dripped with acid.

Frowning, Creede released her and Laurel opened a bag and reached deep into it. Her fingers scraped smooth leather and she pulled out her second journal. Such a plain looking object, yet the truths inside were ugly. She handed it to Creede and noticed her fingers left damp spots on the cover. "Read this and you'll understand."

Creede didn't even glance at the book, but peered at her. "Promise you won't leave until after I've read it and we've talked?"

One last promise.

She nodded and walked into the cabin without looking back.

I am not God, yet that is what is asked of me—to choose who lives and who dies. My soul cries for everyone I cannot save. But outwardly I must do my duty and not let anyone know how much I am troubled by this responsibility. I can only pray that some part of my soul will be left when this horrible War is over.

Creede closed his eyes, but Laurel's words echoed in his mind. He was sickened not by her actions, but by what she'd been forced to do. To have a woman as compassionate as Laurel separate the badly wounded from the less badly wounded soldiers was one more tragedy of the War. The reason for her nightmares and need to keep her promises to those dying soldiers were no doubt rooted in the guilt she carried. Yet the doctors simply considered her reaction part of a woman's "sensitive nature." Creede would like to see a man go through what Laurel had and come out of it unscathed.

He rubbed his burning eyes. How could she believe he couldn't love her after reading her journal, which was stained with teardrops and blood? If anything, he loved her more for her strength and will.

"Are you done?"

Laurel's soft question startled him and he turned to see her standing behind him on the porch.

He nodded.

"So now you understand why?" she asked with a catch in her voice.

"More than you know." He rose from his seat on the step and handed her the journal. "You did the best you could, Laurel, and there are men like Augustus alive because of you."

"And boys like your son dead because of me."

"No, because of you he can rest in peace." Creede's throat grew tight. "Thank you, Laurel, for delivering my son's message and comforting him as he joined his mother."

Laurel's breath caught and stammered. He'd read what she'd done and still he thanked her? No, he must not have understood. She fought back the hope she thought was extinguished. "I killed them, Creede."

He grabbed her shoulders, but his grip wasn't punishing. "You did everything you could to save them. The doctors trusted you to make the best decision and you did that. Think of how many lives you saved." He paused and his intense blue gaze drilled into her. "Only God could've saved everyone."

Laurel's head pounded and she jerked out of his grasp. She held up her hands to ward him off. "I have to think."

She ran across the yard and into the barn. With tear-blurred eyes, she entered an empty stall and sank onto the straw. She pressed her hands to her temples to force Creede's words out of her head, but they wouldn't go away.

Think of how many lives you saved.

Only God could've saved everyone.

Creede was right. How many times had she heard overworked, exhausted doctors utter those same words? Those same doctors had confidence in her to choose the soldiers who had the best chance of surviving. She'd done what she could in the most horrible of conditions. Maybe the guilt wasn't hers to bear. Maybe the guilt lay in the manner of war itself.

The cat meowed and joined her on the straw. He rubbed against her and purred so loud it vibrated Laurel's arm. She cradled the cat in her arms and buried her face in his soft fur.

For the first time she allowed hope into her heart. Silent tears coursed down her cheeks as she finally grieved for those who'd died. And gave thanks for those who lived.

Just as she'd brought peace to the families to whom she'd delivered the messages, so too had Creede gifted peace to her with his words.

She raised her head and peered at the stubborn cat who had never given up on her. He reminded her that ignoring love didn't make it go away. Her love for Creede welled within her. She hadn't wanted to love him—or this stupid stray cat—but she did.

"Laurel," Creede called out.

She glanced up to see him enter the barn. A lump filled her throat and she rose, keeping the cat tucked in an arm. "Creede."

His troubled expression eased when he spotted her and he crossed over to her. "I was worried about you."

"I'm fine." She smiled without fear of ghosts and held out her cat. "I'd like you to meet Hope. And the answer to your question is yes."

$\mathcal{E}$PILOGUE

LAUREL heard a rider coming and looked out the window to see Creede returning from town. She smiled and wiped her doughy hands on a towel, then walked outside to greet him.

He dismounted and tied the reins to a post. With one stride taking the three steps, Creede joined her on the porch, and wrapped his arms around her, kissing her soundly.

"Did you miss me?" he asked, his blue eyes as mischievous as a boy's.

She laughed. "You were only gone two hours."

He stepped back to scrutinize her. "You didn't do too much, did you?"

Instinctively, she rested her hand on her growing belly. "No. I know what I can and can't do."

He shrugged and his face reddened. "Sorry. I just . . ."

Laurel found herself reassuring him just as she'd done numerous times since she found out she was expecting a child. She didn't mind. He'd lost his first wife and son so he was bound to be more nervous. But then, oftentimes at night, it was his turn to reassure her.

In the six months since they'd married, the number of nightmares had decreased, but she still hadn't gone a full week without one. There were also times when she grew irritated and short-tempered for no reason. Creede had learned to recognize those instances and give her time alone to deal with them.

However, each day Laurel loved Creede more, and never regretted becoming his wife. And with his love and support, she had faith that someday she'd remember more soldiers who lived rather than died.

"I, uh, have a letter for you," Creede said.

There was only one person from her past who knew where she lived and that was the doctor who'd told Creede how to find Laurel all those months ago. "I just got one from him three weeks ago."

"It's not Dr. Lampley. It's from Massachusetts."

Lightheadedness assailed Laurel and only Creede's strength kept her upright.

"How did they find me?" she asked faintly.

Creede met her gaze. "I sent them a note."

Anger replaced her shock and she drew away from him. "Behind my back?"

"They're your family, Laurel. They have a right to know you're all right."

She wanted to argue, but she'd learned that hope could never be completely lost. "Wh-what did they say?"

Relieved, Creede reached into his back pocket and withdrew an envelope. "Read it for yourself." Although his tone was neutral, expectancy gleamed in his eyes.

With a shaking hand, she took it from him and studied the familiar handwriting. Her father himself had addressed the letter. She stared at it, mesmerized by what she thought she'd never see.

"Go ahead, Laurel, read it," Creede prodded gently.

Startled from her reverie, she pulled out the letter from the opened envelope and unfolded it carefully, as if it would disappear. It took her a moment to focus on the words instead of her father's cursive.

Dear Laurel,
*I cannot describe my feelings when I received the letter
from Mr. Creede Forrester informing me of your welfare. Suffice it to say I have many things to tell you but I
cannot do so in such an impersonal manner as a letter.
We will be arriving to visit you and your husband as
soon as I can procure passage. I am sorry for the pain I
caused you and we look forward to seeing you, my
daughter. Mother says to tell you we all love you and
miss you.*

With greatest regards,
Father

A tear slid down Laurel's cheek and she wiped it away.
Between her condition and the letter, she had a gamut of
emotions jumbling through her, the main one being gratitude.

"Thank you," she whispered.

"Family is important," he said softly.

And if anyone knew how important family was, it was
Creede Forrester, the man who'd given her a reason to
live . . . and love.

TURN THE PAGE FOR A PREVIEW OF THE
NEXT HISTORICAL ROMANCE FROM
MAUREEN MCKADE

A Reason to Believe

COMING SOON FROM BERKLEY SENSATION!

WITH supper on the stove and Madeline taking a nap, Dulcie went out to the porch to clean the vegetables she'd taken from the garden earlier. She paused to watch Forrester washing up by the well, using the dented tin basin, soap, and threadbare towel that she'd put there for his use. With her floppy hat shading her eyes, she glanced over to see that he'd finished replacing the corral poles and had chopped the old ones into firewood. Impressed again by his labor, she managed a slight smile when he looked over at her.

Taking a seat at the top of the porch steps, she tried to ignore him, but could see his movements at the edge of her vision. Picking up a carrot, she trimmed it and tossed the greens into a tub. She'd only done a few carrots when she felt more than saw him approaching. Her fingers tightened on the knife handle.

"Mrs. McDaniel," he said by way of greeting.

Steeling herself, she met his steady blue eyes. "Mr. Forrester. I see you've finished for the day."

"I figured it was too late to start something new. Hope you don't mind."

How could she mind? She had never expected him to be such a hard worker, given his pay. She shook her head. "As long as the work gets done."

Dulcie kept her focus on the carrots as she continued to lop off the tops, but the strength of his perusal sat heavy on her.

"Got another knife?" he suddenly asked.

She jerked her head up. "What?"

"If you have another knife, I can give you a hand."

She thought of the dull, worthless knives in the cabin and shook her head. "I don't need any help."

He shrugged. "I don't mind. I'm not used to being idle."

It struck her that someone like him shouldn't have any problem finding a paying job, rather than working for only room and board. However, she shied away from that thought, unwilling to look too closely lest she lose the badly needed help.

She shrugged. "Suit yourself. If you're bent on doing something, you can snap the ends off the beans."

He grinned. "I haven't done that in years."

She snagged the large kettle that she'd put the beans in and handed it to him. He took it and lowered himself to a step, setting the kettle on the ground.

From her position above him, Dulcie could see his long fingers pick up a bean and snap one end off, then the other, tossing the ends into the tub with the carrot tops.

"Looks like you haven't lost your touch," she commented.

"The orphanage used to have a huge garden. All of us kids had to take care of it." He kept his head turned to his task so Dulcie couldn't see his expression, only the top of his damp hair. "If one of us didn't do our share, we couldn't eat. It didn't take many missed meals to get us to work."

Intrigued in spite of herself, Dulcie asked, "How many children were in the orphanage?"

A shrug of his broad shoulders. "Numbers changed, but usually anywhere from twenty to thirty."

"Did many get adopted?"

"Some. Mostly bigger kids who could do the work on a farm or ranch."

"What about you?"

He grinned boyishly. "I was a skinny one. Those who came looking for a boy said I was too small, wouldn't be able to pull my weight."

Dulcie stopped cutting in midmotion and studied his broad shoulders, wide, strong hands, and the muscles that flexed beneath his tanned forearms. She couldn't imagine him as skinny or small. "These people who came to adopt didn't want children to love?"

Forrester chuckled, but it wasn't a pretty sound. "Maybe a few of them did, but mostly they just wanted cheap labor. At least I was spared that."

Dulcie continued her work, but her mind sifted through what Forrester had said and, more importantly, hadn't said. Her memory flashed back to the sad orphan girl. "How old were you when you got put in the orphanage?"

Forrester paused, his motions stilled. "Six. I had two older brothers. Creede was sixteen so he didn't have to go there. Slater was eleven."

His voice was even, almost flat, but Dulcie had the impression his control was hard-earned. "At least you had Slater," she said.

"Not for long. Someone took him away a few months after we got there." He resumed his task and snapped off the ends of a handful of beans before speaking again. "I haven't seen either of my brothers in nearly twenty-five years."

Dulcie gasped, unable to imagine having family but not knowing where they were or even if they were still alive. In spite of her father's drunkenness, he'd been family. "I'm sorry, Mr. Forrester."

He glanced at her over his shoulder. "Call me Rye. And no need for you to be sorry, ma'am. It was a long time ago, and I've made my own way."

Ill at ease and uncertain what to say, Dulcie finished

lopping off the carrot tops. "I can give you a hand with those beans."

Forrester—Rye—set the pan on a step where they could both reach. As they worked, the quiet snaps blended with birdsong and the far-off barking of a dog. Occasionally, a hawk's haunting cry echoed down from the hot blue sky.

"So what about you?" Rye asked. "You live here all your life?"

"Most of it," Dulcie replied, uncomfortable talking about herself.

"When did your ma die?"

"Pa said about a couple of years ago." Fresh anguish squeezed her lungs, bringing a lump to her throat, which she cleared with a cough. "I wasn't here."

"Were you with your husband?"

Dulcie's defenses, which had lowered, slammed back into place. "Yes."

"I didn't mean to pry, ma'am." Obviously he'd picked up on her renewed guardedness. "I just figured since you said you were a widow."

She relaxed only slightly. Too accustomed to men wanting but one thing from a woman, she had to watch her words. "He was in the army. Died about five months back."

"So you came back here."

It wasn't a question, but she nodded. She kept her focus on her hands as she worked, afraid if she caught his eye, he'd ask more questions. Questions like how had her husband died and what kind of man had he been and how she'd made the journey back home.

Time lengthened and Dulcie finally breathed a sigh of relief when it appeared he wasn't going to continue his interrogation. He might be merely curious, but she couldn't take that risk. Her failures were her own, not things to be held up in the light of day to gain pity or charity. Or to be used against her.

"I'll check on supper. Could you get rid of the greens?" she asked.

Rye nodded. "I'll give them to the livestock, then wash the carrots and beans."

"Thank you." She rose and dusted off the seat of her breeches, then hurried into the house. The potatoes were boiling, as were the peas and corn. All she had left to do was fry the salt pork and slice the bread.

She got Madeline up so the girl had time to wake and wash up before eating. Twenty minutes later the meal was ready and Dulcie had settled Madeline at the table. Before she joined her daughter, she carried Rye's meal out to him.

Rye had swept the porch and only the two pans of washed carrots and beans remained.

"Thanks for taking care of those," she said stiffly.

"It wasn't any hardship, ma'am." He accepted the tray from her. "Smells good."

"Salt pork," she stated with a shrug. "It's all we have for meat."

"Did your father hunt?"

"He used to, but not since Madeline and I came."

"What about you?"

She shook her head. "I never learned, and even if I had, I wouldn't have trusted Pa to stay sober long enough to watch Madeline."

"If you can spare me, I'll go out tomorrow morning and see what I can find," Rye said.

She'd hoped he might offer, but she was unable to bend her pride to give him her gratitude even though guilt twinged her conscience. "As long as you aren't gone all day."

"Yes, ma'am."

She couldn't tell if he was mocking her or not.

"Done eating, Ma," Madeline shouted.

Saved by her daughter's call, Dulcie fled back into the cabin.

That night, after the dishes were washed and Madeline was asleep, Dulcie settled in the old rocking chair, a tin cup in her hand. Silence filled the darkness and with it came the familiar emptiness.

Memories filled the void, chilling her with their mocking accusations. She lifted the cup to her lips and welcomed the whiskey's heat that burned her throat and belly, and dulled the voices for a little while.

PREDAWN found Rye riding away from Mrs. McDaniel's place. His mare, unaccustomed to days of inactivity, tugged at the reins and Rye let the horse gallop down the road. He closed his eyes to fully appreciate the cool morning breeze against his face. After three months of endless days where there had been only dank, stale air, Rye had sworn he'd never again take anything as simple as a morning ride for granted.

It was good to be away from the woman and her daughter, if only for a few hours. It was tough keeping up his pretense of not knowing Mrs. McDaniel's husband. The lie of omission grated on his conscience, but he was convinced he'd done the right thing in keeping the truth from her. The proud woman wouldn't have accepted his help otherwise.

Two hours later, he had two rabbits skinned and tucked into the flour sack tied to his saddle horn. He'd spotted signs of deer, but never had a decent shot. With his money and supplies low, Rye didn't want to waste even one rifle cartridge.

As he headed back to the cabin, his horse suddenly shied and Rye, lulled by the morning's warmth and peacefulness, was nearly unseated. Regaining control, he patted the mare's neck and glanced around to see what had spooked her. A flash of color not twenty feet away caught his attention.

"Who's out there?" he yelled.

Leaves rustled and a group of finches rose up not far away, startled by something. Unwilling to let go of the mystery, Rye dismounted and looped Smoke's reins about a nearby branch. He ducked under branches and pushed through spiny brush.

"Who's out here?"

Even as he called out, Rye cursed himself for being ten kinds of a fool. If it was someone who had nothing to hide, he would've answered him. If the stranger didn't want to be found, Rye was probably going to be shot for his trouble or, at the very least, have his horse stolen.

Hoping he hadn't gotten smart too late, Rye retraced his steps back to his mare. He spotted a figure standing by Smoke and drew his revolver. As he neared the opening, he realized the person was very small or very young. Or both. Then he recognized the too short and oft-mended overalls. He stuck his revolver back in his holster and strode through the brush, not bothering to mask his approach.

"What're you doing out here, Collie?" he asked.

The boy who worked at the bathhouse shrugged as he continued to stroke the mare. "I'm out here a lot. I heard the shots. Looks like you was hunting."

Rye had to take a moment to process the boy's seemingly unrelated statements. "I wanted some fresh meat."

"You mean you and the widow?"

Rye pressed his hat back off his forehead and crossed his arms. "So how do you know I'm working for her?"

"I seen ya."

Mrs. McDaniel's farm was three miles from town. "Why have you been out there?"

Another indolent shrug. "Nothin' else to do. Ain't many folks that use the bathhouse."

"What about school?"

He wrinkled his nose. "Don't like it."

"What about the family you're staying with? Don't they worry about you?"

"Why?" Collie seemed genuinely curious. "It ain't like the Gearsons is my real folks. They only took me in 'cause they said it was their Christian duty."

Rye considered the boy's words. He'd known people like the Gearsons and oftentimes their Christian duty included working the adopted children like slaves under the guise of teaching them a work ethic. He fought down a wave of anger. "Do they give you chores to do?"

"Nah."

Startled, Rye tried to see past Collie's indifference. "None?"

"The other kids do 'em. I'm just underfoot."

The way Collie said "underfoot" made Rye suspect the Gearsons used the term a lot around the orphan. "So they don't miss you when you're gone?"

"Hard enough to keep track o' their own."

Rye eyed the boy's skinny frame. "They feed you?"

Collie turned his back to Rye and rubbed the horse's nose. "Yeah."

Something told him the kid wasn't being entirely truthful, but he didn't want to push him too hard. "Want a ride back to town?"

Collie spun around, his eyes wide. "Sure, mister."

"The name's Rye, remember?"

"Sure, Mr. Rye."

Smiling, Rye mounted his mare. He leaned down to grab Collie's wrist and hauled him up to sit on the horse's rump behind him. "Hold on to me."

Collie wrapped his thin arms around him, and Rye tapped Smoke's sides.

"You ever ridden before?" Rye asked the boy.

"My pa used to let me sit in front of him."

Collie's wistful tone stirred Rye's own memories. "When did your folks die?"

" 'Bout a year ago."

"Do you have any brothers or sisters?"

"I had a little brother, but he got sick and died when he was a baby."

So Collie was alone.

"How many children do the Gearsons have?"

"Seven."

Rye was surprised a couple with that many of their own would offer to care for an orphan. "You like them?"

He felt Collie's shrug. If Collie spent so much time roaming around alone, it was doubtful he did much with the Gearson children.

"Mrs. Gearson was Ma's friend. She said she was obla . . . obla—"

"Obligated?" Rye guessed.

"Yeah. Obligated to take care of me. Mr. Gearson didn't want to." Collie tightened his hold around Rye's waist. "At least he don't hit me."

And for a young boy alone that was probably the best he could do. Rye patted the boy's arm. "You mind stopping at Mrs. McDaniel's place before we go into town?"

Collie stiffened. "Don't want to."

"But you said you've been there already. This way you can meet the widow and her little girl."

"No!" Collie released Rye and wiggled backward off the horse, dropping to the ground.

Rye halted Smoke and turned to see the boy climbing to his feet, his eyes wide. "Why'd you do that?"

Collie merely shook his head, his shaggy hair falling across his eyes. He shoved the strands back and, without a word, turned and fled.

"Collie," Rye shouted. "Come back here. Collie!"

Only the sound of crashing brush answered him. Rye was worried about the boy, but he knew that if Collie didn't want to be found, Rye wouldn't stand a chance of locating him.

Why was he frightened of Mrs. McDaniel?

The answer was plain to see. Collie probably feared her for the same reason the townsfolk shunned her. She was the daughter of a supposed murderer.